THE EIGHT

The Gods of Chaos

GLENNIS GOODWIN

First published in 2022 by Blossom Spring Publishing
The Eighth Deity The Gods of Chaos
© 2022 Glennis Goodwin
ISBN 978-1-7391561-0-7
E: admin@blossomspringpublishing.com
W: www.blossomspringpublishing.com

CHAPTER ONE

In the dusk of early nightfall, the lowlands from the valley lay beneath the chilling evening sky while overhead, the dark grey clouds gathered thick and tight across the rising moon, giving little hint to the slow progress of this heavenly body as it began its nightly crossing high above. Beneath the shadow of the overhanging trees, which ran their course along the canyon's ridge, the six riders from the far-off north sat motionless after their long hard journey; their thick cloaks wound tightly around their broad backs to ward off the chill which crept in low across the desolate lands far behind.

Earlier, as the dusk had descended over the lands in the east, the riders had quietly negotiated the last of the scrublands. Arriving at the craggy rim which guarded this side of the vale, they had left their horses under the safety of the trees and now sat in wait for the moon to guide them down the treacherous slopes and into the heart of the ravine where the city and their prize lay.

As they sat, they spoke quietly amongst themselves, their talk sounding bleak and harsh as it constantly turned to the forthcoming riches and rewards that were to come. Before finally, a silence settled, and they each found time for some rest. Here they remained long into the dark of the night, unable to guess at the passing of the hours as the moon continued its slow journey above the overhang of the clouds. Until eventually, the faintest of movement high above and at their backs signalled the rise of the wind, and the moon appeared directly above them, flooding the valley floor below with its soft, cold light as the misty haze sped away west.

Quickly preparing themselves, the men gathered their

blades and tucked away their knives, keeping them close to hand for ease of use. Lofting their packs high on their backs, they stepped out from the protection of the cover and looked out along the tree-lined edge from where they had sat. A huge granite boulder could be seen beneath the overhang further along the rim, the moonlight picking out the ancient writings as it shone down upon them. While before it, leading off downwards, a lightly pebbled track began the start of their pathway. Gallius, the leader of the men, quickly led them forward past the marker.

Blending into the gloom of the swaying trees which lined either side of the trail, they first passed down through an area of light woodland before it came to an abrupt stop, opening out into an area of massive boulders, some smooth and rounded while others carried hard razor-like ridges which threatened to cut deep. Both appeared devoid of plant life as they clung precariously to the slope as it dropped away, and each held its own concern. The pathway had now vanished, and there seemed no easy way over or around it except to tackle the ridge head-on. Climbing across the top of the smooth surface and using the razor-like ledges as purchase for both hand and foot, the men slowly scrambled over with caution as they often glanced down into the drop of the valley which opened up on their right, while the abyss at their back lay wide and threateningly perilous in the glare of the moonlight.

Arriving on the opposite side, somewhat bruised from the hard rocks and with their hands feeling the slight nicks and grazes from their gripping of the edges, the men took a moment to gather their breath. Finding that the path had once more become tree-lined and broadened out before them as it twisted and turned gently down the valley side, their progress became easier. One moment, the moonlit valley was in full view, and the next, it had disappeared behind the thick hedges and brambles which littered the slopes only to reappear again some few steps later. But in each sighting, they could see their progress as the lowlands slowly grew nearer. Finally, the brambles thinned at the side of the path, disappearing altogether as the vista opened up, and they could see the city just below them at the southern end of the vale. The huge city gates stood open in the moonlight, and a thin stream of smoke filtered out from the topmost tower. Underneath a thin light shone from its windows, and the shadows of the passing city guards could be glimpsed in the glare of the firelight as they moved around unconcerned and unaware of the threat which sat so close.

Gallius now produced the map which he had carried hidden away in the pouch around his waist. Dropping to his knees, he spread it out in the moonlight on the mossy turf. His men gathered around to study it. It was a plan of The City of The Vallenti and its surrounds which his master, Dedrick, King of the High Places in the North, had given him before he left, and it was yellowed with age and torn and crumpled at the edges where the timeworn map had been folded many times in its history. But it still showed the streets and buildings, and although named in an ancient hand which few could now read, Gallius alone knew where he was and placed his finger immediately upon the map.

"Here is where we are at this moment," he whispered, his voice sounding out of place in the stillness which had gathered, "and this is the north gate where we shall be entering the city." He moved his finger slowly over the parchment before coming to a stop. "And here," he jabbed his finger near the centre of the map, "here is where our goal is!"

He sat back on his heels, letting the men pass the chart around as they memorised the route into the great city, and as they did, their talk turned again to the reward which awaited them at the end of the journey. Their whispers gave evidence of the greed which was rife among them as they dropped their packs and pulled out their rations, drinking the last of their bitter wine as they settled in sight of their goal. Then they waited again for the moon to do their bidding, for now, it was the darkness and silence of the midnight hours that they needed to provide cover for both their attack and retreat, and everything depended upon them remaining undetected throughout these early hours of the morning and having placed a great distance between themselves and the valley by break of day.

Gallius moved away from his men and sat at some distance in the shadows; the fight with this duty placed upon him again playing through his conscience, and although he thought he knew a little of the reason for the coming event of the night, he did not carry at that moment any certainty of its outcome. Only that he would not disobey the order given to him by King Dedrick.

Rumours had been rife throughout the streets of the High Places for many years that the king had already taken possession of a number of ceremonial statues stolen from the surrounding cities, and this one, *Amaunet*, Icon of The Vallenti, Gallius knew would be his next. For in the only certainty that he now carried, he was stealing this statue to save his daughter, Daina, whose life depended upon his return with this trophy, and if he failed, then he would die in the action.

Suddenly his second-in-command, Roth, appeared out of the growing gloom which was slowly descending, and reaching out, he roughly grabbed the man's arm and brought him down to his level, Roth's dark face coming close to that of his own as the smell of bitter wine hung heavy on the man's lips.

"The moon is doing our bidding, Roth," he growled as the darkness gathered around, "and is now in hiding, so we must make our attack soon."

"Yes, let's move. The men are getting restless," Roth replied firmly, his dark eyes looking across to where the shadows of the men stood on the downward path, their packs once more shouldered. "Let's get this job done and be on our way!"

Loosening his blade, Gallius got to his feet. Leading his men, his eyes moving slowly backwards and forwards across the dark shingle of the sloping path, they moved towards the city walls as the air became increasingly warm and stuffy under the overhanging trees. The path seemed to go on forever until, at last, the wood finished abruptly, and they came out into the open, the freshness of the sweet air filling their lungs as the ground once more sloped gently upwards until it met the walls towering some fifty feet high. Here before them stood The City of The Vallenti.

This ancient city was old beyond the ages of man and had long stood as a monument to the greater generations which had gone before. Here in the long ago past, the warrior tribe of the valley had built their mighty city to the glory of the gods on the backs of their slaves and with gold and jewels from the far corners of their known world. The city walls had been carved with huge hieroglyphs, and a towering procession of gods and goddesses, forty feet high marched around the city perimeter while at each corner stood sixty-five-foot-high obelisks; their tips at one time covered with beaten electrum which had reflected the powerful sun rays across the fruitful valley.

Then had come the peasant uprising and the ensuing war which followed, and the pestilence of famine and disease had swept its corruption across the rich fertile lands of the north and south and laid waste to the regions between, leaving behind large barren areas and a once proud land split by its differing races and tongues. And each city had retreated behind the safety of their high walls until year after year, decade after decade, the five great cities of the north and the four in the south had slowly become isolated islands surrounded by seas of spoilt withered wasteland.

Occasionally in time past, a lone traveller had journeyed from one city to the next, but as suspicion between the nine cities grew, even that frail link was severed, and it had been many decades since a traveller had been seen in the once great City of The Vallenti and thus it had fallen into disrepair. Ancient crafts had been lost, and the common knowledge of the ancestors that had once been revered now lay forgotten in the vast sprawling libraries of the temple scribes. The followers had even deserted their gods, *Amaunet* now being the only one left. For in providing protection over her valley, she was still accorded her feast days and was tended by a legion of priests and altar tenders, and to her, all men looked for blessing and guidance.

The Vallenti had then become a peasant people, tending their flocks of black-backed sheep and harvesting the fertile lands which lay within the valley domain of the goddess, and the ancient times lived on only here and there in the small rituals of home and in the stories passed down from generation to generation by the priests and scholars at the temple altar.

Now the city guards, sitting night after night in the light of their lamps, held little fear of the dark and the land beyond their walls, and with that, the northern men, aware of the honest nature of the people, expected little resistance on their way into the city. Gallius had ordered his men to shed no blood on their raid; however the four

6

watchmen, although surprised at meal and only being lightly armed, had put up a better fight than expected. The men with who they fought, therefore had to be swift to act to keep the silence, and as blade was thrust deep into gullet and cut sharp across throat, the order was disregarded and the guards were soon stilled, their lifeless bodies falling dead to the ground. No alarm was raised at the finish, and the defence of the city was breached.

Following the city map, Gallius led his men quietly through the undisturbed sleeping streets before arriving at the temple complex. With some feeling of relief at their unseen arrival, he quietly ordered his men to remain outside to guard the gilded doors, and he entered the temple alone. Passing through the dimly lit interior where the people worshipped and walking across the ornate tiled floor, the leader passed between the richly carved kneeling stools and embroidered seats, which lay in an informal pattern near the middle of the high domed building. Here the air was thick with the scent of burnt candle and incense as he approached the shrine.

The altar of *Amaunet* lay beyond heavily embroidered curtains which swung gently from their hooks high in the domed ceiling, the breeze from the open door causing their disturbance. Hidden within the gloom of the temple the gold-outlined figures of the gods and goddesses inlaid upon the fabric appeared to move gently across the rippling curtains as though the altar itself had breath. Here *Anubis,* the jackal god, stood, the body of a man with the head of a dog looking off to the right following the gaze of *Hathor*, the cow goddess who was placed before him, her huge horns delicately outlined against the richness of the cloth. While upon the left-hand curtain, the eyes of both *Thoth*, the ibis god and *Bastet*, the cat goddess, mirrored their stares. All were beautifully inlaid with reds and blues to match the fiery gold of their eyes, which looked out into the dark, and here Gallius hesitated. His mouth felt dry, and his heart beat fast while with restless hands, he gripped the curtains edge as he fought the inclination to flee empty-handed. But then his thoughts turned to Daina and his last sight of her as she sat pale and upright on the left side of King Dedrick as he sat upon his throne. The pleading eyes she had turned upon him in her anxiety left him in no doubt of his duty; he was doing this to save her in the only way he could.

Slowly his hands parted the heavy curtains, and passing through he let them swing together behind him with a sigh as he faced the simple stone altar which was directly ahead. Edged by a pale blue cloth, the black granite shelf held only a simple ring of flowers placed in offering at the feet of the goddess as she looked down. She stood only five inches tall, her snake head held high as the ruby eyes flashed a defiance, but in her body of solid gold, she expressed a power and strength which many would desire. Men would kill for such a beauty, he thought grimly, and grabbing away the altar cloth, he let the flowers scatter across the floor before snatching down the statue and hastily wrapping it away from sight. Turning with a haste to be out of the city, Gallius swiftly returned to his men and directing them back through the stillness of the silent streets, he paused briefly at the city gate to look down with a sadness upon the scattered bodies of the guards. They had already begun to cool and stiffen in their downfall before his thoughts quickly moved away from the violence they had received. Focusing once more on his own duty, he stepped out from the opened gateway, steering his men eventually back up the valley side and away from the coming chaos.

***

The sun rose in the east, lighting up the cold blue of the morning sky, and the valley was left behind at their backs as the men headed north, their horses feeling the freedom of the rein as they moved off through the openness of the land. And first, they found themselves travelling through a bleak scrubland of boulders and stunted trees, heading towards the mountain pass which lay beyond the wasteland and between the white peaked ridges of the Marn Mountains, and they knew that many weeks of hard riding lay ahead.

Their passage through the mountains would then take them through the Plains of the High Rush and on away beyond the Sleeping Caverns before finally the borders of their own country in the north would be seen, and they would once more stand within sight of the gates of the King's city. But for now, with the wintery sun rising, they were surrounded by the disorder of wasteland, and through this, they moved with some caution.

Here the land was a confusion of boulder and stunted tree where man and beast could so easily lose sense of direction. The ground on each pathway was strewn with granite boulders of every size imaginable, and here and there, they had been piled one atop the other, balancing like some grotesque statuary as their shadows, distorted and twisted by the advancing sun, fell across the dry, dirty soil. The thorn trees growing amongst and around the boulders were small, their roots buried deep to provide an anchorage against the strong winds which blew fiercely at times from the east. While their thick waxy leaves curled around, covering the stems that bore the thick inch-long thorns which could so easily injure if encountered, and through these the horses made their careful way guided by their leader. The men of the north, travelling down in haste towards the valley, had been wise enough to leave a trail for their homeward journey, and following this, Gallius led the way, his eyes moving this way and that as he noted each of the small brightly painted stones which had been dropped and which stood out in his eyes from the background colour of the natural rock. Guiding his horse around the boulders and through the wilderness, he left Roth to follow on as, bringing up the rear, he walked and threw aside the signs as he passed.

They spoke little as they moved forward, the silence of the land echoing only the stumbling footfalls of the beasts as they brushed aside the thorn trees. But on the rare occasions that they came upon a barren area, they would gallop flat out to make up the time, the horse's hooves beating a fast drum on the dry earth. On this first day, with the sun reaching its full height in the sky, they had put a good many miles between themselves and the valley, and so they stopped to eat and rest at the first sight of water.

The small stream bubbled up between two huge boulders, its clear waters running cool into a vast dish-shaped stone, and the horses plunged their noses in with little hesitation. Then the men drank gratefully too, filling up their water pouches before moving away to rest their backs against the large rocks where the mid-day sun warmed their faces. Here they sat and rested, eating their rations, and although surrounded by the dry and desiccated thorn tree wood which littered the ground, they made no fire to make a warm drink. In this arid and dusty region, any sight of billowing smoke would be an instant indicator of their presence, and this was something they wished to avoid.

Here in the daylight, however, with the sun above their heads, the men did feel some security gather around them, and gradually, one by one, they fell into a deep sleep with their heads nodding gently before finally falling onto their chests. Until, as the men snored and the insects of the mid-day wastelands buzzed and droned their constant noise, only Gallius and Roth remained awake to talk, the two sitting together in the shade of an enormous rock.

"Let them sleep while they can," Gallius mumbled as he stared over to where his men rested, "for tonight, we must travel fast and keep our advantage." He took a gulp of the cooling water before continuing, "The Vallenti must surely be on our trail by now, and we must reach the Marn pass before the new moon, and then our journey north will be the easier." He suddenly spat out a hard piece of food which landed at his feet, and seeing the remains of the dried-up fruit it reminded him of their provisions situation. "The food will be even lower by then, and hopefully, the Mountains may provide some sport to catch a rabbit or two."

"The craving for rabbit certainly grows after these weeks of dried fruit," Roth complained, staring down at the last piece of dried food which would have to see him through the day, "and mountain deer sounds even better. Let's hope that at least our supplies have remained hidden from the mountain people, or I'll see some sport there if it hasn't!" He lifted his hand, placing the shrivelled segment into his mouth and began to chew.

"Well, that may have to do just as well as roast rabbit if the supplies have gone," Gallius honestly replied, glancing again over to where his men snored in the warmth of the day. "We can't make it much further without fresh meat or provisions; the men are almost skin and bone now!"

The journey had certainly made its mark on all the riders, for the bitter conditions in the north followed by the searing winds and trials of the dry High Rush Plains had left them all with a deep tan, and their weathered, lined faces bore evidence of the harshness through which they had passed. They were all tired and had not seen a friendly fireside since leaving their homes many months before. But they were all good men. The two brothers Marke and Rogan and the trackers Statte and Brann had each been handpicked by Gallius for their bravery and skills, and he knew they would stand by him. He would not fail them either; he had made promise of that.

Suddenly he felt very tired himself, overcome with sleep, and he closed his eyes and rested his head back against the hardness of the boulder. The sounds of the wasteland receded as the rasping sound of Roth sharpening his blade came soothing to his ears, and at first he didn't hear the question asked.

"What's the statue like Gallius?" Roth had asked in a casual whisper; as continuing to edge the blade, he looked sideways to where his leader rested, the man's head thrown back as the whiteness of the throat lay exposed and vulnerable. "What's it like?" he again repeated, his voice taking on a slightly darker tone.

"What are you talking about?" Gallius finally managed to reply as the darkness which had begun to take him slowly faded, and the surrounding sounds once more became noted. As Roth repeated his question, it made him bring forward his head and open his eyes.

"The statue, Gallius." Roth's voice came louder, and he stopped in sharpening his blade. "You must let me look upon it!" he demanded. Bending closer towards Gallius, his breath coming in short gasps, his face became set dark and grim against the light of the day. "Let me see it!" he then commanded, "Let me see it!"

Gallius was instantly on his feet, sword in hand, as all traces of tiredness dropped away. And as Roth, too, stood up, blade ready at his side, a wave of panic and rage swept over him, and he stepped back. He could feel the threat as they stared face to face across the dirt-ridden expanse, and all around seemed to darken on the periphery of his vision as a chill wind blew in from the east, salty and tangy on his lips as if blown in from the sea. Before him, Roth was fixed in stillness, his face contorted by a savage grin, the lips drawn back as a noise, animal-like and savage, grew in his throat. His eyes appeared blank, holding little emotion as they stared out towards where the leader stood in astonishment. This was something that Gallius had never seen before. He and Roth were like brothers and had grown up together in the shadow of the increasingly darker times which plagued the north. They had trained together too, taking their turns to lead as they practiced their swordplay and schooled their men. Each knew the other's strengths and could call each other friend as well as equal.

Slowly Gallius managed to step further back. Placing more space between himself and the man who appeared rooted in his spot, he looked away to where the other riders still lay in undisturbed sleep, and his eyes followed on to where the horses stood tethered close by, and he quickly estimated his chance. He could see his mount, the dark grey horse standing nose down at the cool water and knowing that the statue lay hidden in the saddle pack, his mind began to judge his opportunity. Suddenly, Roth, his breath coming heavier, swung his sharpened blade out before him, and Gallius immediately and instinctively brought his own up in defence, the metal of the blades shining out against the brightness of the day.

Moments passed as they stood there, the tension building, but neither made their move. Until, with no warning, Roth let out a long groan, and dropping the unused blade to the floor, he toppled forward to his knees, his whole body gently sinking to the ground. He lay flat out, face pressed hard against the black harshness of the grit and dust while his whole body twitched and jumped as if a fit had overcome him, and a whiteness foamed at his mouth and gathered on the dry earth. Gallius again moved away, wary and unsure of the event happening before him. Stepping even further back, he came hard up against a boulder while still holding out his sword, ready to strike if needed.

Slowly, the erratic motions subsided, and the body of the man became quiet and noiseless against the ground until finally, he gradually began to move to sit up. He was still sweating as if in a fever, but his eyes at least held some recognition, although he seemed like a man aroused from a bad dream. Looking around and up at Gallius in confusion as he scrabbled against the looseness of the land, he appeared as if drunk.

"What happened?" his voice stammered as, with shaking hands, he wiped across his eyes where a veiled mist swirled before them, clouding his view. "I feel so cold!" Sitting up, he wrapped his arms about his body and, gently moving backwards and forwards, attempted to work away the coldness which gripped him. "Were we attacked?" he eventually asked, his voice growling harshly as he looked at his situation. "I remember seeing shadows, and someone was calling my name!"

"No, there has been no attack," came the reassuring reply, "but you appear to be unwell. Here let me help you." Gallius came forward, putting up his sword now that the threat had seemingly passed, and aiding the man to rise, they moved back towards the boulders. "Come and sit back down in the shade, and I'll risk a fire for some extra warmth."

Within minutes the collection of dried thorn tree wood had been made into a small fire, and a warming drink was soon prepared, and Roth sat next to the growing heat wrapped in both his own and Gallius' cloaks. He was still shivering slightly but less so now, and the drink which was soon placed into his hands added further comfort as he gripped the hot mug. His pale, ashen face was gradually returning to normal, and Gallius felt able to leave him for a few moments while he checked on the horses and ensured the safety of *Amaunet*. But he now could not put to mind any rest in regard to the statue and knew with a growing unease that for certain there would be trouble ahead in its respect, and he would have to be on guard.

***

Hours later, as the chill winds began to increase their severity, the men awoke from their much-needed sleep and found their leader and second-in-command seated in front of the embers of the slowly dying fire. Unaware of what had passed earlier, they eagerly gathered around the heat to enjoy its last warmth and rations were handed around as they watched the sun fall slowly into the west. Now the shadows around the boulders and trees continued in their lengthening until just before the sun disappeared over the reddened horizon, they repacked their saddle bags, hoisted the replenished water pouches onto the rested horses and prepared to move on for the long night's ride.

The deep darkness of the night sky descended rapidly across the wastelands, and the riders soon found themselves wandering through the ghostly landscape of shadows which seemed to move and follow them as they continued northwards on their return. Gallius remained riding out in front, still picking out the secret trail of painted stones that shone out against the black soil as they lay reflected in the cold light of the full moon, and Roth now rode next to him. And although the second-in-

15

command no longer shook with the chilling coldness, he still felt cold to the core inside. The icy chill which he could not shake, gripped his chest and stomach, and after many hours of riding, his head too began to throb, each jolt and stumble of the horse beneath him becoming like a sharp dagger to his mind. Soon after, his recalling of the voice he had heard returned to him, shouting his name from the misty shadows, and in its familiarity, he fought to recognise it until finally, in the aching dullness which filled his head, he said the name of Serdos, The High Priest.

Gradually as they rode deeper into the ruined land and the hours of the night passed with each step of the wandering horses, the pain reached its peak and then suddenly stopped. His thinking became quite clear in its instruction as the High Priest's orders once more burned deep in their remembering within his mind. Gently he caressed the secret talisman of the Brotherhood of the Snake, which lay hidden deep and secretly beneath his shirts, and as his cold fingers touched the silvered token, he remembered his given task. But for now, he thought, he would wait his time. For with both restraint and patience, he knew it would come.

CHAPTER TWO

The chime of the dawn bell awoke Malian, the altar tender at its usual time, its sound ringing out wide and clear across the city and its surrounds, the same has it had done on previous mornings for many centuries in the past and would do according to the city laws for centuries to come. And in the time-honoured tradition of the Ancients, he prepared himself carefully for the morning rites. Abstaining from food and cleansing his head and hands in water blessed by *Amaunet* from the Sacred Lake, he moved slowly around the bare cell, which had been his home for many years, as the grey, early morning light filtered through the small window high above his head. As he shuffled his tired feet, he hummed softly to himself, aware as ever of the sleeping priests who shared the austere rooms of the temple tenders close by.

Once prepared, he stepped out from his room into the dim stone corridor, and closing the door with care, he looked out into the greyness of the courtyard. Here twelve doors led off from this side of the corridor, and the pattern was repeated over on the far side, the other two remaining open to the lush gardens. While there at its centre stood the clear pool of crystal waters, the marble figure of the Solar Scarab rising from its middle where a fountain played, and large tubs of dwarf orange and lemon trees lay placed around its perimeter. Above his head, baskets of herbs hung low around the corridors, giving out their heady aroma, and all who passed beneath breathed in the fragrance of their flowers.

Malian paused for a while, mentally preparing himself for his first task of the day, that being the cleansing of the altar of *Amaunet*. Taking in the first fresh breath of the morning, sharp and sweet with citrus and herb, he softly

17

whispered to himself a venerable chant to *Nut*, the goddess of the sky and to the coming of the sun, which would soon wash over the tips of the eastern valley. It was a simple piece, one remembered from his childhood and one which captured the simple life of The Vallenti, and it cheered him to once more repeat the words.

Finally, he finished, and standing head bowed, hands clasped to his chest, he took in again the morning's heady scent. Until, with a sigh, he moved off slowly along the worn cobbled corridor and out into the start of the temple gardens. Today he felt old, very old. Older than his sixty-odd years and older than he thought bearable, and scuffing his sandalled feet across the grass and on past the beds of flowers and tall birch trees with their slender weeping leaves, his eyes remained firmly fixed on the ground ahead. Unusually he felt cold and chilled this morning, and he hugged his thin cloak around his shoulders for warmth. He was sickening for something, he thought, as the Sacred Lake appeared before him, and a large flock of water ducks took flight at his approach. Perhaps he would later call to see his friend, Mosera and get some of her medicinal advice.

The weak sun was now beginning to light the edge of the eastern valley rim, and Malian lifted his eyes to watch its rising. As the thin golden rays flooded down the valley side, an unease and disquiet gripped his heart, and he looked away towards the celestial courtyard at the end of the lake and beyond to where the doors led into the temple buildings. All at once he stopped, for he felt something was wrong, and lifting his head higher to watch the flash of the ducks as they screeched black and white against the icy blue of the early morning sky, he found his eyes being drawn back to the buildings in the far distance. Suddenly he found himself running towards the temple in concern of what he might find, his legs finding an unexpected strength as he ran along the pathway between the hedges and into the courtyard. There he could see the gape of the temple doors as they stood wide, the rising sun glancing off the gold inlay, framing the darkness of the opening which yawned ahead.

A freezing cold wind suddenly appeared from the east, blowing wildly the swirling motes of dust around the court and gathering them around Malian's feet as he came to a stop before the violation. And not daring to enter at that moment for fear of what lay inside, he stood still and remained unable to move. The wind around grew stronger and colder by the second, and the whole of the courtyard was caught up in its movement as the slender trees swayed back and forth. The huge pots of grasses and roses crashed to the ground, the petals torn from the withering blooms racing across the temple forecourt before being tossed high above Malian's head. The same force also worked on Malian, tearing at his hair and clothing, and worse, penetrating his mind like the scream of far-off spirits. Slowly he sank to the ground, giving his mind and body over to the power which he could no longer fight.

Many hours later, when the first worshippers approached the temple to pay homage to the gods, this was where they found the old man lying face down in the white dust before the temple doors and covered from head to foot in the gold-red petals torn from off the roses.

***

He slept, trance-like, for two days and two nights in the house of Mosera, the healer, while around him, the discovery of the theft of *Amaunet* and the chaos of her loss gathered and increased, and the valley underwent a shift from warmth and sunshine to the depths of winter. For on the very day that Malian had been found, the first heavy frost had attacked the higher slopes of the valley while overnight, a scattering of snow had arrived, and the following day, the citizens had awoken to a white dawn.

Set'al, the High Priest of *Amaunet*, had quickly called his advisors, sending each away, in turn, to consult their books until a meeting between all of the elders was called in expectation of some findings. And on the evening before the gathering, Malian opened his eyes and spoke his first words through dry lips to the young boy who appeared at his side.

"I must speak with High Priest Set'al," he croaked weakly as the boy gently raised his head and placed a drinking cup to his lips. "I must see him straight away."

"You need rest first, Master Malian," the boy replied softly, "for you are too weak to rise and must not upset yourself."

But as he helped Malian to a further drink, he rang for Mosera, his mistress, and she was quick in answer. Within moments she appeared, her gentle fat face smiling encouragement as she peered deep into the altar tenders eyes, and patting his cold hand, she then felt his brow for signs of fever, nodding her head at her findings.

"Well, Malian, you have certainly had us worried," she said, looking hard at the older man she had known for many years, "but I would say you were over the worst now." She smiled over to where the young boy was busying himself around the room, filling the flask with fresh water and tidying over the bedcovers. "Pieter has looked after you well, but you still need plenty of rest before you go jumping up and speaking with Set'al."

"But I must speak with him," he demanded, his voice edged with determination. He tried to rise before dropping back against the pillows, a fatigue overcoming him as he lay breathing heavily. And with eyes half closed, he shook his head gently.

"See," the woman scolded, "you've little strength with lying abed these past days. Rest now," she advised, "and Set'al can see you tomorrow after you've had chance for both rest and nourishment. Shall I get Pieter to fetch some hot soup?"

Malian nodded weakly, and the boy disappeared through the carved door opposite. While he was gone, Mosera spoke to him of his finding outside of the temple doors and the discovery that *Amaunet* had gone, stolen by thieves who had killed in their effort to take her. She went on to say that Set'al, on report of the loss, had immediately sent out trackers. The men, though, had soon returned, bringing only news that they had lost the trail of the thieves in the wastelands but that they appeared to be heading north, possibly making for the Marn Pass. Worse still, she said to Malian, was that the weather within the valley had changed on *Amaunet's* disappearance, and the city had fallen into the deep cold of winter. The majestic trees around the city had decayed overnight, their leaves dropping to the ground, while all the blooms that sat atop the flowering bushes had withered in the first heavy frosts. The elders had talked in hushed tones of the coming of the first snows, which, according to the scripts they had hurriedly consulted, would blanket the grasses and meadows where the sheep grazed, only to awaken the next day to find the valley enveloped in white and the sky full of heavy clouds ready to deposit more.

While she spoke, Malian lay listening, his eyes searching deep into hers as she told of how Set'al's advisors had given little to offer and the meeting of the elders on the following morning was seen as their last hope for the valley and for *Amaunet's* return.

"Set'al has had the elders scouring the archives for

scripts to ward off this murderous weather," she finally said sadly, "but I can't see them being any salvation for us." She turned her head away, not wishing to show her anxiety and despair. "Our only hope now, Malian, is for the return of *Amaunet*."

"Then I must be at that meeting," he replied decisively, finding a strength in his own words. "For I am feeling better already, no doubt to your care and attention." Managing a weak smile, he gently squeezed the healer's hand to show the return of his vigour. "But I do need to hear if the elders have found anything, and I have much to offer myself, as my mind has wandered far in the long dark hours I have slept."

"That may well be true," Mosera said, turning as the door slowly opened. Seeing Pieter carrying the tray of hot soup and freshly baked bread over the threshold, she finished, "But first, you can forget about the meeting and eat." She helped Malian to sit up, propping the large cushions at his back for support. Then sitting at his side, she watched while he slowly ate. Eventually, every last drop of soup was finished, and the bread was eaten and more fetched before the altar tender finally pushed the tray away and leant his head back against the pillows.

"Now I really do feel better," he said, smiling at his friend, "I felt like I'd not eaten for months!"

"Good," the woman replied, rising quickly from his side, "and now you must rest for the night. Pieter will be in the next room if you need anything. You only have to call." She picked up the empty tray and headed for the door, stopping before she left. "I'll say goodnight now, Malian, and I hope you find some rest." Looking down at the empty dishes, she finished, "I'll make sure we have plenty of bread for your breakfast tomorrow; we must put some more flesh on those bones." She laughed and was gone, but Malian could still hear her voice sometime later as she instructed her staff for the morning.

Finally, he sat back in the softness of the bed, watching the boy Pieter as he closed the thick curtains and placed wood on the fire, and for the first time, he was able to look around at his surroundings. The room was sparsely furnished, the big wooden bed in which he lay taking up the majority of the floor space. While a small table and chair sat close by near the window, and a huge carved wardrobe took up the opposite wall next to the ornate door. This was all that stood within the room, but the curtains and the bedcover of matching material made up for the shortage of decoration, for although being simply trimmed with design of tree and foliage, they gave an elegance to the starkness. Beneath this, Malian slid himself down, the mustiness of the bedcover filling his nostrils as he felt the warmth surround him. Covers of such thickness had always been rare and seen as unneeded within the valley, but the colder weather had seen those that remained brought forth from attics and basements after untold time in storage, and those who had been gifted of their finding had been grateful as was now the altar tender.

That night he slept ignorant of the deepening outside cold and undisturbed by the dreams and voices which had haunted his previous nights, and when he woke the next morning, his mind was clear and uncluttered of the images of the past. Opening his eyes, he found Pieter already at his bedside, a tray of warm bread and fruit ready for his breakfast.

"Good morning, Master Malian," the boy said gravely. "I shall put the tray near the window, and you can sit out." Placing the tray and moving the chair aside, he drew back one of the curtains letting in a flood of cold light, and standing beside the frosted windows, he wiped away the frozen moisture with the cuff of his shirt and looked down. "It's been another heavy snowfall this morning," he remarked, his glance taking in the whiteness which had collected below, "it looks just like a drawing from the Book of the Skies."

Malian eased himself gently onto the edge of the bed, his feet touching the chill cold of the bare floor before they found the warmth of the slippers placed at hand. Slowly rising out of the softness which had encased him, he unhurriedly walked over toward the window, the feeling of the chill air collecting in his bones as he wrapped the blanket around.

"You have read such a book, Pieter?" Malian questioned as he lowered himself into the wooden chair. "I would have thought you far too young!"

"Well, I've only looked at the drawings," he reluctantly admitted, "but Mistress Mosera is teaching me the words, for she wishes me to be instructed at the archives when I come of age." He turned away to tend the smouldering embers in the fireplace, and soon the flames blazed brightly in the hearth while Malian settled himself at the table to start on the tray. As he ate, he stared through the frozen window and saw for himself the heavily bowed trees which lined the street below, the starkness of the whiteout glaring into his eyes as he looked beyond to where the houses stood opposite, their shutters closed tight in their uncommon silence.

It was the first time he had ever in his life seen such a thing, and he too, like Pieter, straightaway thought of the Book of the Skies, for it had also been his first instruction so many years ago when he had felt the desire for knowledge. Now, remembering its script, he recalled it to be an easy first book to learn, containing many of the basic texts which had seen him through school. But still, he pitied the boy the hard years ahead, for the archives held their own order, and all had to bow to the Masters.

Thinking back, he brought to mind the drawings of the Winter Seasons, which had so fascinated him with their intricate drawings of harsh bleakness, the hunched figures of the people wrapped in their furs as they trudged through the deep snow shepherding their flocks along the thick valley slopes. These images, he had been told, were from beyond the ancient times, before the coming of the sun god bearing his gift which banished forever the cold, winter winds to the far corners, or so it was said in the long history past. Now, though, with the stealing of their beloved protector *Amaunet*, the winter had returned, and this snowfall would only be the beginning. Things would only get worse as time went by, and many people would perish if they had no store of crops to feed themselves or their herds, and Malian felt a sudden urgency.

"Pieter, are any clothes ready for me to wear?" he swiftly asked as he made his way back to the bed. "And I'll need a thick cloak and some boots for this treacherous weather. Could you find some for me?"

"Everything is already here, Master Malian," came the reply as the boy opened the large wardrobe beside the door, showing where his things hung. "The Mistress thought it best for you to remain here for a while and so had your clothes bought over. Some boots are already warming here by the fire while a cloak hangs ready in the hall."

Bringing across the boots and garments which had also been placed beside the fire, Pieter helped Malian to quickly dress, the altar tender finding the boots being somewhat restrictive after the sandals he was used to wearing. But once clothed, he stood, and Pieter addressed him formally.

"I am to take you to the Court as soon as you feel fit, Master Malian," he politely requested. "The meeting is just starting, and High Priest Set'al is anxious for you to attend." Bowing his head in respect for the older man before him, he stood aside and opened the door.

"Well, I'm as fit as I can be, Pieter, so lead the way!"

Pausing only briefly in the hall for Malian to wrap a cloak around him, the boy led the way out into the side of the frozen courtyard, where the sharp drop in temperature caused Malian to catch his breath and hug the cloak tighter around. His eyes quickly dropped to where the worn courtyard slabs lay covered by ice, and he cautiously moved across them as he slipped and slithered his path towards the gateway. Passing through into the street beyond, he witnessed with his own eyes the damage which the white snow had done in such a short time. Everywhere he looked, the plants had died, their blooms curling black against the frozen stems, while beneath the naked branches of the trees, the leaves either lay fallen in untidy piles or had been windblown in the bitterness and had gathered in the corners of the yards. The brightly painted birds, which had so delighted many with their song, either sat huddled together under the bare eaves of the houses or else lay stiff upon the ground, a blanket of frost and snow covering their dulled wings.

But it was the silence that Malian found most disturbing. For as well as no bird song, there was neither the raucous chatter from the workers as they made their way out into the paddocks on their noisy animals nor the sound of children playing in the streets. The whole valley seemed smothered in the blanket of white, deadening all sound.

Many careful minutes then passed as they walked the short distance to the roofless building known as the Open Courtyard, Malian leaning heavily on Pieter at times as the thickly iced and frozen streets lead through the city, and here they found the regular meeting place of the elders. This was usually a bright and sunny place for them to gather and discuss all things meaningful, but now it lay abandoned and left to the icy fingers which hung off the columns surrounding the seating. Passing through, Malian and Pieter entered the small Inner Courtyard where the warmth of fires blazed in copper pots, the firelight glinting off the polished statues of earlier High Priests and off the ceremonial armour worn by the two courtyard guards who stood to attention at the door to the Closed Court. Here Pieter stopped, for it was forbidden for anyone so young to enter the great brass doors, and solemnly bowing, he bid Malian a farewell.

"I will leave you here now, Master, and shall see you later on your return to the house." Turning quickly, he was gone, and Malian had no time to make reply. But he was sad to see him go, for he was a reminder of himself all those years ago.

Now though he put aside these thoughts, as approaching the doors to the Closed Court, the guards saluted. Bowing low, they let him through into the corridor beyond, which stretched off ahead, the doors behind him closing as silently as they had opened.

Malian stood in a soft light that led off into the distance as the corridor drew his footsteps along the polished floor, and swiftly he walked his way towards the brighter light and headed into the sanctum of High Priest Set'al. It had been a long time since he had been this way, and he was, as ever, awestruck when he emerged into the light at the end of the corridor, and the vastness of the domed building reared above his head. While beneath the span, the colourful fountains played into their pools, and the exquisite furnishings appeared lavish against his own austerity.

The elders were already gathered around the carved meeting table, Set'al standing at its head, his cloaks thrown back from off his shoulders. Leaning heavily on the table, he let the long grey hair frame the grimness which had etched itself deep into his features. His face was strong and handsome with eyes of intense blue, and the kindly smile which was normally at his lips, appeared absent as he spoke. Malian paused patiently at the doorway until he was finally noticed as the high priest raised his head and with a nod of recognition from both sides, he stepped forward to the table.

"Welcome, Malian! Please come and join us; we have been expecting you," Set'al said, his voice soft yet forceful. Indicating a vacant chair on his left he waited for Malian to sit before asking, "We trust you are feeling well again?"

"Yes, my Lord, much better, and I give my apologies for my late arrival." He now sat quietly between two of the elders and waited patiently his time to speak.

On Malian's entrance, the talk had been on the sending out of another force to rapidly hunt down the thieves with a hope of a swift return of *Amaunet* and the restoration of balance within the valley. But no advice had been forthcoming from the men of the council, and the meeting was soon turning to some hope of guidance from the archives and the scribes who pored over the folklore and tales of the past. Finally, Alrynn, the head of the elders, slowly stood and addressed the gathering.

"The people must be given some hope," he demanded. Studying the open books and parchments which lay before him, the half-remembered legends and myths of a past time gave little comfort. Carefully closing each one in turn, he let his head drop. "All of this means nothing," he indicated, spreading his hands over the useless papers, "for without our protector, we are damned, and our faith will fail, and the city will fall into dust at the feet of the gods. *Amaunet* is our only hope, and she must be returned to us!" Slowly he sat down, his empty hands upturned at the tables edge, and all eyes turned back to Set'al.

"Brothers, as we already know, our findings have been few. What we have gathered helps neither in the return of *Amaunet* nor in the plight in which we now find ourselves. Of this, we have already spoken, and to keep going over it offers little joy. But I ask again in hope of reply, does anyone here have something which will offer up some salvation? Let anyone speak who will!"

Malian slowly rose to his feet, an inner strength willing him to rise, and standing before the council, his plain temple robes looked shabby against the richness of the garments of the elders. He cleared his throat, and all eyes turned to him.

"Malian, you have risen to speak," Set'al declared, bowing his head towards him and fixing him with his blue gaze. "Do you dare give hope where even the most learned cannot?"

"My Lord," Malian's voice spoke softly, "I have little to give, 'cept what the gods have given me in my dreams, for with them I have been on a journey and seen such visions few eyes have seen." He stopped, looking around the vast table at the faces, some expectant while others fearful of his words, and suddenly he found a strength to speak with conviction. "I have been on a passage with the gods themselves in search of *Amaunet*, and with their guidance, I travelled over the plains and under mountains into the darkest corners of the earth itself." Here his voice rose as, looking along the length of the table he finished, "The journey I took began at the Gates of *The Duat*!"

On hearing these words, the whole of the table suddenly arose in uproar, the elders shouting their opposition as fists were raised, and Malian's voice was no longer heard against the shouts and commotion. Until finally, Set'al raised his hand and restored the order.

"Silence," he thundered, "silence, everyone! Let Alrynn speak for you if there is any misgiving."

"My Lord," Alrynn said, slowly rising as the other elders resumed their seats, "we all know the way through *The Duat* is the sacred realm of the dead. The way into the divine fields beyond this world, and the path is not known to living man. It is the way of the spirits," he continued, looking around at the faces of his men, "and the way of the departed who take their steps towards their final judgement…No," he finally said, turning to face Malian, "*The Duat* will not and cannot be our salvation!"

The elders immediately thumped the table in agreement as Malian remained calmly standing before them, his face turned towards the high priest until gradually the noise died down, and he turned to speak directly to Alrynn.

"My Lord Alrynn, I am not asking you here for the way to *The Duat*," he softly replied, "for that has already been given and the journey laid forth and taken out of our hands." Moving away from the table, the altar tender turned to face the whole of the assembled men. "I come only to this meeting to ask for assistance in making it, for the gods have chosen me in this undertaking, and whether I go by myself or not is the question I came to ask here!"

Returned to his seat as the commotion again rose, he sat down quickly, his legs giving way beneath him as the enormity of the challenge became clear, and he thought on the dreams that had filled his sleeping hours. In them, he was not alone, as the guidance of the spirits of the gods had shown him the deep waters at the northern end of the valley. Here they had taken him down into *The Duat* and through the Seven Gates, which stood shut to all except the dead and along which they walked the path on the slow passage to *Ma'at*, the Truth.

He had descended into the darkest depths and entered

the Gates where his dreams had been filled with the creatures of these paths, but now sitting at the table of elders, he remembered little beyond that, only that the spirits would once again return to him when the first challenge had been passed, and he stood on the far side of the Gates. And his thoughts, as he stood in the Closed Court, were now only of the dread of the days to come if he was sent out alone.

Set'al had remained seated in his chair as he listened to Malian speak, but now he sensed that in the quieting room, the whole of the gathering was looking to him, and presently he stood.

"We have all come here hoping to find some comfort in the teachings of our forefathers," he declared, "but no help from them has been forthcoming. Now, this man has come forward with his dreams, and so I say, speak Malian. Speak the words which we hope will ease our fears."

Malian once again stood, but this time he walked up towards the table's head where the high priest remained standing and looking at Set'al, he spoke directly to him, blind to the others who sat in wait.

"My lord, I have been given this task by the spirits of the other world, and even to my ears, it seems as wild and fantastic as it is to yours. But I believe it is given with the knowledge of the gods and must be taken as such." The silence of the room surrounded him, as he then said, "I cannot give you hope beyond that which is given to me, and should you say that this journey is not to be, then I will go without your blessing or that of the elders and will face whatever the fates hold in store." He looked away, dropping his gaze from the cold blue stare before finishing, "I only ask that I'm not sent alone, for my age is against me, and my strength has weakened of late. But in that, I shall leave it to you and the elders to decide who will accompany me."

"My dear Malian," the head of the elders replied, his face holding concern for the man who remained stooped before the high priest. "You know we are no longer men of much action or fight, for those days have long past us by. The hardest work these many years has been with plough and shovel, and our warriors of yesterday are no more!"

"Then Alrynn, I shall take any who have the faith to come with me," the reply came back. Turning away from Set'al, the simple altar tender again faced the assembled men, and his voice sounded small in the vastness of the room as a silence once more gathered.

Suddenly a voice was heard rising from the back of the room. "Surely no one would be foolish enough to believe this old man and his ramblings," it scoffed from the far end of the table, breaking the silence, "let alone join him on such a foolish adventure! Let us be honest about this, for we are surely just clutching at straws here, are we not!"

"Hold your tongue, Tarnik," Alrynn shouted his demand, looking down to where the agitated man had pushed away his chair, "I would have thought better of you. But if you are unhappy about the hope given by Malian, then I suggest that you, and any others who hold such a feeling," his gaze worked along the table sides, taking in the looks of each man in turn, "and any of you who cannot accept the word of Malian, leave the Court immediately and go about your business." He waved his hand in a final dismissal for any who wished to leave, and Tarnik and the elders either side of him stood and were joined by a number of the seniors' from around the table. The group gathered around the doorway before leaving the Court amidst a growing clamour.

"I'm so sorry it has come to this, Alrynn," Malian

came forward to the elder, his face holding a look of shock as he realised the upset, "I had hoped to bring some unity in our cause, but it would seem we are already at each other's throats."

"Don't worry yourself, Malian," the head of the elders encouraged, "at least we know where Tarnik and his men stand, and I can at least know I have my most faithful around me in these troubled times." His eyes fell upon the remaining elders who had turned expectantly in his direction as the departure had unfolded, and he smiled encouragingly at them. Many were the younger men of the elder council and less experienced than those that had followed behind Tarnik, but he was sure they held no corruption and would take his orders with little recompense. He wondered, fleetingly, what hold Tarnik had over his men, for surely some of them who had left the Court seemed reluctant to go, but he had forced them to stand and show their loyalty. Suddenly the voice of the high priest broke into his thoughts, and guiding Malian back towards the table, he and the altar tender sat down once more before High Priest Set'al.

"Come now, Malian," he had then said, himself seated again at the head of his table, "we can now surely talk freely and with little fear about this whole business, and you can tell us your dream from the beginning."

Malian paused in gathering his thoughts, finding it difficult to know where to begin. But slowly, he started to tell of the dream which had filled his unconscious mind as he lay in a trance while around him, the remaining elders listened in amazement.

"First, there was a wind," he began, "loud and unbearable, and I found myself lifted high above the valley, the whole of its fertile land mapped below me in its greenery and abundance. While around and about, the barrenness of the vast scrublands stretched away in a greyness in each direction." He paused as if remembering some torment, and the high priest reached forward, placing his hand upon his shoulder.

"Please go on if you can," he said, "we cannot know your pain, but sharing sometimes can make it more the bearable."

"I'm sorry," Malian quietly replied. "It was just that as I watched from above, the greyness began to creep its way down beyond the valley side, engulfing all in its path, and there was nothing that I could do." Leaning forward, he placed his head in his hands and closed his eyes for many minutes while he summoned his courage before moving back and straightening himself within the chair. "I travelled far into the dark night," he continued, "like a ghost across this grey land until I reached the lakes at the northern head of the valley. There sat the boatman, the Lord Aken, in his royal barge, waiting to row me across the black lake of sorrows and beyond down into the Gates of *The Duat*." He stopped suddenly, aware of the silence which had increased around the table and looking to where the elders sat, and seeing their looks followed by the twitch of the hand to ward off any evil, he made a decision to speak no more.

"I'll say nothing else in this place," he then quickly finished, "only that the gods were with me every step of the way, and I would call the journey well favoured by their presence."

"Bless you, Malian," Set'al said, "for in your god-given task to rescue *Amaunet*, we can hope that you will be ours and the valley's salvation in seeing her return. But, now name your number, for I would not have you go alone!"

"That too I leave to the gods," Malian replied, "and I'll take all who they commend!"

"And we shall all help in the planning, Malian." A

voice suddenly came from the table's end where Hahan, the scribe, one of Alrynn's faithful, had stood. "I know where sits a map of the valley which should guide you along to the lakes in the north, although I fear it may be a bit torn and faded in places. I'll get a copy drawn and hope it will be useful."

"Well now," Set'al said, banging his fist heavily on the table, "the journey would seem to have a starting place and destination. And a time will surely be given by the gods. So come, the morning grows dark, and we should eat and find some refreshment."

Leading the way across the Court, he paused only to throw aside the heavy curtain which concealed the doorway to the inner halls where Malian could already smell the baking of bread as he stepped through, and following behind the high priest, he was accorded a place at the top table.

Remembering little of the simple meal which passed as he sat in the surrounds of the priest's court, he found the wine was the best the grape growers could offer, and it soon played its part in the tiredness which overcame him. Dozing in his chair and lulled into a light sleep by the music which played in the background, it was many hours later when Alrynn came to disturb him. Shaking him gently by the shoulder, he said, "The afternoon grows old, Malian, and you would seem to be still needing your sleep. Let me see you back to Mosera's, and you can rest further."

Malian could find no need to disagree, for the room was nearly deserted. The musicians had departed and the assemblies of the elders had broken up sometime earlier, and rising slowly from his seat, he asked, "Did I miss out on anything important? The wine went straight to my head, and the music was so delightful that I just drifted off."

"Only that Set'al has called another meeting for the morning," Alrynn informed as he led the way along the tables, "but the scribes will be busy this night, and messengers have already been sent out to the Great Houses. Hopefully, news will come soon as to who will go with you."

"Has no one come forward from within the city walls?" Malian quietly asked, falling into step alongside the elder as they passed the chair of the high priest and pausing only to bow low and accept his blessing, they made to depart the hall.

"Not as yet," came the reply, "but we have hope that the Great Houses will bring news tomorrow."

"Yes, tomorrow will bring some hope," Malian encouraged, "for I can feel it in my heart."

The two walked in silence for many minutes, passing out of the cover of the court into the frosty afternoon sky which twinkled high above their heads, and looking upwards, Malian wrapped his cloak tightly about him and hunkered up his shoulders to keep warm.

"Tomorrow is going to be very cold again," he declared, "and we must hope that the gathered crops will sustain us, or we shall all be going hungry before the Feast of Light is celebrated."

"And we must supply you with food for your journey," Alrynn also reminded him before stopping suddenly. Bending down, he carefully picked up the body of a small bronze bird that had fallen to the ground at their feet, the tiny heart still beating as he gently wrapped it in his cloak edge before he held it up to his chest for warmth. "Poor things," he said, "they shall also perish if we don't provide for all."

"I fear we shall all suffer in our own ways, Alrynn," Malian sadly replied. "And I know that this trial will separate both weak from strong and sick from healthy, and I suspect that disease will not be held back long."

The house of Mosera could now be seen through the bare branches of the low-hanging trees, the torches blazing brightly either side of the doorway in the fading light, and a small wisp of smoke curled its way lazily up from the kitchen chimney as the cooking fires worked in the depths of the ovens.

The two men stopped, and Malian turned to farewell the elder.

"I had always hoped that someday I might be asked to join your company, Alrynn," he said, "but now," he paused as he grasped the outstretched hand, "well, who knows!"

"Yes, we are in troubled times, my friend," he reflected, smiling down at the man who appeared to be their only hope. "Now in you go, get a good night's rest, and we shall see what tomorrow brings. Good night, Malian and give my regards to Mistress Mosera." Striding off into the coming night, the little bird still wrapped warmly in his cloak, he was soon lost to Malian's tired eyes as he stood outside on the porch. Here the heat from the torches warmed his chilled face until finally, he was forced to retreat indoors from the bitter winds which blew around his legs and feet.

***

Dark clouds now gathered at the northern end of the valley, and with a frozen wind behind them, they moved south, bringing with them more misery which would enshroud the city the following morning. And as the large snowflakes descended from the gathered gloom, Malian was wrapping himself warmly under the thick bedcovers, and there he hoped to sleep peacefully.

CHAPTER THREE

The next morning Malian awoke from an undisturbed sleep to the greyness of his bedroom. Outside, behind the thick drapes, he could hear a soft dripping noise that he could not place, and fumbling his feet into the slippers Pieter had left nearby, he dragged open the curtains to let in a stream of cold hazy light. Wiping a small space in the frost-covered glass, he peered down into the yard below to where the trees stood in a covering of snow, and the ground was many inches undercover. Someone had already been about as a trail of footsteps could be clearly seen crossing the white expanse to the little shed which supposedly housed the wood for the kitchen fires, and a small four-legged animal, possibly Mosera's cat, had left its prints alongside.

Shivering at the sight of the white death, he turned quickly away and returned to the warmth of his bed, and wrapping the covers around his cold body, he was suddenly overwhelmed by a great fear. How had he come to this, he thought, a mere altar tender chosen for such an enormous quest. The very thought left a terror in his heart, and a nausea came to his stomach, and the taste of last night's wine filled his mouth. He sat for many minutes, huddled against the pillows with his eyes closed until a slight knock was heard at the door, and Mosera's head appeared in the doorway.

"Ah, Malian, so you are awake. I thought I heard you moving around." Opening the door wider to admit the breakfast tray she carried, she nodded her head towards the window. "You'll have seen the weather?" Settling down the tray on the small table, she puffed out her cheeks. "It is truly bitter this morning, and if this wind keeps up, then none shall venture far from their hearths."

38

"I hardly feel like getting out of bed myself," Malian replied slowly. But somehow or other, he roused himself and making his way over to the table, the cover still wrapped around his body, he quickly sat as the smell of freshly baked bread and warm meat issued its temptation.

"You have been out this morning?" he asked Mosera, and seated, he watched her move around the room.

"Just for wood for the fires and ovens," she replied, tidying up the vacated bed. "How did you know?"

"I saw your marks from the window," he answered. Helping himself to a large slice of bread and placing meat on his plate, a cup of steaming tea was downed in one go and instantly refilled from the pitcher which had been placed by his side. "It must be very heavy for it to have settled so deep?"

"Yes, I think I will send Pieter next time and save my poor feet from the cold. They still feel like ice, and this chill gets into the bones very quickly." Walking over to the fire, she stood silently by its heat, warming her hands and feet at the glowing coals while watching Malian continue on the tray. He too, remained silent for his part, for his thoughts had turned to the forthcoming meeting and on who would accompany him on his journey, for news travelled quickly within the city walls, and he hoped and prayed that someone had stepped forward. As if reading his mind, Mosera's voice suddenly caught his attention.

"Set'al has sent word that the meeting will be held as soon as possible," she said, "and I hear tell, that three have already come forward. All newcomers to the city, but here within these walls when the word went out. Or at least that's what the rumour says." Moving away from the comforting heat of the fire, the woman stood at Malian's side and, laying her soft hand on his bowed shoulder, said, "I expect the news will take longer in this weather to reach the Great Houses along the valley, and even then they will have their own to look to for they will be the first to suffer if the harvests have not yet been gathered."

Up and down the valley, the Great Houses had been thrown into an urgent panic since waking only a few days ago to that first frozen dawn, and the herdsmen had fought desperately against the driving winds which whistled down from the ridges to gather their herds and shepherd them to the safety of the homesteads. The farmers too, had not been idle either, out since early light to assess their damaged harvests, and they had hastily gathered anything that was ripe enough for storing. However, little had been saved, for the damage had already been done, and soon all within the valley would go hungry, for the Great Houses and their farms provided the city with meat, grain and wines throughout the year, and in return, they received the protection of *Amaunet* over their flocks and fields.

"Yes, I feel that is to be understood, Mosera," Malian reasoned, thinking on the distress the sight of that first snow must have caused, "the Great Houses must look to their families, it is only to be expected. But it surely lifts my heart to know that some have come forward in our hour of need." Reluctantly pushing away the tray and patting Mosera's hand, he then made ready for the day. "Well, I mustn't keep them waiting."

A while later, refreshed and dressed, he was escorted solemnly down to the front hall by Pieter. Here Alrynn was already seated by the large oak door, his tired eyes hidden under hanging lids as he fought off the sleep that his body cried out for, but on seeing Malian, he felt somewhat refreshed and was at least able to rise and welcome the man as he approached. "Greetings, Malian, I trust you slept well?"

"My dreams were nothing that couldn't be forgotten in the light of the morning," the altar tender quickly replied, grabbing his cloak from where he had left it the previous night.

"Come then, we must make haste to the meeting. News already awaits us, for I hear that weary messengers have been coming in since first light."

Alrynn led the way through the cold snow of the courtyard, now messy and dirty underfoot with the crisscrossed trails of both animal and man. And leading out onto the freshly swept paths which lay beyond the walls, they moved along the lanes as fresh snow drifted down from the skies. Looking up, no break could be seen in the thick grey clouds which covered the valley from rim to rim. Continuing carefully through this snow-covered landscape, Alrynn talked of the evening's work which the scholars had put in at their tallow-stained tables, and reaching to the bag at his waist, he withdrew a small barrel, holding the object beneath his cloak as the snow whipped around their feet.

"You remember Hahan from the meeting, with his map of the valley?" he asked. "The one showing the way to the northern lakes? Well, he has done you here a copy as promised, which he hopes will be of great help." He handed over the barrel, which was tightly bound and encased in leather, an intricate pattern of markings adding decoration.

"My thanks to Hahan," Malian said, nodding his head as he took the map, "for already the journey seems the easier for his troubles."

"But that's not all," Alrynn continued, a sudden excitement heard in his voice, "for late last night, he brought me another scroll. The gods alone know where he finds these things, but he's always nosing around in some dark corner." He paused on the pathway underneath the light of an overhanging fire basket. And producing another small scroll from the depths of his cloak, he unrolled it before Malian as the flames above their heads flickered wildly, casting long shadows across the papyrus. "It appears to be an ancient scroll of the dead," he quickly explained as he handed it out, and the two men looked down.

"This would appear to be very old indeed," Malian agreed. Taking the proffered scroll from the elder's hands, he quickly rolled it up to protect it from the elements. "Do you know what it says?"

"No, the text is beyond my reading, but it is definitely a scroll of the dead," he declared, "for the Seven Gates are clearly marked." Taking Malian by the arm, he gently continued his lead towards the Court as he explained further. "They were written by the ancients as grave gifts to guide the souls of the dead through the Gates of the underworld and out into the Field of Reeds beyond, where their spirit would rest for eternity. But of course, you would already know of this," he acknowledged as Malian nodded his head in acceptance of the explanation. "Seven Gates are marked on this one," he continued, "but there may be more, we do not know, but for each gate, there was a keeper, and a secret keyword or password was required for safe passage through. The keywords are also marked on the scroll but mean very little."

"Perhaps in their time and place, they may mean more," the altar tender then said, "and I shall study this one in great depth and hope the gods will guide me when the time comes. Oh, but Alrynn, will it be too hard a test for me to walk the paths of the dead?" Stopping quickly, he turned a tired face towards the elder and told of his doubt. "Even with the knowledge that scroll may give, it will still be a hard test for even the bravest to endure."

"Take heart and trust that the gods would not choose foolishly," Alrynn replied honestly, hoping to encourage Malian in his moment of misgiving. "For it would appear you have their blessing, and in that, you can hardly refuse their task."

"Well, yes, you can hardly turn down the demands of a god," he said, a slight smiling crossing his face, "and thank you for showing such faith in me. Please also give my thanks to Hahan for this scroll, for every little may help us on the right road."

"That I will do for you, Malian," Alrynn then added, "however, I feel it best not to mention the scroll at the meeting, for all of the elders will be attending, and I feel sure that Tarnik is up to something, and will try and disrupt your journey."

Arriving at the Court, they found it full and noisy, and all the elders were already there, including Tarnik and his followers, who stood at the back of the chamber keeping their own council. While the high priest's advisors, their plain white robes contrasting against the rich colours of the others, stood at the left hand of Set'al. Pushing their way forwards before finding their seats, they quickly took up their places along the marble table, and as the high priest seated himself at the table's head, a hush descended slowly through the crowd, and his voice rang out.

"Now that we are all gathered," he said, 'let Malian come forward, and you also, Alrynn, for both good advice and guidance will be required before we finish this meeting."

The two men came forward, moving slowly through the packed crowd around the table to stand alongside the high priest's chair, the advisors stepping back to make way, and Malian could now see the others who stood gathered around. On entering the swarming court, he had noticed three strange figures at the right-hand side of

Set'al's chair, and as he came nearer, he was able to regard them with a keener eye.

The first was a tall, gaunt man wearing the clothes of a scribe about his spare frame, the head of light grey, slightly lowered as if too heavy for the neck to support, and his eyes darted brightly around the room until his gaze reached that of Malian. Here they had lingered, and a hint of a smile crossed the thin lips, and he nodded his head in recognition, and Malian had bowed his head in quick reply. The hands of the scribe were not visible, but he knew the long ink-stained fingers would be calloused from the endless flicking amongst the ancient scripts and parchments. However, this man was more than just a scribe, for his eyes were not dulled from a lifetime of dimmed candlelight, nor was his back bowed from long, hard days poring over his work. This man's soul stood as straight as a reed, and in that, he held his authority.

The second man was an even taller individual and broad too, a giant of a man with a dark complexion and eyes as black as night. His hair and beard were both woven in an intricate pattern, and he was clothed in what appeared to be animal skins, but his cloak, which he wore fastened at the throat and thrown back over his shoulders, was thick and ornate, giving more to the man than just a fighter. This man, Malian had noticed, did not look around the room but stared straight ahead, his mind seemingly lost in some privately known vision, and he remained aloof throughout the continuation of Set'al's address.

The third person was a young man, barely much older than Pieter, Malian guessed, who stood silently at the very side of the chair of the high priest. His eyes held expectation, and he fidgeted his feet around on the polished floor until the tall scribe beside him laid a gentle hand on his shoulder and whispering a few words; the boy became stilled as Set'al spoke.

Standing on the other side of the high priest's chair, Malian and Alrynn waited as Set'al finally finished his opening address before he handed the meeting over to Alrynn, the head of the elders, who took up his position alongside him at the head of the table.

"Welcome again, my friends," he said, in sober greeting as he looked intently around the room at faces long known to him. "We are, as I'm sure you are all aware, assembled here on a matter of dire urgency for this city and all the people of the valley, for our whole existence is in danger, and all here are equally vulnerable in our position." His voice rose as a low murmur filled the room, and he held up his hand for silence. "You must know that no one will be spared," he continued, "and so all must come together in strength and support."

Stepping away from the chair of the high priest, he came forward to address his men in earnest.

"You all know that we are here this morning to choose the companions to accompany Malian on his journey," he established, "and I now ask formally. Have any searched their hearts and found the faith to attempt such a deed?" He looked around the assembled court before adding, "Remember that Malian has been named by the gods, but great faith will be required to attempt the Paths of the Dead, both for him and any who come forward. So think wisely before committing your soul to the journey!"

He moved back, and Malian took his place, the altar tender approaching the silence of the crowd as they awaited his words.

"This journey is not for the weak of heart," he began, looking intently at the gathering, "and I will not take any who have faltered or done wrong in the eyes of the gods. If there are any amongst you, pure of heart and ready to give up their comforts, let them come forward and receive the blessing of this meeting." He stopped in wait and expectation while all around the assembly, the elders looked at each other in apprehension. But there was little movement from within the hall until finally Set'al arose from his chair, and indicating the three newcomers to come forward, he presented them to the gathering.

"Here I have three who have come forward, Malian, and all are here of their own free will." Gesturing first to the tall thin man to speak, he seated himself down as the grey-haired man spoke.

"My name is Mentu," the man said softly in introduction, "and I'm sure that some of you may have already heard of me, for I have devoted my life to the learning of the dark secrets of the scrolls and for the last twenty years the Great House of Ran Agua in the south of the valley has been my home. There the parchments are equal in number to your great city, and I have been in study of them for years beyond remembering." He turned to the altar tender at his side before continuing, "Malian, I can only offer the gifts which the gods have bestowed upon me, these being my knowledge of the scrolls and the magic of the temples, and if you will have me, I will be your eyes and ears as you journey through *The Duat* and beyond." He then offered both his hands to Malian, who found himself instinctively coming forward to grasp the thin, cold fingers between his own.

"Welcome, Mentu. It will be a great privilege to walk with you, for surely no better teacher could be found from within the valley." Quickly releasing the hands of the scribe, he again moved towards where the two figures remained, and he asked for them to come forward and make known their names. Suddenly he turned away, distracted by a sound that rose up, and looking first to Set'al and then back to the crowd who were swiftly becoming restless, he saw the commotion within the elders. The voice of Tarnik could be heard rising above the others as he and his group of followers held their own meeting at the back of the group, and heads were slowly beginning to turn that way until Set'al intervened in the growing disturbance which was sweeping across the floor of the Court.

"Silence! Silence!" he roared to the elders. "Tarnik, you wish to speak? If so, then come forward and address the Court in the proper manner!"

"I tried to voice my opinion yesterday," Tarnik spoke arrogantly from the back of the room, "and I was ordered out of Court to go about my business. But I will repeat it again for the sake of those who were not present then." Pulling a chair forward, he stepped up and stood disrespectfully above the heads of the gathering so that all could see him and he could look down upon them.

"This venture of Malian's is doomed to failure," he began, "for no one would be foolish enough to follow a simple altar tender or attempt the Paths of the Dead." His followers now showed their support, and he quickly held up his hand for quiet. "I say we should pursue the tracks of the thieves, hound them to the ends of the lands if necessary." His followers again burst forth with loud approval, fists held aloft this time in support of their leader. "And for this, I plan to set forth this day to trail in the cold footsteps of the heathens who dared to steal our beloved *Amaunet* from us."

"I have not given leave or my blessing to this venture," Set'al responded. "Would you go without either, Tarnik?"

"Yes, that I would," the man spat out. "For any fool who journeys with Malian will surely be lost forever. Consumed on the Paths of the Dead if they ever reach them, and *Amaunet* will never be returned to us!" Turning his defiant eyes on Set'al, he held his head high and stood exposed to the whole of the Court.

"Very well, make your journey," the voice of Set'al rose thick with anger. "But know this, Tarnik, the gods themselves are with Malian, and in his ventures, he stands protected. Who will you take as your keeper?" Tearing through the astonished crowd, he finally halted before the raised figure of the elder. "Tell me!" he thundered. "Who shall protect you in the barren lands and the wastes that lie beyond!"

"I give no answer to you," came the stark reply, "for already you do me a great dishonour speaking thus. But know this, we do not go unprotected, for I too, have not been idle in these days." He alighted from his chair and descended amongst his followers. Emerging into the space which was developing between the two groups, he placed himself before the high priest. "We start our journey immediately, Set'al, and on our triumphant return with *Amaunet*, we shall be blessed by all, and the city will be rebuilt to the glory of the Ancients." Turning away from the outraged priest and from the gathering of the dumbstruck elders, he strode from the Court. His followers surged after him, until finally, all had left, and the door banged closed against the aged lintel.

After many minutes to compose himself, Set'al slowly turned to face the silenced Court, and a pathway back to his chair opened up in the crowd and along this, he made the weary way back to the head of the table.

The confrontation seemed to have sapped the very strength from him, and he slumped into his chair, and there remained throughout for the rest of the meeting as Alrynn, seeing the distress of his high priest, endeavoured to maintain the purpose of their gathering.

Without delay, he introduced the second of the strangers, the tall, heavy built warrior.

"Here is your second companion, Malian," he quickly

announced. "Tragen, from the lands in the south, come forward and state your purpose."

The large man walked heavily forward to the front of the table where he stood, face impassive to those before him until Alrynn gently touched his arm as if to awaken the life within.

"I am Tragen," the deep voice resonated around the Court, "son of the Chief of the City of Lights, and I have been travelling for many months over lands which are new to my eyes for such a change as come over the south that my heart is heavy at the memory. Forgive my appearance," he said with some regret, "for I arrived barely an hour ago and although my body cries out for sleep, I cannot rest until I have spoken and told news of our plight."

"Welcome then, Tragen," Malian gently replied, sensing the distress of the man before him. "Come, tell us your news, and we can see what it is that you require of us and be better able to judge your circumstance."

"My city is under a great spell," the man eventually began. "All the crops in our fields have turned to dust, our wells run dry, and our warriors lie dead or dying from a grievous plague which ravages my people, and the women folk cry for the loss of sons and daughters." The huge man hung his head in weariness and exhaustion. "I have come forth from my city to seek that which has been taken from us, our protector and guardian, only to arrive here and find that your city is also blighted and no joy is to be found."

"Your guardian is an Icon like *Amaunet!*" Alrynn asked in astonishment.

"Yes, she is one of the Eight Deities. *Naunet*, her name in our tongue and in the language of the Ancients. She has been lost to us now for months longer than a year, and our city is dying for her return."

"And what would you have us do, Tragen?" Set'al's voice slowly asked, his head raising as he felt the weight of his burden. "We cannot come to your aid when our own need is so great. Our people suffer too, and the suffering will get worse. All we can offer is the hope that if we can reclaim *Amaunet*, then also *Naunet* can be returned."

"Then I shall take that offer and will journey with you," Tragen declared, "for I see no other course and cannot return empty-handed to my city." He turned now to the altar tender. "Let me join your quest, Malian, in the hope that if *Amaunet* is returned to her rightful place, then so too, *Naunet* can be restored and the lives of many saved."

"May our journey then be the quicker," Malian replied, sensing the growing urgency as awareness of the growing dilemma increased, "for the sake of those here and those you yourself have left behind." Coming forwards, he joined hands with the large man. "I gladly accept you into our small group of travellers, Tragen. Strong men are hard to find here in our valley, and I shall consider us well blessed to have your company."

They then parted, and Tragen stood alongside Mentu as the third and last figure came forward.

"Now let me introduce you to Darric," Alrynn spoke encouragingly as he urged the smaller figure of the youngster forward. "A humble but very essential person for the journey. He will be in charge of the pack animals, which will soon be laden in the stables."

Approaching Malian, the youth's eyes remained fixed on the floor where the light played in pools around his feet. "My Lord Malian," he announced nervously, raising his dark head slightly and casting a quick glance around, "I have been well schooled in horsemanship and have been trained in the ways of the woodsman and fields craftsman, and with that, I offer you my services. Will you have me on your journey?"

"Darric, you are gladly accepted, for a steady hand with the reins may well be of need along the paths which we choose to tread, and the arts of the craftsmen are welcome on any journey undertaken. So here I give you my blessing." He placed his hand on the young man's shoulder, and together they joined the other travellers at the head of the Court.

Alrynn, sensing that Set'al would have little more to say on the choosing of Malian's companions, as each had come forward with no undue influence, now welcomed the group together. However, in his conclusion, he noted that there remained an absence from within the Council or elders.

"Is there no one else to come forward from this meeting?" he finally asked the upturned faces.

Eventually, after a long period of silence, a small, hooded figure shuffled into the space at the foot of the high priest's chair and holding forward wizened hands as if in prayer, the figure slowly dropped to its knees. Pushing back the hood, which hung heavy over his features, it revealed the long-forgotten face of Psamose, the pilgrim.

Alrynn alone gasped in recognition, and clasping the outstretched hands, he quickly helped the figure to rise to its feet.

"Welcome, Psamose, my old friend," he said. "Many long years have passed since we've seen your face amongst us, and my heart fills with gladness at your return." The joy in Alrynn's voice spread amongst the gathering as a chorus of "Welcome, Psamose, welcome," resounded around the room.

Immediately, Set'al felt the darkness lifting from his body, and leaning forward, beheld the face of the elder who stood before him, the piercing blue eyes and hooked nose set amidst the small, wrinkled nut-brown face, topped off by a sparsely covered dome of white hair. Here was one of their own, an elder wanderer from the Vallenti, not seen within the Court for many long years.

Stepping up towards the high priest, the old man turned and addressed the whole Court, his voice cracked and craggy.

"I bring news and greetings from the House of Abu Salama in the central plain," he announced before continuing, "Far have I travelled these last days, and in great haste, for I was away in the north when the snows came, and I was forced to return quickly to the Great House. There I heard rumour of our loss and, on hearing such, felt compelled to set out immediately to join here with the elders and the council to find out the truth." The pilgrim's face was lined with fatigue as he recalled his journey, arriving at the city walls with the snow covering his stooped shoulders and his hands almost frozen to the carved walking pole which he carried with him. "It has been a long road, and my task is not complete until I deliver the message from Master Salama, which I carry with me." His hands disappeared into his robes before emerging with a small packet that he handed up. "Please, Alrynn, take the message from my tired fingers."

The spokesman of the elders did as he was asked, and unfolding the packet, he presented the contents to the high priest.

"The message is indeed from Abu Salama," Set'al informed the gathering after some few minutes. "He sends his wishes and hopes that the return of *Amaunet* will be swift and the thieves quickly vanquished beyond the borders. A wish that we all share. He also offers up any help which we deem he can give, either from his own table or from the outlying farms and homesteads which fall under his protection." He looked towards the gathered group at his side. "This is indeed pleasing news, Malian, for surely your journey must take you along the side of the valley before you reach your destination in the north, and where better to put up for the night, my friends, than at a Great House noted for its hospitality." Set'al smiled at the little company, knowing himself the warmth of Abu Salama's reception, and placing the message down in his lap, he finished, "We can only hope that the other houses and farms will also show such graciousness if your journey takes you near their borders."

"The friendship of the homes throughout the valley has been tested time and again in my wanderings," Psamose said and speaking with a conviction, he ended, "and I have always found them hospitable and been made ever welcome."

"Yes, of course, my friend, I meant no disrespect, and now you are welcomed back here in your own city," Set'al announced, "and here you will find rest after your hard travels."

"My Lord, my journey does not end here, for I too, will be setting out tomorrow with Malian and his companions. I have left unfinished business back at the House of Salama, and a swift return is called for."

"But surely you will not be rested enough for the morning, Psamose," Alrynn said, a concern rising in his voice. "The travel here has surely severely fatigued you?"

"Yes, that it has, but I require very little sleep these days," came back the reply. "For such is the way of the aged. All I ask is for a warm meal and drink and a few hours at rest and prayer, and I shall be ready to walk beyond the Mountains themselves."

"So be it," spoke Set'al, his voice rising upwards into the roof of the dome, "for the day advances swiftly, and all are in need of refreshment and rest from the Council. The tables will be laid forthwith. But before this meeting is closed and all go about their business, I must ask this question of you all one last time. Are there no others to journey with Malian?"

The elders and the Council now continued in their silence, the courage to undertake such a venture not to be found in any of their hearts, for they were men long since used to the comforts of their tables and of the kitchens which provided for them.

"There is no one?" Set'al asked for a final time, the pause lingering long before he finished, "Very well. Then, Malian, your companions stand before you, and the blessings of all here and in the valley go with you. And now let us eat."

Set'al led the way through into the feasting halls, which Malian remembered from the previous evening meal, but this time found himself seated alongside his travelling companions, and as he glanced around, he wondered if they would all pass the tests which awaited them. As the other tables slowly filled around him, his mind then quickly turned to the food dishes which passed across from one side to the other, for surely they seemed sparse and less well-laden than the previous meal he had attended. It would seem that even here in the Great Hall, there was becoming a need to ration supplies, and the kitchen staff had been given their orders, which would affect both scholar and elder likewise. Now though, he had to banish such thoughts, and helping himself frugally from the dishes which passed before him, he turned to Tragen, who was speaking at his right.

"My Lord Malian," the large man spoke, his dish of meat and bread left aside for a moment. "We journey tomorrow, but in what direction do we start?"

"I think that is a question for Psamose," Malian

quickly replied, "and Tragen, please let us forget formality. Stop calling me my lord, Malian will do fine, thank you." He smiled encouragingly at the man before turning and addressing the one at his left. "Psamose, will you enlighten us on the direction to the Great House of Abu Salama, for I'm thinking that we will head there first?"

"That will be our initial destination, for I have cause to return there, and it is a path that I have travelled often in my time." He took a long pull from his mug. "West will be our direction, with the rays of the morning sun at our backs, and a journey of two or three days is usual, though the snow may delay us and our speed greatly reduced, I fear. Also, we have to find places to shelter on the way and that may be in the remotest of places." Seeing the look of dismay cross the faces of the group, he quickly added, "But I do already have one place in mind for our first night's stop, just off the path, but it should not delay us unduly."

"Your knowledge, Psamose, will indeed be a blessing." Malian raised his mug in salute to the pilgrim, who returned the salute in kind.

"It is given with the favour of the gods, Malian, and we should use it to the best of our means."

The talk then turned to their destination in the north, first to the Great House before taking the route along the river, which would see them journey to the lakes at the head of the valley, and while this discussion continued, Darric diligently emptied his plate. Feeling content, he excused himself to see to the horses in the stable and to supervise the packing of their supplies for the morning.

When the meal came to an end, Malian and his three remaining companions then retired to the warmth of the blazing fireside. Seating themselves in the comfortable chairs placed at hand, they stared into the depths of the flames and talked of the coming hard journey through the snow-laden valley, for this was surely of concern and remained uppermost in their minds.

"The report is again not good for the weather tomorrow," Mentu offered, for he had overheard the conversation between two elders who had been watching the changes closely, "and they say it only will get worse!"

"The weather will surely deteriorate as we move further north," Psamose agreed, "for even as I left the Great House, the frosts had attacked the berries and the vines, and the field crops lay withering on the snow-covered ground." Sitting back in his chair, he sighed and closing his eyes, brought to mind the sights he had recently witnessed along the valley.

"It is only to be expected," Malian's voice came sadly, "for we are living in such troubled times. But let us take comfort that the weather will also be hindering the thieves, even if they are used to the cold of the north. And let us be thankful that our journey does not take us through the barren lands, for we have no map for such a place anyway."

"We have no map for the underworld either," Mentu stated, slowly rubbing the head of a hunting dog that had found the warmth of the fire. "So, who will guide us through this uncharted domain?"

"Well, that's where you may be wrong, Mentu," Malian spoke in a whisper as he gestured for the men to come closer. "Alrynn has given me this scroll," he said as he retrieved the papyrus from deep within his clothing. Spreading it before them on the low table, he continued, "It is an ancient script detailing the Seven Gates through *The Duat*, along with the keywords required to pass through unharmed."

The three elder men studied the scroll with deep

interest while Tragen looked on, and in the light of the fire, it could be seen to be highly ornate, with the Gates enclosed in their cartouches shown in great detail. Even so, it would only be of service when each Gate stood before them, and they could see each for its worth. But its great importance was obvious, and Malian was charged with keeping it safe until needed, and surreptitiously he returned it to the deep pockets of his cloak. The men sat for many minutes in silence while they contemplated this formidable journey ahead before Psamose finally spoke up.

"I fear the evening grows swiftly old, my friends, and we should soon be thinking of rest, for we will need an early start tomorrow," he instructed, "and I would like us to be away before daybreak to make safe camp for our first night in the valley."

"Surely there is little to concern ourselves within the valley, Psamose?" Tragen asked, his own mind knowing the shape that fear could take, "I'd thought only the weather our obvious adversary while the valley sides protect us."

"I wish that were all we had to contend with," the pilgrim said as he rose stiffly from his chair, "but I have a growing unease that horrors which had lurked on our boundaries for many years, have now set foot within our unprotected valley and my heart feels heavy with dread." He stopped, noting the looks which passed across his companion's faces. "Nevertheless, at least for this evening, let us talk no more of such things and be at rest or prayers as each feels necessary."

The four finally went their separate ways to spend what little time remained in preparation for their travels, and Malian returned briefly to Mistress Mosera's house to pack the few belongings he would require on his journey. He did not encounter either Mosera or Pieter

while he was there but left each a short note before
returning to the Court of Set'al, where he would spend
the last of the night in discussion with the high priest.
When at last he got to his bed, he slept fitfully but awoke
refreshed in the grey dark of the morning while the sun
was still many hours below the horizon.

***

It was dark in the shadow of the western gate where the
four travellers and Malian made ready to start their
journey. Only the flickering torchlight gave weak
illumination to the gathering, and here both Set'al and
Alrynn, along with a small group of elders, had
assembled in the snow to bless and wish the journey well.
Standing there stamping their feet on the cold ground,
with thick cloaks hugged close to keep out the chill cold
wind, they said their farewells as the horses were brought
out through the gate, their hooves scrapping the frozen
ground as the warm air blew out in gusts from their
muzzles. There was a mount for each man, and two pack
animals, strong and sure-footed which carried the food
supplies as well as some fuel for the fires, and Darric
busied himself checking the straps and packages carefully
for any slippage while each made ready to mount.

Once they were ready, Psamose spared no time in
starting the journey. Leading the way across the snow and
into the shadows of the overhanging trees, the group was
set on the road with Darric and the pack horses bringing
up the rear while Malian remained half twisted in his
saddle until the gate could no longer be seen. Finally
saluting the great city, he turned his back to the walls and
setting his mind on the campaign to come, he could only
look ahead and wish for guidance from the gods.

Under the trees, the five moved silently along the

sloping path overhung with snow-laden branches, and as the minutes turned into hours, the darkness gradually grew less, and Malian could see a good way ahead and to each side of the path as they moved forward and downward. Forest animals could be heard and occasionally seen as they went about their business, but as the light grew, these sights became less, and finally, Malian and his companions had the forest to themselves. Travelling many miles and for many hours along this path, they rode past the ruins of firesides and deserted dwellings long since forgotten before emerging at the forest edge into the light of a cold crisp early afternoon. Psamose immediately halted the group, and they rested themselves and their horses, and while they ate from the supplies, they looked out over the valley floor to where the snow lay deep. They were still high up but had made good progress and would need to continue downwards and across the wetland area, which was the beginning of the river which ran away north.

"We must make for the path on the other side of the valley," Psamose said as he repacked his saddle bag. "And then the going will be the easier, I hope." He pointed his long thin finger in the direction they must take, and the snow could be seen lying thick all along the valley side. But a track of sorts, outlined by a line of trees, was seen winding its way up from the valley floor to disappear behind a small ridge in the distance. "But first, we must negotiate the head of the river, so we had best get moving again."

The steep path down into the valley was open on each side, and the weak sun had melted the top of the snow, causing slippery rivulets of water to make the ground underfoot even more difficult. The men did not dare ride but guided their horses safely down into the valley bottom and towards the wetland area. Here the river usually flowed up from underground at many outlets of sodden tussock grass with, in between, areas of dark pools which made the area difficult to negotiate at the best of time. However, this water, with the onset of the sudden sharp weather, was covered in a film of ice and the grass was frosted white and hard and lay snow-covered in many places. The only way to navigate across appeared to be by using the islands of grass as stepping stones and allowing the horses to make their own channel alongside. Darric went first, steering his mount and the pack animals out onto the first of the large grassy tussocks. Feeling forward for firmer ground with his feet, he negotiated the grass islands as the others prepared to follow in his steps.

"Be careful, Darric," Psamose warned as he watched the boy edge forward. "It was not like this a few days ago, and the ground around here can be treacherous at the best of times."

"Let us then go in single file," Malian said, looking across to the other side, "or do you know another way round, Psamose?"

"No, this is the quickest way, and Darric seems to be doing alright. We shall just have to go carefully and watch our step."

Darric was some way out into the channel, and using the islands as resting places, he appeared to be making light work of it as the others cautiously followed. Slipping and sliding across the streams of melting ice, they eventually arrived a good while later at the opposite side. Fatigued and irritated and with soaking feet, they had landed in an area where small snow-covered bushes sprang up, and the ground had started to improve, getting firmer under their weary feet as their pace quickened towards the path up the opposite side of the vale.

Once on this snowy path and protected by the trees,

they were able to move slightly swifter, and after a good hour's climb upwards, Psamose halted the group. On checking his bearings, he turned to lead them off to the left into a large thicket of snow-covered Alisander bushes. The late afternoon light was soon seen to be failing as the men followed him towards a dark expanse of rock fastened onto the valley side, and a few moments later, they found the opening into a dry cave which would be their resting place for the night. Water could be heard at the back of the cave, and once Darric had lit a fire, it could be seen that a stream ran along the back wall before disappearing into a smaller cave on the right. While the men warmed their chilled hands at the blaze, the younger man first attended the horses, and once satisfied of their comfort, began to prepare a warm supper.

Later, as they all sat around the flames, they talked softly in the gloom until eventually, one by one, they settled for the night, each wrapped in their thick cloaks, close to the warmth of the fire. Here they all slept with no thought of fear, for they were safe within their valley.

Around the hour of midnight, when the sky was thick with cloud, the snow began again, the first flake drifting gently to the ground, followed quickly by another and then another until the whole sky was full of dancing shapes chasing each other earthwards. The ground outside the cave was quickly covered, new snow on old, building up around the bases of the trees and drifting under hedges as the winds whipped around furiously. Around the door to the cave, it settled thick, building up as the night progressed and sealing the cave and its occupants to the outside world.

CHAPTER FOUR

The fire in the cave did not last through the nightfall, and when Darric awoke the following morning, he was cold and hungry. Opening his eyes to the semi-darkness of the cave, he tried to roll over, but during the night, the men had instinctively bunched closer together to get what warmth they could from each other, and he found himself between the cloaked figures of Malian and Mentu and unable to move. He could hear the horses becoming increasingly restless at the rear of the cave as they searched the ground for any morsel or crumb left over from the previous night, and sensing the urgency to get a fire started he eventually managed to crawl out, stretch his legs, and stand.

Wood for the fire was his first thought, but on checking the packs, he found little comfort, perhaps enough for this morning, but that would be all. He had hoped to replenish their supplies as they travelled, but the opportunity had not yet presented itself, so there was no choice but to look outside for more. Finding the cave mouth sealed, he used his spade to dig his way out and soon stood outside in the snow-covered landscape which surrounded the trees. With the realisation that no dry fuel would be found close to hand, he quickly returned back into the cave to escape the cold, where he found the others awakening from their sleep.

"My bones feel set solid," moaned Mentu as he stamped his feet and rubbed his hands up and down his arms, and soon the others were doing the same in an attempt to get some warmth into their limbs, and Darric was urged to make quick with a fire for them to warm at and to make a hot brew. As the men finally sat drinking, the young boy began his preparation of the horses for the day ahead.

Later after a meagre meal of oats cooked over the dying flames, the group made ready to move on, washing pots and filling their water flasks from the stream and leading their horses out into the cold light of the morning. Here they followed Psamose back through the snow as he made his best attempt to lead them to the Alisander bushes where they had turned off the track the night before. And eventually, after several wrong turns and a few anxious moments, they were again on the path between the trees which had led them out of the frozen wetlands.

Now they turned the horses' noses left to carry on upwards over the snow-covered ridge which had been seen from the opposite side the previous day. Once over this ridge, they halted and could again see downwards towards the river, and for the first time, their gaze took in the deep canyon within the valley floor. The river, once out of the wetland area, Psamose explained, descended down three huge waterfalls before disappearing into a black riverbed that ran through an area with steep sides. This formed a dark yawning fissure and made the river inaccessible, and this was what they could now see, a deep rift within the valley, and they were also now able to see why Psamose had brought them this way to reach the House of Abu Salama, for it was the only way over the gorge from this end of the vale.

While they stopped and the weak sun warmed them, he pointed out the general direction of that day's journey. First, they would be travelling along the ridge for a good few miles and then back down towards the valley floor, still heading north, while keeping the river gorge to the right before finally on to their next overnight rest. This was the usual way of the carts and wagons bringing wine from the Great House to the traders they met at the wetlands, who then took their purchases on up into the city, and the path had been safe and freely travelled in past and recent time. Now though, lying deeply snow-covered, it seemed that the ridge track would need careful crossing. The ground to the right sloped steeply down a vast area of white blanketed scree into the valley below, and one false step would see an animal tumbling down, never to return. While the men studied their route, a cold wind started to blow up from the valley, and the decision was made to move on as quickly and safely as possible while the light was with them.

Psamose again went first, still leading his horse and testing the ground with his walking pole for fear of rocks or hidden holes underfoot, and Malian followed with Mentu and Tragen directly behind, each leading a pack horse as well as their own. Darric trailed along in their wake, grateful that the two had offered to share in the leading of the pack animals. As the miles passed, the wind increased, and the company moved along the ridge slowly, with heads covered to keep out the chill and bent forward to watch their footing, until eventually, it ended at another tree-lined pathway, this time heading down into the valley. Quick to make the descent and get out of the wind, they moved under the trees and stopped to give the horses and themselves a brief rest before continuing down. The light was again fading, and once the group had descended and reached the valley floor, Psamose gathered them around him under the protection of the trees and reminded them of the next step of the journey.

"We shall be going a short way along the valley," he said, "keeping the river gorge on our right until we reach the Old Cedar Tree, which will be our nights resting place. Shelter has always been guaranteed there in the past along with provisions," he continued, "but who knows these days!" He shrugged his shoulders. "It seems there are no certainties left in this world." Turning, he led his horse out of the trees, and directly above the river gorge, he headed off to the left along the snow-covered ledge where the deep drop gaped at his right.

"I thank the gods we have Psamose with us," Malian said to Mentu as they followed along the bank above the river which coursed below them.

"Yes, but for how long will he be with us?" came the reply. "He has unfinished business at the Great House, or so he says, and with that, he may not journey further."

"Then we must let the gods decide, for I see no answer to that," Malian said before moving closer to Mentu and letting his voice drop.

"There is, all the same, another concern which bothers me," he whispered, "for I am surely troubled by Tragen. That look that sometime comes across his face makes me fear his mind wanders to the sufferings of his city and a depression sits around his shoulders. Will you watch out for him, Mentu?" he now asked.

"I think he is well able to look after himself," Mentu replied, glancing back in the gloom towards the huge bulk of Tragen as he led his horse. "I would certainly think more than twice about picking any sort of fight with a man of such size and dress."

"I was thinking more of his mental and spiritual wellbeing rather than his bravery," Malian further explained, "for I'm sure we have no doubt that his fighting skills will be tested in the near future, and he will show us what sort of warrior he is."

The scribe then quickly nodded his agreement, and Malian satisfied that he had done his best for the Chief's son, moved apart from the man, and their journey continued along the gorge side in silence.

In the course of time, the light faded further, and they reached the start of an area where the path divided around the base of a gigantic cedar tree which stood at its centre, the vast overhanging lower branches completely enclosing the space and forming a canopy above the men's heads. Here as the pilgrim led them off and around the pathway, the woodland trees encroached on one side as the gorge dropped away on the other, and above this, it was impossible to see the dark which was descending.

"Follow me," shouted Psamose as he led the group toward the great tree, and guiding his horse around the far side, he disappeared into a black hole at the base of the trunk. The others quickly followed and found themselves in the shelter of the cavernous heart of the hollowed tree. Here the darkness which initially greeted them gradually gave way to a lighter dark which became a greyness that filtered down from above, although no holes or windows could be seen. There was a warmth too, not overly great but gentle, which surrounded the men as they entered, leaving the cold and the chill of the growing night behind them.

"A fine shelter for man and beast, Psamose," Malian said as he softly stroked the hand-worn walls of the tree and peered upwards through the grey gloom into the dizzying heights above his head. Around him, the men quickly began unburdening and settling their horses before looking to themselves and shedding their cloaks.

"A sanctuary in time of need, my friend," Psamose replied, seating himself on a log bench that was hidden in the shadows. "Many travellers have rested here before us, and long have we been glad of its protection. Even in better times, such places have always had their need."

"Well, our thanks to the travellers for guarding such a place, for never was its need greater than this very moment," Malian replied, grateful for the refuge.

"So, are there more trees like this, Master Psamose?" Darric asked as he hurriedly dried off his shivering pack animals, placing feeding bags over their noses before coming to sit close to the pilgrim.

"There were once. Many existed in Ancient times, Darric, and whole towns were built around and under their protection. But when the uprisings began in the forgotten past and the wars split the land, these trees were left to rot and decay, for such trees need tender care and attention to flourish."

"Then is this the last one?" the boy cautiously asked, lifting his head to look up into the heights above his head.

"To my knowledge, this is the last one," sighed Psamose with great disappointment and regret in his voice. "And so we must take our care while we rest here."

"There was once such a tree in my city, too," Tragen's deep voice spoke out of the gloom as he shook off his cloak, and sitting down, he stretched out his thick legs before continuing, "It was long before my time, but a marker stood at its position in the courtyard close to the water well which refreshed my people as they passed." He then shifted uneasily on the bench before suddenly rising and pacing the floor, and with head hanging down and such bleakness in his voice, he finished, "But no one meets there anymore, for the sickness started at the water well and the elders forbade its drinking. The women had to walk many miles for clean water running from the southern lakes and glad we were to drink of such, but still, the sickness spread and the elders could do no more. *Naunet* was our protector and goddess of the water, but once she had gone, we were doomed." He slumped back down onto the bench, shoulders stooped forward like some great black bird and became lost in his sorrow. There he remained seated for many hours while the others settled themselves for the night ahead, and their thoughts finally turned to food.

Psamose decreed that no fire was to be lit, for this was forbidden within the protection of the tree, and although the group did not require warmth for themselves, their food would remain uncooked while they sheltered within. Nevertheless, after a well-needed meal provided from the provisions Psamose thankfully found stored within the tree roots and washed down with the fresh cool water collected at the cave, the men made themselves comfortable and slept safe within the roots of the tree.

The next day dawned cold, with snow falling slow but steady, and saw the group making an early start to their third day. Psamose, still leading from the front, continued to guide them along the side of the gorge with the white-cloaked sentinels of the trees to his left. However, they were now able to ride as the path was level, although deep in snow, and the horses instinctively seemed to pick out the best path. This time the journey along the gorge side was longer than the day before, and after many slow, hard miles, they finally reached an area where the trees stopped, and they came out into a cleared, long sloping bank that wound gently upwards on the left. Here was the start of the farmlands around the House of Abu Salama, and large amorphous lumps could be seen under the snow, where trees had been dropped to let the sunlight from the east flood the lands beyond onto the grape vines, which made the celebrated wine. The snow, having briefly abated at this point, saw the men choosing to rest for a short while.

"We shall soon be at the Great House," Psamose informed them as he passed around a drinking flask, "and Abu Salama is famed throughout the valley for his hospitality, so we shall all have warm beds to sleep in tonight."

"The thought of a warm bed brings much cheer to these old bones, Psamose," Mentu laughed as he eased himself in his seat before dismounting and shaking off the snow from his shoulders and stretching his cramped legs.

"And young bones, too," Darric said solemnly, repositioning himself in his saddle. "For I have heard say that the Great Houses have beds with mattresses filled with down, and it is like sleeping amongst the clouds." He suddenly thought back to his old bed in the apprentice's dormitory and the thin hard cushions which covered the boards on the creaking beds, and the remembering made him shiver.

"You shall have your night in a feather bed, Darric, for Abu Salama has many rooms filled with such items," Psamose enlightened them. "But enjoy it while you can, for come the morning, you will all be setting out again on a journey where even a safe place to rest your bones will soon be in short supply."

"Will you not be coming with us, Psamose?" Malian asked, picking up on the words said as he stamped his feet in the cold snow.

"I do not yet know if it's my destiny to go further with you, Malian. I shall need to consult with the wise woman, for her judgement in the stars will tell me which path I am to take and in her words, my destiny lies."

"You would be sorely missed if the stars choose not in our favour, for already you have saved our group, and we shall be forever in your debt. But let us speak no more until a decision is made, for the light is fading, and we must be knocking on the doors of the Great House before dark."

After their brief rest, the track took them upwards and eventually on between the vines themselves, which should have been, at this time of year, filled with the sound of the workers as they tended the rich vineyard harvests. However, with the sudden change in weather, the crop had been gathered in great haste and well before its time, and the grapes stored in hope of their survival at the Great House. While the stubby stems of the vines had withered and been left to poke up here and there from the snow. Frost had claimed the orchard fruits too, which had hung heavy on the trees, and the orange, mandarin and tangerine had turned black and dropped heavy to the ground. This scarred landscape expanded either side of the riders as far as the eye could see in the descending dusk, and as they made their way across this bleakness, their first sight of the House of Abu Salama was of the torch lights on either side of the huge wooden entrance. Eventually, as the group approached, a horn sounded out, and the doors immediately swung back to invite them to enter.

The courtyard beyond was well-lit with many lanterns which picked out the highly decorative timber windows and doors which opened there, but the rest of the entrance remained empty save for a watering trough that had been placed to the left. The men entered, dismounted and now stood on the frosted but freshly swept cobbles with reins held lightly and heads bowed in respect for the Head of the House who appeared, framed in the doorway before them. He was a small man, bare-headed and clean-shaven, with a vast waist indicating his status. All of his clothes had a flowing quality about them, giving the impression that the body beneath was forever on the move, and the richness of the colours added to his mystery. Many bangles were at his wrists, which jingled as he stepped forward and shaking each of the men by the hand, he welcomed them into this home, the freedom of the House being bestowed on all who entered.

The mounts were now left in the capable hands of Darric and two of Abu Salama's stable hands while the rest of the party entered the hall of the Great House.

It was warm and welcoming in the huge chamber which opened out in front of them, and a fire burned at the far end to which the weary riders needed little encouragement to approach and to seat themselves before its warmth. Here Abu Salama personally gave each a silver tankard of hot tea laced with rich red wine and taking one himself, he toasted the safe arrival of the group. They in turn, raised their tankards to the health of the house and its owner before toasting their own health and prosperity for the journey ahead. Then, with the formalities over, they settled down to enlighten Abu Salama of their journey so far. Malian did most of the talking, and the darkness had crept in from all corners before he finished, the lamps being lit at the windows as they discussed the events of the last days.

"But of course," he finally concluded, his face glowing in the light of the fire, "we now need to make decisions on the next part of our journey. The guidance of Psamose was never guaranteed, and we are somewhat sightless in our headway."

"Psamose is not going further with you?" Abu Salama asked in surprise as he turned to the pilgrim. "This is surely news to me, Psamose, for it's not like you to pass by a visit to the Lowlands. What do you say?"

"The stars will guide me in my choice," came the quick reply. "For I see no further than the end of my nose in this affair, and I need to seek the wisdom of Shuma."

"Ah, Shuma! She will be pleased that you seek her service, for she knew you were on your way; the bones never lie! She has grown ever restless as the days pass and awaits you in her rooms, and it would not do to keep her waiting too long," Abu Salama advised.

"Then I shall keep her no longer, and with your leave, I will go and face my future." Psamose stood stiffly from the cushions, and leaning heavily on his walking pole, he bowed first to his host and then to the others before melting into the darkness which had filled the chamber.

Silence followed his departure until Abu Salama yawned, and stretching out his arms, he bid the men to rise and follow him.

"Come let us eat and put aside our fears for a short while," he said as he led them through into a smaller room filled with shelf upon shelf of books and scrolls where a table had been set for an evening meal. Gesturing for them to sit, he invited them to make themselves comfortable.

"Please help yourselves to whatever you wish," he announced, "and take the seats nearest the fire, for the chill creeps in even here at the heart of the house."

The men quickly settled into their meal, but the scribe, having helped himself to a generous helping of dried fruits, wandered around the room in a daze. The books which lined the walls from floor to ceiling would keep any scholar busy for ten lives over. The room may have been small, but this was no ordinary collection. This was a collection of books and scrolls to rival even the Library in The City of The Vallenti. No wonder Psamose chose to spend time at such a Great House, he thought, as his fingers gently moved along the shelves.

As the evening wore on, the men remained seated, enjoying the hospitality of their host, and sometime later, Psamose re-joined them, looking grave and announcing that he would be continuing on the journey with them the following morning. He was not alone, for Shuma, the daughter of Abu Salama, accompanied him into the room. She, like her father, also wore dazzling flowing clothes but intricate symbols and stars adorned them to indicate her profession. She was taller than her father, dark-haired but slim and graceful, with a hint of strength cloaking her limbs as she moved around the room. She did not speak until she approached Malian, and they stood face to face.

"I give a great welcome to you, Malian," she said, her voice coming soft but strong, "and a thanks for your safe arrival at our home. We have been expecting you." She held out both hands, her long fingers adorned with rings of silver and gold, and Malian took them in his old hands and gently lifted them to his lips.

"Such an honour it is to meet a Lady from a Great House!" He bowed his head as he released her slender hands, "And one which will be with me for the rest of my days."

"Oh, Malian, you know how to flatter," she laughed, "and I see now that the gods have chosen well, for you will not disappoint the people of the valley. I see a strength within that even you do not realise you possess, but one which unfortunately will be tested in the very near future."

"Of the testing, I am well aware," came back the sure reply, "but I put my trust in the gods and hope that I will not fail them. Also, my companions give me much strength, so I am most fortunate."

"Good, then the news that Psamose will continue with you will not fail to please. The stars have shown us the path which he must take and the one which you must follow too. Your journey will continue alongside the tumbling river which flows into the Lowlands and on into the lakes at the north."

She continued her telling as, turning away from Malian, she addressed all of the men as they sat in the library. "Tomorrow, you must all ride with the greatest of speed, for the stars tell of another who searches and who is already gaining on the thieves."

"You must mean Tarnik and his men," Malian said, knowing of no others in the search. "For he left before us in his haste."

"That name does not mean anything to me. Only his spirit and his black heart are open to my eyes. I see the evil which is contained in them both." Her voice was suddenly deep and dark, and the shadows seemed to gather further around the little group as she spoke.

"Such news must surely spur us on, Malian," Mentu's voice broke into the silence that followed. "We must be away at sunrise, or we will lose the only reason for going on."

"That advice is well given," Shuma said, "and if you will have me, I shall join you on your journey through *The Duat*." She held out her hands again to Malian and looked deep into his eyes. "The stars do not tell me of your decision, but I have a saddle bag packed and will be ready if you say the word."

"The gods told me to take those who were willing to journey into the very Gates of the Underworld," the altar tender said, his eyes resting on each of the three companions who stood nearby, "and I already have four trusted friends who will follow me. But your offer is not one I can easily dismiss." He paused and, turning away from the fire, thought long and hard. Finally, having come to a decision, he turned back and smiling gently at Shuma said, "Very well, you shall join us and be my fifth willing companion. But," and here he held up a warning finger, "if in the cold light of the morning, your faith fails you, then I, nor any other man here, shall apportion any blame."

"I have strong faith and an even stronger desire for the return of *Amaunet*, for you have surely witnessed the destruction of our vines and orchards. It is plain to me that we cannot survive without our Icon." She held her proud head high, and her eyes flashed defiance. "I will fail neither you nor the Great House that carries my name."

"Then welcome, Shuma, for your faith and gifts will hopefully smooth our journey." Malian embraced her, and gathering all around him near to the fire, he questioned Psamose about the direction of their journey for the next day.

Psamose, however, said very little, only that they must prepare themselves well for a long expedition into the Lowlands before they reached the lakes and that the going would be made even harder by the weather conditions which would surely deteriorate the further north they went.

With this thought in their minds, the men found time to take in more of the refreshments provided by the Great House before eventually, as the midnight hour approached and Darric returned to the group, they all retired to their sleeping quarters. Abu Salama personally escorted each in turn up the long flight of twisting stairs, a bright candle held high over his head to light the darkness as they ascended. Mentu was the last to retire, reluctant to leave the book room which had so enthralled him, but eventually, he followed the shadow of Abu Salama up the stairs and retired to his room. The last sound he heard before falling asleep was of Darric making himself comfortable on his feather mattress in the adjoining chamber.

CHAPTER FIVE

While Malian and his men journeyed along the canyon's edge with the guidance of Psamose, Tarnik had been steering his followers, who numbered twenty of his leading elders, through the wastelands above the valley. And on the very evening that Malian sat in the library of the Great House of Abu Salama, they had arrived at the Marn Pass with neither sight nor sound of their quarry. They were all exhausted, being mostly men of prayer and ritual, and hard riding on short rations had pushed them and their horses to the limit of their endurance. They had at first made good progress up and out of the valley and on into the start of the wilderness, but this had slowed greatly when the snow had started to fall both night and day, and they had soon become lost amongst the boulders. Tarnik, however, persisted in leading them in a general direction northwards, as he knew by his maps that the nearest shelter could only be found in the Pass and that itself was the only way through the mountain ranges of Marn and beyond into the northern lands.

That evening they made their camp at the very entrance to the Pass that twisted its way through the high mountains which had been seen snow covered in the far distance. Up close, these ranges were shrouded in a thick wrap of cloud collected on their steep slopes, and the snow-covered peaks were no longer visible in the darkening mists which crept ominously down towards the upturned faces. The men worked quickly to make camp, for the night was rapidly upon them, and they dared not risk the shelter of the Pass in the dark. It was rumoured that there were many paths within which led to dead ends and walls of solid rock which blocked any escape from the labyrinth of avenues that snaked around the foot of the mountains. Worse, too, was the whispers and reports, either true or fabricated, of the hordes that lived in these harsh Mountains. Of vagrants and heathens who supposedly hid in the high caves and fed on the flesh and souls of any man or beast who had the misfortune to cross their path. With all of these concerns to mind, the men knew they would have to be on guard both night and day, and watchers were posted while the remaining elders attempted to settle for the night.

Later, as the snow-thick sky lay heavy overhead threatening to fill the night with more misery, Tarnik, and the three men he had named that day as leaders, sat apart from the main camp under a flimsy cover and discussed their plans for the coming days of travel.

"The Pass should be easier in the light of day," Tarnik said as he looked to where his appointed men sat, their heads lowered deep in thought, "and we should hopefully have no trouble from the people hereabout. I have heard tell that they are mainly creatures of the night if they even exist," he scoffed. "But we must all be on our guard, for we are heedless travellers in these parts and may be tempted and our feet forced from our path. So tomorrow, I shall be splitting up the group. I shall be taking five men and yourselves four each, and you shall have total command over these, for if one group fails, then another may make good." He glared around quickly at the bowed heads before him before demanding, "Does that reach with your agreement?"

He was answered with quick nods of approval from each of the men but would not have expected anything otherwise from those who sat before him as he had been careful in his choosing.

"Then I will now bid you goodnight," he finished, "and let us rest for what remains of this day and gather our strength. Tomorrow we must be alert for any eventuality." He rose and, wrapping his cloak around him, left to check on the guards, leaving the three elected men sitting in the gloom of their shelter. Here they sat, wishing for the safe haven of a roof over their heads and a warm bed to crawl into and not another night in the open air, their cold bones groaning on the frozen ground.

Having finished his tour of inspection of the unfortunate men who had been chosen to protect the camp, Tarnik eventually returned to his tent and sat in the soft light of the fire, which was giving out what little warmth it could muster. He felt little need himself for sleep, for tomorrow he would be leading his men into the Pass, and with the help of the writings he had found, he hoped to guide them safely through to the other side. How fortunate, he thought, to have remembered the scrolls and even more fortunate to have been able to place his hands upon them before they left. Here they now lay opened before him, and for many hours, he sat in dark contemplation of both the journey and of his men.

Finally, as he gently rolled up the scrolls and returned them to the safety of the leather tube in which they were carried, he wondered where the riders were. They could not be too far ahead, for surely this weather would have also caused them a delay. Laying back on the hard ground and covering his shivering body with his furs, his eyes remained open. Already a lightness was creeping into the sky and the dawn would shortly be upon them, and the riders would surely soon be within his reach.

As the daybreak spread its light, the elders could be heard rising early, for they had slept little and were glad to stretch their limbs and forsake their hard beds. Sitting huddled around the smoking fires, they concentrated their attention on the meagre meal that was breakfast and considered the day ahead. Not one of them wished to be entering the Pass, and if they had a choice, all would have given up the quest and returned to the protection of the valley which they had left so few days ago. But they could not return, for Tarnik had, over many years, been devious in his choice of followers. He had found out each and every little secret and deed thought hidden, and he had been very patient, allowing the elders to quarrel and bicker amongst themselves, and neither picking nor favouring one side or the other, he had waited on the side. Notes had been taken as alliances had formed and then crumbled, and when he made his move, he had been swift to gather favour. He now had many supporters but few that he could call friend.

Later, as the camp was hastily cleared and they prepared to enter the Pass, Tarnik stood before them with his black horse at his side, and the elders arranged themselves into the four groups as had been discussed the previous night. However, on hearing this news that morning, there had been a general argument within the men about who was to be in Tarnik's group and the three appointed leaders, who had felt it unwise to make choices, had eventually solved the problem with the roll of a dice which unfortunately for the men, Tarnik had not been blind too.

The groups were then due to set off at short intervals, with Tarnik's group being the first to leave the campsite and venture into the deep cleft of the Pass that stood yawning at the base of the Mountains. Here twisting around a huge outstanding buttress, the entrance presumably led on into the canyon itself, and the snow seemed less deep here and patchy in places. The path beyond hardly seemed touched by the snow at all, having been protected by the huge overhanging rocks which arched above, but the men still feared entering the place.

"Mount up!" Tarnik's voice came dark and hoarse on the chill morning wind as he roughly guided his horse towards the opening of the Pass. "We have wasted enough time here already." The five luckless men who had lost to the dice now slowly mounted, and reluctantly joining him at the canyon's start, they looked down to where he pointed.

"Behold the Path of *Horus*," he announced, his gloved finger extending towards the carving etched into the granite slab, which was set deep into the earth of the canyon floor. This showed the falcon head of the god *Horus*, his tight beak pointing its way into the ravine. Raising his hand, Tarnik gestured along the gorge to the first of the deep bends, which led away to the left. "This will be our guide through the Mountain Pass," he explained, "for the falcon points the way to the next stone and gives guidance for a safe passage." Here the shadows were already cast long and dark even in these early hours, and the men felt a sudden dismay as they looked onwards.

"What of the others that follow, Tarnik?" One of the men asked. "Will they know that this is the sign they must watch for and follow?" The speaker was Theroc, one of the senior elders and a man who had been much respected within the councils of the city.

"The others have already received their orders, Theroc and will know the signs they must follow," Tarnik snapped back, "so now let us make a start, for the way ahead is clear for the present."

Turning his horse and following the line of the Mountains, he moved off slowly down the Pass, and the others fell in behind him in single file. And with many looks back to the elders who remained watching, their hands were swiftly raised in hope of blessing and farewell. The first bend was quickly reached, and the safety of their campsite was soon out of sight and the true nature of the Pass could be seen. It was hardly more than a crack between the two halves of the Marn Mountains, which towered unseen overhead and which seemed to slowly creep in on them as they made their way along. Here enormous disfigured slabs jutted out over their heads, and the wind cascaded snow and a silvery brown rain of dirt onto their cloaks as, in places, they bowed their heads to pass beneath. These rocks, weather-torn and sun-bleached, leered down on them with dark holes that became eye sockets and cracks and crevasses, mouths of rotten fangs waiting to bite deep.

Within a short space of time, more than one of the men had begun to glance nervously over their shoulders, and none more so than the elder who brought up the rear. As the hours dragged on into the afternoon and early evening approached, he became more convinced that they were being watched from above. There was an almost silence too, not complete, for the horses' hooves slushed through the soft earth and occasional patches of light snow which had been blown down into the depths. Also, the wind sighed between the rocks and through the rock holes. But there was something else, just beyond the perception of the men, which gave a feeling of weight pushing down upon them, and the ears of the elders ached in its press.

Later as the light seemed to be fading, a chittering sound could be heard at their back, like insects caught in a trap, which they became more aware of as they slowly dismissed the surrounding sounds and focused on the higher pitch. The horses sensed it too and snatched and fought at their bridles as they moved their heads wildly this way and that along the tight confines of the canyon, and the elders had to fight desperately to stop them galloping frantically forward into the growing dark of the Pass.

"Keep a tight hold!" bellowed Tarnik as the noise rose

and the emerging bats, like a black cloud, caught up with them, passing low over the heads of the terrified elders. Finally, the rush of darkness disappeared like a scream into the night as they made off north to hunt in the grasslands far beyond the other side of the mountains.

The elders, having dismounted to calm their nervous horses, then struggled to advance as fast as the canyon walls would allow, for in some places, it was barely wide enough for them to lead their saddled mounts, and they made slow progress as the light faded even faster. Finally, in the dusk, they reached a major fork in the canyon which gave off two pathways standing like hollow eye sockets in the walls of the mountains.

Tarnik walked slowly to each entrance in turn and scraping his foot across the black earth, first at one spot and then another, he peered down, searching for the falcon-headed god to show them the right way along the Pass. While he did this, the other elders remained with the horses, until finally sensing Tarnik's frustration, they too joined in the search, scrambling around in the growing dark. The slab of carved granite was finally located in the exact middle of the clearing, the cruel curved beak of *Horus* pointing the way while the empty eyes stared into the blackness of the sky above. Tarnik was quickly on his knees, brushing away the remains of the dirt engrained in the carving to confirm the direction.

"It's the left-hand tunnel we must take," he muttered into his cloak, which was pulled up high into his neck to keep out the chill winds that had increased along the Pass. "But we must wait for the coming daylight, for I dare not lead you into the darkness. We shall sit out the night here and wait for the others to catch up."

The elders, both with relief and reluctance, made their camp for the night in the growing gloom, their horses being tethered together against the Canyons wall. But no light nor warmth would Tarnik allow so far into the Pass, and so they themselves sat miserable and cold, huddled close together in the deepening darkness which closed around them. Each sat in their own anguish and misery as they anticipated the arrival of the others.

Eventually, as the time moved slowly on in their wait, the elder Theroc whispered a question into the dark, his thinking having brought it to mind. "Tarnik," he asked, "why should we be troubled by the Mountains?" He bent forward closer to where the leader sat as the wind whipped away his words. "The defilers of the temple must have surely travelled this very same path, both on their journey down and now in their haste before us?"

"It would appear that the Pass may be easier for some," Tarnik's voice replied coldly, acknowledging the question. "For the hordes that they say live here will surely have their allies in the north and also the reverse. But who knows, our fears may be ours alone, and we can only hope for a quick passage."

The dense darkness now seemed impenetrable to the men's eyes, the cloud-filled sky above barely visible from the cleft of the canyon as slowly each of the hunched figures became bowed down with the weight of the night. Sleep would not come, and each man sat with his own fears. And when the remaining groups of elders failed to appear, an even greater terror and unease started to fill their minds.

Suddenly, a terrifying noise, the sound of sharp metal on rock, burst into the darkness bringing the men to their feet as a shout arose in each throat and then died just as suddenly as the silence closed around them.

"What in all the heavens was that?" a frightened elder asked out of the dark.

"My imagination would have me believe the worst," Tarnik replied, his voice loud against the resounding hush which filled their ears. "But we must have some light, for the very darkness itself holds such fear that it alone could be our undoing. Theroc, prepare the lanterns!" he shouted.

The torches, once lit, produced a harsh glow around the heads of the elders as they crowded back-to-back in the centre of the pathway, the slit of the dark sky pressing down on their heads. The flickering lights which they raised aloft reflected and passed wildly across their petrified eyes as their short swords were held at the ready. Slowly, as they became used to the growing light, they could see shapes and shadows crowding into the clearing, the dancing light sending them spiralling across the rock face to hang hideously above the heads of the elders before they came crashing down amongst them. Instantly the light of the lanterns was extinguished by a cold breath that assailed them, and the darkness became complete. The fight was brief, for the men panicked in the dark and could only guess the direction of attack and the numbers which assaulted them, and although they put up a brave fight, none escaped the onslaught.

***

Hours later, as the weak sun filtered through the cold light of the morning, the elders awoke to the jarring sound of cold metal against hard rock as the mountain people, known to themselves as The Pagan worked their axes and swords in the darkness of the cave. Vague outlines of these hard men could be dimly noted as they passed in and out of the flames of the lanterns, and the ragged arm and shoulder of a Warrior loomed large across the rocks as the flames flickered. Many others could be seen busying themselves at the opening of the cave bringing in the frightened horses and the elder's bundles taken from the canyon floor.

The elders themselves had been caged high above their heads, suspended in a structure from the cave ceiling which slowly rotated in the chill breeze, there sitting hunched and bowed within its tight confines. None seemed badly hurt, a few scrapes here and there and clothing torn by eager hands as they were captured and carried away, but they were all still alive, or at least five of them were, for Tarnik was not among them.

"A fine state we are now in," one of them lamented as he eased his body into a squatting position and peered down into the depths of the cave. "We would seem fated to be skin and bone by the end of the day."

"Have faith, Rusan, all is not yet lost."

Theroc, the senior elder, spoke from his huddled corner, his face catching the leap of flames from the lanterns. "I imagine these vagrants are not ones to keep their captives alive nor to take prisoners. Let's be thankful we live for the present."

"Little hope if we remain in this cage with no food or water," the man came back as he continued to look down. "But perhaps they mean to starve us to death."

"I fear we would be of no use to them as fleshless remains," Theroc replied darkly. His voice a whisper against the frantic noise of the terrified horses as they stood tormented at the front of the cave before they were quickly driven off into the darkness of the mountain, the clatter of their hooves against the rock floor slowly dying away into silence.

The Pagan that remained below could be seen to be stunted and small, their clothing wrapped around to keep out the cold of the high mountain. And while they busied themselves about the floor of the cave, none glanced upwards to the swinging cage high above their heads as they eagerly tore open the packs of foodstuff and bundles of clothing that the elders had carried with them from the city.

Now at least the elders had a chance to observe them from their height and assess their situation.

"Do you think we would have any chance to outfight them?" Rusan whispered hopefully as he moved closer to Theroc, the cage spinning giddily in the process. "They seem quite a ragged bunch to me, except for that one." He pointed to an especially large man who stood in the shadows near the opening of a side tunnel, a heavy sword at his belt and many sharp blades about his person.

"Yes, well, I agree he would not be an easy fight," Theroc said, noting the stature of the man, "and of the others, I would also be unsure. We ourselves remain defenceless without our own weapons, and none of us are fighting men like these, and so I would say 'No,' let us wait and see what is to come!"

"But we could so easily overcome these few!" Rusan declared sharply, his voice full of anger as he looked again at the stunted men who worked below, "and then we could at least try to deal with any more that may attack."

The three other elders were quick in agreement and could only answer that it would be foolish to remain captive if there were even the slightest chance of forcing their way out and escaping their predicament, and Theroc found himself outnumbered.

"Very well," he finally had to concede, "but first…how do we get down from this cage?"

This question was never answered, for a sudden disturbance at the back of the cave sent the smaller, stunted Pagan scrambling to get out of the way as a group of the larger Pagan Warriors entered. Held firmly between the first two was the robed figure of Tarnik, the elder's leader, while behind strode the tall figures of

Gallius and Roth, who came to a stop beneath the slowly swaying cage.

"Cut them down," Gallius immediately ordered, looking up towards where the elders stared down, "but see and bind them well. They are men of principle and as such, will deem it their duty to try and escape."

The cage was roughly lowered to the floor with many stops and jolts until it lay upon the roughhewn stone of the filthy cave floor, and the door was opened wide for the men to emerge. They did so slowly, stretching their cramped limbs at the taste of freedom but wary of the sharp-tipped blades of the assorted weaponry that the Pagan Warriors held lightly in their huge hands.

When all had been released, they were bound in a line with Tarnik at the head. And, with Gallius and Roth taking the lead, they moved slowly out into the cold of the mountainside with the Warriors in the rear. They could now see that they were high up in the Mountains with a sheer steep drop to their right and were soon being guided along a heavily trodden track. Hanging on to each other for protection on the slippery path, they saved their breath for the hard toil while above them, a weak sun shone down. But they could not lift their heads for a comforting glimpse and concentrated on putting one foot in front of another as they battled forward.

Slowly, as time passed, they started to descend, and the track became easier on their sore feet, the hard ice-covered path giving way to a softer snow-covered soil while the walkway broadened, and the bowed heads of the elders were released from the tight grip of the wind as they raised their eyes to judge their position. The snow-covered Marn Mountains surrounded them in each direction they looked, but the canyon floor was nearer to hand as they continued downwards. Eventually, as the path seemed to be rising again, they were finally led into another cavern in the rock face. Here the air was dark and rank from the sullen fires which flickered from the fire baskets hanging on the walls, and the shadows of the elders danced across the roof as they were pushed towards the rear and away from the doorway through which they had come. Here there were many more mountain people, though no more of the Warriors, for these were the caves of the lower classes, and their young could be seen playing in the dirt and squalor which surrounded them as a stench of decay pervaded the air. The Warriors then quickly left them, returning up the face of the Mountain to their higher domains, leaving Gallius and Roth to take charge of the huddled captives.

"You shall certainly not want for fresh meat, my friends," Roth laughed as he addressed the small group which gathered around, their laughter joining his as he prodded the nearest elder with the end of his sword. But Gallius remained grim-faced and quickly raised his hand to halt the fun.

"Enough of that, Roth," he commanded. "We shall have no more bloodshed here. You know my orders."

The long journey across the wastelands had seemingly taken its toll on Gallius in more ways than one, and Roth knowing him more as a friend had been first to see a difference in the leader and suspected it was from close contact with the statue. But he had been given his orders to follow, which suited him better in his own outlook, and for the moment, he thought, he would show patience and would wait. It was useful to him at this time to keep Gallius alive and appear to accept his rule alone.

"Very well," he slowly conceded, putting away his blade. "But on the first sign of trouble from them, they will all be slaughtered!"

"We shall give you no trouble if you return that which you stole from us," Tarnik spoke boldly from his position where he lay flat across the floor. "That is all we want, but I cannot give my word if that is denied."

"Then you shall remain bound and under guard at all times," Roth replied, and with that, he and Gallius left the chamber leaving the elders to their fate.

***

For two long days and nights, the elders were kept confined to the cave, and the riders did not return. And although they were not treated too badly, they remained loosely bound and unable to stretch their legs beyond the cavern. Food was offered and refused to a large extent, it being mainly meat and unrecognisable as to which sort. But bread and water were freely given and warmth was provided. Here they had time to think on their dilemma and that which no doubt had befallen the other groups and could find little comfort in the outcome. Tarnik did not join in any of their speculations, keeping himself aloof and often sitting by himself and spending his time in prayer, and the other elders felt content to let him be.

On the morning of the third day, they were awoken early and their ties completely removed, and with a guard of armed Warriors taken to meet with Gallius and Roth on the slopes slightly lower down the Mountainside. They were still fairly high up in the Ranges, but they continued downwards back towards the Canyon in a slow procession, and the trek became somewhat easier in the making. As they reached a fork in the path, one way leading upwards, the other down, they came to an area of a vast pit with a sheer cliff side at its back. The path then took them along a ridge where they could look down into the waste which the Pagan had thrown down from on high. Here was surely the resting place for some of their fellow Citizens of the Vallenti, for piles of freshly gnawed bones and tatters of clothing could be seen amongst the filth and waste that lay within, and the elders openly wept as they recognised pieces of cloak and clothing, and here and there they glimpsed the personal items of their friends scattered around.

"What will become of these remains, for with no decent burial, their spirits will wander the land, lost forever!" Rusan cried as he stopped before the sight, whilst quietly thanking the gods that he had not eaten of the meat offered.

"We must pray for them," Theroc said as the tears of anger raged. He quickly knelt to bow his head. "Pray that the goddess *Amaunet* heard their last cries!"

"Be quiet there," growled Roth, who was bringing up the rear, "and keep moving, or you'll find your bones joining them!"

The Warriors roughly picked up Theroc as he remained on his knees and urging the elders on swiftly, blades piercing the backs of any who lagged behind, they continued to move downwards. The descent was then made more briskly, the older men half carried and half chased, arriving at the base of the Mountain and the canyon camp of the riders exhausted and unable to move any further.

"You have two hours to rest, and then we ride," Gallius informed them as they lay breathless and prostrate before him on the dusty, cold canyon floor. "There is food ready for you, so eat quickly."

"I can't move," Theroc gasped, his face looking up in exhaustion before he collapsed.

"Then I shall leave you behind in the company of The Pagan," Gallius replied harshly, "and that goes for all of you, either eat or be eaten." He stalked off in the direction of the horses and left Roth in charge.

"You heard him." Roth grabbed Theroc by the hair

and pulled him to his feet. "Get moving."

The six slowly made their way over to the fires, each assisting the other and found that hot porridge and tea were brewing. There was also meat, but of that, they did not partake, for who knew where it had come from. Even though the riders did not appear to be like the Mountain people, the elders feared the worst. There was, however, plenty of oatmeal along with the thick Pagan bread, and the plates and mugs were filled and filled again before the two hours were up. The men now rested from their weariness while they could, and as they sat, Rusan quietly voiced a question that was on all their lips.

"Why do you think they are keeping us alive?" he asked as he pocketed a piece of bread for later. "And why have they been delayed in the Mountains? They should have been long ahead of us, shouldn't they?"

"I don't know," replied Theroc. However, in remembering that Tarnik had seemingly spent some time with the riders after their capture, he looked hard at the man who had his head lowered as he worked industriously to empty his plate. "Perhaps our leader can enlighten us on this?"

"Me," the man replied through a mouth full of porridge, his eyes never leaving his plate, "how should I know their reasoning? Ask them yourselves, if you want answers!" He wiped his hand across his mouth, and moving off, he once more turned away and kept his own company.

There had begun a slow change in Tarnik since their capture, one that had not gone unnoticed, especially by Theroc. In his spending more time by himself, a distancing between him and his men was becoming felt. However, the senior elder had let it be, for his thoughts kept constantly turning back to the dilemma of their capture and the possibility of escape. Now he voiced a question.

"Do you think that Roth is unhappy with Gallius as leader?" he suddenly asked in a whisper, looking across as he moved to sit closer to the fire. "I sense perhaps there is bad blood between them, and I wondered if we could use this knowledge to our advantage!"

"I'd not made note of that, Theroc," Rusan replied, swiftly glancing up as a sudden interest showed in his face, "but if so, it would be useful to know who was for Roth and who for Gallius. Then we could play each other if possible and work it to our advantage."

"Yes, that's a possibility," Theroc quickly came back, hearing the eagerness in the man's voice, "and perhaps it's in our interest to watch and wait a while. What do you all think?"

The others were all in quick agreement to this, nodding their heads as they saw sense in waiting their time and gathering their information. But for Theroc, a sudden extra anxiety had seemingly fallen into place. Having again seen their leader once more turn away from his own men, he knew he would also need to be watching Tarnik.

Roth eventually returned as the elders were finishing their meal, and kicking the fire across the cold floor, he poured the remains of the brew over the ashes and signalled that the two hours were over and they would be moving on.

The northern men could be seen making their final preparations, checking packs and repositioning such items as necessary as Roth led the elders over to mount up. There were horses for them all, good strong beasts which no doubt had been spared by the Mountain people, but none that were recognised as any of their own fine Vallenti stock, and so the elders mourned their loss in the caves. However, they did not mourn the fact that they were getting away from The Pagan, and their hearts lifted slightly at the thought. Now, all mounted, the prisoners with their hands tied to their saddles, they headed off down the Canyon in a long line with Gallius in the lead and Roth bringing up the rear.

The journey through the Mountains was then in the charge of the northern men who had their secret routes along the Canyon floor. And through hollowed-out caves and tunnels unknown to others, the days flowed into nights, and the elders lost all concept of time as the mountains engulfed them. As they moved slowly north, the cold diminished, the snow disappeared, and the air became slightly warmer until eventually, the mountains became hills, and the land flattened as the Canyon ended.

Before them, a high grass-covered bank hid the swamps from their eyes as the sun was rising higher in a clear blue sky, and huge dark insects swooped and dived in the first warmth over the heads of the trees. The buzz of their droning eventually disappeared down into the misty, murky depths of the canal which surrounded the High Rush Plains. Plunging over this bank and on through the trees, Gallius quickly led them on into the thick undergrowth as the day advanced and the sun rolled its way across the land.

CHAPTER SIX

Malian had risen late from his soft bed, the early dawn chorus having failed to awaken him. He had slept through the night and long past the dawning day and had woken refreshed. And in greeting this new sunrise, he was pleased that the company was complete and the journey could continue with the blessings of the gods.

There was no sound from the other rooms, and after his morning rituals, he found himself quietly descending the twisting staircase back down into the great hall, where he found the others already up and awaiting his arrival.

"Welcome, Malian. I trust you slept well." Abu Salama came forward, and extending his arms in greeting he guided the altar tender towards a table set for breakfast. The others followed, and although they had already eaten, they still found room for more tea which had been placed fresh for them. Malian helped himself liberally to the morning meal and settled himself next to Abu Salama when his plate was sufficiently laden while his fellow travellers seated themselves around. Looking closer, he noticed an absence from the evening before.

"I see Shuma has not joined us yet," he noted, "I pray that she is not having any doubts about her faith in this matter?"

"Have no fear, Malian," Abu Salama replied. "My daughter will be true to her word in every sense. For in that, she is so like her father."

"She certainly has spirit." Malian raised his cup before picking up his fork. "And I certainly slept the easier knowing of her decision to join us."

He then started his breakfast, and the talk turned to the journey ahead, with the conversation moving on to their destination in the north and on through the Gates of *The*

Duat. Each knew that this would be the hardest part of the journey, but their faith remained, even if, in their own private thoughts, they had doubts and fears. Eventually, all fell silent, and Malian finished his breakfast as Shuma, dressed in her travelling clothes, arrived in the hall from the gardens.

"I do like to see a healthy appetite, Malian," she said as she approached the table, noting the empty plate which sat before him.

"Welcome, Shuma." Malian embraced the woman as she joined them. "You have been missed this morning, and we feared a change of heart."

"Never," she quickly replied, "for that would bring a great dishonour upon this house." Standing behind her seated father, hands resting gently on his shoulders, she explained her absence. "I have been saying farewell to my friends and countrywomen, for they deserve to hear of my leaving from my own mouth and not as some hearsay or message sent on my behalf." She paused briefly before continuing, "Also, they deserve to know of the dangers and perils that I may face and that I may not return."

"Well, let's not speak of such at present," Psamose voiced a feeling held deep in each of their hearts. "I would prefer to think on the positive side, my lady."

"And I would prefer that my kinsmen know that I may not be coming back, Master Psamose," came back her reply. "Each to his own!"

"Enough!" Abu Salama decidedly responded, himself fully aware that his daughter was in peril the moment she left his side. "You will have plenty of time on your travels to agree on who speaks the wisest. And now, I sense that your departure draws near, for I feel you are eager to be on your way, Malian." Turning to look upwards to where Malian stood, he looked long and hard into the face of the altar tender, sensing his eagerness to be away until he could bear to look no longer and dropping his gaze, he got to his feet and quickly stepped away from the table.

"Yes, we must be away soon," Malian smiled at the assembled group, "for the morning grows longer, and already we lose any advantage over those we pursue." He stopped as he looked at those who would be journeying with him. "But let us delay for a short while, for to leave in such haste would be disrespectful to such a Great House. We will assemble at the doors in thirty minutes, so let us use the time wisely."

The group broke up, with Darric, accompanied by Tragen, departing to check on the pack animals. While Psamose and Mentu remained seated in the comfort of the Great House, for both were already packed in readiness, and their meagre luggage stood at the front doors awaiting the off. Shuma immediately disappeared to her tower, ascending the steep steps to spend her last minutes in her home with her sister, Tellia, the youngest daughter of Abu Salama. Tellia suffered from a rare physical disorder that confined her to her bed, and having shown great distress that day on hearing of Shuma's departure, the older sister strived to spend the last moments quietly in her company to quell her fears.

Abu Salama himself had taken Malian to one side, and when he was sure no one was looking, lowered his voice and thrust a small, wrapped parcel into the altar tenders' hands.

"In our parting, Malian, I should like to give you this," he whispered. "Please take it. I feel it has brought good luck to this house over the years, and although I shall be loath to see it go, I fear your need may be greater than mine."

Malian deftly unwrapped the parcel and found a copy

of *The Book of the Two Lands* in his possession, its outer covering delicate in its stitch and leatherwork. Here was a very rare book indeed, he thought, seeing its title etched before him. The original was believed to have been destroyed in the long past, and copies were known to be few and far between, but here in this respected house, he stood amazed as he realised that it might help them in their travel northwards and hold guidance for the journey ahead. The book itself was written both in hieroglyphs and the common tongue and was richly decorated with scenes from the lives of the Ancients who lived before the lands had split and of the gods, they had worshipped and who walked the earth alongside them.

"It has been well looked after," Abu Salama continued as he also looked down upon its decoration. "It has been hidden away from prying eyes, but," he declared, uncertain of its worth, "it has always held a mystery to me, and I only hope that my gift to you will be a good sign and may help you on your quest."

"That I can surely hope for, too," Malian replied, "as I fear I shall need all the help I can get in the coming time that lies ahead." He carefully wrapped away the book, covering over the deep letters of the engraved title, before grasping the man's hand. "The gods have given where it is most needed, Abu Salama, and so I accept your gift with an open heart and with great thanks, and long shall I remember your hospitality."

"I only wish that I could aid you further."

"You have already helped in a way in which you could have least expected," Malian replied. Before in hoping to ease the man's regret, he finished, "You have given your own daughter to such an undertaking, and that goes beyond the call of most men!"

"Shuma is her own woman and made her own decision. Know this, Malian, that even has her father, I had little to say in this matter save for wishing her a safe and speedy return to us."

"We will all be praying for the same, I especially, for the burden lies heavy with me. My fellow travellers are unaware, in the main, of that which lies before them." He nodded now towards where the other men stood in wait. "But let us talk no longer, and let us make ready."

Leading, Malian walked back to the warmth of the fire where Psamose and Mentu stood warmly beside its heat, and the two stopped in their company.

The group assembled in the hall, Shuma being the last to arrive from her farewell, while Tragen and Darric waited at the doors. Slowly they filed back into the courtyard where the light of the mid-morning shone full down upon them and where a small gathering of well-wishers waited to see them off. Already the snow-laden clouds could be seen filling the sky, but at least the bitter wind had ceased, and the birds could be heard singing above the rooftops.

The horses had long been packed and stood stamping impatient hooves on the hard ground as Darric and Tragen checked their packs. Overnight the mounts had been tended well and were fully rested after their stop in the warm stables where Abu Salama kept his fine stallions, and they had been joined by another pack pony with extra bags of provisions hanging heavily across its broad back. There was also an extra riding horse, a fine pure-bred, light-footed mount that Shuma had ridden for many years and whose loyalty was hers alone. As the group collected before the gates, the company was seen to be complete in its number, and a sense of anticipation gathered.

Each busied themselves, checking straps and rearranging saddle bags, as Shuma alone bid farewell to her father and received his blessings. Finally, after one last embrace, she vaulted nimbly into the saddle of the waiting horse, and they began the day's journey with many a look back at the House of Abu Salama and countless raised hands in farewell.

Out from the doors of the Great House, they turned the horse's noses north and skirting the desolate vineyards, their path took them alongside and down through the snow-covered orchards of blighted trees until they reached the river gorge back along the valley floor. Here the trees carpeted the steep valley sides where they met the trail, and Psamose continued to lead the way along the gorge's edge. The journey into the higher lands was known to him, and the track, although snow-covered, could be picked out easily enough if you knew the way.

"Shall we see the northern lakes in the next few days, Psamose?" Malian asked as he jogged alongside the pilgrim on the frozen path.

"Perhaps," came the quick answer, "but only if we keep up this pace. First, we must negotiate the ranges through into the Lowlands of the lakes before we see the water. Then we must move back down towards the valley floor. The ranges here are high," he further explained, "and very difficult in places, but there is a way through for those that know, and that is where we are heading."

"We'll be camping out tonight then?" the question came, the wind beginning to bite into the altar tender's face as the breeze changed direction, gusting the coldness from deep within the gorge.

"Possibly, but there is a place I know if we reach it in time. But it will be no luxury, for there are no more houses, great or small, this side of the gorge or this far north in the valley." Turning, he raised his voice back towards where the horses followed behind in their line. "We shall not see a feather bed for many a long time, Darric," he shouted to the boy who brought up the rear, "so I hope you made the most of your bed in the Great House, as tonight you shall have only your pack and the hard ground to sleep on."

"I shall have warm memories, Master Psamose," the boy called back, expertly guiding the pack ponies along the frozen track, "and I will remain in hope that they keep my spirits up in the coming days."

Their journey continued for many miles in silence along the gorge side while Malian's thoughts drifted back and forth at their own will as he sat and allowed his trusted mount to pick out the path ahead. And so engrossed was he in his thoughts that he was unaware of the gently hand of Psamose taking the reins out of his hands and leading his horse until suddenly the voice of Mentu aroused him.

"Are we stopping for food soon?" he asked, a thought which had been slowly growing in other minds. "My belly is starting to complain, and I would like to see it quietened!"

"I suppose here is as good a place as any," Psamose reluctantly said, peering into the depths of the trees to the left, "and we have been riding for many miles, so perhaps a brief stop would surely refresh us all."

He led the little group off the track, first checking this way and that before stopping under a large overhanging tree, where they dismounted into the thick snow which had collected under the boughs. Here it was cold and chilly as little sunlight found its way through the thick foliage, although the snow-covered branches gave off a lightness that lit up the figures as they sat and rested. Above their heads, the air drifted damp from the fog which wound among the base of the trees and hung like ribbons from the lower branches.

"This rawness is getting into my bones," Tragen complained after a short while of sitting. "I think I'll stretch my legs and see how the land lies up ahead." Quickly getting up and collecting his bow from his saddle, he disappeared onto the snow-covered track, and after a few moments, Darric followed him.

"Those two seem to be getting friendly," Malian remarked through a mouthful of salted meat as he watched the boy disappear beneath the trees, "and it will be a friendship in which they will both find benefit, I think."

"Well, the youth will certainly learn some skills, at least in the art of hunting, if I'm not mistaken," Psamose replied. "But what do you think Tragen will get in return?" he queried.

"Probably that which he requires the most," Shuma wisely said, for the warrior's grief had not gone unnoticed to her, "a reliable friend and a companion in times of need."

They now sat quietly only for a short while, and as the gloom deepened and the increasing wind could be heard whipping the branches above their heads, they stowed their packs and moved back onto the track where the snow had once more started to fall.

"We'll catch up with Tragen and Darric as we go," Malian shouted above the wind as he mounted his horse. "They can't be too far along the path unless they have strayed off."

"Surely they would not go off wildly without leaving a sign?" Mentu queried, as having climbed atop his mount, he pulled Darric's and Tragen's horses behind in his wake.

"No, I think not. Both are more skilled in the art than that," Psamose replied, gathering up the reins of the pack ponies and starting off along the track. "We shall meet them further along!"

Riding slowly, bent almost double over the necks of

their horses, the path took them under the snow-laden branches, which threatened to drop their icy burdens onto the heads of the riders until they reached a place where the path divided. The wind was instantly swirling the snow in their faces, and the easiest way appeared to be towards the right, where the trail continued to follow the gorge downwards. Psamose, however, consciously moved his horse to the left and urged the others to follow the path leading up.

"Let's hope Tragen and Darric did not go the wrong way," Mentu said as he trailed behind Psamose. But just then, a shout was heard from further up the path, and the warrior and his companion came into view carrying a limp sack between them. Their cloaks and breeches were wet and covered in snow through crawling under the trees and hedges, but they had each received a rich reward for their efforts. The bag contained a number of fat dead duck who had been sheltering out of the snow and who had been easily caught unawares.

"Well done," Malian praised as the sack was opened and the ducks, necks snapped like twigs, were revealed, "we shall have a feast tonight and thank the gods for providing for us."

"We won't if we don't keep moving," Psamose reminded them darkly. "The wind is getting stronger, and I sense the snow will be getting much worse. We must reach the Neferu Passage before we get caught out in a storm." He set off swiftly up the path urging his mount onwards, and Tragen and Darric hurriedly mounted, setting off after Psamose and following the others in their haste.

The ground got progressively heavier as they rode upwards into the ranges, and the snow was unceasing, but they made better time than anticipated and arrived at the wide entrance to the Passage with a few hours to spare before the night was upon them. Making camp in the mouth of the tunnel for protection from the wind and the tumbling snow which fell constantly, they relaxed for the night with the thought of the roasted duck to satisfy their hunger, and each found rest around the glow of the fire after the efforts of the day. All except for Mentu, who could not settle, and pacing back and forth, he peered into the deeper black depths of the passageway at their backs as a feeling of misgiving grew within him, and he frequently glanced over his shoulder as if being watched.

"Will we be able to see the other end in the daylight, Psamose?" he eventually asked with little hope in his voice.

"No, we shall be carrying torches," came the reply. "The passageway leads deep into the ranges, and there is no natural light to reach into those depths."

"You have been this way before, Master Psamose? Through this passage?" Darric asked as he skilfully turned the ducks over on the fire, and their fat dropped sizzling into the flames.

"I have, although it was a few years ago, and things can change in the remembering. But I feel there is little to fear." He quickly glanced up towards Mentu, who remained standing ill at ease. "Except perhaps for that which you take in with you…and then again, a fear of the dark if you are so inclined. But let me tell you a folktale."

He went on to tell a story from long ago when the gods were on the earth, and the land was fruitful and warm, and man was but a servant who gave thanks to the gods for their benevolence. There in those days, in these southern lands, a people gifted with the art of carving, design and sculpture lived. These people were a kind and gentle race, skilled in the craftsmanship that the gods had bestowed upon them and master craftsmen at quarrying the limestone and granite for the building of the tombs and monuments in veneration of the gods, and which they carved in such detail for their dedication.

At that time, a young family, who had been well chosen by the gods, were blessed with a child in the early years of their marriage and had dedicated this child to the god *Ptah*, the supreme god of craftsmanship who accepted her from the day of her birth. She was named Neferu, and she was a happy and beautiful child.

Ptah watched over her in her early years and saw that she was brought up to believe in only him as her god, which she did as a dutiful daughter would. And as the many years passed, she blossomed into a fine sculptor, and her parents were proud of the fine pieces which adorned temples throughout the land. But Neferu grew restless, and thinking her talent was wasted in the carving of *Ptah* alone, she secretly went up to the caves in the hills and set up a workshop. There she carved the most beautiful statues that she wept at her own perfection and wanted to share them with the whole of the land. Her work was placed in the finest temples in the largest cities, and all wondered who this talented sculptor could be.

Ptah, however, recognised her work and appeared to the girl in a dream, where he questioned her closely. Under his penetrating gaze, she admitted that it was she who had done the work, saying that her eyes had been bewitched by the beauty which had arisen from the stones as she had carved and that her hands had been guided by unseen spirits. She knew that she would be punished but begged the god for forgiveness and to spare her life. This *Ptah* promised, but commanded that from henceforth she would "see darkness forever" and that her hands would wither and rot, never again being able to bring forth such beauty from the rocks which surrounded her.

The next day, when Neferu awoke, it was as if she had

not opened her eyes, for the god had been true to his word, taking away her precious sight as punishment. And as the tears flowed from the opaque spheres, she knew the dishonour this would bring to her family, and so silently and without saying goodbye, she left and never returned. Instead, she made her way to her cave in the hills where her withered hands carved crude sculptures from the rocks, and then growing tired of this, she attacked the very walls of the cave, carving from floor to ceiling until every inch was used up. Then in her madness, she started to excavate into the back, carving as she went until the cave became a channel, which in turn became a tunnel that eventually became a huge passageway. She required no light to guide her work, and none was offered by her god, who watched her progress from afar until finally, she had burrowed right through the mountainside and felt the wind of the lakes on her face. Here she lifted her blank eyes to the gods and, with one last plea for forgiveness, fell dead upon the grass-sloped mountainside.

It was said that *Ptah* himself collected her soul, and then, in the lands beyond where the spirits lived, he forgave her and gave her back her sight and the beauty of her hands.

"So, is this the same passage?" Darric asked as the story came to an end, and he looked up into the dark towards the ceiling above their heads.

"Well, this one certainly dates back beyond many years, and the walls are indeed carved very coarsely. But who knows? Let me just say that I have passed through here before and have no fear of the dark it holds, and I trust the telling of the story will help you all tomorrow?" he finished, and accepting a piece of roast duck from Darric, he raised his mug in toast.

"Well, I for one, shall hold no fear of the passage,"

Shuma spoke from the depths of her cloak, which was drawn up around her neck to ward off the night chill, "for such love, devotion and courage to complete such a task as Neferu accomplished must have left strong echoes in these very walls, which even the strongest woman would be unable to resist." She glanced around, aware that there was a certain sacred feeling about the place and finished, "I can feel her presence here already."

"We shall come to no harm, that I can promise," Malian reassured them, "for I have already been this way in my dreams, and the journey was blessed by the gods. So come, let's eat and find our rest for the night." Standing at the far side of the fire, the altar tender sat himself down alongside the woman, for already the duck were cooling, and their wholesome smell was filling the air. Now as all gathered around the comfort of the fire, even Mentu seated himself with reluctance, and peace came about the camp.

"So, shall we be in sight of the lakes tomorrow?" Shuma asked Psamose, helping herself to the hot meat.

"No, that will not be tomorrow. Once we are safely through the passage, then hopefully, we shall see the lakes in the distance. But today, with such a late start and the difficulties on the track we must be grateful to have got this far in one day." He bit deep into the roast meat of the plump bird which Darric had passed to him before continuing, "If I had been travelling alone, it would, no doubt, have been the swifter, but we can only travel at the speed of the least quickest. That said, we are now here, and here is as good a place as any to spend our night."

They sat in silence as they finished their supper before retiring in the darkness to their packs which had been placed around the fire. Settling for their night in the protection of the cave, they one by one let sleep overcome them, for the day had been exhausting, and each felt weary to the bone and drained of energy. All that is to say, except for Darric, who offered to stand first watch and who sat long into the cold night before waking Shuma to stand her turn.

**

The night was good to them, however, and as they slept, the thick clouds had gathered, keeping off the bitter winter chill that had threatened in the early hours, and they awoke to a bright morning with the light of a weak sun on their doorstep. After breakfasting, Psamose immediately set into action and started by advising them on the journey ahead, first suggesting that the water skins would require filling and that rushlights and candles should be made ready from the start. Darric was quick to respond, gathering up the skins and filling them with the melting snow from around the cave mouth while the rest made ready the packs and the horses and prepared the necessary illumination for the off.

"Fill the flasks to the brim, Darric," Psamose instructed as he watched the boy scooping the cold snow. "We must take enough to see us through to the other side. For note well," he advised them all, "the water inside the passage should be avoided at all costs. It is foul and bitter from its course through the rocks. Also, eat nothing that you may find there nor touch anything that grows."

"You did not mention this before," Malian snapped. He had awoken anxious and worried after a troubled dream, and an uneasy feeling was growing as each minute passed. What if the gods had deceived him, he thought? And what if the path through the mountain was a trick, and he was leading them all to their deaths?

"They are just a few wise words, Malian," Psamose answered, noting the tone of the altar tender's voice. "For darkness breeds its own life, and we must respect that to maintain our own." Looking around the group as they busied themselves for the departure, he saw them all restless to be on their way and into the passage to face the gods knew what. He knew that although he had been graced with plenty of time in this land, strange days were upon them, and he too, held a doubt where once was certainty.

The horses were to be blindfolded, and Darric and Tragen had left this to the last before binding each with great care and joining them together on one restless line. Psamose led the way in, and with the aid of his long stick and holding a blazing torch aloft, he walked slowly to the opening at the back of the cave and plunged into the darkness of the passage. Malian paused only briefly before following, and the others came singly, with Darric and Tragen bringing up the rear guiding the horses, who stamped and flared their nostrils at the acrid smoke which the torches gave out and which lingered around their heads as they tagged along.

The darkness before them was complete, and their meagre light hardly illuminated the walls and the ceiling, whose distance could only be guessed at, disappeared high above their heads. Within moments the scant morning light at the mouth of the tunnel was gone, and the darkness enveloped them as they moved forward.

The silence was initially broken only by the heavy breathing of the horses, but soon the constant dripping of water from above added subtly to the background, which, as unseen time passed and they moved slowly forward, became a focus in the minds of those travelling beneath. Tall encrusted growths started to grow up around their feet, making their passage troublesome, and causing many a stumble for them and the horses before Psamose stopped to inspect them.

"These have grown bigger since I was last here," he whispered, as he gently touched the clammy tip of a growth, "and these I have not seen before!" He bent down and illuminated a large pale fungus that sprouted up out of the cave floor, a faint musty aroma rising as he gently touched it with his foot.

"It must be the damp," Tragen said, his voice echoing into the unseen heights. "The melted snow water must get down here eventually."

Malian bent to examine the growth, for it gave him a nasty uneasy feeling, and on standing, he urged the group to move forward swiftly and not to dwell too long.

"Yes, the sooner we are out of here, the better, I think," Psamose agreed, "and we must remain silent from this point if we don't wish to disturb any spirit that may rest here." He turned away before any questions could be asked and started off again into the darkness, which seemed to open up and then just as quickly close behind him. While the rest of the group immediately followed, stumbling forward to keep up and hardly daring to think of who or what may be resting in the darkness around them.

Their journey went on forever, with only the briefest of pauses for rest and nourishment and the intense cold bit deep into their bodies as they moved ever onward. Time meant nothing in this place, and outside in the valley, a day and night passed, and a new day dawned unnoticed. But the feeling of dread continued its rise with each footstep, and the unspoken imagination was soon filling minds with unseen horrors, and the horses rapidly started to become restless.

"Do you hear something?" Tragen's voice suddenly echoed out of the darkness from the back, and his hand instinctively went to the weapon at his belt. "There's something coming up the tunnel behind us." The horses were now pulling hard at their reins, pushing forward in fear, and Darric and Tragen held on tight until finally the reins were ripped from their hands, and the beasts fled into the blackness before them, scattering the others aside who led the way. The group instantly gathered, and holding the torches high, they all strained their ears to catch any sound above the dripping of water and the receding of hooves as the horses disappeared into the dark. Slowly, a high metallic scraping noise, like nails on stone or like talons on rock could be heard, far off but somehow getting closer by the minute. The darkness seemed to increase if that was at all possible, and Psamose urged the group to move onward, torches held aloft to light the way, while he led them forward along and up the passage. In growing fear, their steps began to falter, and in their terror, they pushed past each other, the strong overtaking the weak, with little thought but of escape. And when the foul odour hit them, a mania came upon them all, and it became each man for himself.

***

When Malian opened his eyes, it was to the bright of the morning sun, and a fresh but biting wind blew across his bruised and battered cheeks. He lay on his back in the snow and watched the ragged clouds skim fitfully across the cold sky which stretched above him. High up, he could see a flock of birds, tiny shapes to his naked eye, flying across the heavens and their distant trumpet call came sharp and clear to his ears. How he wished he could follow them, to leave the earth and soar high above it, and with long hard beats of his wings, disappear into the distance and never return. He shivered and suddenly felt very cold as he remembered the tunnel, and raising his head, he saw the others in the snow around him.

CHAPTER SEVEN

Their bodies lay scattered across the hard white ground as if thrown down from high above, with arms and legs flung aside like dolls cast away from a child's hand. But each was alive, and as the horror and stampede of the passage slowly left them, they lifted their heads and looked around. The tunnel had brought them fairly high up on the northern mountainside where the forests had disappeared, and the land before them could be seen down to the Lowlands and the lakes at the end of the valley. Here the mountain ranges stood proud with jagged white tops disappearing into the far-off north. The group, each bruised somewhat in the crush to escape the passage, took time in overcoming their fear and, in the process sought some understanding of what had happened to them, and the silence eventually gave way to questions. Tragen was the first to speak, kneeling in the snow and wiping great handfuls over his face to awaken his senses.

"What happened in there?" he asked, sitting back on his heels as the snow dripped gently onto his massive shoulders.

"I think a great madness came upon us and fed on our fears," Psamose eventually replied, struggling to make some sense of the situation, "and each of our fears merged and became as one." He remembered the sheer panic which had overcome him and the thickness which he had felt in his lungs and mouth as he tried to breathe. A sourness still remained, and he quickly thrust a handful of the pure snow into his mouth and immediately spat to his side. A dark sprinkling of fine grey-black grains there coloured the snow, leaching into the whiteness and possibly providing a reason for their flight.

"Look," he said, pointing to the debris while noticing the smell which arose from it, "could this have been what caused our terror?"

Malian was instantly at his side. "So I was right to be troubled by those growths," he reflected, quickly recognising the particles for what they were. The spores of the pale, thickened lumps, which had been disturbed and kicked into the air by their passing had brought on the madness and mania, and he hastily urged the group to wash and cleanse themselves, both in body and dress and to have no more fear.

"But we all heard the scratching, didn't we?" Darric announced as he shook out his cloak and wiped down his breeches with handfuls of snow. "That wasn't in our imagination, was it?" He looked to each companion in turn, who were busying themselves in a similar manner.

"It must have been in one of us," Malian replied, "and then in our collective delirium too, for such fear can so easily be passed on in challenging situations. But let's not apportion blame, for we all had our own trials to face, and let us be glad that we all overcame the dread which assailed us." He glanced around at the group, who took some comfort in his words while they finished dusting themselves down.

Tragen, however, took little cheer from the words, for he knew it was he who had alerted the others to the following sounds in the passage which had set them into the panic and flight into the darkness. And he knew it was his own past fears which had unknowingly fed into the insanity which had descended. Hurriedly he moved away from the others as if to distance himself both in body and mind and all the quicker restore stability and soundness within the group and headed back up through the thick drifts towards the northern passage which had so powerfully disgorged them onto the mountainside.

Malian followed as speedily as the snow would allow, catching up just as Tragen arrived at the cave mouth where he had stopped, afraid to enter.

"Our woes can make us weak, Tragen," Malian spoke softly, reaching his side, "but they can also make us strong, and that is for us to decide. For I feel we should be masters of our own free spirits."

"My misfortunes are great indeed," came the reply. Tragen turned and looked at Malian, his face wretched with the misery which haunted him, "And I have carried them with me for many a long time, and they have ripened and festered within my heart that even my own courage now fails me."

"Perhaps if you shared your fears, they may lessen?" Malian asked quietly, in some hope that the telling would bring some purpose back into the warrior's life and that it would all be for the good. He indicated for the large man to enter the cave, and they both stepped into the shelter of the passage end, which they had so quickly fled in their confusion.

There still remained a feeling there that became a tightness around the chest of each man, but the terror of previous had gone, and the brightness of the snow chased away the darkness into the passageway beyond. Tragen, however, still remained troubled and paced back and forth as the other members of the group slowly followed them off the mountainside and back into the security which the cave provided.

"The horses are lost," Darric reported as he arrived last at the cave mouth. Snow encased his lower legs, for he had followed the hoof marks in some hope around the side of the slope before losing them in the deeper drifts which cloaked the treeless heights, and he now stamped his feet to dislodge the ice which had gathered around his boots. "But I found a couple of packages." He threw them down between the group, and the snapped and broken straps dangled and snaked across the cave floor, indicating the force of their removal. On inspection, however, they were found to contain some small items of dried food which would hold off complete starvation.

Yet Malian's concern remained with Tragen. For he could not carry his fears into *The Duat* and risk again all who travelled on this path, and he now pushed further for the man to ease his mind, and in the telling, throw off the nightmares which haunted him. Formally, he asked them all to sit, and in his tone of voice, each realised the seriousness of this and quickly settled, wrapping themselves around in their cloaks to keep out the cold from the stone floor.

"Tragen," Malian began, his voice coming forcefully, "you must purge yourself here and now before you take another step on this path!" Approaching the tall figure, he looked deep into his eyes. "For you must know that your fears risk us all." Sweeping his hand across the seated group, he turned to face the others and looked into their tired faces as he continued, "And the consequences cannot ever be imagined. I have journeyed through *The Duat* in my dreams and know that fears can become deformed and monstrous in our perception. But we must all enter with a pure heart and soul to pass through the Gates and accomplish our end." He then addressed the group as a whole. "My friends, we all must do as Tragen, for if not on this journey, then on our inevitable passing in the future. Know now that we shall all eventually face the Weighing of the Heart and the judgement of our souls, and to fail does not bear thinking!" He looked at each in turn, knowing this last judgement was common knowledge within the valley, but so often it was taken lightly until old age compelled such contemplation and the chance to change or make amends had long passed.

Tragen presently stepped forward alongside Malian, lifting his shoulders and nodding his head in awareness and understanding of his duty to do away with the inner terror and guilt which had driven him almost into the ground. His whole appearance was remade, and a self-composure fell around his large frame and strengthened his determination to speak.

"I stand here in your judgement," he began, "for my wrongdoings are many in my city and also since I left my home, and all are none to be proud of. But let me tell you my story." He took a deep breath before continuing, "The City of Lights was once a great and prosperous place to dwell and to raise our children under the blessing of our goddess *Naunet*, and the fields overflowed with plenty for all.

"Then came our downfall when she was taken. And so soon the crops failed, wells ran dry, and water couldn't be found to hand, and the women had to walk for long miles to fill their flasks. Disease and plague quickly followed, taking not only the weak but the strong among us and leaving few untouched. My daughter, Tess, was the first of our family to fall ill and the first that I sent off into the wilds in hope of protecting my sons and wife. But it was of little use, for the spread was quick, and even banishment was to no avail, as many other families also found.

"I never saw my daughter again or know where her body lies, but my wife and sons I buried together and dug deep alongside in readiness for my own passing. My wife and youngest son, still only a babe, both died at my own hands, for she begged me not to let them suffer as she had seen the others." Here Tragen's head fell to his chest, and he sobbed, "This I did with my love, trusting that I would soon join them, but that was not to be." He turned away, unable to go on or face the dismayed looks which he had briefly glimpsed, and the silence within the cave slowly wrapped around him.

"You must go on," Malian said, lightly reaching out his hand. "For your heart must be fully free of all failings, and I sense that the worst is passed in your telling."

"No, no, there is much more!" came the desolate reply as Tragen gradually turned around to again face their inquest. "How some of us survived, I don't know, but as Chieftain's son my only goal for my people was to reclaim our guardian and, in the doing, revenge the wrongs which had been done in hope of returning our City of Lights to its glory. There were so few left, but each man came forward to accompany me, and out of those, I chose only the strongest for the hardships which I saw ahead.

"And so we set off leaving behind misery and misfortune for those who remained." Here he paused, wiping his huge hands across his face before continuing, "Our journey took us far into the wild lands to the north of our city, but within days, we were hungry and disorientated, and a madness descended in which I fought and slew the broadest of my companions and we all feasted well with no guilt or shame of our actions. This happened time and time again, getting the easier with each event as we each fought for survival, and my own life could have so easily gone the same way. But somehow, I withstood and endured. Until finally, I alone stood at the southern edge of your valley and arrived at your city walls, Malian, on the morning that you were choosing your companions. And there you accepted me into this group." He hesitated a moment and then, speaking strongly and with conviction, said, "I stand here now before you with my heart relieved and my soul unburdened by my admission of guilt, and I ask only for understanding of my crimes and the circumstances in which they were brought about." He looked to the others, who sat or stood before him, for their reassurance in his weaknesses and in the opening of his soul to receive their support and acceptance of his conduct.

"Tragen," Malian said, quietly approaching the warrior who stood before him, "your first actions were done with love for your wife and family and at your wife's request. For she feared greatly for their suffering, and for these, no stain should darken your soul." A murmur of agreement echoed around the chamber as the group arose and came forward to indicate their support of the wise words spoken.

"But what of the other?" The large man asked, pulling away and putting up his hands to hold off their advance. "How does that fair among you?"

Psamose now moved close, wrapping his cloak further around him, aware that his life of wandering and pilgrimage had given him some little idea of the ordeals in the wild, where the presence of starvation was never very far away, and the thought of the next meal could unbalance any mind.

"Survival is a hard undertaking," he began knowingly addressing them all, "and for some, it is too easy to give in and give up than fight on. You, Tragen, are a warrior and a fighter in life, and this means having the courage and aggression to battle on whatever the outcome and however hard the decisions are. You took your men's lives and in so doing, gave yourself the means to continue your search for the overall good of your people. With that comes not only awareness of your guilt but also a clarity of your actions and forgiveness from us for the events in your past. You know what you are capable of, and in forgiving yourself, you give us no cause to condemn you!"

Psamose quickly marched forward, and embracing

Tragen, he gathered the huge man back into the company where he had so recently felt forsaken. Gradually there was a feeling of recognition and acceptance within most of the group, for each knew that they had their own souls to cleanse in the coming days, and each hoped that their own admission of their failings would grant some redemption and bestow upon them a safe passage. Darric, nonetheless, remained shocked at the disclosure, for someone so inexperienced had done little, so far, to blemish or taint a spirit that had grown up in relative friendship and security. And so he struggled with the knowledge of Tragen's actions and quietly left the cave as the others gathered in support. Malian noticed his going and hastily followed, catching up as he stepped out onto the frozen mountainside.

"Darric," he said, as he watched the young man walk away from him, "do not judge Tragen as a wicked person for his actions. They were done when a man's spirit has been brought down, and no one can tell how he or she would behave in those given circumstances."

The younger man stopped and turned and lifting his head, looked back at the altar tender who stood framed in the mouth of the cave. To Malian, the slightness of the youth seemed even more diminished by the vast landscape at his back while the thick, cloud-laden sky soared overhead and a darkness tinted the edge of the valley in the east.

"My mind struggles with this, Malian, for this is beyond my understanding of the ways of man," Darric shouted back in a voice angry with pain and disappointment.

"Yes, that I can understand, but both our friendships and thinking are sometimes tested," Malian replied, remembering the youth of the person who stood before him, "and in so doing, they can become stronger with our acceptance of each other and our outlook can be opened up to their capabilities. Come, put your mind at ease and come back in." He waited for a moment before finishing, "Nightfall will soon be upon us, and the mountainside offers little in comfort. We all must face the night in companionship and the safety of the shelter, and with some thought, hopefully, tomorrow may bring some recognition of Tragen's conduct for you."

Darric did not move for many minutes, then looking round and realising his situation, he slowly retraced his steps back towards Malian, and they entered the cave mouth together. Back inside, the others awaited their return, aware of the reasoning behind why they had left the cave, and Psamose was the first to come forward as they approached.

"Darric, you have a right to be disheartened with Tragen's disclosure, for it is in your very nature to be caring," he said as he took the boy's hand. And leaving the rest of the group, he guided him to sit in the shadows near the back of the cave. "But you must also recognize in yourself the need for mercy when you see suffering. You would not let a sick or badly injured horse endure, would you? No, it is not in your nature to be uncaring in that aspect. So do not rule others' actions when it comes to compassion for their loved ones. As for the other," the pilgrim went on, "I know you have already killed animals to eat, for we have all shared in the food you have caught and prepared for us, and in its roundabout way, this was no different to that, was it? We all need to eat to survive, and survival is steadfast and tenacious in every man."

"I don't know, Master Psamose, for I do see your reasoning and to some extent understand that which Tragen did for his family," came the reply, "but I'm struggling with his actions towards his own men. Surely they would have been better in support of each other over fighting and killing?"

"Well, yes, but reasoning does not come into this when survival takes over. You still have a lot to learn in that aspect, but I would rather you were unsure of yourself in this regard sooner than being heartless. Nevertheless, are you dismayed in your friendship with Tragen now that you have seen him in this light and are aware of what he can do?" Psamose asked.

"Yes and no," Darric responded in a small voice. "I know that I have to accept these facts, as you all seem to have done, but I need to think, and I need to settle my mind on this matter. So leave me for a while," this last demand came out in a whisper. "And I shall let my mind think."

Psamose knew he had done his best and, being at ease with the reply, left the young man to his thoughts and contemplation and joined the group sitting huddled near to the doorway where Tragen met him as he approached.

"Do you think Darric will be able to stomach what I have done, Psamose? Would it help if I spoke further to him?" he said in a low, anxious tone.

"Leave him be for now, Tragen, for he has enough to think on." He hesitated for a moment and then continued, "But I was wondering if you could help him in another way. What do you say about training him up, pass on some of your fighting skills or defence instruction? If he agrees to it, of course?"

Tragen thought for a little while and then said, "Well, I've seen him hunting and tracking, and he's fair with a blade for butchering, but he needs toughening up in his build. He needs some muscle adding to this frame, and that only comes with months of hard work and exercise. Then, perhaps, he could be taught the techniques and tactics, but that would have to be at his bidding, not mine, and I'm sure we don't have time on our side."

"Well, let's leave it at that for now and see what the morning brings. Now we must eat and settle, and pray the gods are good to us."

Darkness was closing fast over the valley, and although a moon could be seen rising, the cavern was soon in gloom and permanent darkness. Without wood for a fire, the evening promised to be long and cold, with the only benefit being that they were now out of the wind. The dried goods, which they found in the saddle packs, were mainly oats and grapes from the Great House's table, and they were soon divided up and passed around. Malian took some back to Darric, who accepted them and who, on eventually realising his situation, reunited with the others to keep from freezing to death overnight. Water was provided by the snow at the entrance, and warmth only from their thick cloaks and body heat as they huddled closely together and sought to rest.

The dark hours, in the dead of night, were long in passing, and they all attempted to keep warm and conserve their strength. In recognising this, they set no watch at the door, for the intense cold ensured that deep sleep did not come to any, although each dozed in their own silent way and prayed to survive the night.

After what seemed an eternity to the group, the darkness began to pass, and the sky slowly lightened in their eyes and a sense of relief and realisation passed through them with the awareness that they had endured and remained alive, and they moved to stand and shake life back into their chilled limbs.

"By the lord, I don't wish to see another night like that." Were the first words out of the cracked and frozen lips of Malian as Shuma reached to help him to his feet and steadied him. "We must hasten down into the valley today for we can't spend another night on this mountainside and hope to live."

Everyone was in full agreement, and with no camp to dismantle, food to prepare or gear to stow, it was not long before they were ready to move down the frozen mountain and make for the lakes at the head of the valley, which could be seen glistening in the distance in the morning sun. Psamose was, however, a little reluctant to leave without first attempting to find the horses and their precious cargo.

Although the night had been bitter to the group, the animals were better equipped to stand the intense cold, and so he and Shuma moved away slightly above the cave entrance and scanned the scenery. While they did this, the others, wrapping their thick covers around them, had started down the slope immediately outside the cave. Here the ground was met with apprehension in places, as the recent snowfall concealed areas of frozen slippery ice. Malian and Mentu slowly brought up the rear, assisting each other when needed. And in allowing Tragen and Darric to move forward in their own company, they gave them the opportunity to join in a conversation that needed to be had between the two.

"How was the night for you, Darric?" Tragen hesitantly asked in way of opening after the silence become too much.

"Cold!"

However, there was little coldness in the voice, so Tragen sought to continue. "Darric, can you accept what has happened in my past and how I had to act to survive? Why I did what I had to, even to those known to me? Do you still make judgement of my honesty?"

"No," came the reply, "I have thought long through the night and can now accept your actions. But only as a kind of madness that came over you." Struggling through an area of deeper snow, the youth sought to maintain his direction while the heavier man at his side waded through with ease.

"Madness! Yes, that was what it was. Madness and grief at my own loss," he said, having some relief that his behaviour had become reconciled in the youth's mind, "and it heartens me that you have the ability to think this way."

"I overheard what Psamose said to you about training me," Darric announced after a few moments. "How does that sound to you today?"

"Well, you must also have heard that I have little or no failing in your basic skills," Tragen answered back. "But you are lacking in strength and build, and that is the first that would need undertaking, wouldn't you agree?"

"I've always been spare of frame," the boy openly admitted, "and I know I need to develop my skills too. But the question is, would you teach me?" He stopped and looked at the heavyset man at his side before continuing, "I'm not asking to replace your sons in your memories, Tragen, for you have your own images and recollections of their training and also of your family. But I would be willing only if it would help both of us in some way and not be to the detriment of the journey."

There came no reply to this as Tragen reflected on these words, and so they waded on in silence until suddenly, a sharp whistle rang out behind them. Stopping and turning back, they caught sight of Psamose and Shuma leading the horses down past the cave entrance. Malian and Mentu had also come to a halt and were looking back and waited for them to descend to their level. The animals, in various stages of fatigue, had been found occupying a slightly sheltered position off to the east and upward of the cave, and Shuma's mount, who had lost its blindfold in the flight from the passage, had kept them corralled together through the night even though the tethers had been broken. All of the covers had now been removed from their eyes and joined together again, the troop could now calmly and gradually be brought into line. Most of the bundles remained, although some were lost, and broken straps hung down around their legs, but the little pack pony had faired best and was bringing up the rear of the team virtually as fully laden as they had set off through the passage.

Tragen and Darric waited for the whole group to gather together where they had stopped, and they could each take control of their own horses, relieving Psamose and Shuma of the responsibility. Malian quickly inspected his horse over first before moving on to the saddlebags and checking for the scroll which Alrynn had given him before they left the city and for the book that Abu Salama had given him only a few days ago. He felt sure they would be needed on their progress through *The Duat* and beyond into the Plains, and both were thankfully found safely tucked away. The others equally checked out their mounts, reassured in what they found and what remained of their supplies, and tidying up the loose straps which dangled annoyingly for the horses, they then, as a group, began to tackle the slopes down into the valley.

The day that they found on this northern side of the passage was crisp, cold and bright for them as they slowly journeyed down, with the icy, snow-covered areas gradually giving way to just thick deep snow, which set its own challenges. The Lowlands at the head of the valley could be seen in more detail at this height on the slope, the three large lakes shining against the backdrop of the barren lands. And the mountains which rimmed the basin amidst the snow-covered Mountains of Marn marched off into the far distance to the north.

As they moved down, the view changed, and the top edge slipped out of sight with the valley wrapping itself around them again. Their progress was made the more difficult with the horses who faltered in the heavy conditions, and the hours passed by before the valley bottom felt any nearer. Here, at last, the river gorge could be seen to be less deep, for the sides had gently widened out, leaving the river running in a broad channel that eventually formed three arteries which ultimately ran separately along into their individual lakes. The group, almost down the mountainside, stopped briefly to rest and Mentu asked a question.

"Which lake do you think we head for, Malian? And do we cross it, or is there a path alongside?" he asked, shifting the pack on his horse's back which had started to slip sideways.

"I'm not sure," came the answer, "for in my dreams, I was above the valley, and the gods were guiding me. It all seems so different here on the ground, especially with the snow." He hesitated a moment before continuing, "But I think we should aim for the middle one, for the point of it seems to vanish into the back of the valley, or that's what it looks like from here."

This middle lake appeared to be narrower and less daunting than the broader ones which dominated either side, so this suggestion was quickly agreed upon and accepted, and the company moved off down into the valley itself. Heading north and following the river on their right, the banks became broader, although the thick snow collected deep in places, and the group could still only go as fast as their surroundings would allow. But a sense of achievement was at long last felt as the mountainside was put behind them. Moving along, Malian had drifted towards Tragen and coming apace with the warrior, he asked how it had gone between himself and Darric.

"Well, he certainly thinks older than his youth,

Malian, and he's given me some cause for thought." They moved along in silence for some moments.

"Is it something I can advise or guide you on?"

"No. Unless you have knowledge of being a father!" Tragen came back, knowing full well the answer.

"Aagh, then that will have to be between you and him. But I will say only this…you both have your needs in different ways, and if each can support the other, then where is the wrong in that?"

"I would agree, for he is certainly keen to learn, I think. Yet I also think he fears for my thoughts with regard to my family, and for that, we will both need to respect and keep our limits."

"Well, that is a good place to start," Malian advised. Seeing the nod of the broad head, he moved forward to catch up with Darric and left Tragen to resume his thoughts.

The river shortly came to an area where the branches each split off to run into their own separate lake, and the course running off to the left crossed the path on which the group assembled. The water was not deep, and the horses crossed easily with their respective riders on board, and they remained mounted for a short while as they pushed further along the left-hand side of the middle lake. This tapered towards the back of the valley and their intended stop for the night. The lake appeared to hold no life, for no reeds or grasses decorated the edge or floated in islands over its surface, and even the wind failed to swell the black veneer, which sullenly reflected the light back into the sky. The water felt dead, and even the horses refused to drink from it.

As the afternoon light slowly paled in the west, they reached the top of the water and found themselves in a stone-covered bay where they made camp in the shelter of the valley side. The area turned out to be a disappointment to the whole group, although none could say the reasoning for this, but each had held some expectation of what they would find here at their destination at the valley head. Malian, especially, felt helpless as he looked around for some assurance that his leadership had not led them astray. However, they could go no further this night, and so while the others settled, unloading their mounts, brushing away snow and gathering driftwood for a fire, he set off along the water's edge. But finding no help in that direction, he slowly wandered back. The evening was again guaranteed to be dark and cold and this time without shelter, although they now had their additional clothing and bedrolls, which made the prospect of a better night's rest on the frozen ground. And they would also have a fire.

"We'll move on at first light," Malian announced on his return and seeing the questioning and uncertain faces, he continued, "and head further round the valley for we do need to be at the top of a lake, but perhaps it's not this one."

"This one doesn't feel right for you, Malian?" Psamose asked, looking up from his bedmaking.

"I'm not sure. It feels right in its way, but I don't know where we go from here. I don't know the way in." He instantly sank to the cold, hard ground, resting his head in his hands, before going on, "In my dream, I was with the gods under their guidance and protection, and they showed me the way into and through *The Duat*." He wavered briefly before deciding to continue, "Now I feel it is the time for me to take up the telling which I swiftly cut short in the Closed Court many days ago. None of you were there at the time, so take my word that I abandoned the recount for the sake of those around me and for their peace of mind. But you all need to know the whole, for the time of resolution is here, and we all must make our final decision."

He went on to unfold the dream which had sent him on this journey and which now included them all in its tale. Initially, the others continued to move around fitfully in the half-light, attending to their horses and preparing beds, but on sensing the importance and disquiet of the moment, they finally came to rest around the altar tender as he sat in the chill air near the spiritless water's edge, with Mentu and Shuma being the last to settle.

He recounted how the spirits of the gods had shadowed and protected his soul along the valley and where, at the head of a lake, he was given over to the charge of the Boatman and placed within the prow of his ornate boat to commence the voyage along the starlit meandering waters and through the *Seven Gates of The Duat*, which lay open to them as the god's boat advanced.

"Seven?" Mentu asked from the gathering dark. "My books and readings have instructed me there are at least twelve, one for each hour of the night which the dead must traverse before their souls see the light of the beyond." He paused and then concluded, "However, the scrolls are not always very precise in their detail over this!"

"Yes," Malian agreed, "I had heard the same, but I was only shown seven. Perhaps, for the dead, the journey is of a more testing nature for their souls to pass through the afterlife gates and out into the Field of Reeds. Possibly the number of gates is governed by their mortal behaviour in the real world. We are not dead," he continued, "and so I don't know or have answer to that. But of this, we will find out, have no fear." He went on to reveal that the Gates were guarded well, with each having a herald, a doorkeeper and a god, and the demand was to give the password to progress through and along the rivers course unharmed. He also attempted to recount the nightmare of his visions where grotesque animal-headed beings had assaulted the boat from all sides as they moved forward. But as in any dream, Malian explained as way of solace, these had quickly become slightly muddled in the remembering. Nevertheless, in the main, his own journey was there, bright and clear in his recollection.

"Then you were given the passwords?" Mentu enquired with some hope in his voice. "For it seems to me that unless we know what to say, then we stand no chance of getting any further." They all nodded in agreement in the gloom, aware that they had come to the time of decision-making.

"The passwords were not given," Malian regretfully disclosed, "but I do have a scroll from the city which I hope may shed some insight." Collecting the Scroll of the Dead, which Alrynn had given him, from his saddle bag, he passed it to Mentu, who unrolled the papyrus with his long thin hands before slumping forward to study the markings, once again revelling in the expertise and practice of the scribe.

"Yes, it shows here Seven Gates," he eventually declared, somewhat surprised, "and it displays the passwords too, I think. Here look." He pointed to the devices which shone in silver along the right-hand side edge of the scroll. There were seven in number, each with its own corresponding gate showing a simple drawing of a stone-surrounded portal encased in an oval cartouche running down the opposite left-hand side. Above all of this, the writings of the Ancients declared the document to be in the name of Sanuu and for his benefit as a given grave offering from his loved ones.

"These are each of the Gates." His finger moved left to the cartouches. "Stone clad by the look of them and all varying in decoration and stone, I would guess, for the writings differ in their naming. See, the sign of the stone is written in each portal, and perhaps that has some meaning along with the password."

"Can you read the names of the stone?" Malian asked the scribe, for the writing was in script form but not in a common hand and appeared foreign to the others as they looked on in the growing gloom.

"I have seen such writing before, and I'm sure it would have been known to our ancestors and indeed known today to our priests who perform our ceremonies for the dead. For the journey through the Gates is one which we all must still undergo at our end, and perhaps the passage through was not meant to be daunting for either king or worker alike. It is the final test, though, The Weighing of the Heart which is the ultimate and that which sorts the good from the bad!"

Mentu, in this saying, had answered a number of smaller questions that had been forming within the group. But left one big question, The Weighing of the Heart Ceremony.

From an early age, they all had been schooled to some extent or other in this one rite that would guarantee everlasting eternity in the heavenly fields beyond the underworld. But only if you lived a life of order, harmony and respect and were true to your own heart. Upon the great golden scales of the goddess *Ma'at*, the jackal god *Anubis* would place the heart of the spirit to be balanced against the white feather of truth while *Thoth*, the ibis, looked on to record the findings. Meanwhile, *Ammut*, with crocodile head, lion shoulders and hippo tail, sat beside the scales, ready to devour the souls of those whose heart weighed heavy and were assumed unworthy.

An innocent imagination had been left to grow and run wild regarding this fable, but each had conducted themselves in a childlike way, not knowing fully that their actions would be accounted for at their end. However, like many things, a child's belief had been overtaken by older age and by life itself, and choices and decisions made were not always simple or painless or without regret.

"I think I was presented for the Weighing of the Heart," Malian declared quietly, aware of the silence around him, "but remember little of this dream. I was still under the protection of the spirits, and with them, I stood on the far side and was then taken up into the grasslands."

"What was that!" Psamose suddenly interrupted, rising sharply from his bed. "Did you hear it?" he exclaimed. Walking quickly towards the shoreline, he peered out. "There it is again!"

The dark was descending rapidly, and a half moon appeared rim wards over the valley casting its light and disturbing the slickness across the water, while the gentle lapping along the waters shores, which had slowly soothed their minds, came more to their attention as it increased in their awareness.

"Malian, something is coming over the water!" Psamose announced as the soft ripples enlarged around the bay, casting the waterline further up the shingle.

"This must be it! Prepare yourselves!" the altar tender declared, his voice rising sharply as he rushed to gather his bags and collect his belongings from his saddle bag.

"If anyone wishes to leave, it must be now," he shouted, making clear that the choice was still open, "for there is no turning back once we enter the underworld." Striding forward, he headed in the direction of the shore and focused his vision on the increasingly disturbed water.

Behind him, there was an immediate panic and response from the camp as most of the group hurriedly made ready according to their needs.

"What about the horses?" Darric cried out while frantically collecting together his gear and removing his tools from the saddle bags before stuffing them into the pack which contained his personal items.

"I shall see to the horses," Psamose replied, calmly remaining seated, "for my job here is done, and I can guide you no further."

"You're not coming with us?" Darric stopped in mid-stride and turned to the pilgrim.

"No," he affirmed, "I will be returning the way we came. Back to the House of Abu Salama." His decision had only recently been made and had surprised even himself. But he had been aware for some time that some of the others had already foreseen this eventuality. And so, for now, he stayed seated next to the fire while around him, the camp was swiftly broken. Goodbyes were then said and blessings given, and the five figures eventually assembled nervously down by the water.

The moon had risen further now and shone down obliquely across the lake, except for where an area of absolute pitch darkness pushed slowly across the depthless water, dragging a thick forbidding smokiness along in its wake while a feeling of trepidation cloaked the whole as it advanced. Minute after minute passed until the sweep and slap of oar eventually broke the silence and grew louder as the darkness approached. On the shoreline, the five waited fearfully with a growing amount of dread. Finally, the huge shadow stopped someway in front of them, its obscurity covering the water as a frigid cold settled over the group where they waited for a signal.

Suddenly, a deep and resonating horn sounded over their heads, driving a chill into the hearts of those standing and causing Mentu to drop to his knees in sheer horror and panic at the harsh sound. And as he clasped his hands over his ears, he pitched forward headlong into the water. Malian and Shuma immediately rushed to his aid, each grabbing an arm and helping the scribe back to his feet, and clinging tightly to his hands to hold him steady the echo of the noise slowly faded out across the lake and down into the valley. The three stood ankle-deep in the blackness of the frozen lake, while Tragen and Darric brought up the rear, and as they paused, the horn sounded again, and the knowledge came over them that now was the time to board. Slowly striding and supporting each other through the water, with word as well as gesture, they advanced towards the boat where the blackness accepted them, and as each melted slowly into the dark, they moved out of an earthly dimension and became surrounded and encompassed in their own folklore.

Above the waterline, Psamose watched from the fire as his friends disappeared into the oblivion, and as the blackness of the shadows passed, he raised his cup. "Farewell, my friends and good fortune in your travels."

CHAPTER EIGHT

Absolute darkness and freezing cold instantly filled their minds as the night took them up and left them sightless to their surroundings, while under their feet, they felt the assurance and firmness of a sturdy base as they blindly boarded the vessel. Around, they could hear the breathing of each other and sensed a nearness, although an understanding of their bearings remained lacking as a great fear and dread continued to rise and swell in the hearts of the five. Malian could still feel the hand of Mentu in his, and he squeezed hard to gain a reaction. The hand responded forcibly and with a certain amount of urgency, giving immediate awareness and a comfort to both that they were not alone. The group, under some hidden force, eventually came to a halt upon the ominous flat platform that filled the expanse within the boat, and here they waited.

Slowly, a sense of motion could be felt, and the forbidding sound of oar dipping through water could once again be heard as the horn sounded out for a third and final time directly over their heads and was followed by the penetrating voice of the Boatman.

"I am the Lord Aken, keeper and protector of the barge, **Meseket.** *The ferryman has awoken me, and I stand here in the service of those who undertake their final journey."*

The group as a whole instantly fell to the floor, handholds broken, as the voice stormed through their consciousness, and they lost all sense of being. Now as they lay spread out across the boards, the voice came again.

"Hear me, travellers into **The Duat,** *for you are entering the Kingdom of* **Osiris** *and will there be judged*

and receive his judgement at the end. For such is the way for each soul to enter 'Aaru,' the Field of Reeds or else receive divine reckoning and be assigned to oblivion."

The oar continued to dip in and out of the water, slowly moving the powerless figures onwards in the direction of their inevitable fate, while the boatman continued in his declaration.

"Yet, your hearts still beat, your blood runs and your souls remain fast within their confines...And whether judgement will be given or taken, I know not. Nevertheless, I have been commanded and instructed by the Lord Ra, *he who escorts the sun, that you journey along his Path with his blessing, and so I do his bidding and take you into my charge as we enter the underworld."*

As he spoke these words, a calmness descended over the exhausted bodies and the nightfall took them completely.

"Open your eyes, Malian," Shuma's voice came out of the dark, distant at the first but stronger as the darkness waned. "Malian, open your eyes."

The brightness was dazzling, and Malian instantly lifted up his hands to cover his face until gradually the vividness ebbed, and he inched his fingers down and slowly looked upon *The Duat*. He was lying along the platform of the boat, facing up into a dusky star-filled sky, while Shuma stood over him with a lightness shining over her shoulders. Bending forward, on seeing that he was awake, she placed a cup to his lips to drink.

"I expected it to be dark," he said with some conviction and after some few moments of drinking, "but this light is so astonishing while the sky is so at odds. I really can't believe we are here." He lay in complete amazement at his surrounds as the solid black sky, star-streaked and studded, drifted slowly over his head, and a sense of movement endured as the boat rocked slowly in the water as it continued forward. Finally raising his head and sitting up into the brightness, he instantly witnessed the start of *The Duat*, the Path of The Dead. And that which was also called the Path of *Ra*, where every night the solar disc was guided on its voyage through the underworld, and his heart soared at what he beheld.

To each side, the river was broad, and silver coloured where the oar entered the water, sending ripples to the margins which splashed noiselessly against banks dominated by boundless carved cave walls. The colossal pantheon of the gods and goddesses strode forward into *The Duat*, while the decorated walls were filled top to bottom with their ceremonies and observances which they executed, and the painted star-filled sky arched overhead. Altars bearing food were carved in great detail, overflowing with offerings to the gods, and the rich lushness of the grasses and palms decorated the backdrop. The colours were astonishing, the yellows unbelievably gold, the blues as rich as gemstones, and the whites of such a brightness they hurt the eyes, and Malian had to look away.

Turning his head, he looked back towards the way they had come and sensing more than seeing, he witnessed the greatness of the Lord Aken standing at the rear of the boat. There oar in hand, he propelled the craft onward with the Light of *Ra* surrounding him as the solar rays illuminated *The Duat* on their journey through the night-time hours. It was like looking through a gleaming misty curtain that moved gently in a breeze, for the outline shifted as he sought to make some sense of shape and colour until finally, he glanced away, back towards the direction of travel.

Shuma remained at his side while Mentu, Tragen and Darric were at the front of the boat, staring anxiously first along the river and then frantically back to the scroll of Sanuu which Mentu held in his hands. The First Gate could not be too far away, and the password had still not yet been unravelled, although Mentu had deciphered the Gate cartouche, which had shown the boat of the afterlife with the word GRANITUM written in the portal.

"Granite," he had declared, "the First Gate is of granite."

The river soon after started to become less broad, with the banks closing in on either side, allowing the walls to tower over and encroach upon the group in the boat and a pathway alongside both of the river banks could be seen along the waterside. Soon shapeless formations could be noticed along these paths, which soon became recognisable as the bleached bones of a hand or foot or the roundness of a wispy hair-covered skull sticking up out of the shingle.

"Behold, those who knew not the word to pass through the Gate," the Lord Aken declared, pulling hard again at his oar and steering the boat into the middle of the river before adding, *"And here I now command and warn you, DO NOT leave the boat or touch any bones where they may lie, for The First Gate approaches, and you must make yourselves ready."*

Malian and Shuma, in great haste, quickly joined the others at the prow, and looking over Mentu's shoulder down onto the scroll, they aspired to help in uncovering the password. The silver inlaid designs running down the right-hand side shone brightly on the scroll while the cartouches detailing the Gates sat opposite.

"This is the first password," Mentu hastily reminded them in his panic, "it's in script form, too, just like the Gates. But it makes little sense to me. Here look." He thrust the scroll towards Malian, who eagerly looked down.

The word read INEBE SIBUNA, with the first word sitting directly atop the other:

$$\mathfrak{I} \; \mathfrak{N} \; \mathfrak{E} \; \mathfrak{B} \; \mathfrak{E}$$
$$\mathsf{S} \; \mathfrak{I} \; \mathfrak{B} \; \mathfrak{U} \; \mathfrak{N} \; \mathsf{A}$$

"Does it make any sense if the letters are moved about?" Malian asked with some hope, quickly looking along the water to where a darkness was rapidly looming.

"I have already tried that," came the distressed reply.

"Well, it can't be too hard, or no one would pass through," Tragen shrewdly said before quickly suggesting, "What about if you read it backwards? What does that read?"

"EBENI *ANUBIS*!" Mentu said in relief and surprise that it could be so basic while he held the scroll up to the light.

"Does that mean anything?" Tragen asked.

"The word *Anubis* is easy enough, the jackal god of the dead and of the afterlife, and perhaps a fitting start for the First Gate along the Path," Mentu announced. "But Ebeni could have a number of meanings in my understanding."

As the light of the solar rays lit up ahead, the First Gate came directly into sight. An immense structure of light-coloured, coarse-grained red granite with darker minerals running through filled the tunnel from the ceiling downwards, cutting across the starry sky above and straddling the pathway each side of the water. The stone was sculpted in great detail with carvings and scripts of *Anubis*, the god affiliated with the art of mummification and of the afterlife. Here he was depicted with the body of a man and the head of a wolf, black-skinned to embody the colour of death and embalming, and surrounded by mummified statues of the dead.

"Ebeni! Ebeni! Ebeni!" Mentu repeated frantically, wishing for enlightenment and understanding of this one word as the boat slowed before the portal, and the others looked on in dread at the vast Gateway before them.

"Ebony!" exclaimed Shuma, "Ebeni *Anubis*! Could it be ebony jackal? The god of the dead?"

"Ebony jackal!" Mentu declared hopefully. "Yes, the god who greets the dead on their journey. So simple if it's without error. But now, I fear, it's too late to decide otherwise." He looked in haste towards the looming Gateway, "For the truth will be in the saying, or our bones will soon be adorning the path."

As the boat stopped before the huge doorway, a horn blared, and a voice rang out across the water from the left side of the river.

"BEHOLD THE RIVER GATE OF GRANITE," the herald announced. **"ADVANCE AND PRESENT THE KEYWORD."**

The boat moved carefully forward, its prow piercing the Gate, bringing the group within the shadow of the great entrance as the doorkeeper advanced from the left-hand side, clothed in flowing black robes. He was human in size and shape, however, his head was covered with a great dog's head mask, and he carried a towering staff that was thrust forward and across the Gateway, barring the boat's complete entry. Slowly he turned his head to overlook the group which had drawn back to the midpoint of the boat, where they cowered, panic-stricken and with fear of the consequences of their actions.

"COME FORWARD AND SPEAK THE WORDS OF ADMISSION," he demanded. **"AND PREPARE YOURSELVES BEFORE THE OVERSEER OF**

THE GATE."

The silence of *The Duat* gradually wrapped itself around them as the reverberation of the voice faded away and the moment of truth came to hand.

"I shall go first," Malian announced, standing quickly and decisively in some hope of giving courage to the others whilst carrying little of that for himself.

"No, Malian," Shuma swiftly replied, grabbing his hand, "we cannot risk your loss if our thinking is unsound, for your task goes beyond this first challenge. I shall go first!"

"No, let me go," Darric instantly reasoned, "for I am, by my own judgement, the least essential of the group." And rising, he moved forward with purpose before any chance of being stopped.

"Kneel before the doorkeeper," the Lord Aken proclaimed as Darric slowly advanced forward, inch by inch, along the boards in the harsh light before dropping to the deck on reaching the front, where the staff blocked his way. Here he was dwarfed by the Gateway, which stood over him, but raising his eyes and hoping that Shuma was correct in her deduction, he spoke the words, "EBONY JACKAL," strong and loud before hastily dropping to his knees and bowing his head to await the uncertain outcome.

The doorkeeper slowly inclined his huge head, and dipping the staff slightly in acknowledgment of the response, then said, **"PASS, BELIEVER IN THE GOD *ANUBIS*, MASTER OF THE HEREAFTER."**

Darric, turning with great relief and satisfaction to the others, was then quick to his feet, and on witnessing his success, Malian swiftly followed. Then the three remaining travellers, with renewed keenness, eagerly awaited their chance to approach the doorkeeper and state the password to grant them through the First Gate. Once all had declared and been given access, the staff was withdrawn from across the entrance, and the boat slowly moved off into the Gateway proper. As the massive portal passed overhead and alongside, a sense of reprieve flooded the boat, and the company could draw breath whilst congratulating Darric for his bravery and courage in this opening test and trial.

Through this First Gate, the water became darker, taking on a bronze sheen to its surface, which reflected the painted stars above and gave a hued colouring to the very light within the tunnel. The walls remained exquisitely decorated, showing again as the light flooded across them, the gods in all their glory and with their abundance and richness of wealth. The pathway remained snaking along each side of the river, but here the shingle line was at least thankfully free from bones on this side of the Gate.

"Thank the gods, for that seemed easy enough," Mentu said, relief washing over him as he settled between Shuma and Malian in the bottom of the boat. "But now there is no going back. So let us be better prepared for the Second Gate, for it will soon be upon us, and I wish to have more authority on the subject."

Drawing out the scroll, he spread it along the planks between where they sat, and he and Malian bent forward to study the writings.

"Let's look at the Gate cartouche first, for that is our initial source of insight," Mentu suggested.

The Gate details on the left read QUARZEA, and the Gate itself was edged with flowering stalks, possibly depicting plants and vegetation.

"Quarzea?" Malian queried. "That sounds similar to quartz, but my understanding may not be correct."

"I think it's more likely to be quartzite, for the ending of the spelling differs slightly," Mentu added knowingly.

For with the deciphering of the First Gate, it gave the scribe insight and some knowledge of the writings of the scribes who had prepared the scroll, and he felt more confident in his judgements. "But the name of the Gate was not included in the actual password, so do you think we need to know the exact name for it?"

"No, perhaps not," Malian pondered. "Let's concentrate on the password and see how that goes." Bending their heads again, they became engrossed in the design which represented the Second Gate.

This password was also in two lines, one atop the other, the same as the First Gate:

$$S \ A \ A \ D \ S \ B \ K$$
$$M \ R \ G \ I \ O \ E$$

"It makes no sense either forwards or backwards," Malian said straightaway. "So it's not exactly the same as the first."

"No, it's not, but if we move the letters around, it's got to work out. All the letters are there, it's just reading them in the right order," the scribe figured.

Time passed, and the boat was propelled ever forward, and the two moved the letters around in their heads and attempted to make some sense of the whole, until eventually Malian said, "The last three letters on the top line and the last two on the bottom, make up the name *SOBEK*. Look, you need to take one from the top and then one from the bottom and then back to the top again." He pointed out each of the letters in turn and read out, "S..O..B..E..K."

"*Sobek* is the crocodile god of the water, and the water governs the fertility of the land," Mentu said, aware that Malian would not be ignorant in these matters. "Aagh, so our understanding of the Gate cartouche is also important too," he reasoned, "not in its material structure but in what is depicted there." He pointed back to the cartouche on the left. "The plants depict the fertility of the land and the god who protects it. *Sobek*, the crocodile god!"

"And if we do the same to the other letters, what do we get?" Malian eagerly asked, moving closer alongside Mentu.

"S..M..A..R..A..G..D..I," Mentu spelt out, starting with the first top letter and copying Malian's actions. After some thought, he added, "Smaragdi means green, like a precious stone, I think, in the script form."

"Green, precious stone," Malian repeated. "Like malachite or jade?"

"Well, yes, but I think it may mean something more splendid in this sense and in keeping with a god. Perhaps something like emerald."

"Emerald crocodile!" Malian declared. "It's the same as 'ebony jackal,' an animal's name preceded by a colour, for the want of a simple term. Surely it's got to be correct," he reasoned. Sitting back, he observed Mentu as he continued to look over the scroll, checking and rechecking his findings to be sure of their conclusion.

While the two elders sat and figured out their workings, Shuma, Tragen and Darric had moved further back along the platform and sat huddled together in the shadow and the presence of the Boatman who towered above. Backlit by the solar rays, the Lord Aken gently progressed the boat forward into the slightly undulating river of *The Duat*, dipping the oar ever slower into the bronzed water and propelling them onward past the towering figures carved deep into the walls where their gaze looked fixedly along the path towards the next Gate.

"Is this how you imagined the underworld?" Tragen eventually asked Shuma in hushed tones as the three sat powerlessly imprisoned within the limitations of the boat, and their dread steadily increased. An unease and doubt still remained, gripping them in a tight hold, and although the First Gate was passed, the Second would soon be upon them.

"I don't think I'd ever really thought much about it," she whispered back. "I would judge that most folk don't." Here she paused and then continued, "But it does perplex me that the passwords seem challenging in one aspect but childlike in others." Suddenly she realised that in their panic, it had taken all contributions to solve this first puzzle concluding with Darric putting his life on the line. "I mean, though, '*Ebony Jackal*,' it's not like it's been too confusing for us to work out. But what about the field workers and the housewives," she went on, "would they know these passwords? And what about the children? Not everyone sees old age or dies with loved ones at their side."

"Perhaps that's what happened to the ones on the approaching side of the Gate," Darric's voice rang out darkly and suspiciously as he stared along to where Mentu and Malian appeared to be coming to some conclusion.

"Not all will see beyond **The Duat,***"* Lord Aken suddenly declared from above their heads. *"And note well, the passwords are given in accordance with the eminence of the soul and for the life lived…and so for each, the challenge will be clear or harsh."*

"So, when our final day is at hand, the passwords will not be as those said along this journey?" Tragen asked, somewhat in dismay.

"No! Your judgement will be yours alone!"

Malian and Mentu had risen suddenly, and coming back towards the group they quickly sat and again produced the scroll.

"We've done it, we think. We've worked out the

password for the Second Gate!" Malian announced. "And it's also of help for our solving of the others. If it's correct, of course," he quickly added while showing the working out of this next password to the others.

The boat was again slowing, and the darkness ahead became lit up by the rays of *Ra* as they slid along within the constraints of the water. Now the heaps and stacks of bones gradually reappeared on the footpaths, and either side of the river, the skulls once again stared out with vacant eyes as they gathered before the Gate. As the brightness advanced before the boat, it picked out each one before impacting on the solid structure which traversed the river.

"Prepare to speak the password," the Lord Aken demanded. *"For the Second Gate approaches."*

A horn again rang out, though twice now it split the air and a voice once more resounded from the left-hand side of the river.

"BEHOLD THE RIVER GATE OF QUARTZITE," the herald of the Second Gate announced. **"ADVANCE AND PRESENT THE KEYWORD."**

The Lord Aken once again navigated his vessel towards the portal, pulling hard on the oar to slow the barge in its advancement as the Gate reared up above their heads. The white, grey quartzite sparkled vividly in the light, revealing the pink, red and purple staining of iron that tainted the rock and which highlighted the detailed carvings. Here the god *Sobek* was chiselled into the tough rock face, crocodile head atop the body of a man, while a vista of vegetation grew up around his knees and plant life trailed around the exquisite carvings.

The doorkeeper now appeared, again from the left, wearing a long cloak of sparkling white with the crocodile mask weighing heavy on his shoulders.

Carrying his staff forwards, he slowly lowered it into place across the portal to impede the travel of the craft before turning his elongated head towards the group and speaking, **"COME FORWARD AND SPEAK THE WORDS OF ADMISSION, AND PREPARE YOURSELVES BEFORE THE OVERSEER OF THE GATE."**

Again Darric chose to go first, walking with slightly less heart towards the prow, prior to slowly kneeling and lowering his head before the doorkeeper, where the staff was again placed to hinder their progress. Once again, the others waited and appeared more unnerved in the following, fully aware that in the saying of this Second Gate password, it would either uphold or disprove the reasoning of the two elders for the Gates which lay ahead.

"EMERALD CROCODILE," he spoke out in a strong voice. Then nervously and with some panic, he glanced upwards to receive judgement.

The crocodile head slowly swung round and down towards the stooped figure, and the jaws gaped opened to expose jagged white teeth with a blood-red tongue disappearing into the darkness of the throat. Suddenly the doorkeeper proclaimed, **"PASS, BELIEVER IN THE GOD *SOBEK*, MASTER OF THE WATERS AND OF THE LANDS FERTILITY."**

A relief instantly washed over Darric and passed likewise to the waiting group. Again, with regard given to the doorkeeper, they then individually moved forward to repeat the words already spoken and once completed, the staff was raised, and the Lord Aken pushed forward, bowing his head and shoulders to avoid the boundaries set by the arched Gate.

As they passed through, the water again changed its colour from a deep burnished bronze to the shade of old blood, not bright red but of a deep wine stain and the colour of ripe grapes before the autumn harvest.

"My Lord, what happens to those who don't answer correctly?" Darric humbly asked with curiosity and some petition to the Lord Aken as they passed below the Gate. The saying of this second password had unnerved him more than the first. "Are these their bones which litter the ground?"

The remains which had been seen collected around the face of both preceding Gates had not continued onto their rearward sides nor continued along the pathways, but on nearing the portals, they had somehow massed as if in wait.

"The bones lie in hope of restoration with the passing souls of the recent dead. For they are unable to pass, and their spirits are doomed to wander desolate through **The Duat** *for eternity,"* came the explanation as the voice echoed deeply along the enclosed chamber of the underworld. As they left behind this Second Gateway, the god himself straightened up into the canopy of stars on the far side, and he pushed slowly forward.

Darric shivered and hastily turned away to join the body of the group gathered together once again in the midsection of the boat where Malian and Mentu, with scroll again unfurled between them, contemplated the password for the Third Gate. The design read:

The two men, having successfully solved the mystery of the Second Gate, were now even more convinced that it detailed a colour and the name of an animal, and it was just a matter of working out the pattern to achieve the end.

The Third Gate cartouche, down the left, showed the portal topped with a half-moon and with the word SABULI lengthways down the centre. The word itself was quickly identified to be sandstone, which therefore denoted the structure of the Gate, but the half-moon gave for some thought.

"We do need to look at both pointers," Malian reminded them, and Mentu promptly nodded in agreement. But in looking from one side of the scroll to the other, it became no clearer, and the design itself eventually became the focus of attention. Reading it as the previous and trying other ways, the letters made little sense. Until Mentu suddenly read them in the round, starting at the letter A at the top before moving down the left-hand side and around the bottom and then climbing back up the right.

"A..R..G..E..N..T..I..B..A..B..A," he spelt out the letters before quickly declaring, "Argentibaba, and with the association of the half-moon symbol! Does that make any sense?" he asked, as they all looked on.

"The time of the half-moon is the time of the dead. Sort of halfway between life and death and a time of great omens," Shuma volunteered, with some hope that her knowledge in these matters may be of benefit.

"Right, and an animal that is embodied with the strength of the dead is the baboon. BABA!" Malian quickly added, noting the last symbols. "That would then just leave us with ARGENTI."

"Well, that can only be the colour part of the password, but I only know it has money or payment in coin," Mentu said. Thinking for a short while, he took up the scroll and studied it further and then ventured, "Or I suppose you could say silver if you are talking about coin. That's it, silver baboon!" he concluded.

Suddenly sitting back, he eased his bones as a sense of relief washed over him. This quickly spread to the rest of the group, who looked on in some sureness that another design had been likely solved and the Third Gate would possibly, be negotiated with the ease of the earlier two. But Mentu would give it no rest for long, and in a short time, his mind focused lower down the scroll, and he bent once more to regard the following Gates and designs which lay before him.

The rest of the group, however, felt a small amount of assurance for the Gates, which waited up ahead, and Tragen, Shuma and Darric left the scribe and Malian to their contemplations. Gathering together their bags, they returned again to the hush and stillness of the shadow of the Boatman as he moved them onwards along the watercourse.

"I don't like those bones," Darric said with some fear in his voice, for a feeling of deep unease was growing, and he was unable to let it pass. "I feel like I'm being watched!"

"Many have lain here for an eternity, but they can still sense the beat of a heart, and their souls reach out for connection and affinity with the living," Lord Aken's voice spoke from above. *"But give them little concern, for you are in the Light of Ra, and in his path, you are shielded. BUT,"* he stressed, his voice echoing into the depths, *"again, I remind you DO NOT leave the boat, or touch any of the bones where they lie, for their souls are voracious in their longing."*

A quietness and inaction soon came over the three, and each sat with his own thoughts, lulled into a false sense of ease as time carried them forward on their eternal passage. Until eventually, after some time had passed, *The Duat* began to gently curve away to the left with the procession of gods, goddesses and their table offerings disappearing from the Light of *Ra*, only to slowly reappear as the boat and its light advanced around the bend of the ruby river. Once more, as the Third Gate approached, the bones started to gather, and the skulls, with their blank stares and bony hands protruding in supplication, assembled on the river's edge to observe the boat and its cargo as it passed, and a nervousness overshadowed the occupants, urging them to quickly collect near the prow in haste and readiness for the Gate ahead.

Straddling again the river, the massive portal came into view, matching the two former in size. But being of a softer bleached sandstone mass composed of minerals, rocks and organic matter, the framework appeared less overpowering than the last, with the matrix of rock allowing only for the most basic of carving, which appeared crude and savage over the previous. Here the baboon was portrayed in all his manliness, with scenes showing his stiffness and virility, and the course images and markings left little to the imagination.

A horn blew three times, and a voice again rang out from the left-hand side of the river.

"BEHOLD THE RIVER GATE OF SANDSTONE," the herald of the Third Gate declared. **"ADVANCE AND PRESENT THE KEYWORD."**

The group quickly assembled near the front while Lord Aken guided the boat gently to rest before the Gate. And as the tip of the prow stopped dead in the archway, the doorkeeper appeared on the left in his sweeping grey robes, a huge hairy, unshorn baboon's skull covering his head which overflowed down his back. And with the dog-like face, its mouth agape and huge fangs protruding, he quickly thrust his staff forward to bar the way before proclaiming in a harsh tone, **"COME FORWARD AND SPEAK THE WORDS OF ADMISSION, AND PREPARE YOURSELVES BEFORE THE OVERSEER OF THE GATE."**

"I shall go first, this time," Shuma spoke with conviction, moving up to the prow and past the others, "for Darric has twice taken his chance and risked all for us."

The now familiar rite took place, with Shuma kneeling and lowering her head before the keeper of the door, and the password was spoken, "SILVER BABOON."

While the response, **"PASS, BELIEVER IN THE GOD *BABA*, BULL OF THE BABOONS AND MASTER OF THE POWERFUL DEAD,"** came swiftly with the staff rising slowly as the last came forward and the final password was given. The doorkeeper, now bowing his head and conceding the Gate, melted back into the darkness, and the group made themselves ready to proceed, moving around the vessel as the Boatman slowly made to move off under the overhang of the gateway. But in his speed and hurry, Darric brushed past Shuma, and in doing so, his shoulder roughly disturbed a small, outstretched hand of white bone which overhung the bankside, sending it askew from its line. The cry was instantaneous and painful to hear, and as an immediate lament followed, the group stood rooted in their tracks, and Darric instantly recognised his error.

"A soul has been aroused!" the Boatman woefully announced before addressing Darric, *"And now you must be swiftly through* **The Duat,** *for the soul will follow your beating heart in hope of its redemption and escape from its suffering, and in its place, you shall become of*

the dead. Come, we must make haste!"

Moving rapidly, he thrust the oar into the water, guiding the craft under the portal and on into the next stage of *The Duat*. On passing through, the river once again formed a unique colour change, with the water becoming of such a rich translucent green that the surface looked like a mill pond except where the oar disturbed the surface in its rush to move the boat forward.

"I'm sorry, it was an accident!" Darric pleaded as the sounds of sorrow and misery followed behind them and as he looked back in horror towards the receding Gate, he half expected to witness the soul manifest itself before his very eyes. The group had swiftly gathered towards the middle of the boat, sensing the immediate urgency that the Boatman had made known, and there Darric dropped to the platform in his fear and anguish. Their only hope now was to swiftly get through the other Gates.

As Mentu went on to explain his success in arranging the device letters for the Fourth Gate, pointing them out on the scroll, the voices of mourning gave chase.

"This fourth cartouche shows the Circle of Life atop the portal," he quickly indicated, "with the word LIVIDA down its core and livida in the sense of stonework stands for slate," he continued, "and the circle along with the design which reads from left to right, and line for line, gives us AHENIBASTET."

He went on to clarify that *Bastet*, the cat, was the protective goddess for the fight against evil spirits and disease and, therefore, the guardian of life. This left only the word Aheni to decipher, and this in script, he added, stood for a brazen cooking vessel, pot or cauldron usually made of bronze. He, therefore, had reasoned the word for the Fourth Gate should be BRONZE CAT. To Mentu's relief, there came an instant acceptance of this as the next password, and their attention immediately turned to the importance of their speed in traversing the waterway.

The river here was bent almost like a sickle, and the walls curved tightly around, leaving little view forward, for the canal too had grown inwards, and the banks still with their paths could almost be touched as they brushed the side of the boat as it pressed forward. This, unfortunately, slowed down its advance and gave great cause for concern for those on board, for it allowed the spirits of the dead to gather in their lament.

Suddenly and without warning, Darric was pulled to his feet and away from the group as they stood near the prow, and feeling a massive tug at his chest and shoulders, he was dragged physically backwards along the boat and dropped at the feet of the Boatman. There he lay, struggling for breath. The others immediately rushed to his aid as an overwhelming clamour and wailing noise surrounded them, and the very air seemed to condense, slowing them in their advance.

On the towpath ahead and to the left, there slowly emerged the outline of a small body, head drooping forward off the rack of bones which made up its chest. And with tatters of clothing drooping off its shoulders and covering its extremities, it raised its head, the jaw falling open as the vacant eye sockets looked directly to where Darric lay, and slowly it raised its small bony arms in petition.

"Let the light surround him," the Boatman roared, *"and let the Lord* **Ra** *give him protection through the*

coming Gates." Quickly drawing the silver blade which he carried at his side, the Lord Aken held it forward over the figure at his feet. Instantly the solid brightness which had escorted them flooded around and directed itself to the prone figure, wrapping him in its sheer radiance and guarding the youth from the spirits. The stern of the boat was in complete brightness, and even the Boatman had disappeared into the very rays of the sun while the leading beams continued to light the river ahead. Turning away from such sheer brilliance, the others, unnerved by the events and fearful in their dismay, hurriedly returned to the prow in hope for the best for both Darric and the remainder of the journey.

"We can do no more for him," Malian spoke loudly in his panic, "for he is now in another place." He looked around at the shaken, and dismayed group collapsed at his side, then said, "So, we must look to ourselves and hope that the Lord Aken will continue to row and we can persist in working our way through the Gates, for we can only look forwards and prepare ourselves for the next challenge."

The boat did, thankfully for those on board, continue to move onward while the lamentation of the spirits continued to follow them as they progressed. But on passing the bony figure on the left, its raised arms had fallen to its side, and it had collapsed and became just another collection of rags and bones littering the path, again joining with those which had already begun to gather together and amass in expectation of the next Gate.

Negotiating left around the bend of the emerald river and feeling like they were again going back on themselves, the Fourth Gate soon came into view as the leading Light of *Ra* lit the way. Clad in a dark grey material which lightened to an almost dusky silvery shade as it reached up toward the star-covered roof, this Gate was adorned with carvings of such a delicate nature showing the cat-headed goddess *Bastet* in her tight white gown and with the "*ankh*" of life held firmly in her hand. Here she was surrounded by discs, representing the sun in its circle of life and rebirth, which happened each day, and in some of these, medicinal plants could be seen in respect of her guardianship over disease and evil spirits.

As they approached, the lamentation of the dead faded until it finally ceased altogether as a horn blew four times while again a voice rang out, this time coming from the right-hand side of the river.

"BEHOLD THE RIVER GATE OF SLATE," the herald of the Fourth Gate declared. **"ADVANCE AND PRESENT THE KEYWORD."**

The boat, almost of its own free will, advanced and came to a stop well before the Gateway giving the occupants the time to take in the rich carvings as they moved to the front in readiness for proclaiming the password. The doorkeeper emerged on the right-hand side of the waterway dressed in a shimmering white dress with a sleek black cat head adorned with piercing blue eyes and turning her gaze upon the boat she waited.

"Why has the position of the herald and the doorkeeper changed?" Malian softly whispered as he slowly bent his head toward Mentu as they stood in the prow, concerned somewhat that this seemed an added complication to their progress.

"This Gate is surely female," Mentu immediately whispered back, "while the others we have already passed have been male. The Left side of the Passage is male, and the Right-side female. I think it is nothing to be worried about as the password must be given just the same!"

They both concentrated ahead as the boat inched slowly into the portal, while the doorkeeper now came forward, extending her stave to forbid passage. As the boat came to a halt and the four waited, she stared at each one in turn before announcing, **"COME FORWARD AND SPEAK THE WORDS OF ADMISSION, AND PREPARE YOURSELVES BEFORE THE OVERSEER OF THE GATE."**

The password, "BRONZE CAT," was then given four times, as one by one, starting again with Shuma, they approached in confidence. And for each, the response was acknowledged with, **"PASS, BELIEVER IN THE GODDESS *BASTET,* MISTRESS OF THE LIGHT AND GUARDIAN AGAINST DISEASE AND EVIL SPIRITS."**

On the final saying, the staff was finally lifted, the boat mysteriously moving forward and off through the Fourth Gate, leaving behind the green water before eventually emerging into where a deep sapphire blue coloured the waters of *The Duat*. The moaning of the spirits, which had stopped before the Gateway, now resumed in its pursuit of the boat as it moved onward along the river that gently curved around a long right-hand bend. As the rear side of the Gate disappeared, and the boat advanced on its course, the group remained at the front, unable to bear the brightness which filled the rear of the craft. Powerless to help Darric except, in the only way possible, they looked to the next Gate and their escape from *The Duat*.

"Only three more to go," Mentu said with some conviction as he sat and tried to make himself more comfortable upon the boards, "and we must look towards the next Gate and its password."

The rest of the group settled around him in their shared agitation, and the scroll was once more unrolled and studied. With the gathered knowledge, they could, at last, be more confident in their assumptions and also in their working out, which was progressing quicker at each Gate. And while the banks of *The Duat* slid past, they carefully examined the evidence as the pursuing sounds slowly faded into the background, and they concentrated on the puzzle before them. This fifth cartouche had the portal ringed with, what looked like eyes, one at the base of each pillar and the other surmounting the top, with the word MARMORIS down its middle. Mentu explained that marmoris stood for marble.

"But what do the eyes mean?" Tragen questioned as he and Shuma closely scrutinised the scroll before he handed it back to the scribe.

"Eyes can stand for many things. Such as honesty, truth, and intelligence. However, in this case, I think they can stand also for 'Judgement'," he explained, "and this must be taken in addition to the design read from left to right and line for line, which gives us "AURI*THOTH*."

"*Thoth* is the god associated with wisdom, justice and the science of writing and magic, and is depicted as an ibis-headed man," Mentu continued, "and the remaining letters, A U R I as we now understand, must be a colour." He added that he had often seen workshops of the goldsmiths in the valley with the letters A U R I engraved over their doors to advertise their trade and that they must have some meaning in their world for the word gold. The password, therefore, for the Fifth Gate must be GOLD IBIS.

The four quickly agreed, and with this next password hopefully solved, Malian, Tragen and Shuma turned their attention forward along the waterway. The paths were once again starting to fill with the ragged heaps of bones, and the skulls began to jostle in line along the riverside in anticipation of the Gate ahead. With the eyes of the dead staring off into the distance, Mentu remained concentrating, scroll unrolled before him, as he seriously contemplated and examined the remaining two Gates while the three made ready for the next undertaking.

The craft had begun to quicken as the river widened slightly at the approach of the Fifth Gate, which soon came into view on the very bend of its waters. Again, the lamenting ceased as the colossal portal was neared, and the Gateway straddled the banks as ahead the gleaming white monument grew larger, and the boat came near, the finely carved details of the god *Thoth* and his attributes easily picked out of the carvings. Here he stood ibis-headed and with staff in hand while around him grew the papyrus plants that made the scrolls and reed pens of his vocation. Above his head, the all-seeing-eye looked out in judgement of those who passed beneath, and in the background, the lesser gods sat in anticipation of souls unworthy of advance.

The challenge of the horn blew five times, and the voice rang out from the left.

"BEHOLD THE RIVER GATE OF MARBLE," the herald of the Fifth Gate declared. **"ADVANCE AND PRESENT THE KEYWORD."**

The boat once more moved slowly forward, prow almost touching the Gate as it swung around to take up position in the centre of the water, and the four stood highlighted in the sun's rays, awaiting the doorkeeper who emerged from the left, his iridescent blue robes shimmering as he strode forward to the waterside. The figure was again male but with a bird-like head, with long slender beak which moved from one side to the other as it observed the boat and the four who stood in its prow. Here the long staff was once again thrust across the opening of the Gate, and the voice rang out in command, **"COME FORWARD AND SPEAK THE WORDS OF ADMISSION, AND PREPARE YOURSELVES BEFORE THE OVERSEER OF THE GATE."**

Again, each took their turn as before in proclaiming the password, "GOLD IBIS."

And each received the assent of the doorkeeper, **"PASS, BELIEVER IN THE GOD *THOTH*, MASTER OF WISDOM AND WRITING AND GUARDIAN OF THE LANDS JUSTICE."**

Once again, the huge staff was gradually lifted as the final assent was spoken and the boat moved off through the Fifth Gateway and into the waters beyond the portal, which had transformed from the comforting blue into a deep greasy-looking blackness that sucked sullenly at the boat sides as they advanced. The river immediately started to bend as they emerged through the Gate, but the procession of gods remained in place, escorting the dead along the pathway and on to their reckoning. The occupants of the boat, once again quickly and with knowledge gained, worked out the password for the next Gate with the guidance of Mentu, who had already, with the help of the cartouche, started by detailing the Gate word SILICIA as meaning limestone. Moving on to the design, they had been puzzled for a short while until it was worked out that it was to be read from the S at the right-hand bottom and working up the word in a snake-like fashion. This gave the word, S A P P H I R I *T A W E R E T.*

Taweret, Mentu was able to enlighten them was a fertility goddess and a protector of women during childbirth and child-rearing. Going on to add that she was also protector of the young and vulnerable and was more likely a household deity rather than a major god, but of equal importance when one was helpless and in dire need. She was, he said, represented as a hippo standing on its back legs while holding an ancient sign for protection in her hand. The word Sapphiri translated as a blue gem or, as Mentu made clearer, sapphire. So the password for this next Gate was SAPPHIRE HIPPO.

"There are stars detailed in the cartouche," Shuma asked, "and their heavenly meaning in *Taweret's* understanding must be for our offspring."

"Yes, Shuma, our children are the stars in our eyes," Mentu instantly responded before realising what he had said and looking sharply towards where Tragen sat opposite.

Tragen, however appeared unmoved unless deaf to the exchange, and the small group, content that this next password had been solved, remained confined to the front of the boat where in their mental exhaustion, they attempted to rest and make ready for the oncoming Gate. Shortly, as the wailings and lamentation of the spirits ceased but the unsettling bones again gathered on the path, the portal came into sight, and they advanced within the rays of *Ra.*

The Gate of limestone appeared to be pure white, giving a clarity within the carvings and an unsullied look to the surface as it towered into the passageway. The images etched into the soft whiteness showed the goddess

Taweret as a hippo, standing on her back legs with a crocodile tail advancing down her back and with large drooping breasts hanging from her chest. Her hand was placed on the *"Sa"* sign, which stood for protection and safety, while the carvings themselves were surrounded by a multitude of star-shaped fossils, large and small, which enhanced the appearance of fertility and propagation.

As the boat continued to approach in the greasy waters and the Gateway slowly grew overhead, the horn blew six times from the right, an indication that the Gate god was again female.

"BEHOLD THE RIVER GATE OF LIMESTONE," the herald of the Sixth Gate declared. **"ADVANCE AND PRESENT THE KEYWORD."**

The boat, as at earlier Gates, started to slow again before stopping in the Gateway itself, where all looked to the right to where the doorkeeper advanced from her cover. She was as depicted on the Gate, hippo headed with open mouth baring strong teeth and with a crocodile tail down her back, and pendulous breasts reaching down almost to her navel. However, as doorkeeper, she wore entwined around her heavyset waist a flowing kilt of yellow sunlit fabric which offered a certain modesty to the overall. Moving forward, she planted her long staff over the Gateway before exclaiming, **"COME FORWARD AND SPEAK THE WORDS OF ADMISSION, AND PREPARE YOURSELVES BEFORE THE OVERSEER OF THE GATE."**

For a sixth time, each of the four came forward to announce the password, "SAPPHIRE HIPPO."

And one by one, they accepted the grant of the doorkeeper, **"PASS, BELIEVER IN THE GODDESS *TAWERET*, MISTRESS OF ABUNDANCE AND LADY OF THE HORIZON."**

On the raising of the staff and the final inclination of

the huge head, the boat once again moved onward in the Light of *Ra* under the towering Gate and into where the river changed from its dark and oily course into a rich golden waterway that radiated the beams into every corner and facet of the passage, bathing the gods and goddesses in a celestial glow as they continued their progress along the walls. The effect was dazzling, and the four quickly crouched down at the front of the boat, the hoods of their cloaks pulled up over their heads in search of some relief from the light. Mentu, seated between Malian and Tragen, informed them that he had already worked out the Gate cartouche at the bottom of the scroll, which read ONYCHINA signifying onyx. Whereas the next and final password for the Seventh Gate from the words which lay at the base of the scroll design read as,

$$\text{ꝗ ꝗ U S R H}$$
$$\text{N B R U O}$$

He explained that it translated as H O R U S R U B I N I, starting at the top last letter H before moving downwards to the O and then back up to the R and so on. The sky god *Horus*, the hawk, was recognised by all who sat within the boat and needed little description. But the word rubini, Mentu added, was likened to the word rubinea, which meant a red or ruby colouring in the markets of the dye and cloth sellers. Thus, he had translated the password to be RUBY HAWK.

This agreed and considered to be solved, their thoughts gave way to other concerns, and while the boat slid soundlessly through the waters, the four remained undercover from the light and in contemplation of the other side of the Seventh Gate and whether judgement would indeed be carried out. Shuma appeared the least to be concerned and concentrated her time on carefully checking over her pack, while Tragen, having already disclosed his failings to the others, remained troubled that there may be somehow a reckoning for his actions. Malian and Mentu, however, both felt a certain contentment within themselves of a life lived within the boundaries of the scholarly world and would go to the test, should there be one, with little fear but perhaps a trace of sadness for a life not tasted to the full.

"I think the Seventh Gate approaches," Shuma suddenly said after unseen time had passed in reflective silence, "for I feel a slowing of the boat." Uncovering her head and looking over the hunched figure of Tragen, she saw the Gateway coming into view with the radiance of *Ra* focused through into its very heart. This last Gate stood out like no other, having no carvings but decorated with parallel banded onyx gemstones of black, white and red, studded into the rock face in the shape of ornate crowns representing kingship. There were no depictions of *Horus* here, and the backdrop to the Gate remained free from other images and renderings. Noticeably absent, too, was the collection of bones that had been seen massed at the previous Gates, for the pathways running alongside the golden river were barren of any bones leading right up to the Gate itself. Even the voices of lament had not followed them through and had ceased in their pursuit. The four companions quickly readied themselves for this Seventh undertaking, and as the Light of *Ra* extended further onwards, they prepared to once again face the doorkeeper.

The horn blew seven times, followed by the call ringing out from the left for a last and concluding time.

"BEHOLD THE RIVER GATE OF ONYX," the herald of the Seventh Gate declared. **"ADVANCE AND PRESENT THE KEYWORD."**

Finally, along the banks of *The Duat*, the boat slowed

in front of the massive Gate with the prow coming to rest before the portal where the doorkeeper, standing on the left-hand side, was already awaiting the boat's arrival staff in position across the Gateway. He stood, more than double the size of the former keepers, with an immense hawk head and brown and cream feathered cape which encased him from shoulder to foot. Turning his sharp thick beak and bright eyes down towards the boat, he spoke, **"COME FORWARD AND SPEAK THE WORDS OF ADMISSION, AND PREPARE YOURSELVES BEFORE THE OVERSEER OF THE GATE."**

One by one, they then approached as before and declared the password, "RUBY HAWK."

To which the doorkeeper granted, **"PASS, BELIEVER IN THE GOD *HORUS*, MASTER OF THE SKY AND PROTECTOR OF KINGSHIP."**

However, as Malian, being the last of the four, had come forward to declare, the doorkeeper had stepped forward and, bending closer, had looked directly into the frightened altar tender's eye before pronouncing.

"THE SEVEN GATES HAVE BEEN CONQUERED AND ARE NOW CLOSED. BUT TO YOU ALONE, MALIAN, I GIVE THS GIFT, THE *SHEN* STAFF. WHICH WILL ENCIRCLE AND ETERNALLY PROTECT YOU IN YOUR SEARCH AND BEYOND."

He passed to Malian a short golden staff which was topped off with a crosspiece surmounted with a large circle attached to the middle, and bowing his head low before straightening up, he returned to his post, lofted high the staff which had prevented the boats passing and the craft moved forward. Has it made its pass under this final Gate the voice of the Boatman suddenly addressed the four from the brightness at the stern.

"Your journey is now at its end, and in the Light of **Ra,** *you shall be re-awakened from this dream without trial and returned into the light…but note well…that in good time we shall again make this journey together!"*

Drowsiness quickly overcame them followed by a confused sleep, and the light which surrounded Darric had enclosed them all in its warmth and protection. While beyond this last Gate, the water had again remade its colour, and the golden river had turned into the clear light of a blue sky, cloudless and wind free, and the boat had come to a stop. Time had meant nothing as they travelled along *The Duat*, and minutes passed could have been hours or days in their reckoning. But they had finally reached the end and, in the Light of *Ra*, were again reborn into the new day.

CHAPTER NINE

As the sun rose higher, the insects and bugs of the fetid swamps had quickly collected around the heads and shoulders of the riders as they moved further into the marshland, and the horses continually trembled and shuddered in a constant act to rid themselves of the biting flies which swarmed up from the lush greenery. Gallius rode out in front, with his team and the elders trailing close behind. In his wake, Marke rode escorting the elders Tarnik, Rusan and Gaival while his brother Rogan led Theroc, Claud and Petrus. They were then followed by Statte and Brann, with Roth bringing up the rear.

On entering the swampland that morning, the banks of the High Rush Plains had initially seemed at a distance, and the elders rode in dread that the night would have to be spent amongst the dense, rank vegetation of the wet bog. But as the day moved forward, the banks grew nearer, and with relief, the heavy mire eventually gave way to a firmer terrain, and the horses climbed gently up onto the reed-covered embankment, and the land of the rushes spread out before them.

At this distance, they seemed as flat as the eye could see, showing first a creamy off-white border of sand before advancing greenly off into the far distance where the closing heat of the day was sending hazy mists spiralling into the air. And for the riders, at last, the smell of the swampland and its innumerable flies were thankfully at their backs. Quickly descending, the group entered the beginning of the High Rush Plains, where the land first crossed a sandy barren desert before the start of the plains proper. Here the soft dusty surface slowed their progress, and the riders dismounted to aid their mounts and to lead them quickly onward. Their camp that evening was in a low dune that offered protection from the north-western wind with its gusting sand and provided a place to eat and then a soft bed for them to lay their weary bodies in their exhaustion. Warmth was not needed for the powdery grains radiated a gentle heat, and lightly wrapped in their cloaks, they all huddled down to see the night through.

The next day they were on the move before the rising dawn had coloured the sky, the prisoners being woken roughly from their sleep by the sharp feet of Marke and Rogan, who ordered them up and to ready themselves at once. The brothers had started to show a distinct hostility towards the elders and had taken a dislike to their appointed task of caretaking to which Gallius had assigned them. Marke, the older of the two, had particular cause, for he resented the subtle whisperings and furtive glances which he saw as their attempts to antagonise and irritate him, and he took his frustration out on Claud, the youngest man, with much enjoyment.

The day that unfolded saw the riders continuing across the warm sand, the horses being guided over the formless terrain before the vast tufts and tussocks of the beds of grasses appeared before them, and they passed into the Plains of the High Rush. Here the huge green plants with their broad leaves towered many feet high above them as the stalks of downy, light flower heads rustled and stirred in the light of the day. But the extensive roundness of these tussocks allowed easy passage between each circular outgrowth, and the firmer ground made once again for a quicker speed. With Gallius leading the way in heading to their first stop at the Oasis of Plenty, he initially kept the rising sun towards his right shoulder and worked his horse this way and that around the beds of light and airy greenery which made up the clusters of growth.

The High Rush Plains had been an area of extreme activity where a vast number of field workers once harvested the thick green leaves of the plants to create the ochre-stained parchments and scrolls used throughout the land. The market had been exceedingly profitable, and a wide range of industry had built up, from around the workers themselves to the parchment manufacturers and along to the scribes who provided a document and handwriting service and who decorated the scrolls which accompanied the dead. Now all that remained were the plants themselves, and the villages around the oases and the wells which the workers had built had fallen into ruin as the peasants and labourers had moved on and abandoned them during the uprisings of the long ago, and through these, the men slowly passed.

***

On the day that Gallius, along with his men and their elder captives, travelled towards the Oasis of Plenty, Malian awoke exhausted and weak from his unconsciousness. Resting on the shores of Lake Cannis many miles to the north of the riders and two long days and nights after their own reappearance and reawakening from *The Duat*, he had awoken to the warmth of the day holding the *Shen* Staff tightly to his chest and with Shuma by his side. He remembered nothing of their arrival at this place, for his long sleep had carried him far in his dreams, and Shuma had to recount their arrival as she recalled it from her own disorientated state.

He was told that the morning Light of *Ra*, which had accompanied the boat *Meseket*, had emerged into this eastern basin on the northern side of the lake, and here the Lord Aken had awoken them fully into the warm misty light of a cloudless dawn.

"Awake and behold the new morning," he had announced, as the surrounding light which had protected them rose up skywards, releasing them from its radiance, *"for the Lord* **Ra** *has risen, and the day greets you in all its splendour and possibility."*

Immediately the group had awoken completely to their location, all except for himself, she explained, who appeared to be in a trance-like state although still able to disembark the boat with the help of Tragen and Mentu. Stepping foot onto the sandy soil, he had immediately weakened, and falling forwards had been laid gently to the ground. Once all alighted the *Meseket*, a deep grey fogginess had collected low over the water in the west into which Lord Aken had steered his boat. And as the horn blared out for a final time, he had turned and raised his hand before disappearing back into the mists, ready to meet, once again, the setting sun on its eternal travel. They had made their camp in the bay, unable to move further with no real idea of direction, and awaited his awakening.

Shuma went on to quickly add that there was one crucial and substantial thing that Malian urgently needed to know. For when the Light of *Ra* had released them, Darric, too, had been released from the radiance at the oarsman's feet, and his transformation had been startling. The dark-haired youth who had been shielded in the Light of *Ra* was now altered by the encounter, and the person who stood before them was white-haired and with an awareness about him that hung lightly off his shoulders. Quickly assisting the others in disembarking, he had, however, been unaware of his own physical changes until she had approached him and gently reaching out, had guided him towards the lake where he could witness his own change in the reflection of the waters.

On hearing this, Malian hurriedly sat up and, looking for Darric, saw the white-haired man at the water's edge stooping low over the water.

"How has this gone with him?" he quickly asked. He had heard of such things happening before but usually at times of great stress or overwhelming shock.

"He's accepted it," came the reply, as she positioned a pack to support his head, "and he has grown in his acceptance." Rising and smiling down at Malian, she continued, "I'll go and tell the others that you are awake." Leaving him, she strode off, and he was able to see the sandy beach which they had made into their camp, and which had been his bed for a number of days and nights, with the huge lake which lay in front of him.

Lake Cannis was of the most beautiful clear jade colour and surrounded by broad beds of tall lily plants bearing large tropical blooms of such vibrant red, orange and yellow colours growing proudly out of the broad green leaves. Its source, at its western side, was the swamplands surrounding the High Rush Plains with its vast area of marsh and reed beds before it flowed along and out into two widened areas forming deep bays on its northern rim. There it finally ran its course out to the east towards the great Inland Sea in the Heartlands. The clear green colour of the water was mainly down to the immense flower beds at the mouth of the swamp, which filtered and extracted the pollutants through its extensive network of swollen roots, allowing the contaminant-free water to feed the beds further along the lakesides.

Here Shuma had been able to use her knowledge of these beautiful flowers and their roots, for these would not go to waste while they remained on the shoreline with Malian. She knew that the roots of the plants, as well as the seeds, were edible and even the young shoots could be boiled, similar to a vegetable. The leaves were also of benefit, for placed on the fire, they provided a light smoky vapour which kept away the great thick swarms of gnats that danced over the water as the sun went down.

"Malian, it's good to see you awake," Mentu's voice suddenly sounded from behind him, and turning, he saw the scribe moving closer down the beach. Looking further back, he could also see the high dunes which dwarfed the approaching man. These he knew led on to the Sleeping Caverns in the north and then beyond into the very northern lands itself.

"Mentu! Come and sit, for we have much to discuss," he called back before quickly placing the *Shen* Staff to one side and replacing it with a drinking flask that had been left at his side.

The scribe, seeing Shuma and the others approaching from further along the beach, then hurriedly came forward and quickly sitting, he looked directly at Malian before saying, "Have you been told about Darric?" A concern being heard in his voice.

"Yes, I have been told. But what do you make of it, Mentu, for Shuma said little?"

"I feel there is little to be said," Mentu acknowledged with some feeling, "for the man himself appears changed in looks alone, but I feel that more has gone on that he has yet to find out. Still, you must make your own judgement," he concluded.

The individual that approached alongside Shuma and Tragen strode with some purpose, and although Darric had not grown any taller or sturdier, the young man had been refashioned in other ways, for his white hair certainly stood out, giving him a sense of maturity. Coming close and bending forward, he looked Malian directly in the eye.

"You need to eat," he advised, staring intently at the gaunt altar tender as he lay back against the support.

"I think that would be good advice for all of us," Mentu reasoned, suddenly rising and discreetly leading Shuma and Tragen away. "Let's get ourselves organised with some of that tasty soup!"

Malian and Darric were left alone, and the younger man seated himself in front of the older while the space in between filled up with silence. Eventually, after some time had passed, Darric leaned forward and extending his hand, he gently placed it over the right hand of the old man as it lay open in his lap.

"We have both seen things that the others have not," he began tensely, in a voice deeper than Malian recalled, "and in the doing, we have both been changed by the experience. Still, we remain ourselves at heart, although I remember your advice on the mountainside that our thinking is sometimes tested and our outlook can be opened to other capabilities."

Malian also remembered this guidance, given when the young man had been put to the test by the disclosures of Tragen, and he also remembered how eased in mind he had been at the settlement of the situation.

"You have reasoned well, Darric," Malian noted seriously, "but you always had that ability, and it is one which will be of great benefit to you. But you must always remember, sometimes we need to just be!" He patted the hand which remained over his and smiled at the man before him.

"I did 'just be' while in the Light," Darric replied, sitting back before continuing, "and I survived only in the presence of *Ra*. For the god protected me and changed me as you see." He lifted his hand to his head, touching the white hair. "What do you make of the change? Does it suit me, do you think?" The man smiled broadly, and the concern and tension between the two were immediately released.

"Aagh, Darric, you had us all worried," the older man laughed, "but I can see that there was little cause for concern." Relief suddenly spread through Malian. However, one tiny thought lingered, and that was that Darric himself remained unaware of the extent of all the changes, for the look of the man now went beyond just the physical.

"You need to eat, Malian," the man said again, this time with greater concern, "for we have been here two days, and you have lain asleep all this time." He shouted over to Shuma and Mentu, who sat around the small cooking fire, and straightaway, a bowl of soup was brought directly over while both Darric and Mentu helped Malian to reposition himself.

"The soup has a distinct taste," Shuma advised wisely as Malian raised the spoon. "A bit like onion with a gritty texture!" Her mouth turned down to portray a look of possible distaste.

For Malian, the taste was refreshing if nothing else, and while he sat, the woman recounted further on their arrival and of the days on the lakeside. While she talked, Tragen joined them from his search for firewood further along the beach, and seating himself down beside Darric, the group came together, and Malian was enlightened.

On their landing in the bay, after the Lord Aken had delivered them safely and disappeared into the mists, Shuma told him she had left the establishment of the campsite to Tragen and Darric while she herself had assumed the duty of carer to Malian. Even though he was asleep, he still needed to be attended to and made comfortable. When not looking after him, she had busied herself in harvesting the lakeside and preparing the roots, seeds and leaves for their various purposes.

Tragen and Darric explained that they had swiftly explored and secured the area. The sandy bay was protected at its back by the high dunes which wrapped around the sides and made an ideal camp area, and here Malian was carried, and their packs gathered together. Wood was found in plentiful supply all along the beach, and a small fire was established and kept going day and night. No evidence of wildlife had been seen, not even on or in the lake itself, and so the plants and the soup made from their roots had become their main food source.

Mentu, said that he had busied himself as necessary. Initially, helping with the collecting of plants and assisting either Tragen or Darric, as required, with firewood collections and filling up of water flasks. Then, after he admitted to Malian that he had looked through his bags and there found *The Book of The Two Lands*, he had used his time in study with the hope of furthering their knowledge for the possible days to come. The book, he told Malian, would be of great aid but only if they had to travel into the far north or the border between.

Then it was Malian's turn. While he had lain on the warm sandy beach, he had dreamt, and in his dreams, the gods had once again taken him up. Placing the empty soup bowl at his side, he went on to explain that their journey did not come to a stop here on this beach. They would need to continue north through the Sleeping Caverns and on further to achieve their purpose.

"But surely we are in front of the thieves?" Shuma reasoned. "Wasn't that the intention for going through *The Duat*, for us to get ahead and ambush them?"

"Yes, and we are in front, Shuma, for they should still be many days behind us. But we are not fighters like them." Malian sighed, suddenly feeling very weak and looking around at each face individually, he knew that however ambitious and keen they may appear, they would remain lacking if it came to a face-to-face fight. "We cannot meet them full on and achieve our aim," he continued, sensing the displeasure and aware that this news would not be best received.

"Then we don't wait here for them? We don't ambush them here?" Tragen asked angrily and with more than displeasure in his voice. He had been eagerly planning and preparing for an encounter since they arrived and along with Darric, had reconnoitred the main bay area, noting points that could be adapted if required and areas where an ambush could be put in place.

"No," Malian declared, in little hope of alleviating the rising concern. "We will continue north and journey on through the caverns and into the borders of the northern lands beyond, for the gods have set the direction, and we must follow in their path."

"How do we even know that they still have *Amaunet*?" Tragen fiercely asked. "Tarnik and your elders may have already succeeded, and we would be none the wiser?"

"They still have her," Malian answered, knowing in his heart she was still held captive, "and do not forget, Tragen, that our journey into the north takes us ever closer to your own pursuit and the hopeful return of your own Icon. I'm sure you have not forgotten that!" Malian looked at the warrior, aware that the large man was struggling with the inaction which was being forced upon him.

"No, that I have not forgotten!" the man said in rising before marching off to attend the fire.

Darric moved closer to Malian. "He has been focused on this exercise since we arrived," he informed the altar tender as he watched the large man poke savagely at the fire, "and it's given him some purpose. Our travel along the waters of the underworld, confined by the boundaries of the boat, was not to his liking."

"That I can understand, Darric," Malian nodded his head in agreement while his voice dropped gently to a whisper, "The journey was a challenge to us all in different ways that I well know." The altar tender's head slowly drooped forward, and a sleepiness overcame him, which was seen by the others as an opportunity to withdraw. Shuma and Darric then left, leaving Mentu seated at his side.

Some hours later, as the day moved on, Malian woke again with Mentu still sitting close. The scribe had only left his side briefly in the intervening time to fetch the book, which now sat open on his knees.

"Mentu, bring it over, and show me what you have been reading."

The two older men settled, and with *The Book of The Two Lands* open, they let the afternoon of the bay surround them.

***

The Oasis of Plenty appeared suddenly from out of the late afternoon sun, its tall palms waving gently in the breeze while beneath these, the smaller peach and orange trees enjoyed the shade provided by the large fronds overhead. Emerging between the overgrown grasses, Gallius led his men straight toward the water before guiding them off and around to the left where once a village of mud brick buildings had stood. This now lay in ruins, invaded by the grass which had seeded over time in the strong western winds. Here they stopped on the very edge of the oasis where the crystal clear waters provided a number of chances to refresh and revitalise themselves as well as water their horses.

This area certainly lived up to its name, for the trees were laden, and the ground beneath was deep in ripe pickings with the date palms hanging high and heavy with bunches of the sweet dark fruit. Long past, the oasis had been either the first or last village, depending on the way of travel, in the plains area and had seen much activity for trade and commerce, which allowed it to develop and flourish over time. Now, the low buildings were just lines in the sand where the men quickly made themselves comfortable. Here the elders were also untied but remained corralled together, with Marke and Rogan as disinclined guards. However, on seeing the other riders refreshing themselves, the two slowly moved off to join them, leaving their prisoners alone. The older men still remained at a loss at their survival and were no wiser of why they were being spared. Given over to contemplation, they had come up with a number of reasons, none which pleased or held much hope. They had, as agreed by the five, continued to watch and gather information on how the men fared in their choices, and this had also started to include Tarnik, who remained remote to the elders and who had once been observed in the company of Rogan and his brother Marke.

These two had quickly become associated with Roth, for their dislike of Gallius never seemed far from the surface, and their even greater dislike for the elders had quickly resorted to violence. Both Claude and Petrus carried the scars of a quick blade used in anger, while all of the others, apart from Tarnik, were bruised and injured by frequent kicking and bullying that went on without the apparent knowledge of Gallius.

The other two riders, Statte and Brann, were not so easy to group. They were the trackers of the company, and while the riders were at rest, they were usually off hunting for the next meal and, so far, had been good at their job. Most nights, the menu had included meat of some sort, either lizard or snake and at one time rabbit.

The elders, given the short reprieve from their guards, now had chance to stretch their legs and gathered together under a dark-leafed orange tree to discuss and talk in some privacy. While Tarnik had moved away to sit beneath a palm and chew on the gritty dates which lay in the sand. The water spread before them, with the sun reflecting off its smooth surface, and the tall palms mirrored around the edge formed a fringe that danced in the light breeze.

"I think Statte is also for Roth," Claud ventured, taking another bite from his half-eaten fruit as he looked over to the water's edge. "He looks to do right, I feel, but his eyes are forever watching. See, he's like a shadow," he continued, pointing to where Statte remained half-hidden behind a tree, his feet the only part visible.

"That's what makes him a good tracker, I suppose," Theroc reasoned, "but I would agree, and I've got a feeling he's watching Brann, so we need to note how that sits."

"What about Tarnik?" Rusan asked the group in a whisper. "Any more news?" He looked over to where their leader was sitting, head back against the tree trunk, and where he appeared to be asleep.

"He was talking with Marke again late last night and the night before," Gaival, the oldest elder, advised. Sleep did not come easy to him, and most nights, he rested but remained awake into the long hours, which at times could be of benefit.

"Yes, I too, have seen him with Marke," Claud added, "and I'm sure that something was passed over from the rider while they spoke."

"What do you mean?" Rusan asked, quickly looking up with concern.

"Well, it could have been a blade, but I can't be sure it was too dark. But I'm certain I saw a glint of something."

"A blade? Well, we must be doubly on our guard; what do you say Theroc?"

"I think we have known where Tarnik's loyalty lies for some time," came the reply, "but right now, I am even more convinced of his treason and feel we must urgently look to ourselves and disregard our so-called leader."

This was swiftly and unanimously agreed upon within the group, and later, on Tarnik's return to the circle, he was greeted with silence and a cold reception which he hardly appeared to notice.

Eventually, as the sun set towards the west, the group at the oasis broke up, with Statte and Brann rising from the waterside. Quickly collecting their hunting nets and spears from their horses, they disappeared into the grasses behind the abandoned village while Marke and Rogan wandered back to where the elders sat and resumed their reluctant guard duties. Roth had taken charge of the horses, driving them up from the water and past where the elders sat and on around the back of the fruit trees to an area where the grasses formed a protective backdrop out of the wind where they could be settled for the night.

Gallius remained alone at the water's edge, saddle pack open next to him. Lifting the Icon from its confinement and gently unwrapping the blue cloth, he allowed the slowly setting rays of dappled sunlight to wash over and caress the contours of the goddess which lay in his hands. The ruby eyes, set deep within the serpentine head, still stared out fearlessly in defiance, but the soft, warm roundness of the slight body felt comforting and soothing to the tired rider whose hands worked evenly over the golden form, his fingers granted an intimacy denied to others. His mind was in upset as he stared out over the water, for he also sensed the unease within his men. Of late, he had taken to raising his voice even louder, shouting his orders in restrained anger to maintain some semblance of strength and control of those in his charge. Roth and Brann he had known for many years and would trust with his life but the others, especially the two brothers, were not to be depended on even after the many months of hard travel, and he sensed a need to keep them close and within view. The elders, though, gave him little concern. They would be reduced in number fairly soon, and for that, he felt no worry or apprehension. Looking down upon the Icon, he only saw the face of his daughter, and for him that was his only consideration.

Later, as Statte and Brann returned with their catch, a fire was made under the star-filled sky, and a meagre meal of snake and rat was divided between the men and washed down with the cooling waters from the watering hole. And as the darkness of the evening deepened, the two companies with so many miles between them each settled for the night in their own distinctive ways but with the same aim of a restful and secure night.

CHAPTER TEN

The morning dawned bright once again over Lake Cannis and Malian awoke to the sound of the murmur of wind disturbing the tall reeds at the lake's edge and the sigh of the water as it gently broke over the shingle and onto the sand. A blueness hung heavy in the sky, and a warm wind carried the scent of lily flowers as it flowed across the water and on up over the dunes. He had slept fitfully, somehow feeling unsettled by his waking on the previous day to the realisation that their next course would take them into the Sleeping Caverns on their journey north. In his dreamlike state, he had already passed through the labyrinth of caves, overcome with a feeling of complete imprisonment within its confines. There the vaulted ceilings, which hung heavy with growths, had dripped slowly but constantly, and the Neferu Passage and its fears had loomed once more in his thinking and remained lurking at the back of his mind and would not lessen, for the dread of enclosure lingered. Raising his head, he looked down the beach to see Shuma slowly approaching, a bowl held between her hands.

"It's soup again, Malian," she informed him as she knelt and placed the wooden bowl down before helping him to sit up, aware that his weakness remained and he could do no more than rest, and in the process, recover his strength.

"A simple meal for a simple altar tender, Shuma," he replied in thanks, "for my needs have never been great."

"Well, let's see how you feel about it tomorrow," she responded, laughing. "We have certainly had our fill over these past days." She moved to sit next to Malian and once settled, passed the warm bowl of clear broth, which he accepted gratefully.

"The gritty bits at the bottom are from the stalks," she informed him, "unfortunately, they linger even after boiling." She watched as Malian spooned the warm liquid, and then her gaze drifted across to where the others either sat or stood further down the shoreline.

They had made this part of the beach their camp with a stone-encircled fire pit for cooking at its centre. Around this, they had placed their bedrolls, and the wood collected from far across the bay was stacked to one side. Malian had been placed slightly higher up the shore with the soft dunes at his back to afford him some peace and quiet while he slept. But Shuma had never been far-removed from his side as they waited for him to wake. Some, like Mentu, had used this time in his book and reading and others in activity. Still, for each, the time had dragged, and when he was not collecting wood or preparing the site for ambush had fallen especially heavy on the shoulders of Tragen.

"Tragen desires action and deed," Shuma remarked, looking directly at the warrior as he strode purposefully back to the fire where Darric sat, "for the fighter is never at peace with idleness."

"Yes, I know," Malian replied, laying down his spoon, "and I am just as much in haste as Tragen. The gods have left me at their mercy, and my eyes are blind to their decided end. Do you know how that makes me feel?" He turned his tired eyes to the young woman who sat at his side.

"No," came the forthright reply, "but you can talk, and I can listen if that will help." Her gaze fell on the older man while he finished his meal and then slowly placed the empty bowl down in his lap.

Yet Malian remained silent, unable and above all unwilling to explain or burden the soul who sat at his side and reaching out, he took the young woman's hands in his and, raising them to his mouth, gently kissed the long slender fingers.

"Thank you, Shuma," he said before gradually dropping her hands, "but I shall keep my own council for the present. The next stage of our journey has already been shown, and it's now up to me to regain my strength and for us then to move forward."

Sensing a need for his contemplation and solitude, Shuma returned to her fireside, leaving Malian to take his ease in the morning sun as the bay and its surroundings warmed up. Lying in the warm, soft sand, he slept again for a short while before rising and wandering slowly and stiffly down to the water, where he could see more of the expanse of the lake through the beds of lily plants. The whole area shimmered and glinted in the sunlight which flickered across its surface, and the haze in the far distance indicated the southern banks of the lake where the margin sands of the High Rush Plains met the water. He knew that out there in the plains, the riders were moving towards the north, and he too, just like Tragen, felt at odds with the decision to journey on with little or no sense of their destination or outcome. Still, he could only put his trust in the gods and, with that, have a belief in their instructions.

Turning his head, he looked first along the water's edge and then up the beach to the little camp where Shuma sat preparing the next meal with the help of Mentu. Further back, near the sloping dunes, Tragen and the white-haired Darric stood facing each other. Suddenly, Tragen turned and scrambled up the sandy slope, shouting for Darric to follow, and on quickly reaching the ridge of the small dune, they both turned and barrelled back down to the bottom before once more turning and racing to the top. This they did a number of times before both men returned slowly to the base, where the two began to work and practice with a number of round-shaped boulders retrieved from the lake. Lifting them high over their heads, Tragen appeared to be making light work of the task while Darric struggled somewhat in his attempts to match the warrior. Malian smiled, for it would appear that both men had resolved the matter of Darric's schooling, and he knew that for Tragen, it would give him some purpose and mission over the next days.

"Malian, come and join us," Shuma shouted over on seeing the altar tender as she lifted her head from her work, "you can help Mentu chop the leaves."

Raising his hand in acknowledgment, he proceeded to walk towards the fire, first wandering along the water side where the sun flashed brightly over the black, grey shingle which glistened beneath the clear shallow water before gradually making his way up the sand to the small encampment.

"I see Darric has been set for some instruction," he declared on reaching the fireside, "and it will surely be good for the both of them to keep active." He sat down with some relief beside Mentu and continued to watch the two men in their exertions.

"I think it came at Darric's request," Mentu advised, putting aside the chopped leaves and picking up a number of stalks which he laid across the stone between his feet, "but Tragen's certainly shown his skills and given the man little rest these past hours." He cut squarely across the rock, dicing the greenery into small pieces, which he slowly scraped into the small cooking pot set above the flames. "I fear I would never survive such a regime, but thankfully, older age brings with it its gains as well as its faults, wouldn't you agree, Malian?" He added further chopped leaves to the pot before stirring and leaving it to cook.

"Well, yes," came back the thoughtful reply, "but who would not, in an instant, trade old age for youth if given the opportunity!" The altar tender now made himself useful and under the guidance of Shuma, began to clean and scrape the bulbous lily roots which she had harvested that morning and which would soon become as much disliked by him as they had become to the rest.

As he finished on the last root, placing it to one side for Shuma to chop and add to the stew, the warrior and his pupil ended their morning's activity with a run along the bay before stripping off their outer clothing and cooling off in the waters at the lakeside. Finally emerging, they then returned up the beach to the fire.

"Not bad for a first attempt," Tragen said in a positive tone and looking pleased as he took in the three seated figures, he glanced across to where Darric had dropped to the sand.

"I'll tell you later." The man eventually replied with less vigour, sensing already the stricture in his arms and legs and knowing full well that he was certainly lacking in endurance. "My muscles feel sore already." Rubbing the back of his legs, he felt the tightness grip harder, and the tingle of cramps slowly spread up from his ankles.

"You'll need to work through it," Tragen quickly added with instruction, "sit now, but keep moving your arms and legs, or your muscles will stiffen, and the loosening will be the more painful." He already knew the afternoon lessons he had planned would be just as tiring in their own way, and the man who sat before him would be tasked to endure these extra activities. But he smiled as Darric took his word and began to slowly stretch to extend his legs and work his feet.

The group turned to contemplation while the food slowly boiled down, and once cooked, Shuma topped the pot with a little of the lake water. Adding a few freshly cut young leaves, she served the soup to the others, who accepted their bowls with differing enthusiasm. The area beside the little fire became quiet in the noontime sun, and after the sparse meal, Tragen and Darric returned to their practice, leaving the three to sit around the fireside where Mentu was quick to speak.

"How are you feeling now, Malian?" he inquired, leaning forward before adding, "Any stronger after resting?" He peered long and deep at Malian before dropping his gaze.

"My strength will return, Mentu," came the reply, as the altar tender also looked away and then down to his hands as they lay crossed over his knees, "but perhaps today and tomorrow at ease will see me in full recuperation." He felt like he was being questioned and judged somehow for holding them back from their journey, but he had to consider the Sleeping Caverns and the challenges he alone knew they would bring. He realised he would need to have full strength in body as well as in mind, and above this, he also needed to prepare the others for their progress north. This he would do in the given time and at his own pace.

"I too, feel that is wise," Shuma's voice finally broke into his thoughts, "for today and another full day would be of definite benefit. So rest while you can, Malian." She nodded at the two older men before rising and picking up the bowls and then headed down to the water.

On this advice, Malian also left the camp, leaving Mentu to his thoughts and returned back up the sand to the dune area. There he quickly sank into its softness and dozed in the warmth of the early afternoon sun. The voice of Tragen, as he instructed Darric, gradually diminished, but it did not fade immediately, remaining as a steady drone on the edge of hearing before sleep overcame him completely. And as time marched on, the sun slowly advanced across the sky, and oblivion slowly gave way to a certain awareness, although Malian did not move.

His body felt heavy and warm, and he lay with complete freedom and unrestraint in the soft dish-like depression which had developed and grown around him. The campsite below was quiet, with the only sound being of the reeds as they murmured in the soft breeze, and he imagined himself floating in a bath of softly fragranced water with no urgency to open his eyes or return to existence. Later, after sleep had once again claimed him, he was woken by Shuma as the sun weakened on the western edge of the lake, and the shadows of the lily plants had cast an elongated greyness up the beach towards the dunes. A coolness was in the air, and he shivered and was quick to follow the wise woman and again join the group beside the fire, which blazed brighter in the gathering dusk collecting over the water. Seating himself facing towards the lake where the cooling breezes caught the warmth of the dying day, Malian instantly felt the tenseness around the camp, and although their exchanges were initially confined to the activities of Darric's training, there was an awareness of other things which needed to be said.

As complete darkness blanketed the bay, the talk had finally turned to their objective, that being the return of *Amaunet*, with the knowledge that their next steps would take them into the Sleeping Caverns, unseen in the darkness above the dunes which towered at their backs. Malian now felt the timing to be right to speak of his dreams with the gods and their travels further into the north and as the conversation faltered, he sensed the opportunity had arrived.

"I know you do not understand why we go north when the riders are behind us," he said in opening, "and to me, it seems equally at odds. But the gods have once more taken me into their charge, and my trust in them has again been challenged and resolved." Looking at each in turn, their faces glowing above the firelight with the darkness surrounding their backs, the altar tender gave account of his dream journey through the caverns. He told of the maze and twist of caves and tunnels through which he had moved, and the sense of enclosure and tightness felt along with the fears of confinement which had encompassed his whole being. And he told of the dark and the shadows and the echoing sounds of the unseen creatures which assaulted his senses, along with the smell of damp mustiness which left the air thick, stale and unbearable. But he also revealed that, at times a brightness had encircled him with a great light pouring through his body which had been followed by a sudden rush of clean, clear air passing over him before the darkness and staleness had returned.

"We will be challenged," he advised them, "for a life lives there, and it is not of the gods but of man's own making. We will neither be guided nor escorted as on our journey through *The Duat*," he further announced, "so we will need to defend ourselves and subdue our fears to confront the darkness and whatever it holds."

"So why do the gods want us to go this way? Why can't they help us here?" Tragen asked again his question of the previous day, though slightly differently and with some hope that his planning for an ambush had not been overlooked or of wasted effort. "We are as prepared as we can be, so what difference will it make in our travelling further? We shall still only be the same five as here. At least here we are in the open and can watch and anticipate." His warrior side had now come to the fore and shouted out to be recognised, while the realisation of the caverns left a heaviness in the pit of his stomach, which he recognised as apprehension.

"I don't know," Malian openly replied. "I just know that we must move on and let the riders follow us. The confrontation will be at our bidding and on our terms, and not theirs. I can say no more, for the future remains just as open to me as it is to each of us." He could feel the tension around the camp, weightier on his right where Tragen and Darric sat than on the left, but he had great confidence in all four of his companions and knew that they would resolve the situation and each deal with it in their own way if given time.

"So, do we go tomorrow?" Mentu eventually asked.

"No, I will rest for one more day," he answered. With that, he left the fireside and returned up the beach, leaving behind the four as they sat in reflection.

**

That same day had seen the riders in the south moving swiftly through the plantation of grasses, travelling towards the Well of Shelter in their search for water along with refuge from the heat and the drying westerly wind which constantly blew the fine-grained sand into every gap it could find. These water wells, which had been dug by the trade workers, had once been vital stopping off points throughout the High Rush Plains for the travelling labourers and their long teams, which ferried the harvested grass from the interior to the workshops of the craftsmen. There, at the journey's end, the leaves had been separated and sorted, then stripped and pressed to make the papers and parchment much desired in the great cities, and a huge enterprise had blossomed in its making. The men of the past had once delved deep in their search for water, and the immense covered underground basin which supplied the oases had been tapped at its source with wells being excavated throughout the plains, creating a lifeline for the workers and their mules. These the riders had taken full advantage of as watering stations on their way down from the north, knowing that the water remained pure, for the vast subterranean lake and its many canals lay at a depth unpolluted by the sands, and its confining rocks gave the water a clean, fresh taste.

The Well of Shelter was surrounded by huge growths of grasses, and as the sun advanced, the riders and the elders arrived at their night's rest with the once towering broken down well pole marking its position. Here the wellhead arose solidly from the sandy terrain. The well itself was built of pressed brick and was covered by a lid of solid wood attached and held firmly in place by ornate struts which spanned its width and caught tight around its rim. The girth was not large, and the depth could only be guessed at, but on their arrival, the lid had been quickly removed, and a small bucket lowered, and the water flasks filled and replenished with the clear waters which were brought up.

The riders, like many before them, had then made a camp in the shelter and protection of the tall grasses, for no towns or villages had ever been built in these areas, these being only places of transition where the workers had rested before quickly travelling on.

The elders had been left to make themselves comfortable at the base of an overgrown cluster of grasses where two large tussocks had interwoven to form an enormous backdrop of greenery which constantly moved and whispered in the winds, and here they rested while the riders made their own camp.

Statte and Brann had immediately left the group, returning much later with only three small desert snakes for their efforts which were quickly skinned and diced before being roasted over the flames and passed around as the dark swiftly descended. The riders had then settled, having been meagrely fed and adequately watered and retiring to their packs to see the night through; the elders were left to do the same with little inclination for talk or discussion.

In the night, a tremendous dust storm had descended upon the plains, and the horses had turned their backs to the prevailing wind for protection. Gusting and howling around the grassy dunes and rattling the well lid, the gale had passed around and amongst the group who tightly drew up their cloaks for shelter against the wind and stinging grains which relentlessly bit into any exposed flesh. Tearing across the sands in an effort to escape its bounds, it gradually passed over, depositing a thick layer of gritty sand over the resting men and the well area, before making off into the east and the extensive interior of the plains, leaving the riders to sleep in its aftermath of complete stillness.

***

Miles away, under the bright moonlight on the lakeside, Malian also slept in stillness, and his dreams again took him over the dunes and up into the wide opening recesses of the Sleeping Caverns. There a lightness was seen and felt, and his fears seemed no longer justified as a calmness passed over him. Entering the vastness of the first cave with its vaulted ceiling rising high above his head, he gradually moved on slowly into the darkness beyond. The hard stone beneath his feet gave way to a thin soil that turned into a soft leafy terrain where the fallen autumn leaves bunched together in great swathes and gathered towards the back of the cavern rising up towards the ceiling. The sides of the cave gently moved inwards, guiding him still further ahead, and on reaching the base of the pile, he had quickly clambered up the front of the leaf face before looking down into the vast bowl shape at its centre. Inside, the two enormous eggs, one slightly bigger than the other, nestled deep within the leaf mould and a blanket of soft black feathers surrounded and cradled the white spheres as they lay within the confines.

All at once, in Malian's dream state, the fear again returned, landing around his shoulders like a heavy mantle and gripping hard at his heart. Suddenly the feeling of disaster and calamity escalated as he turned to see the immense black swan appear within the entrance, challenging him with its harsh call, as the leaf face collapsed beneath his feet. Waking with a loud shout which echoed into the floodlit bay and with a great panic coursing through his body, he instantly sat up. Brushing his shaking hands across his face, he wiped aside the sweat which ran down his cheeks as Shuma arrived by his side. She had been quick to rise and in her alarm, had rushed up with her blade to hand, swiftly followed by Tragen and Darric, who feared attack or ambush while Mentu brought up the rear.

"It was a dream, it was a dream!" Was all that Malian could repeat on seeing the alarm and upset he had caused, fully aware of the concerns that the group would have on being woken in such a manner. "It was just a dream," he said again, but this time with more certainty, as the seconds on waking hung between reality and fantasy, for such is the way of dreams, and reality had taken its time to restore order.

"Just a dream!" repeated Shuma under her breath as she put away her blade, knowing full well the thoughts behind Malian's dreams. Turning away to reach for his flask, she held it up to his lips. "Here, drink," she said softly, "and relax now and try to rest," she advised as she made him comfortable. Secretly placing the *Shen* Staff under his cloak, she headed back to the fire where the others had returned in hope of again finding sleep. She, however, lay awake for many hours in uncertainty and concern for both Malian and herself. Restlessly turning over, she reached into her bag and retrieved the gift which her sister Tellia had given her many days before when she had set off on her journey. The simple wooden doll lay round and heavy in her hands and was carved and painted in the likeness of a woman with her hands crossed over her lower body. Holding it close to her chest, she felt a comfort and closed her eyes, and the vision of her sister appeared out of the dark. Around her, the three men had quickly returned to their slumber, but lying in his bed of sand, the altar tender did not even seek out or attempt to sleep. Endeavouring to remain awake and not return to his dreams, he chose instead to stare into the lightening sky and await the morning with its rising sun.

***

In the High Rush Plains, the sun rose over the riders who were many miles on their travel to the Garden Oasis, which was their next stop. They had risen early in the waning hours of the night, and after being roughly awoken, the elders found themselves driven forward into the dark to make the most of the gently cooling breeze. Gallius remained in the lead, following some instinct that led him in a clear direction, as hour by hour, they moved north, and the heat of the day eventually caught up with them. The scenery of the High Rush Plains was now tiring, with the unchanging landscape of grasses becoming monotonous as they continually moved this way and that around each wild and thickened growth of tapering leaves and the Garden Oasis was reached with great relief by the middle of the day. It afforded them similar protection and abundance as that of the Oasis of Plenty, along with the bonus of thriving masses of self-seeded vegetables and herbs which carpeted the ground beneath the fruit trees and palms. However, the enormous stretch of the oasis itself was the main blessing, for the men could refresh themselves and soak in its clear waters.

The elders had once more been forced to one side and left to themselves to cool off. Moving back and collapsing under the shade of the nearest trees, where the herbs provided a soft blanket of fragrant greenery, they rested their bruised and exhausted bodies. Tarnik no longer joined his men. Remaining as a solitary figure at the water's edge, he chose to sit in isolation, and the other elders felt the better for his absence and lack of interest. But still, they could not fully rest, for Marke and Rogan had taken to taunting them with hints of what was to come. They had spoken of the Sleeping Caverns beyond the High Rush Plains where, according to the brothers, they had lost a number of their own men on the way south. They had not yet gone into any great detail, but the planting of seeds of disbelief and apprehension had worked its way into the elders thinking, and the seeds had grown in all of their minds.

"Is this why we are being kept alive, do you think?" Claud anxiously asked when the tormenting had again started that morning. The idea had quickly taken root within the men, and the youngest, in particular, had been fraught with worry and unable to hold down any food that day. They had tried to lighten the situation, for it would not take much for him to become skin and bone, but Marke had been quick to notice his distress and had immediately focused his attentions on the unfortunate man. On their arrival at the Garden Oasis, he had dragged him away from the others as they cooled off before showing the elder a little of his anger and nominating him as their first casualty of the Sleeping Caverns.

Claud now lay between Rusan and Petrus, his bruised and cut face streaked with blood and tears, while Gaival wiped his lips with a water-soaked rag in some hope of relieving his distress. The incident, nonetheless, had not gone unnoticed, and Gallius had been seen to take Marke aside, and words had passed between the leader and his own man. This culminated in Gallius striding over to where the elders sat, and kneeling down he peered into the swollen eyes of the defenceless man.

"This will not happen again," he declared to the elders, "for I will have the head of any man who lifts a blade without my order. But heed well, that applies to everyone here, you included." Rising, he marched off, returning to the waterside where his men had settled from the heat of the afternoon and where the horses stood in the deep shade of the palm trees.

***

The camp in the bay on Lake Cannis, which had held them in place for so long as they waited for Malian to wake, was now feeling confining since the decision had been made to move on, and the day stretched long ahead of them when they woke into the clear morning. Shuma had immediately checked on Malian, finding him sitting up with the *Shen* Staff in his lap and with a more robust look to his overall presence.

"No more dreams, Malian?" she asked as she arrived at his bedside and seating herself next to him she took in the view which was holding his attention. "The lake is beautiful, isn't it?" she said. Getting no reply to either question she turned toward the older man who remained looking ahead.

"We are all with you, Malian, you know that."

"Yes, my choosing in the Closed Court of High Priest Set'al is in no doubt," he slowly responded, "but it is in my own heart that the trouble lies." Looking away from the impressive lake, he looked directly at the young woman before continuing, "The gods are with me, Shuma, for it is my task to return *Amaunet* to our people, but that leaves my fears for you and the others as we enter the caverns. My dreams have left behind a great concern not just for my own life but for those I take along with me." The companions that he had first met had become more than friends and as such, had acquired a feeling of loyalty and responsibility that was hard to push aside.

"We are all with you!" she again repeated, and with much more force this time, placing a hand and gripping the worried man's arm tightly as she spoke. "We are your support and protection. You yourself have said this task is beyond just you alone, so in whatever way we can help you, we will. We want no worry or pity, for we chose to come, and that is what you must remember."

They both sat for some little time, again taking in the vista, before Shuma jumped up and heading back down towards the shore, she shouted back, "Come Malian, bring your stuff down to the fire. It's time to leave your sick bed and prepare for tomorrow."

At the fireside camp, the altar tender dropped his pack and blanket and sat down next to Mentu, who was once again preparing stalks and leaves. Nothing was said as the men sat, but their vision was drawn along the beach area to where Tragen and Darric had once again resumed their practice. A change in the younger man could be seen immediately and did not go unnoticed in the older men's eyes, for after only one night's rest, Darric could now keep up with Tragen in his exertions. And towards the day's end, he was even surpassing him in his strength and vigour, and the warrior was called on to find more challenging tasks to keep his attention.

The day had then moved itself along slowly, and in that time, Malian, feeling that much stronger, had walked far along the shoreline and up to the back of the beach where the dunes met the sand. Here, to the left of the high sandbank, could be seen a heavily used pathway in the soft surface where Tragen and Darric had raced up to the top of this small bottom layer before turning and racing back down. Looking further up, he saw what appeared to be a sudden sharp right-handed turn which ascended onto the next vast platform of dunes, and Malian knew this would be the start of their climb. These then rose farther up and higher towards a third layer upon which the immense caverns themselves opened out. It would be a challenge to make the top, he thought, for the softness of the sand made the climb difficult, and the gradient of the slope added to its difficulty, but that was for the next day. Eventually turning away, he returned to the gathering at the camp and their last night on the lakeside where, as the hours passed, the moon again shone down and sleep overcame them all.

CHAPTER ELEVEN

The dunes had been tough and exhausting, their sandy slopes proving to be more of a challenge than initially foreseen, although the first part from the beach up to the second level had in part, been easy enough. The footfalls of Tragen and Darric as they trained had already trodden down and compressed the sands of these lower slopes into a slightly firmer base on which to tread on their way upwards. There the group had rested briefly on the huge terrace before moving on, with the hope of a continued easy climb becoming less likely as the bank sloped alarmingly and the ground became more unstable. Slipping and losing their footing in the shifting sand, their feet disappeared into its softness with each step, and time and time again, they struggled to rise up the steep incline which sloped above their heads. Their hands had been thrust deep into the sands to find purchase but found nothing to grasp or hang onto to steady themselves as they tackled the terrain, for the dunes were equally lifeless, giving no growths or outcrops of grass to catch hold upon as they laboured.

Clambering and crawling up, and with many stops along the way, it took a large part of the morning to eventually reach the topmost level positioned high above the sandy beach on which had been their camp. The rocky area onto which they finally climbed was sandy and barren but gave instant relief from their upward toil. Coming up over this last part of the dunes, the enormity of the Sleeping Caverns had risen up in the near distance with the darkness of the beginning of the caves opening straight ahead of them. The immensity of these vast gaping holes was astonishing and stretched off into the distance on either side of the massive plateau which they had reached, disappearing upwards where they extended back into the north.

Collapsing on the very edge of the terrace, the climbers immediately dropped their packs and lay drained and weary for many hours, with complete fatigue overtaking them. Darric had recovered the quickest and was soon able to assist the others in moving away from the insecurity which the edge of the sloping brink offered, positioning the group further inwards of the drop and towards the caverns. But the starkness around them offered little in shelter or protection, and the caves themselves appeared to be their only refuge. The structure of the cave entrances was beyond belief, for the framework of the wide-open archways appeared to have no support for the immense spans which hung overhead in each gigantic cavity, while the dark chambers gazed out in contemplation of the lands beyond. But they were not inviting, and there was a reluctance to enter. Malian eventually got to his feet and left the others to rest, and turning his back on the openings, he walked forward to gaze out over the edge of the sloping dunes onto the land below.

Looking back down onto the lake, his vision took in the stretch of water, and beyond, the sand in the south stretched away with no sight of the plains, which he knew lay in the unseen distance. The area appeared boundless, but he knew that they would soon be going into an even more endless domain. In his dreams, the Sleeping Caverns had assumed an eternal, never-ending quality that he disliked, and he found himself out of breath with dread. He stood for a long time while the sun travelled slowly into the west, and a sudden chill blew up from the lake, carrying with it motes of sand along with an uncertainty for the days ahead.

Slowly walking back to where the others had remained

seated, he gestured for them to follow, and leading the way, guided them into the openings under the very arches of the Sleeping Caverns. There they settled in whispered silence, neither inside nor outside, but on the very cusp of the entrance and the gateway into the beyond.

Little sleep was had by any that night, and the dawn saw an early start being made as Malian and Shuma scouted further inwards as the advancing daylight gradually lifted the deep darkness collected at the back of the enormous chamber. The ground, where they had attempted to sleep at the cavern entrance, was of hard stone, but as they walked with many footsteps towards the rear this had increasingly given way to a thin soil. This prompted in Malian a feeling of panic as he recalled his dream of the black swan, and he grabbed at Shuma's hand to steady himself. She immediately responded, and sensing his fear, they stopped with the chamber's vast canopy towering overhead while he maintained to restore a calmness and collect his composure.

"Remember we are with you," she spoke softly, the echo eventually bouncing back to repeat itself, "and we will follow where you lead, fearful or not."

"My fear is not only for myself," he replied, breathing in the stale air which swirled around them, "but I feel a great loss here and whose it is or will be is beyond me, for I am not sure if it is in the past or the future."

"Either way, it must be faced," came back the response, as the dimly lit darkness turned to a lighter grey, highlighting the smoothness of the walls rising above their heads. "And we shall confront it together." Squeezing his hand before letting it drop, she strode onward to an area near the very back of the chamber where a large outcrop of immense rock stood conspicuously against the evenness of the wall. "Look, there is an opening here," she shouted back as she peered between two of the larger boulders while the meagre light flowed around her and was sucked into the massive void beyond.

Malian quickly followed her across the cavern floor, and moving the wise woman to one side, he peered around the stone doorway into the tunnel. The passageway was colossal both in height and width and would have taken an army of men walking three abreast with ease. The darkness, which Malian would have expected, appeared to be lacking as overhead, a twinkling light, out of keeping with its underground location, gave off a steady glow. Treading carefully, he advanced two steps into the gallery before turning and exiting back into the chamber. Taking only a few moments to search for other passages and finding none, the two returned to the sunlit entrance and roused the others to make preparation for their uneasy quest into the Sleeping Caverns.

***

On the morning Malian and his companions made ready to travel into the passages in the north, the riders, along with their captives, had stepped up their pace from their previous nights' brief pause of filling up their flasks at the Well of Refuge. They were now arriving at their last water stop, the Oasis of Illusion, as the sun rose over the High Rush Plains. They had travelled long and hard these last days with little rest after their overnight stop at the Garden Oasis with the plenty it had provided. For there, while they rested in the gardens abundance, Gallius had taken it upon himself to speak sternly with the elder's leader. He had endlessly questioned Tarnik and had eventually been enlightened to the possibility that they were not the only group from the city who were tracking the riders. Initially, Gallius had found the story told unbelievable, but had been quick in his decision to move them swiftly onward. No respite had been given that night nor the following dawning day, for the men had pushed forward in their haste to return north and the security of their homelands.

The Oasis of Illusion lay near the very northern borders of the plains before giving way to the encircling sand bar which marked its frontier. Here the hot, dusty winds coming over the vast desert in the west had given the oasis its name. In times past, the area had been legendary for contributing to the many periods of chaos throughout its history, with countless misconceptions and false beliefs growing from the visions, real and unreal, encountered there. The oasis had therefore become notorious to the workers of the plains, and with this, a certain reputation had enthusiastically grown. The riders were, however, only stopping momentarily before moving on, and the men, after being quickly advised to refresh themselves, were soon back on their horses and once more being urged forward by Gallius.

There had been little opportunity for the elders to talk amongst themselves since the Garden Oasis, but they had been surprised to see that Tarnik, from that point on, had no longer joined them in being bound and under guard. Now he rode alongside Roth, leaving Marke with just Rusan and Gaival in his charge. They had quickly exchanged glances on first noting this, wondering why or for what reason the change had occurred and remaining both suspicious and vigilant, they kept an eye open towards the gathering of more knowledge on the matter.

The next hours took them long into the morning, with the sweltering heat breaking over them as they continued to ride around the loathsome grasses. The elders did not seem overly bothered by the heat of the day, being more accustomed to the summer-like nature of the valley, but the riders with their cooler northern temperaments were now weary of the constant heat and found it to be heavy and stifling, and the water flasks were used again and again without much thought.

Nevertheless, tiredness gripped them all, and they each sat atop their horses like huge birds dozing in the sun, all apart from Gallius, who remained awake and alert in his role of leader. Later in the day, the plains came to an end and the riders moved down onto the hot sandy desert, which indicated the finish of their riding and the start of a long walk. Dismounting to relieve the horses, they steered them through the softness of the sand until the dusk descended and no further progress could be made. Here they found themselves in a ravine of sandy hillocks, which formed a basin of protection from the evening winds, and the riders could not go another step. Throwing themselves to the ground, they had settled themselves and their captives in the warm sands as the air around them cooled, and the stars appeared in the clear night sky to shine down on them in their fatigue.

***

A reluctance to leave behind the safety of the cavern entrance was great for each of Malian and his friends but once they entered the remarkable passageway between the rocks, they had been astonished by the size, light and loftiness that met them on the other side. Tragen had been the last to enter and make his way from the cavern, the fear founded in the Neferu Passage and of the enclosure he anticipated in the tunnel delaying his entry. Pausing on the threshold, it was only with Darric's advice that he quickly resolved his fears and stepped through into the spaciousness of the encircling gallery.

The passageway was not long and soon opened into

another astonishingly large subterranean area where the flickering lights hung limply down from the ceiling on long sticky threads. These moved lazily in the unseen currents blowing in from the many entrances which led off and encircled the space. This cave appeared to be completely round, and Malian anxiously walked to each doorway, counting out each of the corridors as he passed. But they all appeared alike in shape and size, with nothing to discern one from the other. He eventually considered the number to be thirteen, or so he thought as he carefully counted each opening. This included the one they had entered by, but he remained unsure and walked around again to check.

"Which exit do we take?" Tragen asked as Malian again counted. This time he came up with a total of fourteen, but deeming that this second count must be wrong, he gave it little thought.

"Let's try this one," Malian eventually decided, for a strong breeze was felt in the opening giving more than a hint of expanse beyond, and picking up his pack, he led the way in. This passage quickly disappeared around many bends before slowly closing in each side of the group and eventually, after much time had passed, came to a dead end with a well-like shaft drawing down the air from high above their heads.

"Not this one, then," he said, in frustration, "we'll have to go back and try another way."

Quickly turning, they retraced their steps back along to the main cave, where they attempted the next doorway round on their left. Again this one ended at an overhead shaft, the roof gradually sloping downwards as the group moved along. In their irritation and rising concern, they tried a further four exits, each with a similar result, before coming back into the centre of the cavern, where they stood in apprehension and dismay.

Malian was suddenly troubled by the number of doorways and promptly asked Shuma to stand before one of the passageways which they had already tried, while he sought to count around her. Standing in the very middle of the floor and starting where Shuma stood, he slowly counted each opening arriving at a number of thirteen, which he had assumed was correct. However, just to be sure of himself, he counted again, this time the other way round, but the number now came to fourteen.

"Shuma, did you move?" he demanded with great alarm rising in his throat, wondering if the woman had changed her position while his back was turned.

"No," she honestly replied.

Again he conducted the same procedure, arriving at the same disturbing result.

"Well, we seem to have an extra door somewhere," Malian concluded in astonishment before looking around and asking, "Which one did we enter by?"

Confusion in their situation was now creating a minor panic, but the sudden realisation and the hope of returning back to the outside gave some reprieve which Tragen quickly grasped.

"It was this one," he said with absolute certainty before rushing up the passageway in his haste. There he suddenly came upon a solid wall which stopped his progress, and finding his way blocked, he thrust out his hands and beat upon the rock face in his annoyance. Returning back to where the others sat together in the lightness of the glowing canopy, he declared, "No, I was wrong, it's not that one."

With his feeling of failure rising, he went on to tackle the rest of the doors, each time placing down a piece from his backpack to indicate the ones he had already tried before finally realising the hopelessness of the situation. None of the passages led out from the cavern, and in growing misery, he joined the others in their despair on the floor. The awareness of complete entrapment was dripping down upon them, along with the understanding that they were imprisoned with no idea or expectation of escape.

"Let's not yet despair," Mentu eventually said after much thought, "I feel we need some logic to this situation. We got in so we can get out!"

He considered for a while longer before venturing, "The difference in the doors that you counted, Malian, must mean something. Let me count and see how that goes." Rising, he stood in Malian's footprints in the centre of the cave and again asked Shuma to stand in the same doorway opposite. "I'll count from the left first and see what we get." Slowly counting out each entrance, he came to the exact same number as Malian, that of a total of thirteen.

"Now I'll count from the right and see if that makes a difference." Pointing at each opening as he took account, he now came to a result of fourteen, and a sudden realisation dawned within him. "See, it's the difference between left and right again, the difference between male and female, just like we encountered in *The Duat!*"

"Shuma, stay where you are," he instructed. And gathering together their packs, the men, each with an increasing amount of hope, walked in a right-handed circular motion around the circumference of the cavern. Counting down the openings as they passed, they arrived where Shuma stood in front of the fourteenth door. The passageway at her back was no different from any of the others, and they knew that they had already been that way under Malian's guidance and had previously come to a dead end. However, on turning around, it was Shuma who led the group through the doorway and beyond into where the end of the large corridor eventually opened out into a vast open-aired subtropical haven set within the confines of the Sleeping Caverns. Here they came to a halt as they took in their striking surroundings.

The light was dazzling in comparison to that of the cave, and the sudden rush of crisp, clean air in their throats was refreshing to the group as they stared in amazement at the sight before them. A lake of sparkling blue lay at their feet and was surrounded by an abundance of tall lush green reeds housing tangled nests of the numerous ducks and waterfowl, which could be seen darting in and out in their search for food. The sheer incline of the cavern walls, which met the far side of the water's edge, gave the impression that the lake had been dragged down completely below the surface of the ground in an attempt to shelter and enclose it in its depths. The blue of the sky was mirrored on its surface, but as they looked up, the walls arched over, and the sky itself could only be glimpsed through the small fissure which opened way above their heads, and they were instantly reminded that they were still deep within the caverns themselves.

The lake under this vast dome was not deep crosswise where the water gently nudged against its edge on the opposite side, but the breadth of it could not be discerned. It stretched away to the east and west beyond sight, and the growths along the waterside blurred the edge as it wound its way along the border. On its surface, the paddling birds continued to move around undisturbed by the sudden appearance of five people on the waterside which gave an uneasy sense that this was a common occurrence, and the group felt the need to remain vigilant even in such an idyllic location. They stood upon a lightly gravelled pathway that disappeared off to the left and right alongside the overgrown reed beds, and a decision was required in their next direction, either one way or the other, although the temptation to linger was strong.

"I think we must leave the choice to Shuma for the present," Malian advised. He sensed that any decisions made here were out of his hands, and the remaining members of the group were quick in agreement. There was a certain feel to the environment, one which was unfamiliar to a man except in long-forgotten memories of childhood, and they now placed their trust in the woman who had safely led them out of the cave and onto the lakeside.

Shuma was equally at ease with their decision, for she too could sense the feeling and felt in complete calm with her surroundings. Instantly choosing the left-hand route to guide the men along, she led for an hour or so before they came upon an extended pebbled area of the pathway, which projected out into the lake. Here she chose to rest for what remained of the day and through the oncoming night, building a small area for herself on the very lake edge amongst the pebbles. Gathering together the numerous cast-off feathers which littered the ground, she made herself a nest and was left to her meditation. The men were left to settle in their own ways but remained congregated together in a form of unity on the pathway, where they sat with the uneasy feelings which had gathered around them.

"Have you noticed that all the waterfowl and ducks appear to be female?" Darric asked Tragen as they sat beside Mentu in the warmth of the early evening. For one used to hunting and tracking, he knew the difference between the drab colourings of the females against the brightness of the male plumage. "I haven't yet seen a male bird at all," he continued before saying, "look, even the nectar birds are all female." The small birds which flitted in and out of the flower heads were all of a sameness in their colouring and marking, and the brown flashes of their comings and goings streaked the air around the reeds.

"Perhaps the males are away, or perhaps they only come to breed," Tragen offered.

"Yes, perhaps," came the troubled reply. However, Darric could not shake off the feeling that the male of the species was somehow not wanted or required here. Or that possibly being here and being male was not entirely to one's benefit.

The night ahead was spent in much unrest, for the men found it difficult to ignore their anxiety while Shuma, although in complete serenity of the haven that the lakeside provided, was unable to sleep deeply. Waking many times throughout the night, she each time left her bed and, walking along the water's edge, stared hard across the lake before returning in hope of finding sleep.

That night Malian dreamt again of the black swan. In his dream, he was still on the lakeside while the others slept close around him. But the waters of the lake had turned dark, and the enormous swan had appeared slowly out of the water from the left. Gliding over the inky surface, it had approached their sheltered area, its black wings curved gracefully across its broad back, before slowing and extending its long sinuous neck towards where Shuma lay. The black beak had opened, and the head moved forward as the beak pecked wildly at the defenceless woman, and as the attack grew vicious, Malian had thrown pebbles at it to frighten it away. Waking with a start, he quickly looked to where Shuma had made her bed and, on seeing it empty, had half risen before noticing the woman standing at the waterside. She turned, and Malian had seen the anguish that filled her face before they both returned to their uneasy rests.

The noise of the ducks and the birds had awoken them early as the weak morning light streamed through the overhead cleft, and the whole area achieved an instant atmosphere of activity. The mass of ducks was immense, and more streamed out of the dense reeds as they abandoned their nests for a day spent feeding on the water. Slowly spreading out, the birds disappeared left and right in their quest for food, and soon the area in front of their overnight camp was left to a meagre few who dipped and dived in their search for beetles and bugs which swam below the surface. This lake, unlike Lake Cannis, teemed with life both above and below the waterline, and the birds and ducks frequently disappeared in the hunt for the next meal, and none went hungry. Across the water, opposite the extended area where they had slept, the morning light lit up an area where the cavern walls intersected at another huge gaping tunnel opening darkly onto the water's edge. It had not been seen on their arrival the previous day, but it very soon started to bother them, for it had a certain watchfulness about it, and all of the group had found themselves looking across at it with a belief that they were being observed. For this reason, along with the fact that their first night in the depths of the Sleeping Caverns had left them feeling unsettled, Shuma was quick to lead them on along the lakeside and further into the labyrinth, which they knew and felt had now completely surrounded them.

The lake to their right became a constant, and the rest of the day saw them advancing along the water's edge in their determination to reach the end of the subterranean pool. However, many hours into their walk, the end was still not in sight, and they knew they would again be making camp along its banks. As they progressed, the conversation again turned to the lack of male species in the vicinity, with Darric still showing some concern for this observation. However, being unable to find any reasoning for it, the talk rapidly moved on to other subjects of interest.

"I don't think the robbers who stole your Icon would have come down this way," Tragen ventured as Shuma strode out along the shingle path, "these passageways would not be easy for a horse, and as we found ourselves, the enclosure within such a space is not pleasant to beasts used to the openness of the fields."

"I would think there are more ways than this to get through the caverns," Shuma sensibly replied as she watched the pathway stretching ahead of her. "We have come into the caves high up from the dunes, but there must be other ways lower down which must be more accessible."

"Well, why aren't we going the easier way?" Tragen challenged.

"We go the way that Malian was shown in his dreams," she answered back, glancing quickly over her shoulder, "and who said the lower ones would be any the easier!"

The conversation went quiet, with the younger members of the group trudging forward in their progression while the two older men followed in their tracks. Here Malian's thoughts had turned to the journey so far travelled.

"How many days do you think we have been gone from the city?" he asked Mentu, who walked slowly alongside him at the lake's edge. "I feel like I've been away for many months, but not even a full moon has passed in my reckoning."

"I've lost count," came the reply, "but it can't be any longer than twenty nights though my estimations may be wrong." His voice then continued softly, "I wonder how the city fares?" A thought that Malian constantly had to mind and which had many times been forced from his thinking as they pursued their course.

"Badly, I would say if our city diminishes like Tragen's, for the only prospect is to worsen, and the decline may be swift." He stopped and, turning to Mentu, then said, "The loss of *Amaunet* is our downfall, and the Vallenti shall suffer greatly if we fail to get her back. So we cannot abandon our pursuit, even if we despair or lose hope for our people."

"We will not lose hope," the scribe answered reassuringly, "and your dreams must and will give you belief and strength, both in yourself and in us." Looking directly back he stared long and hard before finishing, "The gods are with you, Malian, and in their choosing we must not question nor challenge the decision."

"But many will die," the altar tender said, a sad certainty filling his heart. "Not just in the city, but here on this very path that we tread." The distress could be felt in his voice, and he forced back a feeling of misfortune that threatened to overpower him.

"Yes, many will die," Mentu repeated in agreement and with equal truth, and he nodded his head in extreme sadness for the reality which was to come.

The cavern now appeared to shrink around the two small figures as they contemplated this inevitability before gradually releasing them and allowing them on their way into whatever fate lay before them.

"Less than twenty nights, you think," Malian then asked in surprise before quietly and with some finality in his voice finishing with, "it feels so much more!"

The two senior men then slowly walked along the water's edge in their effort to catch up with the others, the beauty and lightness of the lake forgotten as now their thoughts lingered on their people.

As Shuma guided Malian and the rest of the men further along the lakeside, the riders had once again found themselves walking across the sand as the sun appeared in the sky. This time having rested well and with a sense of urgency, they made good timing, and later that afternoon reached the river which flowed from Lake Cannis out to the east on its travel towards the Inland Sea. The clear blue-green of the river continued in the same colour of the lake from which it flowed, and the lily plants maintained a steady progress along the margins of both the southern and northern banks. The water here was not fast but deeper than horse height, and the men gripped on tight to their saddled mounts as the horses swam across the gap before emerging onto the northern shore. Reaching its banks, an immediate sense of achievement was felt within the riders, for the plains were now behind them, and the north felt that little bit closer in their thoughts.

After a brief rest to dry off, Gallius led away around the eastern edge of the dunes where the Sleeping Caverns swept downwards from their towering heights, and the enormous openings took them up from the shore and onwards into the interior. And as Malian and Mentu talked about their city and the loss of *Amaunet*, the riders were soon making to enter the caverns. There the horses were first guided in, for the enclosure in the caves made them skittish, and the men had to keep a tight restrain in order to control their alarm before they settled them in the dimness at the rear.

The elders, too felt alarm, for the fear of the caverns closing around them gave little or no hope for escape, even if chance had presented one. And a feeling of utter despair descended over them as they were forced into the shadows alongside the horses. Claud, whose face remained badly swollen and bruised, had lapsed into an unnerving quietness that the other elders could not rouse him from, and his increasing behaviour became of concern as his nervous hands constantly picked at his woollen cloak.

"This one's gone mad!" Rogan remarked on witnessing the man's wild attempts to pluck and tear at his covering which was wrapped tight around his shoulders. The rider laughed as he tried to pull away the cape which Claud hung onto in his desperation, and the other elders were quick to come to the support of one of their own. In their despair, their anger quickly turned to outrage at the action and constant taunting, and although unarmed, they could not just sit aside and watch.

"Get away from him!" Gaival had shouted, with no fear for his own life. "Leave him alone!" The old man had pushed his way in front of Rogan, and standing to protect Claud, he raised his hands towards the younger man. The rider instantly responded, handing out a vicious punch to the stomach, which dropped the elder to the floor in an agony of pain. Straight away, Theroc and Petrus grabbed hold of Rogan, each pulling an arm down and round his back in hope of stopping the fight and saving Gaival any further injury, while the commotion at the back of the cave immediately brought the other riders running. Marke being the closest, was quickest in his aid, and knocking over Theroc in haste to release his brother, he kicked out wildly at the stricken Gaival and any other elder who was in range. Then he produced his knife. Thrusting forward, he was quickly stopped by Gallius, who had come up behind, and in seeking to control the situation, he had grasped the man's arm before any contact could be made with the glinting blade.

"Stop this!" he demanded, pulling up Marke's arm.

"Your noise brings only awareness of our presence here."
Pushing aside Theroc and Petrus and helping the
struggling Gaival to his feet, he summoned Roth to bring
rope. "Bind their hands tight," he instructed, "and keep
them apart. Statte, you take first watch with Brann and
allow no talk. Marke, Rogan with me!" He then strode
back to the cavern entrance, followed by the two
brothers, while Roth calmed the horses, who were
increasingly pulling at their ropes in distress of the
nearby annoyance. The elders were promptly bound and
each placed in various areas of the back cavern, and here
Gaival lay in pain for the whole night while the others
listened to his far-off sobbing. None were afforded
anything more than previous, except now they had only
their own company to see them through the dark hours.

The night for the riders was spent in the huge cavern,
which gave them a place to sleep out of the winds which
had been a constant on their travel through the High Rush
Plains. The size and grandeur of the Sleeping Caverns did
not overly bother or impress them, for their travel south
had already resulted in their witnessing of these passages,
galleries and water caves of the interior, and their initial
feeling of awe had been replaced with an urgent need to
be through this area as quickly as possible. Their journey
down from the north had ended in the loss of a number of
men, some in the northern lands and some within these
caverns, although where their bodies lay remained a
secret known only to each soul. And in the next few days,
they knew it would bring further loss, but in knowing it
would be at the expense of the elders, they had little
cause for sorrow or concern, and with no more regard to
the matter, they slept.

***

Many miles away to the west, in the far-off interior of the Sleeping Caverns, Shuma had again found a place where Malian and their friends could rest at the lakeside, and they remained on the path at the water's edge with its stillness continuing in its stretch away to their left. But on this night, no one slept, for the overwhelming feeling of being watched had increased tenfold, and the night crept long and slow as the time passed while the silence of the caverns played tricks with their imagination.

CHAPTER TWELVE

Shuma once more walked the path ahead of the men, and again the flurry and movement on the lake surprised them as they continued onward along the water's margin. The cavern walls, with the bright morning light once more filtering through from above, showed them the way, and the lake on their right remained a hive of activity not in keeping with the name that the caverns were known by, which caused Darric to ask the question.

"Why do they call these the Sleeping Caverns?" Having had no sleep that night, this thought gave rise to questions that appeared to be of equal interest to himself and the others as they followed on the path.

"Is there anything in your book, Mentu," Malian asked over his shoulder, as no reply was directly forthcoming on Darric's asking, "for this area would appear to be known of by others, although not with any great awareness in my experience."

"*The Book of the Two Lands* does, indeed, talk of the Sleeping Caverns," Mentu responded, following in Malian's footsteps. He had used his time well as he sat on the sand in recent days to acquaint himself with the caverns which stood at their backs. "But it says very little about sleeping, just that in times long past, the area was seen as a place for social outcasts. Any poor soul who was unwanted in their community was banished here to live out their lives in solitude and emptiness and were forgotten by their families."

On hearing this, Malian immediately thought about the black swan of his dreams, for there was a sorrow about her even in her anger, and a feeling of immense bleakness shrouded the figure, and he said, "But no one lives here now, do they?" His hope remained that the soul who haunted his imagination was of the past and just an echo imprisoned in the very rocks which encircled them and not of his world.

"I don't know, but I would hope that we are now more civilised in our practices. However, I suppose the area could be used by others and for other purposes, so I feel we must remain on guard."

The five figures slowly moved forward while the lake appeared to be filling up with even more of the slender reeds, which thickened out from both sides into the middle. The cavernous roof also slowly stooped lower and lower, with a feeling of culmination instantly anticipated. It came eventually, but only after they had passed long under the immense overhang of the sloping roof where in its finality, it met the path. At this last stretch, they were compelled to drop to the floor, crawling along with their backpacks scraping noisily against the canopy as they moved forward. The sunlit reeds were too dense to walk amongst, and between them and the cave wall, the small, dimly lit passageway with its fear of enclosure had finally fed them through from the lakeside into an area where the body of water finished at a stone laid dike. Here, a wide stream of lake water filtered through the reeds before cascading over the lip of the dike, where it could be seen entering a vast cauldron-like hole in the cave floor. There the waters swirled energetically around the enormous bowl before draining evenly down into the depths and disappearing further into the drop of the caverns.

The area in which they found themselves could not compare with the vastness of the previous or with the doorway-lined cave from which they had entered the caverns. Here the walls completely surrounded, them and the boundaries encircled with no apparent openings except for going back the way they had come. This left their main focus being drawn to the dark mouth which gaped open beneath their feet and which attracted a certain inevitability to their future course as the water sank out of view. Light in this enclosure again came mainly from the ceiling, where the pendent-like clusters of hanging lights softly illuminated with a gentle glow. The meagre light from these, matched by the weak light filtering through from the reeds near the edge of the dike added an eeriness that bled down and crossed the floor at the groups' feet.

Shuma dropped her pack and, having first checked out the surrounds and found no exits, had come back to the middle of the cave. Kneeling, she peered deep into the huge watery void. The others had, with differing amounts of anxiety, concluded that this was their way forward, and Darric had already slumped to his knees at the very edge to check out any way of climbing down through the cascading water. On circling the hole but finding no steps or handholds, he had noticed that the channel appeared to be like a huge chute and that they could possibly just slide down with the flow of the water surrounding them and pushing them onwards. But this did not go down well with everyone.

"What if we get stuck?" Mentu asked in rising panic. "We can't climb back up again, can we?" He looked long and hard down into the opening. "And what if it just leads to another enclosed lake? What if we get stuck there?" The scribe could be seen to be getting even more agitated as his fear of the enclosing waters increased, and Shuma was quick to respond.

"What if, what if, what if!" she said with little patience for the troubled scribe. Then slowly standing and facing the agitated man, she added with more kindness, "I'm sorry, Mentu, you have a right to be scared, but you must have belief." Her voice dropped. "This is the way that

Malian has been brought and that, in itself, should be enough," she firmly said, before adding with some sympathy, "please control your emotions, for they do more harm here than good, and we all need to be strong for each other." Looking around at the group of men, she included them all in this last advice while taking note of it herself. For a fear and unrecognised emotion boiled through her own heart, and any misgivings which she carried had to be controlled.

There now seemed no reason for any delay, and a swiftness appeared to be the best approach with little time given for any reflection or doubt, and Shuma was brisk to gather and encourage the others as she stepped forward. On picking up her pack, she advised the men.

"I would think it best if we put our packs on our front," she considered, "and we need to keep our hands protected." Crossing her arms over her chest, she indicated the best stance. "This should make us more streamlined and keep a clear area on our backs to slide down, for we don't want anything to catch." She quickly looked at the agonised face of Mentu before moving away and fixing her own pack whilst holding her unease in check. Dropping to the edge of the bowl, she sat and let her feet dangle over before taking a deep breath to control her emotions, and then pushing forward into the stream, she dissolved into the shadows at the men's feet.

Tragen and Darric were keen to assist Mentu, for it would take them all in a combined effort to encourage and see him prepare for this step, while Mentu himself was eager to explain his fears and desperate anxiety in some hope of their understanding.

"It's the water, I've always been fearful of water cascading over my head, it takes my breath away, and I panic!" he explained in his unrest. It was a dread long-held and remembered from some event in the past and which had been with him for many years, growing slowly in its severity as time and recollection passed.

"Best to make it quick then," Tragen advised while they all helped and encouraged the older man to seat himself on the rim. "Just take a deep breath, and we'll help you forward."

The scribe desperately gulped in the air a number of times while grasping hold grimly onto the edge of the bowl as Malian and Darric forcefully uncurled the tense clinging claws. And once the fingers were prised open and freed and his arms crossed tight across his front, Tragen could push the distraught man into the water's flow. He disappeared quickly downwards and out of sight, and the others, each carrying his own concerns, were swift to follow on their slide into the unknown.

The water, which instantly cascaded around and over them pushed them downward and took them all by surprise, for it was slightly warm but had a freshness about it. Thankfully the water tube itself was not overly long but led consistently down in one long slope before emerging onto a wide shelf where the waters gathered again in a huge bowl. Here the stream continued along to the right in a deep gully before once again descending through another opening and vanishing once more into the depths.

Shuma was seated on the ledge with Mentu collapsed, coughing at her side as, one by one, the men arrived wet and slightly muddied from their slide in the torrent which had propelled them down. Mentu had taken a lot of water on board in his panic and was being sick, along with bouts of coughing which cleared both his lungs and stomach of its unwanted intake. But the rest had appeared to come through unscathed. Looking further down from the brink of the ledge, they could see several other water chutes, this time open on one side, which led away into the deep. These chutes hugged the contours of the cavern, funnelling the water down in a right-handed motion around the bounds of the lichen-encrusted walls and gave the appearance of huge intertwining corkscrews. Here the spirals, along with their blankets of moss were dwarfed by the immensity of the cavern, and the deep central chamber yawned gorge like in front of the group. The light was brighter than previous, as the hanging glow worms assumed enormous proportions both in size and mass, highlighting the whole of the cavern and picking out the water courses. These did not seem as steep as the first one, having a much gentler incline to their progress as they swirled around each other. And Shuma was quick to note the lesser descent, pointing this out to Mentu after he had recovered from his convulsions in some hope of alleviating his fears. She also thought that the slopes should give the opportunity for them to sit up slightly out of the water, allowing them to keep their heads up and letting the water cascade around them and move them on towards the floor. But first, they needed to negotiate the hole at the end of the ledge where they sat and which appeared to be identical to the one they had just passed through.

This hole was smaller than the previous, but again the water cascaded around the rim with the knowledge from their first encounter that this would result in water flooding over their heads, and Mentu immediately became disturbed at the prospect. His fear was now twice that of before, as the experience had resulted in a deeper fuelling of his aversion, and he became overly anxious and upset, which quickly turned to anger.

"I'm not going through there!" he shouted, his furious voice echoing wildly around before disappearing into the ceiling of the dome, where the reverberations gently agitated the hanging lights high above his head. Rising from his seat, he fearfully grasped hold of the woman who stood at his side. "I can't go through, Shuma. Please don't make me!" Pleading, he backed off towards the wall and the safety which he perceived it gave.

"There's no other way, Mentu," Shuma gently said. Now aware of the great fear which poured off the older man who had begun to pace desperately in front of her, she quickly looked across to Tragen and gave a sign for him to act.

The blow was only slight, but the warrior caught the jaw of the scribe at an angle that sent him sideways into the arms of Darric, who lowered the fallen man to the ledge, and they had then been quick to descend into the water hole. Shuma again went first, disappearing down into the flow before Tragen swiftly lowered himself into the bowl. Turning, he took hold of Mentu's feet while Darric supported the upper body, and slowly they fed the stunned man through the hole as the warrior disappeared under the flood. Once out of the initial outpouring, the cascade had been concentrated into the deep gully, and Tragen and the unconscious scribe chased after Shuma and were carried as one down the water chutes. Behind them, Darric and Malian followed at intervals, and soon the group was swirling around and around the cavern wall as the force took them further into the depths.

***

The riders had woken that morning after their first night in the caverns on their way into the north. And near the front of the cave, the leader of the riders had been roused from sleep into the dawn by the sound of troubled voices. Rising quickly, he had gone back into the cave to check on his men and found them attempting to aid the horses, who were becoming restless.

"The horses are getting anxious," Roth said, leading two of the nervy mounts past Gallius and on towards the opening, "we need to get them outside before they bolt." Skilfully escorting the agitated animals out, he instructed the other riders to quickly remove the beasts from their confines and out onto the sands which gathered at the cavern door. Gallius then turned away, and without a glance to where the elders lay, he left the back of the cave to its silence and joined his men in the light of the advancing morning.

Gaival had not found sleep that night, and his stomach was painfully bloated after the hard blow he had received. He had, in the depths of the darkness, coughed up a large amount of blood that had dried in streaks around his mouth and which now lay in a dark sand-encrusted pool beside his head. Water had been given by Brann before he left his watch in the early hours, and he had tried to make the elder comfortable. But neither water nor comfort had been expected or forthcoming while Marke and Rogan each stood their turn in the following hours.

As the morning light had entered the cave and slowly reached the back wall, he had struggled to sit up and saw where the other elders had spent their own night against the cold of the cavern walls. His eyes took in the gaunt faces as, one by one, they each nodded in recognition before they finally came to rest on Claud, who sat motionless, close to where the horses had stood. His cloak had been removed along with his shirt, and his half-naked body appeared bleached against the darkness of the cave wall at his back. His head was low on his chest, but he was breathing, and his shoulders, at times, shivered in the cool air which passed across the bareness of his body. At his side, Gaival could see a small water flask which gave some hope that the younger man had been looked after in his distress, but he held little of that for the future.

The horses had now gone, and in their place, the riders had begun to reassemble their packs, and an inevitability of progression into the caves became apparent, and what was to come suddenly started to fill his imagination. Looking further round and away from the tormented man, Gaival found that Tarnik was nowhere to be seen, for he had again spent the night sitting alongside the riders. His voice, nevertheless, could be heard as he spoke with Gallius, although Gaival could not make out the words. Looking away from the group of elders and twisting his head to the side, he saw their traitor standing at the entrance, his back turned away from his own men, and anger and rage burned in his heart for their betrayal.

The morning hastily became a time of preparation, and the riders set about making ready for moving out of their cave and advancing further into the caverns, and the horses were once again brought up to the front, this time with their blindfolds covering their eyes. The packs and bundles were collected from the rear and strung from their saddles, and all made ready to retrace their steps back through the pathways that they had trodden on their way south. Meanwhile, the elders had been largely ignored, although Brann had brought food and water to each of them. But he had said nothing, and it was only when the riders were ready to set off that the older men were once more approached. Hastily they were gathered together and again brought forward and given over to the brothers who organised them into the two groups of previous. Gaival had risen painfully slow and was almost doubled over with the dull aching discomfort of his stomach, and Rusan had supported him as best he could as Marke roughly tied them together, pulling them sharply into the centre of the cave where Rogan had begun tying up his charges. There Theroc and Petrus both had to help Claud, for the man was weakened and wasted from his hardships and out of his mind with misery, and he stood motionless and impassive. Dressing him in his torn-off clothes, they quickly positioned him between themselves with the aim of providing support as the riders coarsely bound them into line.

The elders travelled in the midst of the men, with Statte and Brann leading the horses at the rear as Gallius guided the way out of the cavern which had been their shelter. Once out onto the sand bar, he moved off around the right-hand side and entered another wide yawning opening that mirrored the previous entrance. This time, he carried on towards the back wall and disappeared into an immense tunnel that gaped in the cold stone face looming ahead of them. Into this, the elders were taken, their last possibility of escape dwindling as the light behind them gradually disappeared and the glow of the tunnels took over.

The passage went on endlessly with barely an alteration in its width or straightness while the roof line varied in places from high above their heads to even vaster areas where the long-pointed outgrowths of dripping limestone dropped their cold deposits onto the men below. The floor appeared to remain level as they cut deep into the interior, passing first through one spacious cave and then another as they moved further inwards, but very gradually, they had slowly climbed up. Soon time was lost, and each footfall had carried them further away from any imagined safety and into the heart of the Sleeping Caverns and eventually, as the path gently sloped to the left, they entered an area where the winds could once more be sensed, and the riders came briefly to a stop.

The elders dropped to the cold floor, exhausted and frightened of the enclosure with its imprisonment but at least thankful for the slightness of the fresh airflow which surrounded them with its hope or promise of an ending to their confinement. This hope, however, did not last long, for they were once again ordered up and moved forward. This time it was along a smaller tunnel that led away to the left and on upwards until it finally opened out into the flat waterside end of the lake onto which Shuma had led her group days earlier. The riders had come out at the very eastern right-hand end of the lake, where the dome formed the back and side walls as well as the roof of the cavern.

Here the jagged fissure let in the brightness, and a down rush of wind was felt on the upturned elder's faces. The captives had immediately been taken to one side, leaving the brothers to help Statte and Brann with the horses, which were led down to the lake to drink. This end of the water was not as reed-filled as the main part, for the bird life here was somewhat lacking and without the noise and activity seen along the main stretch. But both the riders and elders alike felt a certain relief in the lack of stricture and restraint that the expanse gave after the past long hours of enclosure within the tunnels.

Their camp was made here for the night, and as the darkness gradually gathered around and the light disappeared from above, the sounds along the waterside increased in the quiet before finally merging into a stillness that held its own unease for the men. However, for the elders, at least, who were seated together along the back wall, this stillness was welcomed, and in the closeness of each other, it gave them some little comfort.

***

Mentu had awoken slowly and found himself flat on the cavern floor, his wet clothes clinging tightly around him. His jaw ached as he sat up, and his hand immediately went to the tender spot which he touched hesitantly while he moved his mouth from side to side to ease the soreness felt along the bruised bone. Sitting close to where the water had deposited them, and with the terrible fear no longer gripping his heart, he could see the large dish shape into which they had all been dropped at the end of their slide around and down into the base of the cavern where it was constantly filled from the swirling waters from above. Eventually, it overflowed at its lip into another gulley before disappearing under the vast archway on their left and into another darkened area.

Shuma and the men were assembled near this archway where the main aim of following the stream further into the caverns was being discussed. The drop through the chutes had delivered them many feet down, and looking back upwards, the immense fall that they had travelled brought with it the realisation of their circumstance. The cavern where they stood was enormously tall, beyond even that of the lake cave, and the sound of the water as it constantly flowed downwards was louder here than above as the echoes bounced around the void. But the watery descent had made its mark, and the decision to rest for the night had been taken with little opposition, and they had resolved to settle themselves and gather their strengths for the next day.

"Certainly no going back now," Darric said while staring out above his head and wringing out his sodden clothes onto the floor. He began to check his pack for any water damage and, thankfully finding none, was able to remove his outer clothing with some hope of it drying.

"Looks like Mentu is awake," Shuma quickly advised Tragen on noting the scribe slowly trying to rise from his resting place, "best if you are first to check on him, I think. For I am sure he will have something to say!" The wise woman went about her own preparations for settling while Tragen lumbered over towards the wakening man.

"It was just a tap," he said in opening as he crossed to where the water swirled down. "I could have done worse if needed. But I'm sorry it came to that." He extended his hand to the man at his feet.

"Apology accepted," Mentu replied reluctantly. Taking Tragen's hand, he was pulled up to stand before the warrior. "You have no idea how the fear takes me, for there is no good sense to it, and it shames me that I cannot have mastery over such a simple thing."

"We all have our fears, and a fear of water is not one to take lightly, for it is one which we all have to master," Tragen said while he led the older man towards where the group was making their camp. "I taught my children to swim as babes and when a fear was unknown to them in their young age."

"It is not the swimming," the scribe further reasoned, "for I can manage myself in the spa or bath. It's just water over my head that unnerves me. It's very difficult to explain," he finished, smiling weakly at the large man at his side.

"Well, let it pass, and let us rest for now."

The group settled at the bottom of the cavern and, in the constant light of the glowing worms, slept with the sound of the rushing water to lull them to sleep. But much later, in the half-dark of the gleaming lights, Shuma hastily roused the men and urged them to dress and quickly pack.

"We must move forward," she said as they questioned her, "I feel we need to get away from here quick!" Grabbing her bundle, she hastily lofted it to her shoulder and, feeding her arms through, she moved the whole onto her back. The men, hurriedly dressing into their cold, damp clothes, were swift to respond and within minutes, were being led off to the right, on through the archway and alongside where the stream fed into the deep. Here the tunnel became small and enclosed, but the path was well illuminated, and Shuma was able to move forward at a pace that did not dampen her unease as she guided them beyond the water cavern and into the depths. The anxiety in which she had woken could not be shaken, and each step intensified the need to escape the pit into which they had descended.

The stream running alongside them on the left was swift and noisy and consistently led downward in its discreet twisting and turning, and all the time, it guided the group into the very base of the Sleeping Caverns and away from the roar of the water as it fell at their backs. The stream and its enclosing passage eventually opened out into an endless blackness where the water flowed across and into another lake. Here, in the depths and shelter of the passageway, Shuma stopped before moving slowly out onto the dark of the encircling lakeside. The ground was sandy and beach-like, very much akin to the shore of Lake Cannis where they had spent many days, and the cavern itself had a feeling of enormous spaciousness equalling that of the first lake cavern, which lay many miles away and high above their heads, enclosed within its own confines of the rocks which surrounded it.

"Best if we wait a while," Shuma whispered, coming to a halt, "for we need some light."

"Perhaps no light gets down here at all," Malian softly responded, his eyes unable to tell the height within the cave. No glow worms lit the ceiling here, but a slight sheen that crossed the water gave a sense of luster to the surface, and a feeling of openness gave an indication of expanse.

"Perhaps," she responded quietly, "but we will wait here unless you really wish to enter the darkness?"

The decision was made to stay where they were, for the group could go no further without light, and whether this was good or bad could not yet be decided. However, they all could sense that they should remain there for the present and await further guidance, and so a camp was made, and sleep overcame them all. Shuma immediately felt more at ease here, and her panic slowly dissipated as she relaxed into the sand and let sleep take her while the darkness and its confines became part of her memories.

When Malian woke, it was to the thought of *Amaunet* and to a greyness and half-light which sullenly drained down from the wide open expanse above their heads into the sandy cavern where they lay. This cavern was completely open to the sky, explaining the lack of glow-worms, and its weed and fern-encrusted walls reared vertically up above the group's head, giving the impression of their being down a very broad bottomless well. The cloud-covered sky drifted across the gaping mouth, which towered high overhead as the passing breeze was funnelled down to the waterside.

The group had slept huddled together near the meagre light of the passageway which had brought them down into this area, and here the stream had passed them continuously and noisily on their left before reaching the water and dispersing into the broad bay, which was the start of the lake. This lake was unlike the one above, for the edge was bare and free from the growths of reeds with its profusion of nests that had encircled and enclosed the lush waterline of the first. But the main note was the lack of activity. This whole lakeside felt barren and sterile of life, and a sadness seemed to radiate from the walls into the air which surrounded them.

Each had awakened after a short, dream disturbed sleep, and the men's sense of ill-ease had grown immediately they had fully woken to their surrounds. The whole place felt wrong to them, just like before, and they quickly expected the worst, as again, the feeling of being male brought with it its own concerns. Shuma held no such fears, for although the whole sadness of the area bit deep into her spirit, there was a realisation and expectation which reached out to her, and she grasped hold of the feeling with awareness. Upon rising, they had spent a short time scouting out their surrounds in hope of finding their way out, and Darric had found a pathway off to the right, which led under a small overhang before it trailed its way around the lakeside. Shuma was quick in making her decision to follow this course.

However, as the group prepared to leave the sandy bay, the water had suddenly been thrown into confusion as the ripples and soft swellings, which raced across its surface, lifted the water line, throwing it up onto the sand where the group stood. Instantly they had backed off in concern. All except for Shuma, who felt a need and sudden urge to move towards the very disturbance which alarmed the men.

Out of the half-light across the lake, the black swan emerged, its proud head held aloft while its broad wings were spread wide, beating the water as it advanced towards the sandy bay and slid soundlessly towards the waiting woman.

CHAPTER THIRTEEN

Gaival had been unwell in the night and had coughed up more blood as he lay alongside his friends and was now in great pain and distress from the trauma of his inflicted injury. But Theroc had, had to wait until Brann was close by before receiving any aid for the stricken man. Both Marke and Rogan had been hateful in their unwillingness to help as they each took their turns to check on the elders, and no assistance had been forthcoming from them. Brann however, had brought water and a blanket to rest the old man's head but could do little else for the weak and rapidly ailing elder. At the last, no words were said from either stand as his friends sat alongside him, and Gaival died later that night, gone from the world with a sigh, as the quietness around turned into sadness and the prisoners sat forever fearful for their own lives.

It was many hours later that Theroc had told Brann of the passing. Time that was spent mourning and in silent contemplation of the life lived. On hearing the news, the rider had straightaway awoken Gallius to inform him of the death, and the leader had immediately risen. On approaching the elders, he had at least shown some regard, and kneeling had held the cold hand of the dead man in a semblance of respect but mainly to confirm the passing. With swift confirmation and a nod towards Theroc, he had left the elders to their sorrow. Both Claud and Tarnik had appeared to be indifferent to the death, although for Claud, it was uncertain as to whether he had realised the loss of a close companion. However, Tarnik neither looked nor afforded the older man any acknowledgment in his demise, choosing instead to turn over in the sand and make himself more comfortable.

The elders had then spent the remainder of the long

night in work and preparation, and when the riders woke into the dawning light, the body of the aged elder had been honoured as best they could and lay towards the back of the cave in a shallow scraping in the sand. Covered by an assortment of bedraggled clothing and topped off by the blanket which Brann had provided, its edges were held down by small stones and rocks collected from around the lakeside, and the depthless grave lay before them in the morning light. Around, the slowly rousing birds flitted in and out of the sparse reeds, and although this end of the lake was less populated, the hush and absence of their song was felt as if even the birds could tell of the loss felt by the elders.

The riders, however, held no respect for any such loss and, on waking, went about their morning business as if there had been no change to their number, taking a meagre breakfast and filling up their flasks at the cold stream which fell over the sloping rocks. The brothers, Marke and Rogan, had even been seen to laugh on witnessing the makeshift burial and had thrown a couple of larger stones that way to help hold down the covering, giving no concern or regard to either the dead man or the elders who watched their actions in anger. Gallius, though, on witnessing their conduct, had been quick to move them away from where they sat and set them about organising the horses.

The camp had been broken with some rush, and the remaining elders had to be quick in their parting, with little time given to their sorrow or the farewelling of Gaival. Then they were being led away from the end of the lake with its growing brightness and on through into another dark tunnel which lay to the right and into an area between two rocky walls that took them along and further into the deeper reaches of the caverns.

***

The black swan had continued across the water, growing vastly in size and threat as it approached menacingly in the spreading light of the day. Finally, it slid up onto the sand with its enormous black breast slicing through the golden softness before coming to rest ahead of the frightened and bewildered group that had backed away, blades held at the ready. The huge wings were immediately brought up and folded backwards as the ebony-clothed creature, which stood proudly in the head, stepped off the prow of the black boat, instantly breaking the fabrication and representation of a swan. Malian was immediately bewildered in his confusion, for this was surely the same black swan that had haunted his dreams, and here in the shadows of the caverns it was revealed in its actuality.

"It's a woman!" Darric had exclaimed in utter surprise as the sinuous figure left the boat. Her head was covered by a black and red veil while a raven-feathered cape was clasped tight around the tall frame. Radiating an immense aura of hostility, she walked slowly over to stand in front of Shuma.

The boat which lay before them in the sand could now be seen to contain four other women, two seated on the left and two on the right, each clothed in black, their heads tightly bound and covered. Each held a small paddle which they had placed alongside before picking up their short bows and arming themselves with arrows, they aimed in threat towards the group at the top of the beach. Their heads were bent forward with intent, and each looked up at the men who stood before them while the stillness was complete, and a dimness merged them into one.

"I have come for your offering," the dark, forceful

voice said, addressing Shuma as an equal, "for offering must be given and taken to the Lower Lake."

"We have nothing to offer," Shuma softly responded, staring directly up into the covered face of the older woman, unafraid of the person who stood before her. "We are, as you see here, myself and my four friends. We have come down from the lake above in search of passage through the caverns. Perhaps you can help us?" She spread her hands before her in appeal and to indicate the absence of threat.

"There must be offering within the Sleeping Caverns," the voice again said with an even greater command as the woman moved ever closer, "and it must be given, or taken, for passage to be granted." Swiftly she bypassed Shuma, the edge of her black cloak catching the wise woman softly against her shins, and marched to where the startled group stood at the top of the sandy bay. Stopping immediately in front of the terrified men, she pushed aside their weapons with little fear before saying in a threatening and hate-filled tone, "I see many offerings here, for sacrifice must be given as deemed by the policies and practices." Slowly she spun to face Shuma, who stood with her back turned to the water as she watched the black-robed woman survey the men.

"Offering must be given!" the demand came finally and with such certainty that Shuma realised the great threat which was before them, and for some unknown reason, her thoughts went to her sister. Suddenly she remembered the Shabti doll, and quickly removing her pack, she reached into its depths and brought up the wooden figure which Tellia had presented her with, along with the parting advice to use the gift knowingly and with belief. The physical shape of the doll, however, now appeared to have changed, for the hazy likeness that Shuma had remembered as that of a woman had become a man, its folded hands grasping a sword to its chest, and she was quick to recognise the possibilities in its implication.

"Here is our offering!" she instantly announced, holding out the Shabti with some hope that she was not wrong in her thinking. "Will you take this as payment for our passage and with the tribute that it is given?"

Immediately the swan woman had turned and walking back to the waterline close to where Shuma stood and where the doll was being proffered, she noted the masculinity of the sacrifice before taking the Shabti from the outstretched hands and accepting the offering with a bow of the head.

"Payment has been made and received," she said, lifting the veil to reveal to the woman alone the heavily disfigured face that it concealed, "but note that this will only see you through to the Lower Lake and further offering must be made there." She paused and stared long into Shuma's face before saying, "My name is Anitta, and I am one of the Guardian's of the Swans."

"I am Shuma," came back the reply, her eyes never leaving those of the woman before her, "daughter of Abu Salama and wise woman to our people."

"Welcome, Shuma." The older woman now lowered the veil, and tucking away the doll into her robes, she instructed the boatwomen to make way for the travellers and invited the group to board.

This passage boat would take them along the watercourses and down into the very bottom depths of the Sleeping Caverns and on into their final destination in the Lower Lake, but Shuma saw the men had many misgivings.

"This is our only way out of the caverns," she said, in hope of giving some reassurance as she saw the hesitancy and fear in the men's actions. They had now hung back and appeared to be in no hurry to board the swan boat. Their apprehension had risen alarmingly, and they were slow to eventually pass the armed women who stood to one side before they climbed into the boat and seated themselves along the benches which filled its interior. Shuma was last to board, and like the men, she too had a concern for them. Once they were aboard the boat, she knew they would be virtual prisoners of the swan women and at the mercy of their tolerance.

The boatwomen were again seated, and the black craft was slowly pushed off the sand by the caped figure and the short oars lowered as the water enclosed them. The front two women began to paddle their way strongly back along the right-hand side of the central lake, and the second two remained ready with their bows. The head of the swan boat who had been last to board had once more resumed her place at the front, and the illusion of the black swan was again in place.

"My dream does not come close in its dreadfulness," Malian whispered, holding on tightly to his pack as the boat began to move swiftly forwards, "for the coldness felt towards us chills my very blood!" He anxiously looked around at the other men as they each appeared frozen in position by some unseen force before his eyes were drawn towards the front of the boat where the guardian stood. Slowly she turned her head; her veil pushed up over her face revealing her features.

"Silence," she spoke directly to him, "you are a man here in a woman's world, and a coldness towards you will be the least of your worries!" She looked away as Malian quickly dropped his gaze, the image of deformity forever inscribed into his mind, and he too, sat petrified in his fright.

The boat did not travel for long, finally reaching another bay where a stone-clad channel fed off to the right, and the boat slowly nosed its way into and along the walls where the area contained two huge wooden gates stood closed off to the main body of water. The front women on either side climbed out and, opening the gates wide, returned to punt the boat through and deeper into the channel before jumping out again and closing the gates behind and swiftly returning aboard.

The waterway gradually started to widen, and the boat was paddled further along for many minutes until it narrowed again. Another pair of open gates invited them in before slowing them at a sealed gate where the front of the boat came to a halt before the heavily fortified structure. The two women again climbed out and, shutting the gates at the back they smoothly opened the sluices on either side and with the sound of the rushing water filling their ears, the boat and its anxious occupants gradually began to disappear downwards into the green slime clad channel as the waterline fell. Eventually, they stopped some many feet down as the water evened up on either side of the front gate. These were then opened, revealing a further stretch of water and the two women left above then deftly climbed down each side of the channel in the hewn-out steps before once more seating themselves and paddling the boat through into the next widening stretch.

The subway through which the channel flowed was again as brightly lit as the caverns it connected above and below, and the shadow of the black swan advanced its way across the dry walls which lined and enclosed the passageway as the paddlers briskly moved the boat onwards. The silence, which was broken only by the oars as they dipped in and out of the water, became intolerable as the tunnel ran on and on and many miles went past as the group felt the fear of claustrophobia gradually rising, which had not overly been a bother to them before.

This channel through was obviously not natural for the chisel marks of tooling and the stone-clad edging, along with the huge wooden gates which held back each section of water, were clearly of manufacture and evident of workings and diggings long past. But this was overlooked by the group as they sat uneasily, their eyes either fixed firmly ahead or else gazing into the bottom of the boat.

After untold time the waterway again began to narrow, and another gate cut across into which the boat slowly moved before once again stopping. The same procedure was performed by the boatwomen, and the craft once more descended further downwards into another distance of water while the roof of the passage also descended, enclosing the boat and its occupants as they moved onwards. Time became irrelevant, and the travellers sat with hope for an end to the silence and a wish for a safe greeting on their arrival.

A further four descents were made, two in close succession where the roof had expanded way above their heads before slowly, once again, crushing down upon them. And in all this time, the Guardian of the Swans neither moved nor spoke, and the two women armed with their bows never dropped their guard. However, on the fourth drop of the channel, the boatwomen had opened the doors to a vast sweep of water which led along to where a brightness beckoned, and the black swan had been paddled forward. Coming out of this last stretch, the boat arrived on the southern shore of the Lower Lake, and the warmth and freshness of the fragrant air immediately revived the feelings of suffocation.

The Lower Lake was completely open to the sky and entirely surrounded by the darkness of many cavern openings, one atop the other reaching skywards, with smaller crevices gaping along the water's edge. This lake was as abundant as the Top Lake, with the reed-filled edges growing strong and thick, and across, this the waterfowl and birds were numerous at its surface as well as soaring and drifting in the deep blue sky which arched across the far-reaching edges of the caverns. The noise was deafening after the silence, and there was also the chatter of women, for activity could be seen along the banks as they moved around the water's edge, although none looked towards the boat as it arrived and pulled into its berth.

Once again, the appearance of the black swan was shattered as the Guardian of the Swans stepped down onto the jetty where the boat was tied up by the two boatwomen. Immediately she raised her hand to call forward the wardens who stood in wait. These well-built women, black-clothed and with covered faces, could also be seen to be armed, some with scimitar-like swords and others with short bows and arrows which they had slung across their backs and with which they armed themselves in readiness as they neared the craft.

"Take them!" the guardian instructed, needlessly pointing towards the men who sat contained in the middle of the boat. "Check them for weapons and see they are detained."

She turned away, looking out over the lake as the men were quickly removed at arrow point from the boat and escorted along the quayside to the shore before they disappeared, without any dispute, into the darkness of an opening below the caverns. Has Shuma stepped over the bow, she had turned back, her veil lifted to reveal the ugly scars which cascaded down the middle and left-hand side of her face.

"Come, I will take you to the Enclosure." She held out her hand to indicate the way, and Shuma stepped alongside.

"Where have they taken my friends?" she demanded

with some force as they walked down the quay. "They are not bad men in my experience, and I can vouch for them if needed."

"They will be kept safe," came the reply, "and whether bad or not, they are still men and must be loathed and feared. Follow me," she said, turning to the left as they reached the shore, "you must meet with our principle for she will wish to meet you. Her name is Olor Ebon, for she is the Black Swan."

Anitta led Shuma around the lakeside, where they passed unveiled women working and sitting along its border, and Shuma became witness to the enormity of some of the wickedness which she had never realised existed in her world. Trying to take her mind off some of the women she had seen, she was quick to ask the guardian a question that had bothered her while they travelled down the channel.

"How did you know we were here?" she said, more than curious as to how they had been discovered.

"We have our spies," Anitta replied, "for the birds told us of your arrival in the Top Lake, and the bats were disturbed on your descent down the waterfalls, which alerted us to your location." They walked on further, the sun moving overhead as they continued to pass the workers. "They also told us of the others who are this moment moving in the upper chambers, but now we know of them, they will be met and attended to, and offering will be given."

"They are not with us," Shuma quickly answered, fully aware of who they were likely to be and even more aware of the possibility of how close *Amaunet* could be at that very moment, "but maybe they are from the same group of men we were trying to waylay. We have had something stolen by them which needs to be returned."

"And what is that?" demanded Anitta as she came to a

stop before a huge gaping fissure, its doorway highly decorated with many small white handprints while the cleanly swept pathway outlined by similarly decorated boulders ran off away to their right. Shuma, however, was loath to say too much at that moment and shook her head to indicate her silence.

"Very well," the woman said, "I am sure Olor will ask you the same, and she will expect answer. Come, you will meet her immediately." Turning with some displeasure and irritation, the swan guardian led them along the short path, under the painted door and through into the Enclosure. Here was the meeting place of all the swans and where the identical chairs were positioned in a succession of circles around a centrally raised dais. Within this cavern, each woman had her own seat in which she was among equals, and the floor was open to anyone and everyone.

"We are all alike here," Anitta explained as she led Shuma through the array of seats, "for some are here by rejection of their communities and others by choice. But in either way, it brings union in our society and support for each other over anything else." Now being guided across to her left, Shuma could see a number of figures seated on the very back row of the outer circle, and Anitta headed that way.

Olor Ebon sat in a chair no different to those around her, but her presence was felt as they arrived before the small group, and Shuma was brought to stand before her. On either side, the women were similarly clad as the others, black-robed and veil-less. But the Black Swan herself, although in similar black, wore around her white throat a necklace of fine intertwined strings from which hung many silver circles. Anitta presented the woman at her side, indicating, on her behalf, that passage had been asked for and granted by the giving of an offering which she swiftly produced from beneath her robes. Handing over the male doll to Olor, she appeared initially hesitant to take it from the outstretched hands before finally accepting it, her hands shaking slightly as the long fingers closed around the figure.

"Where did you get this?" she quietly asked, slowly turning the Shabti doll over before placing it gently into her lap and staring honestly up at Shuma.

"It is my sister Tellia's," she explained, before continuing in her introduction, "I am Shuma Salama, daughter of Abu from the House of Salama in the Vale of the Vallenti; perhaps you have heard of us?"

"Yes, I have heard of you," Olor hesitated before slowly saying, "for I once travelled far in the valley, and its grass and earth were once felt beneath my feet." Quickly looking down at the doll, she caught hold of it and skilfully twisting the body, it fell apart, revealing another doll tucked away tightly inside. "And the sun once shone upon my homeland!"

***

The riders and their prisoners had been moving forward for many hours with no rest, but eventually, they reached an area where the passage widened out, and the left-hand side opened back onto the lake they had left earlier that morning. They were now way down the right-hand side of the water, and the area was rich with the life Malian, and the others had observed days before. In fact, the riders were directly across the water from the extended area where the group had spent their first night, and here they stood in the gaping hole which had so unsettled the others with its watchfulness. Gallius instructed his men to make camp, for the area was known to them and had been used on their way south. They held no fear or concern for stopping here, and even though there were many hours left before dark, they came to rest again alongside the water.

The elders were untied and left to their misery, for now, being one less, they felt their world and the chance of survival growing gradually smaller. And as the riders settled into their routine of making camp close to the water, they were free to sit further along the ledge where the wall met the water's edge.

Positioning themselves with their backs to the cold and looking out over the lake with its blue water, they stared ahead, oblivious to the wildlife and activity that went on before them. The light was fading only slightly, and the rays which fell through the cavern's fissure fell diagonally onto the lake and extended eastwards to where they knew the body of Gaival lay. Claud remained indifferent in his silence, as with legs drawn up to his chest, he sat in his own world with Petrus at his side. But doubts had grown widely in the minds of the three remaining elders, and they struggled to remain confident and watchful.

"Do you think Gallius still has full charge?" Rusan muttered as he turned to Theroc, who appeared to have become the elder's frontman. Over the days watching and observing the leader, a realisation had quickly shown the growing hesitancy in the actions of his men as he ordered them about their tasks, and a feeling of division was apparently becoming more noticed.

"No, I don't," Theroc replied with greater authority. He went on to tell that on the night before Gaival's passing, he had witnessed Tarnik and the two brothers in conversation with Roth and had been surprised to see Statte join them with a shaking of hands. This left only Brann to choose his side.

"Will you tell Gallius?" Rusan asked.

"Would he believe me?" Theroc reasoned. For the leader hardly appeared to notice the elders and appeared totally unaware of the breakdown within the group that he led. Dropping his voice in some hope that neither Claud nor Petrus would hear, he continued, "I fear we are all dead men, my friend, for either way, we are on the wrong side."

***

Tragen could not hold back his anger and banged time and time again violently against the thickness of the wooden door which held them in their dungeon, for with the humiliation they had been shown on their arrival at the Lower Lake, his honour as a warrior had been challenged even in his own inactivity and was beyond his comprehension.

The heavily armed wardens had led them from the boat directly off the quayside and into an area where they had been none too gentle with their search for weapons. Each of the men had been humiliatingly stripped and removed of anything which could be viewed as threatening, along with their packs that held their possessions. Malian and Mentu had been shown no benevolence with regard for their age and had been treated just as roughly as Tragen and Darric, who did not take the search lightly and were outraged as their swords and daggers were forcibly removed and thrown to one side. Finally, they had been taken at knifepoint further into the cavern side and soon found themselves locked away in the dusty greyness of a vast airless guardroom.

Once Tragen had finished his futile assault on the door, and his quick search for any other escape routes had proven worthless, the silence quickly surrounded them, and the realisation of their imprisonment became a solid fact.

"We should have put up more of a fight," the warrior announced, his frustration overcoming the embarrassment felt by his lack of fearlessness in the situation, "we have both acted and been treated as cowards and are now hostages to a band of women!" He spat out the last words as if they were bile in his throat.

"We could do no other, Tragen, for we are in their world, and the laws are theirs to enforce. So we must abide for the moment," Malian spoke from the far side of the room where he had found a corner in which to sit. "Shuma will not desert us, and let us be thankful that she can present our intentions, for if we had been all men, I fear we would be one less already." The altar tender closed his eyes, and instantly the scarred face of the guardian of the swans emerged out of the blackness. Thankful that the others had not witnessed the dreadful image, he quickly pushed aside the remembrance and intently listened to the men as they came to terms with their situation. Eventually, the talk gave way to a silence, with the last he heard being Mentu wondering if they would be fed or left to starve, and with his hope remaining with Shuma, he let the dark take him completely.

***

Tipping out the smaller figure, Olor Ebon remembered the last time she had seen the Shabti and the miserable and unhappy situation in which it was presented so many years ago when she had been a much, much younger woman.

The child had been so tiny at its birth while the deformities appeared grotesque on such a small frame, and the shock at its sight had unbalanced the mind of the father as he took his first look within the basket and recoiled with horror. Olor had been blamed and banished for her delivery of such a monstrosity, but the child had been born with love, and Olor would have cherished her, whatever the outcome.

"I gave this doll in penance numberless years ago," she began explaining, rising from her chair and coming forward to meet the wise woman who stood before her, "for it was given in exchange for my absence, as aid and helper to my beautiful daughter who would need it as she grew." Holding out her arms, she wrapped them tightly around the body of the overwhelmed woman and whispered into her ear, "I am your mother, Shuma!"

Instantly, Shuma knew she was true to her word, for the remembrance of the embrace and the smell of the perfume took her straightway back to the house of her family and the soft bed in which she had slept as a child.

"I thought you had died!" she answered softly.

Her father had always explained her mother's absence in such terms, and over the years the questions had diminished and acceptance had taken their place. Now, with her head buried deep in the tenderness of her mother's shoulder, she wept long and hard, both in happiness of the finding and sadness for time missed and opportunities lost.

Sometime later, the two women sat alone in the Enclosure, the other women having left quickly and quietly to afford the two their privacy.

"Your sister's name is Tellia!" Olor Ebon had been first to ask of her daughter, for the name of the baby she had left had not been hers to decide, and she had been taken away before knowing of her calling. "It suits the child that I remember, and I'm sure she has grown into it."

"She is now a woman," Shuma reminded her, "and

248

although her impairments confine her to her bed, her mind is bright, and she holds an intelligence that I lack."

She remembered her sister, dark hair cascading over her shoulders as she sat up in bed, and as she had taken the doll from her bedside, she had held it out to her in a token of love.

"Tellia is well looked after, and is cherished by all who know her," the wise woman finished as she saw the smile cross her mother's face.

A stillness came between them as the question that Shuma next expected was never forthcoming, and she was unable to tell if her mother was unable to ask or was just ignoring the issue and she had to let it be. The time was obviously not right for any remembrance or memory of her father.

"I hear you do not travel alone," Olor then eventually asked. "Anitta has told me of the men who accompanied you here."

"Yes, we number five altogether, and I would like to know if they are safe?" Shuma said with concern for the whereabouts of her friends.

"They will be under guard," the Principle of the Swans explained, "and I am sure you will understand why that has to be. Here the male is scorned and rejected in all his presentations." Turning her face towards the daughter she had never expected to see, she noted the unease and worry which was held for the men.

"I have seen the lack of male birds on the lakes," Shuma said in answer, staring back intently into the face which she had so quickly accepted in her need and longing, "and I have seen the damages and wounds that some of the women carry. But some are uninjured, although," she hesitated, "injury may take many forms."

"Yes, Shuma, not every injury is something you can see, and you are wise to recognise such. Many here appear unaffected by the abuse sustained by others, but each is here, just as I am myself, at the exclusion of our societies. Or else by their own choice of seclusion." The older woman went on to explain to her daughter about the refuge given to any woman who needed it. "Let me tell you a little more about my friends," she began.

While they talked, the Enclosure slowly started to fill up again as the women finished their work, and gathering in their numbers, they came together to close the day in support and unity, congregating within the safety of their caverns.

CHAPTER FOURTEEN

"There's someone coming," Tragen said out of the darkness as the sound of voices broke the silence, and rising to his feet, he swiftly moved towards the door in readiness for action. Darric too, was speedy in his response and stood opposite the warrior, flanking the doorway. Slowly the dull rasp of the opening bolts scraped into the stillness, and the door swung outwards to allow the light of the lamp to guide the wise woman into the cell.

"Stop!" Darric quickly said, hastily stepping forward and grabbing hold of Tragen's enormous fist as he brought it down towards the figure that was entering, "it's Shuma!"

The light was raised quickly, and the acceptance of the identity could be confirmed both by sight and by Shuma's voice as she asked if they were all safe and unhurt. Has the door closed behind her, the bolts scraping into place, she brought the light into the middle of the room.

"I was so worried for you," she said, looking at the four men who stood confined before her, knowing that many hours had passed in their separation and that the early night was now upon them, "but the swans have cause for your captivity and whatever I say will make no change to their conduct where you are concerned," she sadly advised before suddenly going on, "but I have news that will surprise you greatly!"

Stopping and not knowing how best to explain the joy which she had found in this isolated environment, she first went on to tell of her meeting with Olor Ebon. "She is the Black Swan, the Principal of all the women here, but she does not take the name of leader. For all may speak here without prejudice, and all have influence whatever their folklore, and to them, I shall have to ask for your deliverance and safe passage."

Going on to explain the reasoning behind the women's anger and loathing towards them as men, she went into great detail of her witnessing of the women and the scars they bore, visible and invisible, before finally speaking of the Enclosure where she would address the swans in the morning. Reminding them that they would have to remain imprisoned until such time of their release and must spend the night in the dark cell, she finally said, "There is still one more thing that you must know." She paused only briefly before saying, "Olor Ebon, the Black Swan, is my mother and I was told many years ago that she had died and have thought her long gone for over twenty-five years." Looking at each man in turn, she finished, "Yet in this place of remoteness, I have found her, and we have been reunited!"

Her happiness could not be ignored. However, a certain sadness briefly clouded her face as she thought of her father and the action he had taken towards his wife, the mother of his children, and a feeling of bewilderment in his conduct caught tight around her heart.

"We are so pleased for you, Shuma," Malian said, noting the look of confusion which had passed across her face. Coming forward, he took hold of her hands, "You will, I'm sure, have been shocked by your findings but take your time and do not judge until you know all the reasoning." He looked at her with the knowledge that she would be torn in her thinking both between that of her parents and also that of her friends and the journey which they were upon. Shuma too, was equally aware that Malian understood her dilemma, and she nodded her head in gratitude as the older man let go of her hands, and she hastily and thankfully moved on to the problem of their confinement in the cell.

"You should be out of any cold here," she said, wandering around the bare room, which offered little comfort in its lack of facilities. "I have asked for blankets, but the swans will give no cheer, and so you must make what you can of your circumstance."

Slowly she returned to where the men stood and continued, "But you must not attempt any escape, for it will compromise my delivery for the morning and at this time, I do not know how that will go." She looked at the men intently, especially Tragen, for the man's anger could almost be touched as it poured off him. "You will have food, but I can do no more at this moment."

"We shall put our trust in you, Shuma," Mentu responded, "and the knowledge you have given can at least make us more aware of the actions and the sense behind the conduct shown." He looked at the three men as he said this, knowing that it would be only Malian who thought along these same lines and that Tragen and Darric would have their own beliefs on the matter. The two younger men, with their feelings of hostility towards their keepers, would have difficulty in finding the situation acceptable, which could be a problem for their safekeeping, and a night slept on a cold floor could hardly be of help in its ordeal.

Suddenly the noise of the bolts again jarred out into the dark, and the door to the cell slowly opened. This time it admitted a heavily veiled woman, her head hidden by the black cloth wound tightly round, who carried in a covered tray and jar of water. Either side of her strode the armed warders who watched from the doorway, and as Shuma thanked her and asked for the tray to be put down on the floor, she turned to face her friends and indicated that her time was up and she must go.

Leaving the men, both she and the other woman

quickly departed, escorted by the guards, while the door once more slammed shut, and the men were left to their unlit cell, forgotten for the remaining night.

***

Shuma slept the sleep of the dead, for the learning of the previous day had so overwhelmed her that her restless mind had eventually settled itself into oblivion in some hope of peace. On waking, however, she had straightaway thought of Malian and the others, for her decision had already been made to continue along with her friends, however hard that might be in the given circumstances, and her resolve to solve their plight remained firm in her mind. She knew she had to prepare well for the difficult presentation, but first, she had to speak with the Black Swan and rising from her bed, she went out into the light of the morning in search of her mother.

The Lower Lake, which was before her, was slowly waking to the warmth of the day, and the activity around the water's edge equalled that which went on across its surface as the flying birds dived for their morning meal and the women fished upon the banks for theirs. Shuma looked both ways along the stretch of open water before walking with haste alongside the lake and toward the quay where they had first arrived as she saw the figure of Olor Ebon emerge from the guardrooms below the caverns, her face passive as she looked across the water.

"Mother, I have need to talk," Shuma said, on arriving before the principal, knowing that she had most likely been to look upon the incarcerated men, and whether words had been spoken or not she did not know, and so she continued in her petition, "and you must understand my situation and know that I cannot stay here."

The wise woman suddenly felt a need to plead her case even with the one to which she had already spoken, but she also needed to remind her newly found mother that she would not be remaining. "I have need of all my friends to journey with me, so none can be left behind or given in offering."

"You must present your case at the Enclosure, Shuma, it is our way. And respect must be given," her mother replied as she guided her daughter back along the lakeside.

The two had talked long into that first night, and Shuma had explained to her the journey on which she and the men had found themselves. It was now up to the Black Swan and the other swans to decide the men's fate, but the wise woman knew what was also at stake here, for the finding of each other would once again bring loss.

***

The meeting in the Enclosure was for the early morning, and Olor Ebon had proudly led her eldest child past the circle of swans as they surrounded the dais before leading her up onto the raised platform where with joy and happiness, she introduced Shuma.

"This is my daughter, Shuma," she began, her voice echoing to the back of the lined room, "and we have been long time apart and ignorant of each other for many years. Here I now rejoice at her sight, for the child I had once known has become a woman." She looked towards where her daughter stood proudly at her side before continuing, "However, she has come here with others who are unwelcome here, yet they too ask and require passage through our caverns. Their search takes them into the north, and none can remain in offering, and this is the reasoning behind this meeting." Her voice faltered at this, and the Black Swan slowly stood down, descending the steps to the open floor before ending, "I will let her speak and make presentation."

Shuma lifted her head, alone now on the dais before the assembly of swans, and slowly looking around, she noticed the empty seats around the perimeter. The absence of Anitta and the boatwomen, and others of their kind, led her to believe them about their business along the waterways and caverns. For the security of their territory was foremost for the women, both old and young alike who sat unveiled in their Enclosure, and her thoughts went back to her own home and the freedom she had known and taken for granted.

"The valley where I grew up was once a beautiful, warm and safe place to live," she began in opening of her address, "and I recognise that some of you may already be familiar with it, for you are women from many differing parts of this land and some of you will be Vallenti. But for those who aren't, I shall tell you a little of my people."

She went on to explain the simple principles and beliefs of the valley citizens and of their trust and dependence on their goddess *Amaunet*, and whether rich or poor, male or female, each had lived a life blessed in her abundance, and none had gone without. Her voice had swelled with sheer delight and pride as she recalled her home in her remembrance before slowly subsiding into dismay as she went on to tell of the sudden loss of their Icon at the hands of the riders.

Describing the overwhelming destruction caused by her absence she recounted the dreadful cold and winter which had been brought into being, along with the instant effect that it had on her people, for their dependence on the land granted little hope in their survival, and nobody had been spared whatever their deeds or actions.

"We are here, therefore," she continued, growing stronger in voice, "myself along with my four friends who now sit in the depths of your prison to pursue these thieves. To take back our goddess and restore peace to the people in our valley, and for that, I stand before you to ask only for safe passage and guidance along your caverns." The Enclosure around her remained silent as she paced around the platform's circumference, and in its quiet, Shuma knew she had to confess all, and in this, she felt the burden of disclosure which would change the women's world.

She then addressed the swans with a certainty which she alone as wise woman knew would come and one that the men who sat in their darkness feared. Her gift had shown more than just the loss of *Amaunet*, and with the realisation that other Icons had been taken, including that of Tragen's people, she knew the likely aim of acquisition meant the ending of their world in destruction and the fall of many societies.

"Do not think of yourselves as beyond the reach of civilization, for your Sleeping Caverns here will not go without change and upheaval," she revealed to the swans. "The world outside is changing, and the destruction and suffering will not pass you by as you sit here. Your safety will crumble into ruin, and freewill will no longer be yours to own." Looking down sharply into the amiable upturned faces, her anger grew in their inflated self-assurance. "You will soon notice the transition, and it will be unstoppable. Even now, the coldness slowly creeps into your caves, and the world of mankind will be upon you and overwhelm in its dominance."

Off to her left, one of the swans was quick to rise, and making her way swiftly towards the front, she climbed the steps and stood opposite Shuma. Her head was unveiled, and the flawless image, its dark hair framing the small features looking out with such simplicity, hid the aggression in the harsh voice as she introduced herself.

"I am Berran, and I speak only for myself," she explained as she faced Shuma, her outrage growing as she spoke. "You expect me to believe your words, to fear a world that has already rejected me and for me to worry about what happens outside?" She waved a withered and crippled hand towards the Enclosure's opening. "I don't care what goes on beyond these caverns, but my authority here will not go unchallenged, and I will not let these men journey through without offering!" She ended her demand, her voice becoming silent while a slow murmur of support gradually began to take its place, and Shuma looked around at the women before her.

"We gave offering to the Swan Guardian of the Middle Lakes," she replied softly in some hope of calming the disquiet which was increasing around the Enclosure, "and that was accepted in payment of passage. I presented the Shabti doll, and in its likeness of man, it was recognised and approved."

She again produced the doll that her mother had returned to her, minus one of the inner dolls which had been taken in its acceptance of their travel and held it out towards the women.

"Can this not be accepted again?" she asked before continuing in her explanation. "The Shabti may have already given up one of its offerings, but inside, it contains many more."

Now knowing the extent of her sister's gift, Shuma opened the doll to reveal another male figure tucked neatly away inside. This figure, again fashioned in its strength, bore a heavily carved beard, and in its hands, it grasped a fishing pole while across its front, a belt of small intricately cut shapes indicated its catch. Berran regarded the outstretched offering before turning towards the other women and again spoke her mind.

"This to me, is a poor substitute when a much more legitimate offering is to hand, don't you think?" Then dropping her voice, she finished by saying, "But that is my own settlement, and I will respect the resolution of this given by vote as is our custom." She bowed her head towards the Black Swan who sat before her, "For in so doing, I hope we will be quickly rid of these men who befoul our way of life!"

"There is one more thing," the Black Swan said slowly, her voice holding a note of apprehension, and rising from where she sat, she once again joined her daughter on the floor and looked out into the gathering.

"The man, Malian, has asked to make presentation. He has asked to address the Enclosure, and I am obliged to bring this request before you, and you will each make your own resolution."

"No man has or ever will make presentation," Berran shouted on hearing the demand, and again enraged at the very thought that these men were contaminating their lives, she stormed across the dais to stand before the Black Swan, "and we will not allow any man within our Enclosure. This ground is ours alone and will remain so!" Having said her piece, her words spat out as if poison on her lips, she left the dais with all of the women standing in silent support of her words and returned to her seat.

"Malian has been instructed by the gods to lead our group," Shuma declared firmly in her final summary, glad that the subject of offering was concluded in its ruling to vote but surprised in hearing of this other request. Malian had not said anything to her about making presentation, and it had come as a surprise. "And do you dare ignore the gods? Do you think yourselves above such things?"

On this final note, she finished her presentation before the swans while the women remained standing around the platform, knowing they had two choices to make, and each would decide with their own single-mindedness, gods or no gods.

"We will vote immediately," Olor Ebon finally announced, "and in so doing bring a resolution to this matter, both on offering and on presentation."

Taking Shuma's hand, she led her daughter down from her introduction, and passing the seats of the swans, they moved back out into the sunshine of the lakeside.

***

The Top Lake had once again given the riders shelter for the night, but the elders, fearful of the action of Roth and the brothers, had slept little, and the morning found them exhausted in their tiredness. Theroc had, in the quiet of the long night, come to a decision and knowing full well the outcome either way, he resolved to speak with Gallius in some hope of alerting the leader to the likely standpoint of his men. But he knew this had to be done without the knowledge of the others, and therefore, the timing was crucial in this aspect.

Looking over towards where the riders had slept, he saw the brothers busy around the small fire they had made on the shore; their backs turned away from the water. The three other men had disappeared back into the darkness of the cavern where the horses stood in wait while Tarnik was nowhere to be seen, and it seemed as good a chance as any.

Gallius rested near the lake's edge; his head drooped forward as if in sleep, and Theroc slowly stumbled across the stony terrain, his tired legs aching in their fatigue before crouching down close to where the tall man sat.

Dipping his hands, he brought the cool water up to his face in a pretence of washing in the sparkling waters and turned his head to one side.

"Watch your men, Gallius," the elder advised, his voice barely a whisper over the sound of the awakening lake while the water dripped softly off his lengthening beard, "you must know that you are not without rival, even amongst your own."

Quickly he stood before any reply could be made, but Gallius slowly turned and watching the older man stagger back towards where the three remaining elders sat, he rose and re-joined the brothers at the fire. Kicking aside the driftwood, he turned the pot of hot water over the flames and made ready to continue.

The lake was very soon behind them, and the dark of the passage of the caverns, lit only by the glowing insects, once again became their world as Gallius led them on through the slowly sloping tunnels down into the lower reaches of the system. The elders had once more been bound and tied together in their ignorance of what awaited them, and each onward footfall pained them with its tread as they were constantly driven on. Claud was again supported between Rusan and Petrus, and the younger man was literally dragged forward in his collapse. While the clatter of the horse's hooves became an echoing constant as they were led blindfold along.

Soon the walls of the passage slowly started to widen, and another enormous cavern eventually stretched ahead of them, its vast darkness hiding the walls in shadow while the ceiling disappeared out of sight. Leading them, Gallius took them straight down the middle, knowing that their exit lay dead ahead.

Further into the expanse, and after uncounted hours of walking across the dusty floor, he brought his men to a stop and with hope of resting the group for the long stretch ahead, he allowed the elders to collapse to the cold ground in their exhaustion while his men each took their own time to rest. However, he had first been quick to organise some security and had instructed Roth and Marke to stand guard and in doing so, felt safer in his halt. The feeling of apprehension and tension which constantly followed them had reached a point where it could almost be touched, and the darkened surroundings held their own unease.

Gallius had fallen to his own rest with little worry, and the sudden waking by Marke and Rogan as they pounced on their sleeping leader had come out of nowhere. Waking the startled man with the realisation of the betrayal that was upon him, he was first held down in capture before his men dragged him to his feet. The shouts, which broke the quiet, instantly alerted Brann to the treachery, and rapidly rising from his own rest, he sped towards the commotion. Grabbing hold of Marke, he pulled the brother off and away, allowing Gallius to swing around with his fist and punch Rogan in the mouth. Stunned, the man instantly let go and hitting back, he returned with a blow to the head, and the two fought fist to fist, while the other two clashed in their own contest before Brann was finally beaten by Marke, with the help of Statte.

Breaking free of Rogan, Gallius spun round to witness Roth standing near the horses where the Icon, which meant his daughter's life, had been removed from his saddle bag. The wrappings hastily removed had been thrown to the ground revealing the small statue which was held in the hands of the traitor. And as he fiercely moved towards him, he was stopped suddenly by an agonizing pain that bit sharply into his right shoulder. The short blade, which had been brought down with some force by Rogan, had propelled the leader forwards to where Roth stood and reaching out his hands to steady himself, he had grabbed hold of the man's shirt tearing open the clothing as he fell forward towards the floor. Instantly the heavily inscribed talisman was revealed around the traitor's neck, its ghostly glow ringing the metal disc and lighting the darkness which surrounded it. And as Gallius fell to his knees, he looked up into the twisted, corrupt face of the man he had thought of as friend and brother.

"Why have you betrayed me?" he cried out loudly, the blade sunk firmly into his shoulder as the hard floor brought a halt to his fall while the challenging question echoed through the cavern.

"That I will not say," Roth snarled, clutching at the talisman which governed his unconscious actions, "but the rest are doing it for money and mere wealth, for why does any man do these things?"

The second-in-command moved quickly forward to stand over his subdued leader and holding the small snake-headed figure, he tucked it away in the torn shirt to indicate ownership and possession of the golden Icon.

"Those reasons are not mine," Gallius claimed, the blood pouring down from around the bare metal thrust into the shoulder wound. And as the pain grew into a burning fire, he felt a numbness spread down into his right arm and a weakness overcame him, "For another's life is defence for my actions, and that being I have no dispute with you."

"Another's life," Roth asked maliciously, "and one which must be of great value for you to risk such a venture?" Sneeringly he brought his face down towards Gallius, and the leader could again gaze upon the ornate decoration which hung around the exposed neck, and he remembered where he had seen it before.

"Daina was my cause," he replied, while the vision of

a similar token hanging around the neck of King Dedrick swam into his mind, "and the life of my daughter meant more than just riches. But I ask again, why have you betrayed me? Who are you doing this for?" He struggled to stand with the aim being of drawing his sword and facing Roth full in the face but was stopped as he pushed himself upwards.

"That's enough, let's end it here!" Rogan sneered as he shoved Gallius back to the floor. Viciously twisting and removing the exposed blade, he grabbed the man's hair from behind. Pulling the head back tightly, he revealed the heavily bearded throat and repositioned the knife, ready to make its final cut.

"No!" Roth immediately shouted, seeing the man's intent, as smiling he then said, "Don't slit his throat, for it would be far too quick a demise. Let us leave him here and let the women take care of him!"

The brother also smiled, but in his frustration, he viscously brought down the hilt of the blade to knock out the kneeling man, and the darkness was quick to take him before he was savagely beaten to the floor and left where he fell, the ground turning red as the spilt blood flowed.

Roth turned away and, collecting the horses, he rushed to make his men aware of the need for haste and for them to make a swift escape, and they quickly gathered their packs in readiness and stood before the bound elders as they lay on the cavern floor. The number of men before them had now increased by one, for overwhelmed quickly in his fight against Marke and Statte, Brann had also been bound, with his arms pulled harshly into his back and hands tied. His feet had been roughly roped together with assistance from Tarnik, and he had then been thrown alongside the older men as they witnessed the sight of Rogan grabbing Gallius' head with his intent to kill. The brutal assault upon the leader which had followed his first assault played out in front of the elders, but given their situation and weakness, they had been unable to do anything to aid the stricken man and had been forced to watch as he was overpowered by the sudden strike which had come out of nowhere and which was over so quickly. Now they sat with an even greater fear as the shadows of the men congregated in front of them.

"What shall we do with these?" Statte asked, looking into the upturned faces of the frightened older men and feeling little compassion. "Shall we leave them here to starve and rot in their own despair?"

"Kill them!" Rogan was quick to suggest, also staring down at the elders who sat in dread, for he remained displeased with the lack of murder that his hot blood demanded and although both brothers bore heavy marks from their fights, each was lacking the final blow and the release given on its deliverance.

"Kill them all, for alive they will bear witness to our actions!" This voice was Tarnik's, and it rose in agreement as he viciously and uncaringly looked down upon his own people who he had deserted. In fear of his own reckoning and for any accusations of abandonment, he would see them all put to death and slaughtered, and his soul would hold no concern.

"No, leave them tied and ready for the women," Roth decided with some finality, "and they will be our payment through the caverns. For the women are coming, and we must be away." Quickly turning to Marke, he signalled with a slight nod of his head towards where Tarnik stood in front of the captives.

"Who are these women you talk of?" Tarnik was asking, slowly turning around from his men. This was the second time that he had heard mention, and the menace in the name had given rise to an unknown fear in its

265

speaking. And as he turned, the brothers pounced.

"You'll soon find out!" Marke replied with more than a hint of malice. Lunging forward, he and Rogan quickly seized the unsuspecting man, and the leader of the elders was wrestled to the ground with little regard before being securely bound and flung next to the others. His shouts of terrified alarm were ignored as he protested wildly at the conduct, and in absolute panic and bewilderment, he was swiftly abandoned by the riders to whatever consequence would come his way. The dismayed man immediately felt the hatred and contempt which gathered around him as his own people had looked on with some satisfaction and vengeance at the treatment given to the turncoat.

The four riders had quickly disappeared into the dark with no looking back, and all of the horses were led away, their footfalls gradually fading into the silence, and the stillness left behind was broken only by the breathing of the men. Here they sat, stunned by what had just happened but as the quiet gathered in the glowing light, Brann had been the first to move and break the paralysis of shock.

Hands and feet tied, he had wriggled and snaked himself over the rough floor towards where his leader lay senseless in the pool of liquid which had thickened around his head. Finding the man unresponsive, he had moved around to where Gallius' unused blade remained sheathed at his side. Turning his back, he then used his numbing fingers to gradually loosen the blade by some inches and was soon able to cut away his ties against the half-drawn metal before finally removing the ropes from his feet and standing to work the blood back into his limbs. His thoughts then went to Gallius, and he stooped to check on the fallen man, turning him over to allow the still-seeping blood to flow away from his face. The shoulder wound had begun to congeal slightly though the cut was deep, and the shirt had been pushed aside as the blade had been cruelly removed, revealing the bloody slash which gaped between the collar bone. His head wounds were of equal concern as the severe assault had knocked the man out, and the lacerations bled steadily into the dark hair, which became stuck down over the skull as the redness slowly spread. But he was out cold, and all Brann could do was make his friend comfortable until he chose to wake.

Returning to the elders, he began to untie them one at a time. Allowing the men their freedom, he helped each one to stand while checking on them as they arose from the cold floor. Tarnik, however, was not included in this and remained lying where he had been thrown, his knees drawn up to his chest in defence of any assault which would be forthcoming, and the elders gave him neither concern nor care as they each looked to their own.

"Why haven't they killed us?" Theroc had been first to ask on his release, seeing the amount of damage done to both riders and knowing it could have been much worse. "Why have we just been left?"

"The women are coming," Brann replied, leaning down to untie the ropes which bound Petrus to Claud. "We have been left for the swan women and have been given in offering." Straightening up, he finished the job before collecting his pack, which lay hidden in the shadows. Returning to where Gallius lay, he collected both the side blade and short knife, which the leader did not require at that moment. Hiding the knife in his belt, he held the blade to his side as he stood over his fallen leader.

The elders could do nothing in their release, for they had no belongings or arms and stood in all the possessions they owned, and the fear which had gripped them over so many days with its panic had now drained them of any care, and so they sat in the light of the glowing lights and waited.

"The women are coming," Brann once again said after untold time had passed, and putting away his blade, he seated himself next to his leader and waited in acceptance of the situation, "and there is no escape. So we will rest and hope for their settlement or else die where we stand."

CHAPTER FIFTEEN

Once outside, in the morning brilliance which surrounded the lake, Shuma had confronted her mother about Malian's request for presentation, for her surprise and annoyance in this disclosure by the Black Swan could not be held back.

"You have spoken with Malian?" she asked immediately, knowing that her mother must have done so, or else Malian had sent a message which appeared remote and very unlikely. The swans were now streaming past them in a long line as they moved out of their Enclosure, and turning to the right, they headed towards the Cave of Settlement, where they would talk and finally each would place their vote within the solitude of their retreat.

"The swans may take their time to show their hands," Olor Ebon advised, watching the women pass and aware that her daughter was awaiting a reply, "and we must be patient in our stay. And yes, Shuma," she said softly, looking her daughter full in the face, "I have spoken with Malian."

"Then you will know that he is chosen by the gods," the wise woman responded with hope in her heart, "and that this journey has been blessed by them. In their guidance, they have brought Malian here and in doing, have brought you and the rest of the swans back into the world beyond your bounds."

"The gods have had little to say in the past lives of these women, Shuma," the Black Swan sadly replied gazing out over the water with a growing realisation that the outside world was creeping closer, "for each has been abandoned by both gods and man alike and our borders remain our only protection from a world which we no longer recognise nor wish to acknowledge. And that is what you must come to understand!" Her voice became sadder as she stressed the fear and reasoning behind their decisions. "So we will wait for a resolution in these matters, and that is my final order, for I can do no more."

"Then I must see Malian and my friends," Shuma declared, aware that the time of talk between herself and her mother was at an end.

"There is no one stopping you," the Black Swan replied, equally aware that their talk was over. Looking around at the empty lakeside, she turned to follow the remaining swans where she, too, would cast her vote, and Shuma was left alone to follow her own future.

The wise woman found the darkened cell guarded by only one warden who stepped aside from the bolted door behind where her friends had spent the night and sliding across the bars, she opened the entrance to allow the light to flood inwards. The men had spent an uneasy and cool night in its depths, but the cell had at least provided shelter in its basic form, and the food had not gone to waste as the empty tray could verify. But the men blinked and shielded their eyes as the light advanced, and Shuma left the door open to allow the fresh air to replace the stale.

"You have asked to make presentation, Malian?" she instantly demanded on entering the room, and walking towards the altar tender, she continued, "You know it will not be granted, for no man will ever be allowed to address the swans."

"I have asked only to present our cause, Shuma," Malian replied, his hand covering his eyes to screen the brightness, "and your mother did not say no!"

"And she did not say yes either, for it is not in keeping with the swan's values. It has to go to vote, and if the outcome is no, then we will all have to pay the price."

Her frustration at this extra complication to their situation did not go unnoticed, and Malian became aware of the awkward position in which he had placed her.

"I am sorry," he said gently, "but I have need to address these women, and you must take my word that it will be given with respect for their dominion and rule in this land."

"The rule and dominion are not just over the land, Malian," the agitated woman answered back, "it goes far beyond that to the very core of these women, and I fear the swans will not take your message whether god-given or not."

The wise woman began to walk up and down the cell in her unrest, and the men felt it wise to change the subject.

"You have presented the doll?" Mentu asked hopefully, his tired eyes staring out of the unwashed face as he watched Shuma pace the floor.

"Yes, but that too will go to the vote," she responded, "and it can only go one way as far as the swans are concerned when a more acceptable offering in yourselves is to hand." She indicated the men before her as being more suitable donations. "They are voting on both now, so we must wait, for there is no alternative for your release."

"The door is open," Tragen volunteered in his annoyance and wandering towards the opening, he looked out, "is this not an alternative? Why not just escape while we can?"

"You can't escape the lake, Tragen," Shuma said, setting herself down on the dusty floor as the anxiety slowly dissipated and a feeling of lethargy took its place. "You are surrounded by the lake itself, and the enclosing caverns give no sign of any way out. No, we can only wait and put our trust in these women."

The group sat awaiting the verdict of the vote until eventually, a dark shadow appeared in the doorway, and the Black Swan stood there, the darkness advancing and surrounding her as she paused in the opening, while the veil hung heavy over the face already etched deep in Shuma's memory. Addressing her daughter, Olor Ebon announced, "The votes have been cast and counted, and you must return to the Enclosure for declaration." Turning, she disappeared and moving along the lakeside to take her seat among the other swans, she left Shuma alone with the men.

"I must go and find out the outcome," Shuma eventually said, rising from her seat, a fear of the results causing the return of her unease. "If the vote is in our favour then the quicker we are away, the better, and if it is not, then we must be prepared." Swiftly she left, the door closing quickly with a clang, and again the bolts were shot, and the men were once more left to themselves in the dark.

**

"The women are coming," the rider had said, and for many moments the elders had sat in unconcern and indifference to their predicament while Brann had waited beside Gallius. Slowly the harsh light grew steadily nearer, and their shadows were eventually cast long behind as the glowing brightness lit up the large group of swans who had come up from the Lower Lake and who now stood before them. All were heavily armed with their bows and arrows, and long-bladed knives lay flat at their sides. Each was wrapped head to foot in a blackness that soaked up the surrounding dark while the noise of their blazing torches crackled into the gloom.

"Stand up!" their captain had shouted, and Brann

alone had slowly risen at the command.

"You, I have seen before," the woman said, pointing her long finger towards the rider who stood before her, the dark eyes taking in the tall figure, "and I know you have made offering here in the past, and passage was allowed in its giving."

"Yes," Brann confirmed with a nod of his head, for the loss of men on their way south had been given in one calling to the same group of women at the Lower Lake. While a further life was lost days later to the Guardians of the Top Lake. "Our band travelled south on these same paths some months ago," he explained, "and we now travel back north into our homelands."

"I remember," the swan captain replied. "But that was then, and this is now, and again you will be called to make offering on the Lower Lake." Moving towards the man, she addressed her company, ordering them to attend to the elders. "Take them," she instructed, her voice harsh behind her veil as she looked both left and right, "and bind them all well."

The swans immediately swooped forward in their darkness, and the elders, fearing for their lives, very quickly found themselves on their feet and once more tied and bound and strung out in a line. Tarnik was attached to the very end, his panic dripping off him in a dank sweat that streaked his face as he hung back to the full extent of the given rope, with reason of putting distance between himself and the other elders who he now had cause to dread.

"You are called Gina," Brann said, recognising her voice as the captain kneeled to look at the still unconscious body of the rider's leader, for he now had chance to remember her spoken name as the other swans had called her all those many months ago, and in its use, he hoped at least for some affinity between them.

"I have no name to you," she harshly snapped before demanding, "and hand over your blade and knife." Positioning herself in front of the man, she extended her bow, the sharp-tipped arrow pointing towards the rider's chest, as she made her request clear. Quickly lowering it, she removed both weapons from the rider as he offered them up. Checking again on Gallius, who lay sprawled at her feet and removing the blade from his side, she quickly administered a swift, sharp kick and receiving no response, asked Brann what had happened to them.

"We have been overthrown by our own kin," Brann said in honesty and with no knowledge of the reasoning, "deserted and left here in our misfortune for you to find."

"Where have they gone, and how many do they number?" she quickly and abruptly questioned while watching the elders being brought forward, their fatigue and near collapse causing no patience to be given on the part of the swans as they drove the old men at arrow point into line alongside the standing rider.

"There are four of them," he responded, "and they have just abandoned us here." Was all he would say in answer, as he neither knew where the men had gone nor even if they themselves had been captured, and the captain was biding her time in the telling.

"Just abandoned you," she repeated grimly, staring at the man before her. And then, taking in the weakness of the elders as they stood in wait, she continued, "and leaving behind for us just the old and the infirm."

She gestured impatiently with a quick toss of her head for the swans to lead the men away, and they stumbled forward as their line tightened and caught wickedly around their wrists, and they were pulled, with no thought for their distress, past Brann and his fallen colleague. "You should be more mindful of who you choose as friend." She finished with a sarcastic laugh before

274

instructing the rider. "Come, you will carry your fallen or else leave him behind." However, she nodded at two of her women who shouldered their bows, and as Brann immediately stooped to aid Gallius, they came forward and with the unspoken help of the two swans, he raised the man. Between the three, they carried the still unconscious body into the gloom of the glowing cave which lay before them.

The cavern through which they slowly moved, the elders being dragged forwards while Brann and the two swans struggled with their burden, eventually came to an end at an area that split off into two directions, and here the group of swans came to separate.

The captain instructed the main body of women to continue their search further along and into the smaller channel where she presumed the four men had gone. While she took the remaining smaller party back through into the first cavern and escorting their prisoners down to the Lower Lake, she descended into the depths.

***

Olor Ebon arose, and carrying the woven voting plate before her, she ascended the steps and stood before the gathering of swans as they packed out the Enclosure. Standing alone on the dais, her black cloak thrown off her shoulders to reveal the strings of sparkling discs which hung around the graceful neck, she inclined her head and placed the plate at her feet. Straightening up, she held the two pieces of cream parchment clasped in her long fingers. The cavern was in complete silence as the swans waited in observance of their voting while Shuma sat alongside, the stillness adding to her anxiety and nervousness, which gripped her heart and brought a dryness to her mouth.

"For the vote of presentation, by the man Malian," the Black Swan began, "we have a YES! With the condition that it is given in public to all swans who wish to attend and hear his spoken word. And that it is given away from the Enclosure, for no man shall or ever will enter these walls." She indicated the haven which would not be tainted by any footfall from man before continuing, "The place for presentation, therefore, will be on the lake itself, and the man Malian will be set adrift to make his case, and the waters of the lake will surround him and sit in judgement alongside that of our own."

Shuma was stunned as the silence continued to enclose the women, for on hearing this outcome, she expected the swans to rise up in tumult at its significance. But neither movement nor disapproval was shown, and they accepted the vote with a recognition and respect for their own free will and for the system which they valued.

"For the vote of offering, we have a NO!" the Black Swan then announced, "and the presentation of the Shabti will not be accepted on this occasion. Therefore offering in the form of a physical man must be given, and the reasoning behind it must be understood by all." She went on to explain, for the benefit of her distressed daughter, that the life of a man must be forfeited to allow the safe passage of the others. For the giving up of a man's life in aid of his friends was seen as a personal sacrifice by the outside world. However, in their world, it was given as punishment and penance for the violations done to the swans, and the joy in the taking of these lives brought some payment for the wrongs inflicted by man.

Shuma was in shock to hear this last, although it had not been completely unexpected, but the realisation that one of her friends would be taken in offering brought her into a panic which the Black Swan noted as she finished her speech.

"The voting is done," Olor Ebon quickly concluded, tearing up the parchments into fragments with some finality as she let them fall to her feet, "and the resolutions reached will be accepted by each and everyone present." Looking around at the swans who sat before her, she then finished by saying, "The presentation will take place this afternoon on the lake, and you must make your own judgement to attend or not." Stepping down from the platform and wrapping the cloak around her, she slowly approached the woman who looked back at her with her own eyes, and quickly taking her arm, she led her daughter out of the Enclosure.

"The votes will not all be to your liking, Shuma," the Black Swan said as they exited the Enclosure's doorway, "but they must be respected as the swans themselves respect them."

"The first vote I can accept and be thankful, and I respect the charge that it must be given in the open. But for the other, I have great grief and have no heart to tell my friends of the decision made."

"Let us first hear what your friend has to say," her mother finally said. "Then you can all make a decision on the second vote. But Shuma, you must understand our votes are binding and will be honoured in their practice. Have no doubt about it, a man's life will be taken!"

***

Malian was brought out into the light, and the Lower Lake once again lay before him with its afternoon brightness gleaming across the dark waters as ahead of him, a raft-like pontoon had been brought to the lake's edge. Here the altar tender was escorted onto the unsteady platform where he was left, the tethering ropes allowing some stability as the raft was pushed out and moved across the darkness before the limit of the lines were reached, and the raft came to a halt. The lake now surrounded him, although he was only a short distance from the bank. However, the meaning of that did not go unnoticed, for he already felt adrift and apart from the community of women who had gathered as a black ribbon along the lake's margin.

To his front, the swans had congregated along the water's edge, and some stood with their backs to Malian in their show of defiance but with an understanding that they would listen to his words though neither looking at nor acknowledging his presence. Many others stood clothed head to toe in their dress, heads covered completely by the dark veils hiding their gaze, which looked at the man who dared to stand before them. Again, there was a silence, and the lake itself held its breath as the altar tender began his appeal to the audience which had gathered.

"Your presence here gives me much hope," Malian began, his voice breaking the quietness which filled the basin surrounding him, "for I feared that I would be addressing an empty shoreline and my words would have gone unheard except by the wind, which ripples the water." He paused to look along the shore for the wise woman in the dark line up, and seeing the uncovered head of the tall figure near the jetty he felt supported and reassured in her presence. "I have been given a task by the gods," he continued, "and through them, they have guided me here to your lake. First, though, you must understand why the task was given in the first place." Malian then spoke in detail of the stealing of *Amaunet* with its immediate impact on his valley and its people, and in so doing, he repeated and strengthened the words spoken by Shuma in her own presentation earlier that day.

"Nevertheless," he continued as he finished his report and looked intently at the figures who stood silently before him, "my main address is to show to you that the gods have appointed me with this task. And with their blessing, I have been entrusted with a hopeful resolution to the catastrophe which has befallen my people. I here give evidence of their judgement."

Opening his robes, Malian exposed the *Shen* Staff, which had hung undiscovered around his neck, the golden ring of the amulet catching the brightness as it gleamed in the light thrown up from the waters which lay before him. While a vast sweep of brilliance cast itself forward over the swans as they stood on the shoreline, covering them all in its radiance.

"The great god *Horus* gave me this for my own protection," he declared, lifting the ring from his chest and holding it forward in presentation, "and with this, I have no fear for my own life, for no harm can come to me while I possess this staff."

The silence deepened, and the whole lake became still in its watchfulness as the flat water became calmed along its edge, and the swans, enclosed and suspended in the brightness, felt their very breath was a violation on the earth and its creation, and within themselves, they felt a growing unease of their own destruction.

"Know now that for you and all here and those towns and cities away beyond the Sleeping Caverns," he stated, the watching women unable to look away or move, "there is a war coming. For the stealing and loss of the Icons will bring such disorder and chaos in the world that has never been seen before, and none shall be excluded from its mastery." He stopped as the calm gathered before making his demand, "You must all be aware of the change beyond your borders. Can you not feel it as it reaches its claws towards you?" His voice rose in anger to shout the challenge over the hushed lake while the swans stood paralysed before him. "We are all in danger, man and woman alike, and now is the time for us to show respect for each of our situations and come together in agreement. Our world is in peril, and the gods have given me their authority!" The simple altar tender now turned to face across the water. "Let me show you a little of the strength that has been given to me."

Reaching down, he gently touched the *Shen* to the stilled lake, and as he brought it back up, a small droplet of water, like a solitary tear, fell from the ring and dropped back onto the surface. It caused a small circle to form at Malian's feet. This slowly fanned out across the water, causing and creating a disturbance as it advanced towards the very centre where the goddess of the water slowly came into view. Rising from the middle of the Lower Lake, the red sun disk resting atop the headdress of the lion, she stood before the astonished assembly, her dripping crimson clothing hugged tightly around her body as she beheld the crowd and stood within the sky clad domain of her own making.

"I AM THE GODDESS *TEFNUT*," the dark voice said, reaching within the confines of the frozen and terrified minds of all those standing before her, **"AND I AM THE MOTHER OF THE SKY AND OF THE EARTH, AND MY PRESENCE HERE IS JUSTIFIED IN MY CALLING, FOR THE VERY MOISTURE, DEW AND RAIN CREATED BY ME GIVES LIFE TO YOUR WORLD, AND FOR THAT YOU SHOULD SHOW ME OBSERVANCE."**

Malian looked up, his fear held back by his own inner knowledge, as he faced the goddess rising out of the waters. Bowing before her, he held out the short staff, which continued to glow and burn in his hands as he explained the justification for her calling, and the women along the bank witnessed his blessing and favour, which the gods themselves had shown in this undertaking.

"The great god *Horus* gave me this staff as I journeyed through *The Duat*," he quietly said, his voice lost in the overwhelming sound of stillness, "and with this, he has given me in my dreams the insight to call upon you in my need, for he is the child of the earth and sky and in that, is the outcome of your being and sits alongside you in the heavens."

"YET I AM MUCH OLDER THAN HE," the voice came directly into Malian's mind, **"AND MY POWERS AND ABILITIES ARE, AND ALWAYS WILL BE, FUNDAMENTAL TO YOUR VERY EXISTENCE. FOR WITHOUT WATER, YOU WILL ALL CEASE TO EXIST...AND FOR THAT, YOU OWE ME TRIBUTE AND RECOGNITION!"** Straightening up, Malian beheld the power of the goddess as she extended her hand, and gently touching the burning *Shen* Staff with her fingertip, she extinguished the light that Malian held, and a complete and utter darkness took its place over the lake and over the women who in the witnessing could now testify the man who stood before them.

*** *** ***

On leaving behind both Gallius and Brann and the elders, Roth had immediately taken the lead and been quick to find the second of the glow-worm lit caverns. He knew by reasoning of their journey south that the first would take them back towards the Lower Lake before branching off through the caves, while this second cavern would offer the chance of bypassing the water altogether and hopefully evading the women who patrolled the lower reaches. The horses, however, were proving a challenge, for the tunnels were low, and the pressure felt within them as they moved downwards caused the animals to become skittish even though they remained blindfold, and the riders held the animals tight to stop them from bolting.

Roth had been in the lead for many hours, the dimly lit tunnels constantly heading down, while the brothers followed closely behind, with Statte bringing up the rear. And as the tight tunnels twisted around, they finally arrived at a cold cavern where the walls ran heavy and wet with moisture, causing the whole area to stink of a dampness not seen or felt in the upper levels. The glowing lights here clustered towards the centre of the roof leaving a darkness to fill out the corners, shrinking the vast cavern down to a mere strip of brightness that navigated its way along the middle.

"We'll rest back up the tunnel," he said on noting the smell and aware of another pervasive stench that he could not recognise, "it's too cold and wet here but, we can rest for a short while and then move on quickly through."

The men were quick to agree. The need to be away and out of the Sleeping Caverns had become uppermost in their minds, and the stop was planned to be short and brief. While they paused, the brothers had their chance to approach their newly appointed leader and make their demands known, for the witnessing of Gallius' downfall had brought the Icon to their attention, and with that, the reasoning behind their treachery had not gone unnoticed.

"Well, let's see it," Marke challenged, the idea of Roth as leader sitting well for the older brother. He had never felt easy with Gallius' lead, and Roth was at least one of their own kind and of their own choosing. "Let's see this statue that's paying for our service."

Having a need to keep the men contented for the moment, Roth removed the Icon from his pack and unfolded the snake-headed figure for all to see. The dim light of the slowly moving ceiling lights thankfully gave little justice to the small golden statue which he presented, and he was pleased that the interest quickly became confined to its monetary value.

"Must be worth quite a bit," Rogan ventured, touching the solid coldness which radiated from the figure, "and the market for gold is always in a man's favour."

"It's ugly," Marke noted, and grabbing the Icon from Roth, he weighed the heaviness in his dirty hands before concluding, "but there is good value by my judgement, and split four ways should make us some wealth for our efforts." Handing the figure back to Roth, the leader quickly rewrapped the figure before standing and calling the briefest of rests to a close.

"Right, let's move on," he instructed, hoisting his pack again and gathering together the horses, "we should be soon getting closer to the lower limits, and I have need of some fresh air."

The dank, wet cavern through which they moved closed itself around them in its oppressiveness, and the strip of lights which guided them through the gloom eventually stopped at a low overhang between two walls that led into yet another cave. This one was once again brightly lit across its whole ceiling, and the damp which had crept into their bones as they passed through the previous cave did not follow them through. The men and their horses then briefly stopped as an awareness of a soft current, blowing in from the left-hand side, gave the hope of an end to their captivity and darkness, with the promising feeling of freshness and greenery in its gentle breeze.

CHAPTER SIXTEEN

The darkness had slowly taken its time in lifting, and in its place, a heavy downpour of unexpected rain had replaced the brilliance of the afternoon sunshine which had first greeted Malian on the departure from his prison. The altar tender, now that the dark had gradually dispersed, was then hastily pulled in on his platform as the tremendous rainstorm with its governing clouds swept across the Sleeping Caverns. Shuma helped him alight the raft before escorting him back into the safety and dryness of where his friends sat in anxious wait. Here the three men welcomed him back, for the voice of the goddess had not gone unnoticed even in the depths of their prison, and Malian was quick to enlighten them on her invocation. Even so, he still remained unsure of how the swans would react and if they would accept what their own eyes told them, and there was a continued uncertainty over their future.

With this also in mind, Shuma had immediately headed for the Enclosure after returning Malian to his cell, the door again being locked tightly behind as the wise woman departed. Running back towards the water's edge, she found it empty as none of the swans had remained standing along the rain-washed boundaries of the Lower Lake. The sudden deluge that had descended upon the waters had instantly seen the women seeking shelter and sanctuary in their Enclosure. And here a great shock had descended upon all of them as both their ideology and way of life were brought into dispute.

The water goddess *Tefnut* had appeared before them, brought into being by a mere man, and the very thought seemed improbable and beyond the understanding and acceptance of the swans. Some had instantly called it trickery and the creation of a shaman. Standing in their rain-soaked clothes upon the dais, they renounced the vision as simple illusion and too unbelievable for words, although their voices shook as they spoke, and their uncertainty was noticeable. While others sat in quietness and contemplation of the known actuality which had played out before their eyes. As they talked, the rain continued to fall throughout the evening and well into the long night, the heavy dark clouds reluctant to move away and unveil the troubled waters which lay beneath.

***

Further down the lakeside, above the cavern of Enclosure where the women debated, Gina and her swans had guided their prisoners through the last widening tunnel on their descent, emerging onto the shore where the night's inundation blurred the view over the grey water and the lake itself danced as the heavy drops poured across its surface. The returning guards, ignorant of what had preceded the storm and oblivious to the voice of *Tefnut,* had been quick to escort the elders to their prison cells deep in their own guardroom.

Here they had been untied and abandoned to the cold and dark. Theroc and Rusan, released from their restraints, had however, been quick to take hold of their so-called leader, and making their intense anger and displeasure known, Tarnik had received a vicious assault which left him pounded and beaten and in little doubt that more would be coming his way for the betrayal of his own men.

Brann had been led further along the waterside, and with the aid of the two helpers, he carried the body of Gallius. Entering a cave where a number of smaller, dimly lit chambers led off, they were also left, the door closing and locking behind them as the swans withdrew in their silence. The rider's leader remained unconscious, though the man had briefly opened his eyes as the rain fell upon his face as they exited the darkened tunnels. But the coma had instantly returned, and with that, Brann was able to check on his wound as the man lay ignorant of the pain which his inspection would have caused. Finding the blade's entry point congealed by thickened blood, and with no fear of any further loss, he let it be. Retiring to sit in the gloom, his back resting against the cold wall, he then could only wait.

Returning outside, Gina had walked back onto the lake's edge and, on seeing Olor Ebon standing in the overhang of the Enclosure further up, had been quick to approach and report their return with the captives. She also announced that although others may have gotten away for the present, assurance could be given to the Black Swan that they were being pursued by her best trackers. Olor, on her part, enlightened the captain on the presentation by the man, Malian, which had taken place in their absence. As their conversation came to an end, Shuma came jogging along the rain-soaked lakeside from the opposite direction. Finding her mother in talk at the entrance to the Enclosure, the wise woman stopped before the two swans as they stood looking out into the rain.

"There will be much discussion this rainy night," the Black Swan said, turning to look at her daughter, as shocked and confused as the others by the witnessing of the goddess, "and I shall need to address them. I know their talk and discussion will be troubled, and a strong head will be required to maintain balance and security within our bounds." She moved to enter the Enclosure but stopped suddenly and turning back to face the wise woman and the swan guard who remained in wait; she acquainted the two.

"This is Gina, Guard Captain of the Lower Lakes," she said, introducing to Shuma, the older woman who stood before her. "She has advised me that there are other men here, prisoners brought down from the Middle Caverns. Perhaps they are the ones you are seeking or," remembering that some of them had escaped, "they may know where these men are, and if so, an end to your search may be swift." She looked deep into her daughter's eyes.

"I will go and look," Shuma replied, quickly dropping her gaze. The immediate thought of finding the Icon and returning home brought more than a disquiet to her heart as she fully realised the circumstance before her.

"Gina will escort you, for I must attend upon the swans." And with a quick nod to the captain, the black figure immediately swung round and was gone, the dark cloak swirling as she disappeared into the depths of the cavern and into the confusion which awaited.

Gina briskly escorted the wise woman along the water, for her feeling towards Shuma instilled great wariness. Despite her being the daughter of Olor Ebon, she was also an outsider who had brought discontent amongst them and, with that, carried a fear felt by all swans. Quickly guiding her into the guardrooms she plucked a torch from the wall and descended into the back, where a wide tunnel plunged downwards. Moving into the depths where the prison cells had been cut from the rocks, the guard captain led her towards the locked and closed door behind which the elders sat, and as Shuma peered through the small, barred window cut through the hardwood, she raised the lit torch.

"These are not the ones," the wise woman said on seeing the bedraggled men, their dirty unwashed clothing wound tight around them as they blinked in the light which invaded the dark. "They are old men, elders, I believe. But I would need to speak with Malian regarding them, for they may well be known to him if they are from the city."

Four of the men sat together in the pool cast by the brightness on the dusty floor, but one, his head covered completely by his cloak, rocked gently back and forth while the others sat in stillness, an empty plate set before them. Further in, towards the back of the room, another man remained seated completely alone in the flickering shadows, his badly beaten and bruised body resting against the wall as his torn cloak trailed across the floor, and his crushed and broken hands lay inactive in his lap.

"What is your name?" she then asked the nearest of the men, and seeing him raise his head as she spoke, she indicated him through the grilled opening. "Yes, you, what is your name?" she demanded.

"I am the elder Theroc," the surprisingly strong voice declared. And with no attempt or willingness to offer any further information, the man lowered his head back to his chest, and the four returned to their inner contemplations.

"These are not the ones," Shuma again repeated, the agitation showing in her voice as Gina lowered the torch, "but I have heard the name before, and I will speak with Malian regarding it. Now, what of the others?"

"There are two more, younger men, one of who is injured. They are from a known group, for they have travelled here before and made offering in the past."

Turning and walking back out into the night's rain, Gina led Shuma along towards the Enclosure before ducking into the smaller cave where the two riders remained behind their cell door.

"We've put them in here, for they will be the first to be questioned in the morning. They did not inform us of their intent to pass and so must pay for their reluctance to provide offering," the captain explained. Once again, grabbing a blazing torch, she this time presented another to Shuma.

"We also did not inform you of passage," Shuma reasoned, looking the fair-haired woman directly in the face as the light was extended, "and we were stopped in the Middle Lake where offering was given and accepted. Yet my friends also remain imprisoned."

"That is because they are men, and they will remain confined until further offering is bestowed," the swan captain acknowledged. "For I understand the vote remains that a man's life must be given for your passage to continue, is that not so?" she questioned, looking back at Shuma with no great interest in the woman's misgivings. Her eyes held little feeling of anguish at the loss of a man's life, whether friend or foe. But with this thought once more brought back to Shuma's mind, the wise woman turned her attention to those seated behind the cell door in the hope of distraction from the concern that she was unable to face.

"You said one was injured," she swiftly said, glancing away from the coldness of the woman who stood before her, "open the door, and I shall take a look."

Once inside the small windowless cell, she found Gallius slowly waking from his blackout while Brann was attempting to hold him down as he fought to rise. The man was strong, eventually pushing Brann aside as he moved through the pain and was soon sitting upright with his hand pressed firmly to the shoulder wound, which had begun to bleed again. His head was also weeping, and the matted hair, which had become thickened with caked blood, trickled a line of fresh red liquid across his bearded face before it dripped bit by bit down onto the open shirt.

"Where are we?" he asked, his voice harsh and dry in

its agitation as he looked around. "Where's Roth and the other men?" He tried to stand, but the head wounds made him dizzy, and the cell walls spun violently as a sickness came over him, and he quickly returned to the floor.

"They've gone," Brann said, seating himself beside his leader and supporting the man as the sickness passed, "don't you remember? They turned upon us and attacked us in the Middle Caverns, and we have been taken by the women."

The recollection slowly came back to Gallius, and his anger at the treachery of his friend gave him strength to once again try to stand. The two riders soon stood before the wise woman while Gina held her ground in defence of the doorway.

"I am not one of the swans," Shuma quickly explained, seeing his anger. And placing her light in the wall bracket, she continued, "I too am prisoner here, yet given some freedom for being female and for my position. But my friends are locked away, and I wish to see them soon released." Pacing the floor before the two men, she continued, her voice showing temper toward the riders, "We are here because of you, for we followed you here from our homes in the valley after you had taken something from us!"

"Yes, we took your Icon," Gallius replied, giving no denial and in confirmation of their theft, while his bitterness and despair at his own loss could not be held back, "and it has also been taken from us too. That is why we were left, and the treachery within my own gives me great anguish!" He immediately sat down as the shoulder wound began to throb, the blood slowly oozing through his fingers as he held the wound tightly shut.

"Let me look at that," Shuma said. Coming forward and firmly removing the man's hand, she exposed the knife's entry point. "It needs cleaning, this dust and dirt will only contaminate. Still, let it bleed for the moment, for at least it may wash the wound, and the dirt will be expelled in its flow." Turning away from the bearded man, she then asked, "Can you fetch me some fresh water, Gina?"

However, the captain remained in the doorway with no interest in aiding these men, and the silence which surrounded her indicated that no help would be forthcoming. Shuma finally pushed past her back into the guardroom, where a bowl was found, and the fresh lake water was collected from the shore.

"Why will you not help me!" she sharply asked on her return, the water spilling over the bowl's edge as she again pushed past the swan. And again, the question was met with silence and a blank, vacant stare. Gallius' wound was then washed and cleaned, and his head was bathed, but the wounds would remain undressed and open to the air, for as the wise woman finished her cleaning, the Captain of the Guard requested her to stop.

"Enough," she ordered, "for the time moves on, and I must attend the Enclosure. Come now," she demanded, and turning away from the door, she was slowly followed out.

Once back outside, Shuma asked why Gina was unwilling to help her, and the older woman came quickly and sharply to a halt before the entry to the Enclosure.

"I have no love of man," she began, her voice harsh as she began her own story, so akin to those told by many along the shoreline. "For I will show you what man did to me!" Removing her robe, she turned her back to the other woman, revealing the heavily scarred shoulders before turning and displaying the deeply cut and scored skin that ran down her front, her full breasts pale and livid against the silver lines which crisscrossed her chest and rained down across her stomach. "My own husband did this," she said, looking down at her own disfigured body, "many years ago, when I was young and ignorant of the ways of this world, and nothing I did was ever right for him, and his belt was always to hand." Her voice held such hatred that Shuma trembled at its sound.

"That is why you are here then," the wise woman eventually said, staring in dismay at the maimed figure, "because your husband beat you, and you feared for your life."

"No," she replied, replacing her robe and once more hiding away her injuries, "I am here because I defended my daughter. For the same was soon being directed to her, and her young face and body quickly became scarred, and the freshness of her soul was tainted. My only choice was to stop the beatings." Gina then declared to the woman standing before her, "I am here because I feared for her life, and for that, I killed my husband. I slit his throat from ear to ear while he lay in a drunken stupor, and I laughed as the blade drew his precious blood and sat beside him while his life flowed away. And then we came here, out of reach of man, and made our home in the safety of the lake."

"Your daughter is here with you?" the wise woman softly asked, aware that the captain was unable to completely put aside her deeds, for in her disclosure, she was giving remembrance and recognition of her actions.

"Yes, she is with me," the woman smiled, "and she has recently joined the boatwomen in the Middle Lakes escorting the swan Anitta. You may have met her on your journey down," the captain said lightly, "though she keeps her face covered."

The two women moved on along the lakeside towards the jetty, where Shuma and the captain reluctantly parted. The guard heading back along the waterside as she returned to the safety of the Enclosure while Shuma stood for many moments beside the lake as she looked out into the night. Her mind was now in turmoil over the known decisions which had to be made by the many women who would deliberate into the night, and she hoped her mother would give good guidance.

***

Olor Ebon stood before the women, the unveiled faces staring upwards as she looked around their sanctuary, which somehow had become tainted without even a trace of mankind making its presence. For by the very witnessing of the goddess *Tefnut*, a feeling of uncertainty had been brought into the caverns, and their very sanctum of female safety and purity was now unsound, and it had been of their own doing, as many of the swans were quick to realise.

"We are here at a turning point for us all," she began, her voice clear and strong over the hush which had descended, "for in allowing the first vote to take place, that of presentation by this man, we have all witnessed his favour by the gods and in his telling we must accept and realise that change is upon us." She walked quickly around the dais, the flowing cloak hastily brushing across its surface as she addressed her women, "And change is what we must recognise and put our trust in."

The swans sat in shock and silence as they realised the enormity that faced them, for their safety and security and the very peace of the Sleeping Caverns was no longer a certainty, and as the whispers gradually increased, the women shouted out their fear and frustration before the Black Swan held up her hand and a quietness once again descended.

"What of the second vote?" a voice eventually shouted from the back. "Will that not be honoured?"

Olor Ebon turned to see Anitta, the Guardian of the Middle Lake, rising from her seat, and she slowly walked around the dais to stand directly before her and answer the question. "The second vote remains outstanding and will be honoured," she declared, addressing the woman who stood before her, "for the acceptance of Malian and his friends does not negate our binding vote, which took place before this event. With that, a man's life will be given in offering, by their choosing or our taking. Either way," she finished with certainty, "all will attend the Ceremony of the Reeds, and all will watch its outcome."

"The man Malian must then name their offering," the boatwoman replied, "for it is with his presentation that our security has been destroyed, and he must take some responsibility in the choosing of this man." Seeing the nod of acceptance from the woman standing before her, Anitta resumed her seat.

"And what of these others, these men that I hear have been brought down from the Middle Caverns, they too must make their own offering!" Berran declared as she rose and walked toward the dais, her announcement giving voice to others as she passed.

"We shall have one offering for all," the Black Swan stated, her hands raised to calm and bring finality on the subject, "for then the vote is seen to be honoured, and our consciences must be satisfied in this one sacrifice."

The swans then engaged in a debate for their very existence and which would, in its conclusion, see change coming to the Sleeping Caverns whether wanted or not. For the outside was once again encroaching on their world, and with the stealing of the Icons the threat of man, with his worries and his wars, crept ever closer, and the swans would need to adapt to survive.

***

While the discussion ran on, Shuma eventually returned to the cell where Malian and her friends were imprisoned. Once again, the door was unlocked for her to enter, but this time left ajar to allow some fresh air to penetrate the fusty and humid interior.

The wise woman's mind remained in confusion over the day's many events, and she hoped for some peace and quiet. But her friends, concentrating on the outcome of Malian's presentation and the hope of a quick release, were keen to ask if there was any progress.

"I have no news as yet, for the swans remain in talk," she advised, taking off her rain-soaked cloak before seating herself on the cold floor, "and there will be much discussion this night, and we must await its outcome."

The four men reluctantly returned to their corners, each aware that the time of inactivity and waiting was still upon them.

"Malian, do you know an elder called Theroc?" Shuma asked, stretching her tired legs across the dusty floor.

"Yes, I know Theroc," the altar tender briskly replied, remembering that he had last seen him in the Court of High Priest Set'al, "he's one of Tarnik's followers. How do you know that name?"

Shuma made clear to the listening men that there were other male prisoners in the cells of the Sleeping Caverns, five elders and two riders, all recently taken captive by the swans in the Middle Caverns.

"The elders have been separated from the other two," she advised, "and their health is not good, and one of the riders is injured, knife wound to the shoulder, but it's not serious." Looking quickly towards Malian, she straightaway saw the hope arise in him as he instantly recognised what she had said.

"You have spoken with these riders, Shuma?" The

older man was suddenly at the women's side, his face alight with expectation.

"Yes, I have been allowed in," she responded, knowing that her next words would bring disappointment, "but I am afraid the news is not good." She explained to her friends that these riders were the ones who had taken *Amaunet* and were therefore, the ones they had been searching for. But then a falling out in the Middle Caverns had meant the overthrow of the leader, and four of the other riders had taken the Icon, leaving only two behind.

"They just left the leader, Gallius and the rider, Brann, I think his name is, for the swans to find," she said, "and the five elders were probably going to be given to the swans as offering in the first place."

"Well, at least we now know that Tarnik's attempt must have failed," Tragen's heavy voice rumbled from his corner, "and we know the Icon is still with the riders."

"I was never in much doubt," Malian replied. "But I must get to speak with these two men. Gallius and Brann, did you say? For I need to know their story."

"We can't do much until the swans finish their exchange," Shuma said, a complete tiredness taking over her, "so let's rest and wait for the outcome."

The group took her advice and attempted to settle while the swan warden, eventually closing and locking the door, left the five in the security of the cell as she hurried along the darkened lakeside to the Enclosure and joined the gathering.

***

As the night had come to its end and the rain finally ceased within the Sleeping Caverns, the swans had concluded their meeting and slowly made their way back out onto the lakeside as the dawn lit the eastern border.

"Bring all of the men out, and prepare the boats," the Black Swan demanded, her voice echoing across the water. And the guards instantly obeyed the commands given, unlocking and opening the cell doors wide to let the men out of their darkened prisons while the boats of the swans were made ready. "Let us be away to the east," she declared, "and the Ceremony of the Reeds will give offering to the rising sun, and our Rite of Redress will take place in the light of the morning."

Olor Ebon boarded her craft, taking her place at the front while her four swan oarswomen joined her in the boat, and once again, the semblance of a large black swan became unmistakable in its portrayal.

The men, defenceless yet unbound, had been brought out onto the lake; Malian and his group passing the jetty from the left-hand side while Gallius, Brann and the five elders were brought from the right. Each, in their own way, took in the spectacle which lay before them as the Black Swan drifted over the water and the surrounding lake edge stood deep in a mass of blackness as the swans gathered, ready to board their boats. Shuma was the last to leave their cell, and joining the swans on the lakeside she looked upon her mother in the dawning light.

"We are here to demand your offering," Olor Ebon's voice challenged, addressing the men directly, "and we have nominated the man Malian to select and name only one of your comrades to be given up. In so doing, this will allow the free passage of the remainder." She looked towards Malian, who stood at the end of the line, the large bulk of Tragen standing at his side, as the honest altar tender stared back in disbelief at the request.

"You expect me to choose an offering," he quietly responded, his voice coming out as a whisper, "but of that, I am unable. I cannot name a fellow man, for that goes against my beliefs and beyond my faith." His tired eyes glared defiantly back towards Shuma's mother before he dropped his gaze.

"Are you sure?" she asked, her voice soft and slow as she looked directly back at the man, and receiving a firm resounding nod from the bowed head, she continued, "Then I will make judgement!"

Now the Black Swan, dark veiled eyes taking in the line of dishevelled men as they stood before her, extended a hand to make her choice. The straight finger slowly moved along the line, pausing briefly as it passed Tarnik before continuing along and then making its slow way back. As it once again approached the leader of the elders, the man suddenly shouted out, "I nominate the elder Claud!" And indicating with a broken, crooked finger further along the row to where the sick and wasted man stood supported between the bodies of his friends, he declared, "For the man is witless and his body is ailing, and it would indeed be a blessing for his soul!" The frightened voice gave word to a fear for his own life, and looking at the other elders, he initially received only the blank stares of the men as they stood in shock. Before a realisation of his words caused something to snap within the group, and the fury, outrage and resentment of his actions toward his own men flowed freely and with much vengeance.

"Tarnik! We name, Tarnik!" the three elder's voices rang out together in anger. Daring to move out of line, they stood before their once-valued leader there, pointing their accusing fingers as they rang out his name and condemned him with such hatred for the treason which he had shown them. The beaten man quickly realised his error and he fell to his knees, his broken hands covering his blackened and bruised features, as the Black Swan, seeing the slight nod from Malian, declared him as offering.

"You seem to have few friends in this world, Tarnik," she stated, her gentle voice belying the intentions. Noting the swollen tear-streaked face of the horrified man as he looked up in disbelief, she finished by saying, "But you will be going where friends will be plenty to find. For the Fields of Reeds are brimming with those gone from this life, and their spirits are hungry and in ever need of new sustenance, and your soul will not be long alone." The dark words spread along the shoreline bringing with them an instant dread, and the elder's leader collapsed unconscious, his body reaching out across the lakeside as Olor Ebon announced to the waiting guards, "Take him, for the sun rises, and the ceremony will take place immediately."

Finishing her declaration, the huge swan boat had turned, and moving off, it left the waiting craft along the shore to fill as the swans boarded their boats and the women took to the water. Tarnik was abruptly lifted from where he lay and cruelly thrown into the nearest boat while the men were also taken aboard, escorted by their guards. The waters of the lake then saw the exodus of the swans as they sped swiftly across the calmness of the Lower Lake, the oars of the many women dipping deep into the darkness. The far end came swiftly into view as the light of the morning sun, its brilliant rays gradually cascading down the caverns, slowly lit the surrounds which enclosed the eastern bay, and the flotilla of boats eased up and merged closer as the shore moved into view. The swan oarswomen, slowing their forward motion, eventually began to link their oars to hold their boats in check and to form a floating platform that enclosed the prisoners towards the front. Here the boat of Olor Ebon had come to rest, and there she stepped down off the front and into the lake.

Wading out into the shallow waters, the swan guards removed the senseless body of the elder's leader and carried him behind the advancing figure of the Black Swan as she walked barefoot upon the sand. After them, the swan captains left their boats, and each carrying their bundles of reeds, they progressed up the beach to stand on either side of the offering place. The bleached grains of the bay had seen many past fires, for the dark grey ashen bowls where the burnt and blackened stakes stood, endured and contrasted with the whiteness which surrounded the rings. But these the women had quickly passed by and headed to where a new stake had been placed near the very top of the bay. Here the Ceremony of the Reeds would take place.

**

Tarnik had awoken, and the feeling of his own paralysis coursed through his body as he tried to move, but his broken hands had been tied behind him, and a thick belt of webbing held his shoulders tight to the pole. Ahead of him, down the beach and past the burnt-out stakes of past offerings, the vast array of boats sat on the sparkling water, ringing the shoreline with the faces of all those gathered to watch as he stood bound to the stake at the top of the bay. Before him, he saw the faces of his own men, but the distance between them and the movement across the water blurred their features, and he looked away from their gaze to the two guards who stood either side, each holding a burning torch. While further back, the swan captains stood, their arms full of reed bundles to lay at his feet. Staring downwards, his naked feet were also tied, lashed tightly to the pole. Around them had been placed small bundles of dried reeds, their fluffy, seed-filled heads resting up the sides of his legs, and reaching his knees, they surrounded his body like the hem of a feathered cloak.

The Black Swan stood behind him, and walking slowly round to face the male offering, she placed the wooden Shabti around the man's neck before lifting her veil and smiling calmly into the face of the terrified man as the realisation of his own cruel and painful death dawned upon him. The women before him, she knew, would be the last thing he would see, and as she turned around to face them, their boats moving gently across the waters, Olor Ebon raised her hands and spoke to those assembled before her.

"The eastern sun will rise for its last time on this living soul," her voice descended upon them, "and in the west will go down upon his blackened and charred remains." She walked down to her boat and, collecting her own bundle of oil-soaked reeds, stepped sedately back up the sand before placing her donation at the offering's feet.

"Let the Rite of Redress begin," she announced, turning and raising her hands to the rising sun, "for in his suffering, our own misery and torment will be vindicated and assuaged." Her hands dropped, and she swung around, the wet hem of her cloak dusting the sand. She then looked at the bound man who stood before her, and in her silence, she knew that he would be in absolute terror of the expectation of his fate. Wishing to delay the inevitable no longer, she slowly dropped her head, and the swans moved forward.

The bowl of reeds deposited around Tarnik's legs was then added to as the swan captains, each carrying a bundle of tightly bound stalks, slowly walked past, depositing their bunches around the man's legs. And as the bundles rose up towards his waist and encompassed his lower body, the pyre was lit from the bottom as the two swans let down their torches, thrusting them deep into the heart of the basin at the man's feet. The excruciating pain was immediate as the dry reeds swiftly caught and crackled, and the orange fire appeared around his toes as the base burst swiftly into flame before slowly it made its way up through the reeds and reached his legs. His screams were beyond belief and echoed loud and strong within the caverns and over the lake, while his agonising struggles became more violent as he stood tied in place within the increasing blaze. The riders and elders being the first male witnesses to this ceremony, bowed their heads and turned away from the scene as many agonising minutes passed before the reddening fire had engulfed him, the roar of the flames taking over, bringing first a weakening and then a complete silence to the shrill screeching of the offered man.

***

The stop had again been brief before the riders once more moved on, the breeze tempting them to keep walking. But their exhaustion soon became evident as they stumbled forward, and Roth reluctantly delayed their exit, as unknown to them, the outside evening-light advanced and became night, and the rain had run heavy over the Lower Lake way to their west. Here they had stopped and sheltered in the prison of the Sleeping Caverns for the last time.

The next morning, as the swans had boarded their boats, Roth had been quick to move the men on after their rest. And with the realisation of an ending to the imprisonment of the caves, the riders needed no spur to break their camp and head finally across the last dusty, dirty floor and out of the darkness which had, for many days and nights, wrapped itself around them. Finally exiting the Sleeping Caverns through the gaping cave mouth, which opened onto a raised grassed lawn, the freshness of the outside world greeted them. Here they emerged into the light of the morning with the sun risen high in the east over the wet grasslands which lay gently sloping before them. The sweet smell of pasture caught deep within their throats as they breathed in the forgotten scent of fresh air, and their eyes blinked as the light momentarily blinded them to the openness of the far-reaching views.

"Leave the blindfolds," Roth advised as the horses were brought out onto the grass, "it's far too bright for them. Best leave them in the cave mouth and take the covers off in there."

The horses were reluctantly returned back into the gloom and left to adjust to the brightness while the sweet smell of fresh grass drove them into an excitement at its nearness. Gradually as the time moved on and the four riders relaxed in the light, the mounts were once more brought out into the day and stood, heads down upon the terrace as they pulled at the short stubby grass.

***

Below them, the grasslands stretched away east and west with the promise of openness and space while the winds picked up and blew chill from the north across the pastures before advancing up and over the Sleeping Caverns. There, the wind whistling around the eastern borders of the Lower Lake had reignited the still smouldering blackened body of the elders' leader before moving on in its rush as the remains of Tarnik looked out with empty eyes across the shining water.

CHAPTER SEVENTEEN

Silence surrounded the lake as the Rite of Redress was seen to be met, and with its implementation, the swans could turn their backs upon the burning. Leaving the smoking, smouldering figure of the elder high up on the sand, the women slowly moved away, their boats parting and circling around as the dipping oars steered and cut through the waters as the jubilant swans departed the bay. The men located alongside them in witnessing the sacrifice now sat under guard in a complete quietness, each shaken by the horror which had become firmly fixed to mind. And with the realisation that it could have been themselves blistering and blackening on the all-consuming pyre, the abundance and peacefulness of the lake seemed tainted and took on a dark and dreadful sense in its serenity. Even the reed-enclosed edges now held implication as in their remembering, their dried bundles had burst into flame around Tarnik's feet.

Arriving back at the shoreline alongside the jetty, the Black Swan, her face once more covered by her veil, stepped out of the boat and turned to watch the approaching swans in the morning light. Raising her hands, she ordered that the men should remain seated in their craft, for as offering had been given, they would no longer be kept prisoner on this side of the lake and would be escorted by the swans across the water to the far northern side.

"The Ceremony of the Reeds has been completed and observed, and we no longer have cause to keep you here," the Black Swan stated, addressing the men as the boats bumped against the quay. "We here on our lake, however, still have much discussion between ourselves, but you are free to pass and will be taken to the north side of the caverns. Food will be sent over to you, and there is plenty of wood already gathered. There you can make your camp in safety until you decide to journey further." The Black Swan stepped back, and extending her left arm towards the far shore, she gave leave of the men. The black-clad swans quickly turned their boats away from the quay and moved off out of the shelter of the lakeside, back onto the vastness of the water where the men, still with their accompanying guards, were ferried away.

Shuma's mind was in complete turmoil after attending the sacrifice, and as she exited her boat, jumping out quickly onto the quay, she followed behind her mother, who walked off along the jetty, the sandy edges of her black cloak dragging across the timbers as she reached the end. There, lifting the veil from her face, she strode off the boards and turned left to walk along the shoreline.

"Mother!" the wise woman called out, running towards the end of the platform, "Please stop!" Coming to a halt as the Black Swan turned to face her, she hesitated before continuing along slowly to meet the waiting woman. The other swan boats were once more lining the reed-filled edges, and the guards and the oarswomen, as well as the swans who worked along the waterside, had disappeared about their business. The lake itself had fallen back into a calmness and silence undisturbed by even bird song.

"Come, Shuma, I know you will have many questions," Olor Ebon said, placing her arm around her daughter's shoulder, "but we must again attend the Enclosure, and in doing, I hope you will get your answers." Guiding the wise woman forward, the two entered the vast caverns where the swans had once again gathered and Shuma, seating herself alongside them, watched as the woman climbed the dais to face the assembly.

***

The men were quickly deposited on the northern edge of the lake, the avenue of crevices and caves running along its back providing a cool, dark shelter. While high above, the enormous caverns topped off the arched openings and reached upwards into the cloudless sky. The swan oarswomen had been deft in their landing but were then equally swift to angle their boat off the sands and move away as soon as Malian and the three men were released from their guard. Here they had quickly dropped to the shore in their haste to make land and be away from these women with their need for punishment and sacrifice.

The second boat came in slightly further up, and Gallius and Brann, seated in the front, had been the first to step onto the beach, instantly distanced themselves by walking away up towards the caves while the four elders disembarked. Rusan and Petrus helped the ailing Claud to alight the craft and, on reaching the safety of the shore, looked around to where Malian stood watching nearby. Malian had then been eager to approach the elders, and seeing Theroc, who he knew from the city, he joined hands with the dishevelled man who stood before him.

"Theroc, it is good to see you," he slowly began, his voice coming calm after the witnessing of the harsh scenes, "we last met at Court, if you remember, and much would appear to have happened to both our groups since then." Looking the elder sternly in the eye, he was aware that the man who stood before him had once declared himself for Tarnik, but on studying the tired face, he noted the exhaustion which poured off the man and realised that recent events had been more than unkind yet had given the man a certain knowledge and understanding.

"Yes, much has happened," Theroc acknowledged, his

voice deep in bitterness for the past days, "and much has changed for the bad, and we have lost many men. This is all that remains of our band who set off with such great hope." He spread his hands to indicate the three men who sat upon the sand before dropping them in weary resignation.

"I need you to tell me about these two riders," Malian hastily moved on, and nodding his head angrily towards where the men stood at the top of the shore, he watched as the figures ducked down. And on entering the caves, the two disappeared from sight. "It looks like they may have encountered injury?"

"Gallius is the name of the leader," Theroc began as they both seated themselves alongside the elders, and in the explaining, he confirmed the facts and information that Shuma had already passed to them while they sat in their cell, and Malian gained some certainty of the man he would be facing.

"He's the one that carries the injuries," the elder continued, "for his own men were violent in their overthrow, and he sustained a knife wound. The other man Brann has only declared himself as a tracker, but I feel he's loyal to Gallius or he would have gone with the others."

As they sat in the warming sun, he went on to tell the altar tender the story of their capture in the Mountains with all the despairing days which had passed since, and all culminating with the treachery of Tarnik. While he talked Mentu, Tragen and Darric joined them and the elders felt straight away a growing security in their increased number. He ended with detailing their arrival in the caverns where the riders had been overcome by their own and again he confirmed what Shuma had said.

"Malian, these men may be the ones that stole

Amaunet, but they no longer have her," he declared.

"Yes, I know that," Malian said heatedly, his anger and rage gathering at a pace as he thought of the long, cold suffering of those in the winter-clad valley, "for Shuma has already spoken with these men and confirmed that they are the ones who stole our Icon. Yet even for that, they are guilty of the crime and its damnation which has descended upon our people, and I have a great need to confront them!"

Further up the northern beach, Gallius and Brann had found a deep semi-dark cave where the sandy floor gave some comfort for the riders to seat themselves out of the morning sun. Here Gallius was able to check his shoulder, for the wound remained open, and the pain felt down the whole limb gave little use to his blade arm. He flexed his fingers in hope of instilling some strength and vigour back into his hand. His head also pained him, and the haziness remained, leaving him with blanks in his memory along with a persistent ache that grew worse in the glaring light. The riders, now outmanned by sheer number, then sat in expectation of the coming encounter and the wait was not overly long as Malian, standing looking out over the lake, swiftly turned and progressed up the beach.

"Here they come!" Brann said in warning, and standing at the entrance, he watched as Malian made his way up the sand towards their shelter. The elder Theroc soon joined him to his right while the tall, heavily built warrior, his long beard falling down his front, strode grim faced to the left with the slim white-haired man walking steadily at his shoulder. The rest followed slowly behind.

Gallius remained seated as the first four arrived near the opening but looking up into the altar tender's desperate face, he stood to meet the man's fury.

"You are the ones who stole *Amaunet*!" Malian

308

shouted in accusation, the echo resounding back into the deepness of the cave. For the rage which had been held in check on first seeing the riders earlier that day was suddenly given its freedom, and his anger was unleashed. Swiftly advancing towards the two men as they stood within the overhang of the darkened cave, he further shouted, "You took our sacred Icon," his words spat out with such ferocity, "and you condemned our valley and its people to a cold and wintery death without any thought!" Coming before the riders, his fury was so great and unable to be held back.

The rider's leader then held up his left hand in an attempt to halt the progress of the enraged man, and his voice responded low and harsh as he stepped forward to meet Malian's anger, the taller figure standing over the small.

"You judge and condemn before you even know me," he said, with equal animosity, "for you are unaware of the choices I have had to make or the story which brought me to these decisions."

"And you are unaware of mine!" Malian strongly replied, and bringing out the *Shen* Staff, he held it before him and advanced upon the rider. "I am here with the guidance and favour of the gods," he declared, the staff feeling heavy and weighted in his hand, "and with the bestowing of this gift, I was chosen to recover that which was stolen from us and return *Amaunet* to my people." The men who stood before him, along with the four elders, had not been witness to the lakeside calling of the water goddess and had been oblivious to what preceded the burning of Tarnik and were therefore, unaware of Malian's given command. But on seeing the *Shen* Staff glowing in his hands and the light which encompassed him, they became mindful of his abilities, and the rider reluctantly but wisely backed down from his confrontation. Seating himself once again on the dusty floor, his decision to talk first gave way to his own sense of self-preservation, and he felt a growing need to gather all the facts.

"Yes, I will agree with you, but I feel we both have much need to talk," he said decisively, "for we all have our tales to tell. And all had our choices to make." Aware that the time to fight had passed or was at least on hold, he reasoned, "And perhaps now we must listen to each other and find some common ground to the situation in which we are placed."

Malian's rage slowly ebbed, and he remained silent as the rider began his story, and in his telling, he enlightened the men who had seated themselves in the doorway, to his own situation and that of his daughter, Daina, whose life depended on his return with *Amaunet*. He also told of the other Icons, already held by King Dedrick in his city in the north, and on saying the king's name, he struggled to recall a detail that he knew was of import, but the more he thought, the more it slipped away and he shook his head in annoyance.

"He's collecting these Icons," he was then able to confirm, "a number already to hand to my knowledge. And with my daughter's life at stake, this one would have soon been placed in his control." Speaking of his daughter, the rider's voice had softened somewhat but then hardened as he finished by stating slowly, "I only stole your Icon to save my daughter, and so you must understand why I must get it back and why I must take it to the king." Looking sharply at Malian, he made his intentions known to the altar tender.

"Know then that one of those Icons he already has is from my city!" Tragen's dark and husky voice rose up out of the silence. The bitterness unhidden from the men as he enlightened the riders and the elders of the devastation and loss which had befallen the City of Lights before finishing, "My own family, all gone, all dead and many more buried by my own hands because of this king of yours and his seeming need to acquire. While many more, simple villagers and fighting men alike, rotting away in their graves through lack of water and its goodness that our Icon *Naunet* had blessed my people with."

The large man then turned to the gathering as a whole and looking to reason with all those seated, he made his appeal for the need to act with urgency. "I must get *Naunet* back for my people," he implored, "and there must be some coming together on this, you must all see that. I know we have differing reasons for travelling north, but if we can each help the other, then perhaps we shall all be rewarded in the end." He looked towards Malian, where the altar tender sat slowly nodding his head and making his own decision.

"Yes, maybe you are right, Tragen, and now I too feel we must have a coming together," he agreed, seeing the sense that the man had voiced, "but we need to know and be clear of the end towards which we all work." He glanced towards the riders before continuing, "For me, that will be the return of both Icons to their given cities and also, now knowing of your own troubles, Gallius, the safe release and return of your daughter." He paused before looking around at each man in turn. "What do you say? Will you give guarantee of these terms?" The seated men took little time before each raised their right hand to confirm assent.

"Then, we have an understanding!" Malian said, extending his hand to the rider, who in struggling to raise his right arm, gave notice of the weakness which remained. "If you help us regain our Icons, then we will help you in your attempt to save your daughter."

"Agreed!" the rider quickly concluded, seeing sense for unity, and with a growing anger toward the betrayal of Roth and his own men, he lightly grasped the outstretched hand and gave his word.

***

While the men met in agreement on the northern side of the Lower Lake, the four riders out to the east made ready to move on from their short rest and advance down into the grasslands, where the chill wind remained unabated in its ferocity and strength. Before them, the tall grasses, which stretched ahead moved in waves as the gusts and winds tore across the vast openness, and the horses had grouped together on the terrace, putting their backs into the strengthening breeze. Looking at the collection of animals as they moved fitfully around, Roth swiftly came to a decision.

"We don't need all these horses." Taking the saddle from the nearest mount, he pulled off the bridle before pushing away the horse and letting it make its own way off the raised lawn. "Two each should be enough, one to ride, the other for packs."

He watched as the grey disappeared into the grass, its long tail swishing as it tasted its release while around him, Marke and Rogan picked out the best rides, the strongest being chosen to carry the packs, and the rest were given their freedom.

As the men left their camp, the grasslands were quick to accept them and their horses, and the tall stalks of green were parted and waved as they passed. But within moments of dropping into the meadow, where the softness of the turf felt cushion-like below their feet, they had found that the coldness of a wind had wrapped itself around them, and the gusts slowed their pace as they struggled forward into the long day and on towards the night.

***

The swans sat safely within their Enclosure, the witnessing of offering and Rite of Redress still cloaking itself around them with its feeling of gratification for a suffering handed down to man, along with a reckoning for past injuries. But the world for them was changing, and the once comforting space within their walls had been upset, and the Black Swan had need to provide guidance that she was unsure would be accepted. Standing before the assembly, her eldest daughter seated before her, she steered the forthcoming discussion towards the change which was approaching.

"These men will soon be gone," she began, indicating towards the north, "but more will come if they fail in the search for their Icon, and in the witnessing of the goddess *Tefnut* and our growing awareness of the outside troubles, we must realise that change is upon us and we must each make our decision. Our future sanctuary here in the Sleeping Caverns can no longer be guaranteed!"

The dark figure paced slowly around the platform as she looked into the upturned faces, and the images which looked back, scarred and unscarred, frightened and unafraid, showed her that there would always be a need for protection and refuge for women such as these and unfortunately for many others that would invariably arrive at their borders.

"We can remain here," she maintained, "confined within our boundaries and hope that these men who sit on our northern lakeside will regain their Icon and the world outside will return to its normality…or we sit while the downfall of society ensues." She looked intently around at the women before continuing, "Or we can step out from our borders and help to ensure that these men achieve their goal and, in so doing, secure our protection and retain, to some degree, the world which gives us our security and survival."

"What do you mean 'to some degree?'" the question was shouted loudly from the back. But many of the other swans had noted the same and had cause for concern for the words spoken, and Olor Ebon was swift to provide an answer.

"Change is upon us, whichever way we go," the Black Swan announced, "and even though some of us feel the need to fight flowing through our very beings, the lives lived here cannot go back to the days of yesterday, or even to this very morning."

An immediate commotion overflowed the cavern as her words brought doubt to the women, but the Black Swan held up her hand and, in the ensuing silence, said, "Listen to me, for in the first attending of this morning's sacrifice by these men, there must be an end to this punishment." Again the dissenting voices filled the air with this time some of the swans standing, but noticing their number, they quickly realised their minority and returned to sit as the address continued, "The Rite of Redress just performed on the eastern edge shall be the last seen at this time. For as long as I am Black Swan, there will be no more offerings or punishments for any man who wishes to pass through our caverns, and the lake shall no longer be witness to this act." The swans sat in silence as the tall figure who stood before them walked slowly across the raised podium until she finally came to a stop in front of Shuma.

"I have made my decision," Olor Ebon announced to her swans, "and that is to help and aid these men as much as I can." She paused before continuing, "Tomorrow, I have chosen to escort them through the canyon where the swift river will see them quickly on their way down toward the Great Waters and past the grasslands which neighbour our caverns. Hopefully, this will help their journey and make it the quicker." Stepping forward toward the steps, she declared to the seated gathering, "You will now each make your own decision and in so doing, declare your direction before each other, as I have done to you." Stepping down from the dais, Olor Ebon left the Enclosure to the gathered swans.

"Do you still have any questions, Shuma?" the Black Swan quietly asked as she escorted her daughter back out into the light of the day, leaving the remaining swans to deal with the burden of their own loyalty.

"No, all my questions have been answered." The wise woman smiled as her heart was lightened by the message received.

***

Shuma arrived at the northern caverns much later in the day, the men's packs and arms, which had been impounded before they were imprisoned, taking up small space in the bottom of her piloted boat. While the rest had been given over to bread and flasks of water, which the swans were quick to unload before the boat hastily returned to the other side, the half-light guiding them back across the lake. The wise woman had much need to talk with Malian, and carrying the food up the shore, she found him seated around a small fire in the cave entrance, where she was surprised to see all the men congregated more or less together. The two riders sat somewhat to one side, but the two groups of men had come closer, and the elders and Malian sat side by side, the firelight radiating up into the cave's roof while the wood gave off a faint spicy aroma as the smokiness rose up.

"Malian, I must speak with you," she said, dropping the food parcels at Tragen's feet. And unaware of what had passed between the two groups, she first glanced towards the seated riders before moving further down the darkened sand. Walking back towards the lake's edge, she turned to see the altar tender rise and quickly follow her, leaving behind the warmth of the glowing fire.

"You all seem to be getting on alright." Her eyes intently searched the man's features as he wandered towards her.

"It would appear we have a need for each other after our witnessing of today's events," Malian replied, glancing back up towards the caverns, "although that said, I'm still unsure of who to fully trust apart from my own friends."

Malian then explained to Shuma about the agreement reached between the men. And the wise woman understanding its binding contract with the shaking of hands was quick to pass on her news from the Enclosure where she told of the women being called to make their decision by the Black Swan. Eventually, she slowly informed the altar tender of the recent report from the trackers from the lower caverns.

"They lost the four other riders, Malian, but I'm sure that is not a surprise to you." And with the passing on of this news, it remained that the Icon was still heading north and, with that, dictated the direction of the morning travel for the men.

"Well, we had assumed such would be the case," Malian reasoned before declaring, "and with that, we have come to agreement that we should start through the northern caverns at first light."

"But there is no need!" Shuma instantly exclaimed. And eager to enlighten, she made him aware that the

Black Swan, at least, had given her pledge to help. "My mother knows of a quicker way which should take us faster down past the grasslands which sit above the caverns. Tomorrow she has made promise to guide us through and down the river which leads on to the Great Waters in the west, and then we can head north up the coast."

With that, the wise woman explained further on the meeting in the Enclosure as they slowly walked the sands and returned back to the camp. Seeing no harm in this change of direction if it meant them moving more swiftly forward, Malian addressed the seated men explaining to them their new course.

"Tomorrow, we will not be going through the caverns," he said, quickly continuing, "the gods have seen to help in their guidance." Revealing Shuma's news to the men, he informed them of their new path and that he was happy with this change of plan before finishing with instruction that they should ready themselves for an early start.

"That route is sound to me also," Gallius agreed on hearing the decision to begin by first moving west and heading for the water, "for the way on our journey south was down over the Median Bridge, which crosses the Great Waters northwards of here. It's the only way back into the north in these lands, so Roth too will be bearing in that direction, and we may get ahead of him before the bridge."

"Good, then that is settled. We will be picked up at dawn, so we all must ready ourselves," Malian reminded them, and looking to where the men sat in their tiredness, he finished, "Now, let us collect our packs and let sleep restore our energy for the morning."

"The image will not go away." Unable to find the sleep which he greatly needed, Malian's mind kept going over the events of the day while the dark of the late-night surrounded the cave opening as he looked out across the lake to where the soft lights of the swans defined the southern shore.

"The man would have seen the same done to us if given the opportunity," Theroc whispered back from the far side of the fire, not wishing to wake those who slept around him, "and without any hesitation. Believe me, Malian, the man would have seen us put to death and would have delighted in its doing."

The fire burned bright between the two men, but neither was willing or able to look into its depths as the warming redness of the intense glow gave unwanted recollection.

"Let it rest, Malian," the man advised, "for our actions must now focus on tomorrow. And although our reasoning may differ from those of the riders, we are all on the same search and must work together as pledged." His thoughts then turned to his own men. "But I feel it would not be right to take Claud any further, although I cannot leave him here alone."

"What about Rusan and Petrus? Could they not also be left, for their fatigue hangs off them, and their weariness will only hold us back."

"That was my thought too," Theroc replied, "but will they be safe here?"

"We shall have to put our trust in the women," the altar tender said, "but now let us try to sleep. The morning will soon be upon us, and we must be ready for the swans." Looking eastwards, the darkened tops of the caverns appeared outlined by the coming light while out on the lake, the waking of the birds had already begun.

***

The boats arrived as the red dawn lit the east, and the men had risen early and assembled at the water, their packs sitting on the soft sand at their feet as the craft came into view across the lake. The boats numbered only two, and the crew were sparse, but the Black Swan, veiled once again, stood in the bow of the first as it rode up the beach while the other made shore to its right, the dark figure of Anitta standing in its prow. The men were then swift to board, each carrying a pack, and with a blade once more at their side, they seated themselves within the confines of the black boats where the covered heads of the oarswomen had turned away from their view. Shuma was last to leave the shore; climbing aboard alongside her mother, she moved toward the middle where Malian and Mentu sat ahead of Tragen, and as she passed the black figure, her mother turned and held out her hand.

"Gina has sent you a gift," she said, her voice coming light on the rising breeze. Holding out a short bow with its tube of arrows towards the woman, she handed the offering over. "She thought you might like it."

Shuma was grateful in her acceptance, taking it with the knowledge that it was given to help in the fight to maintain the swan's lifestyle more than to aid the men. But in reality, she knew they were both entwined, and either way, the need for cooperation was now needed. Seating herself next to the bulk of Tragen, she admired the intricately carved bow and the black feathered arrows before looking across to the other boat where the men waited, and the Guardian of the Swans patiently stood facing the front.

"Anitta, are we ready?" the Black Swan eventually shouted over, and receiving a short nod from the guardian, the front rowers pushed off from the sand before jumping back into their boats, lifting their oars over the side and moving off.

Rusan and Petrus, with the stooping figure of Claud stood between them, had now come down the beach to watch the men leave. And as the boats drew away, their goodbyes having already been said around the fire, the men were paddled away along the sandy shoreline, and the three raised their hands in good luck and farewell. The two swan boats then headed west with the rising sun at their backs, and in short time, they reached the end of the lake and could go no further.

Ahead of them, the sun-washed sandy colour of the western caverns fell into the water, and the boats came to a stop at a small walkway where the Black Swan stepped out. She was quickly followed by Anitta, who had that morning pledged her assistance, and both women had turned and removed their veils and cloaks, which they then cast down into the boats before stepping away from the ledge. The swan oarswomen did not leave their seats as their passengers alighted, but as the group disappeared behind the cavern's wall, they slowly moved away, turning the craft around before returning to the jetty on the southern side of the lake where the gathering swans awaited their arrival.

The rapid, fast-flowing underground stream had come as a complete surprise to the men, for the western end of the lake where the boats had come to rest appeared to stop at the embankment. But this only hid the sunken outlet where the water was forced through under pressure, and which could only be arrived at by squeezing behind the boulders before climbing down the short flight of steps to reach its origin. Three canoes which had been carried up from the Western Great Waters below now lay moored before them and were light, sleek vessels to swiftly ride the rapid flow which descended on its course into the depths. These vessels, unlike the wide-bottomed lake boats which were used for paddling across the waters, were smooth and nimble, and each person could sit positioned behind the other in the narrowed confines, with their packs placed tightly between their feet, while a short oar was given to push the canoe along if needed or else help in keeping the boat's sides away from the channel.

Olor Ebon, Shuma, Malian and Mentu sat in the very first canoe, the Black Swan, seated at the front while Shuma sat in the rear. And as Malian and Mentu had each lowered themselves into the middle, the craft had settled its weight, and the foaming waters had crept up the side. Tragen, Darric and Anitta were behind in the next boat, Darric and Anitta at either end while the bulk of Tragen filled out the middle, his long legs stretched out before him to spread his weight. And in the very last, Gallius, Brann and Theroc each sat in equal spacing, the riders at either end with the elder seated in the centre, his feet surrounded by packs.

The canoes had then been quick to move off, Olor Ebon turning and raising her hand before pushing away. Instantly the craft disappeared into the darkness of the flow, with the following two boats quick to rush away with an aim of keeping up. There was no need to steer, as the channel in which they sat gave for little movement except forward into the flow, and the descent within the confines of the canyon was fast within the edges of the gulley, which rushed past at great speed. Around them, the water foamed and frothed in its confines, and overhead the roof was low, adding to the feel of enclosure as the canoes and their passengers flew forward into the dark.

CHAPTER EIGHTEEN

The night in the grasslands descended with little warning over the heads of the riders, its darkness almost instantaneously settling around them as the light rapidly deteriorated. Above, immense black clouds skimmed and chased each other low overhead in the tearing winds, and the four men swiftly came to a halt, although Roth had appeared reluctant to stop. Touching the token hanging around his neck, he felt the summons of the high priest and the need to move north deepened as an unnerving apprehension grew and the obsession to drive forward expanded in his mind and would not lessen. And so he called only for a brief stay to rest the horses.

The surrounds where they made their hasty camp, within the tall whistling grasses, remained constantly wild and windblown and through that dark starless night, the riders and their horses slept restlessly in the cold and uncomfortable landscape. However, on rising in the early hours of the next morning, it appeared that the following day would be no better and struggling again to move forward into the vast blustering territory, the men made progress toward the waiting bridge and their way into the north. And while they led their horses forward into the constant wind, Malian, along with his group had already begun their travel down the waters in the company of the swans.

***

As the boats progressed swiftly further into the canyon, and the noise of tumbling water became a constant, the roof line had suddenly expanded above the heads of those seated within the three canoes, and a lightness began to show, slowly falling around them as they moved out from the area of low ceiling. The walls of the canyon shot vertically upwards from the narrow pathways which lined either side, and the roof was open to the light through the split canopy, which rose high above their heads. To Malian, quickly glancing up as they emerged out into the gulley, it briefly reminded him of the Top Lake, where the blue of the sky had been mirrored, and the sound of the bird life had welcomed them into the Sleeping Caverns, and his heart sank, and he dropped his head as he thought of the events which had passed since then.

The journey through the canyon along the western river could not be given a sense of time for those who sat within the canoes for many miles passed as the water flowed fast in its descent. But occasionally, it had slowed briefly where the river levelled off before once more falling away, and on these few instances where the tumbling waters had slackened, the boats were moved rapidly forwards into the next passage by the short oars digging deep into the watery blackness. Eventually, they had again been moved on, with the flood once more carrying them along and downwards. The light, however, remained constant, and the sandy walls of the canyon shot past in a blur of rough-hewn yellow coarseness while the gulley through which the noisy water ran, fell burnished and smooth after countless years of erosion by the rushing flow.

Finally, the descending river came to an end, and the three sleek boats reached their finish in the vastness of the Western Great Waters. Here the foaming flood seethed and tossed around them as the gushing torrent moved out across the sea, spreading out in its urgency before eventually becoming calmed as it entered the basin which lay ahead. The boats had been thrust from the mouth of the dark canyon into the brightness of the late day and were slowly paddled with great effort out of the torrent and away to the side where the sloping banks of the Sleeping Caverns ran down to the water.

Here the Black Swan brought her canoe around, and heading toward a shallow outcrop of land, she drove the hull up and onto the waiting gravelled shoreline, where quickly stepping out from its confines, the passengers pulled the light craft out of the sea. Each of the other canoes did likewise, and soon all stood on the shingled beach. Everyone appeared wet from the spray and downpour, and the ceaseless sound of the deluge ringing in their ears was suddenly brought to a halt as a hush replaced the steady noise. The group collected, cold and damp, in the small cove after their ride down the stream, and this was the first moment that the men had been able to really look upon the two swans who had accompanied them. For the semi-darkness of the canyon had afforded some concealment for the women who, now without their cloaks and veils, stood uncovered and disclosed to those around them on the pebbly shore.

"Is everyone alright?" Malian asked with great concern, his eyes looking towards where Olor Ebon remained standing tall and dignified near the front of their boat. And seeing her face unveiled for the first time, her eyes so alike Shuma's, there could be little doubt as to the kinship. Staring back at him, she neither answered nor acknowledged him as she swept past to where Anitta had stepped out from her canoe, and in unity, both women had faced the men. The younger woman now revealed her heavily scarred and marked face, which bore witness to her inflicted disfigurement, and the wait for question or sign of compassion filled the space between the two groups. The men however, looked directly back, now aware of the injuries she carried. And neither turned away nor looked on her with pity, and the moment passed in its confrontation.

The group quickly put aside any differences and doubts and moved on to consider their situation. The small beach on which they had safely arrived did not provide much shelter, the smooth slopes of the Sleeping Caverns reaching down to the thin strip of shore. And Gallius, even though he was struggling with his shoulder wound and the weakness to his right hand, was not content to stop there, allowing only for the group to recover their breath before suggesting moving on.

"We need to get dry and make camp," he said, turning away to look out across the churning waters and aware that the night would not be long in its coming, "but I feel we should make the most of this day and move further along the coast before stopping for the night. It will make the travel that much shorter tomorrow." He nodded towards Brann, and each took hold of the boat, and as he strained to lift, they moved the light craft back towards the open sea while the others swiftly followed.

The canoes were pushed out into the waters, the first craft containing the Black Swan once more taking lead, and leaving the foaming outflow of the canyons entrance behind, the group made their way up the shore towards the north. Now the banks along which they moved gradually became tree lined as the sloping hardness of the Sleeping Caverns finally gave way to the softer edge of the greener grasslands. And as the slow dark evening descended, the pastures lining the upper banks could be seen between the windblown stunted trunks of thorned trees which sat along the top of the shoreline.

Eventually, as time passed and the air darkened over the waters, and the paddlers became weary, Olor Ebon carefully chose her spot to bring the canoes in where the shingle beach was shallow, and the boats dug deep into the softness of the shore as they landed. An abundance of driftwood could be seen lying scattered around, and Tragen and Darric had little need to wander far before quickly collecting enough fuel to make two fires. One sat near the top of the shore where the women could rest and dry off, and the other sat slightly further along and down towards the water's edge for the men. Both camps were constantly buffeted by the whistling winds off the grasslands, which coursed bitingly between the twisted trees before disappearing over the water, but the opportunity was given to get dry before a warming fire and the group hastily broke apart.

In the fading light, they were each given a chance to relax and look out over the waters, and Malian stood on the very edge where the Western Great Waters lay in front of him, its soft shallow waves breaking along the pebbles at his feet. This dark sea disappearing off on the horizon was of immense proportions, its limits unable to be seen as they stretched off westwards into both the north and the south, and as the coastal margins expanded from each other, they vanished out of view. Away off to the north, a hazy light indicated the nearest borders, but its scope could not be guessed at, and Malian turned to look along the stretch of shingle towards the direction of their travel. He knew the Median Bridge awaited them, unseen at this distance but sitting crossways over the waters linking the two banks of the north and south.

Eventually, the light faded out altogether, the view retreating beyond sight, and the altar tender, his feet cold against the slippery wet shingle, returned to the brightness of the men's camp. Here he saw that Gallius and Brann were continuing to keep their own council, the men sitting close to the fire while allowing some space to fall between themselves and the others. The remaining men had already seated themselves alongside the elder, and Malian quickly joined them around the warming blaze. His mind was now made up on the coming day and also clear on a decision that had been bothering him. Sitting down between Mentu and Theroc, he held his hands towards the warmth as the night gathered around.

"I think we may be in front by the morning, Malian," the scribe eventually said, wrapping his cloak around him and pulling the hood up to keep off the wind, "and we should have certainly saved a few days on the journey, don't you think?"

"The travel down the river has certainly quickened our progress."

The altar tender warmed his feet at the hot flames, and going quiet for many moments, he let the dark of the evening settle around his shoulders. Suddenly he raised his head and stated, "I don't know how you will all feel about this, but I think we must soon have a change in our leadership." He paused briefly, noting the questioning looks of those around, "And I propose we should leave the future command to Gallius!" His voice had dropped slightly as he made the suggestion, and the immediate lack of support or agreement confirmed what he expected, that there would be opposition to this. Feeling the need to justify his proposal, especially where Tragen was concerned, he continued, "We shall tomorrow be entering the northern lands known well to him," he said, looking directly into Tragen's furious face, "and we should allow him to take lead and in doing so we can all achieve our aims. However," he reminded, "we must never forget that we still have our own say in matters and we shouldn't feel that we are being prevented from that."

The men remained uneasy as he finished, for to them, Tragen's anger and bitterness in the loss of his family and many of his folk was equal to that of their own disaster and all that had befallen them since. And with that, it meant for an uneasy alliance between themselves and the two men who had caused the tragedy brought upon The Vallenti. The very thought of these raiders taking lead seemed outrageous, but Malian realised that further talk was required, and eventually, he knew that with some thought and foresight, common sense would make itself known. So for now, he continued the discussion with the hope of resolving the discontent and accomplishing the desired goal.

While they talked, Shuma had left behind the two swans alone at the top of the shore, and appearing out of the darkness, her shrouded figure arriving ghost-like behind the shoulders of Tragen, she sat herself down between Malian and Mentu while the men carried on with their argument. Eventually, tired of the talk, she left them to their debate and wandered the short distance towards where the two riders sat in the boundaries of the flickering light of fire.

"How's the shoulder?" she asked, seating herself across from the tall rider, "Would you like me to look at it?"

Gallius' right shoulder and arm had been paining him all day, and the exertion of attempting to paddle the canoe had brought upon a sharp cramp that bit into the muscles of his back and arm. But he quickly removed his shirt for the wise woman to check the wound, and lifting his shoulder, he aimed to demonstrate its range of movement as he felt the stabbing pain course down into his elbow.

"It's better than it was," he ventured, his face telling a different story.

"Yes, it's not too bad," she said, peering at the gash in the sparse light cast by the flames, "but the edges need tidying. The dead skin must be cut away to allow the new to grow." Reaching to her side, she removed the short blade concealed at her waist and moving back towards where the men sat around the fire; she thrust the blade into the flames before quickly removing it and heading back towards the rider. Making short work of trimming the dead, blackened edges of the damaged shoulder and seeing the fresh flow of blood underneath, she then checked the leader's head. Here the lacerated cuts had scabbed over between the long dark hair, and the swellings were gradually beginning to recede, and no action was called for in Shuma's reckoning.

"Best to leave the head wounds alone," she advised, brushing back the hair while glancing into the dark face which stared back, "but I think you'll be alright." Her opinion gave no grounds for much concern, and so quickly standing, she turned and walked away. And Gallius watched as she re-joined the men seated around the blaze.

***

In the night, the wind suddenly changed direction, the cool northern winds giving way to warmer westerlies coming off across the Great Waters, and the warm air meeting the cold above the grasslands immediately formed a heavy fog that descended amongst the grass of the plain before thinning out to a grey mist as it neared the Sleeping Caverns. Deep in the heart of the savanna, it surrounded the four men and their horses as they sought to find sleep while towards the coast, the fog also gathered. Then the wind had dropped over the entire area, leaving an outright calm and quietness within the smoky white canopy, which fell and draped itself around both the riders and the sleeping figures on the shore. And on rising the next morning, the groups in both camps, with many miles between them, had awakened to the mist.

"I think this will be set for the day," Olor Ebon said,

as she walked alongside her daughter towards where the men were stirring, "but I think we should be able to follow the coastline northwards if we keep close to shore." The mists had parted as they moved slowly through the haze before swirling and closing behind them as they passed, leaving fleeting, broken images in the chilly air. Ahead the sea had settled itself pacified and motionless under the invisible cloak of silence as the two women neared the fire. Here the men sat, and with the night's discussions having been finally concluded with the acceptance of Gallius, the plan for the coming day had been put in place.

The shoreline camps had been swiftly broken, the canoes once more heading north, but this time with Gallius' canoe in the lead. Keeping to the shallows, they could vaguely see the coastline as it passed their right shoulders, and in the covering mists which swirled around the front of the canoes, the tips of the craft gradually cut through the cold Western Great Waters. The banks which they followed were bordered by wood-strewn gravel, in some places many yards in depth while in others, just a short strip of shale defined the shore. But here, the thorned trees became more abundant, thickening out and becoming like a dense screen the further north they travelled until eventually the shore disappeared, and the trees crept close to the waters' edge, their roots holding the embankments together.

Out of the mist, the Median Bridge had appeared, its vast archway leading from the Western Great Waters into those of the east and beyond up into the cold of the northern bays where the ice floes gathered in the winter. The bridge was an immense structure of blockwork connecting together both areas of water underneath its span, and over its arch, it linked the southern grasslands with those of the lower north. Where it sat, its very position defined it as the boundary not only between north and south but also east and west. In the past, the bridge had been in constant use as the peoples of both regions traded their goods, and the footfall of both man and beast had been heavy throughout the seasons. Recently, however, the only movement had been of the riders who had travelled down into the south. But Gallius knew that this was the only way back into the north for Roth and his men, and as the structure grew out of the whiteness, his hand itched to feel the weight of his sword.

Keeping the bridge to his right and manoeuvring the canoe awkwardly towards the northern bank, he eventually brought the craft to a halt close to the embankment on the northern borders before he reached up and grabbed the exposed roots of the trees. Pulling himself awkwardly out of the boat, he disappeared into the misty undergrowth. Seconds later, Brann had also risen and left the rear, leaving Theroc seated alone as the other canoes came in behind. Moments later, both riders were back, having checked out the northern end of the bridge and its enclosing stand of trees.

"All clear!" Gallius reported, and seeing the raised hand of Brann in confirmation of his own search, he allowed the canoes to tie up alongside each other.

"Fasten the boats safely," he gave order as the three craft emptied, "we don't want them drifting and giving away our presence."

Each group had then climbed up the bank and entered the light mist which had gathered under the trees bordering the bridge. These trees were bigger than the hedge line of the embankment and were more like the tall, thin pines which Malian knew from the valley, but they were also packed in tight and had grown tall in answer to their closeness, giving a feeling of constant damp and a smell of rotting pine needles beneath their canopy. The area surrounding the northern end of the bridge, however, had been left clear, and the cobbled span spread out into a broadened expanse which was mirrored at its southern end.

"Could they have already passed through?" Malian asked, his voice barely a whisper in the cold mist as the group moved through the wood.

"No, there is no evidence of recent disturbance," Brann assured him, for he had already checked the path off the bridge and seen no signs of imprint, either man or horse, "so we must be patient and wait for they can only come this way out of the grasslands." He held up his hand as the group neared the tree-lined edge where Gallius stood looking out. "We'll make camp here," he then instructed, "but no fires." Moving toward where his leader waited, the two men walked out onto the bridge in the gathering fog.

The group now sat heavily wrapped in their cloaks, and their eyes were constant in watching from within the border of the trees, for they knew the men would be approaching, and if not that day, then possibly the next. No fire was lit, and the cold mist wrapped around them, giving them their cover while a thicker dense fog drifted off the water and collected on and under the bridge obscuring its view. In each place, the sense of timelessness gave a heightened feeling to the delay, and Tragen became irritated in his idleness and was unable to just sit and wait.

"I think I'll go and check out the other side." Picking up his blade, he disappeared off into the fog.

***

In the grasslands, the four men had continued to head north but had now taken to leading their horses, for the

332

heavy mist and stillness which had met them on rising, had given little visibility. The ground, although still soft and springy, was soon riddled with unseen holes, and scrapes of animal activity, and the horses had begun to stumble in their weariness. The mist had chilled the men to the bone, their fingers stiff as they held the reins, and the silence around them took on its own shadowy character as it replaced the torrential winds which had so far accompanied them.

The dense fog went on forever, but slowly, as a light breeze was beginning to be felt, it began to darken before them as the southern end of the bridge gradually came into view. Here the surrounding trees were packed just as tightly as the ones on the northern side as they slowly emerged to guide the riders on and through into the clearing, and the men's hearts felt a sudden lift as the entranceway back into their homelands of the north was finally reached.

The expanse of cobbles was soon before them, and they quickened their pace to reach the overpass which lay above the water. But as they arrived at the edge, a figure at the other end of the bridge appeared ghostlike out of the rising mist and the riders, alarmed to see someone there, brought the horses to a stop within the clearing. Roth, Rogan and Statte handed their horses to Marke, who was now ordered to wait, and while the man struggled with the nervous mounts, the three advanced out onto the bridge. The fog which had gathered around and under the archway now began to shred, and thin wisps of white mist moved in the invisible breeze as the men stepped forward and across the span, and over the bridge, the opposing figure did the same.

"It's Gallius!" Rogan shouted in astonishment and with great anger, as the leader he thought dead suddenly emerged from the mist and was recognised standing before them. "I told you we should have finished him!" he growled, and drawing his sword, he swiftly armed himself for confrontation. Roth and Statte also pulled out their blades, and positioning themselves further apart across the bridge, they began to approach the solitary man standing in advance of them and who barred their way north.

Suddenly a violent disturbance near the horses caused the three men to stop abruptly, and turning back, they saw the attack on Marke as the bulk of the huge warrior, his blade held ready, emerged rising out of the mist from under the bridge. Tragen was upon the man before he could realise, and Marke had instinctively released his hold of the horses as his hand went to his side. But he was not quick enough, and his sword and knife would go unused as the warrior bellowed his bottled-up rage. Releasing the full force of the anger at his own terrible loss and misfortune, which had been held back for so long, he swung around with his sword catching the surprised man across the shoulder and slicing open his clothing. The sharpened edge bit deep into the skin of the neck, whereupon the man swore in fury and pain.

The blade then came back and tore across the other side of his body, slashing at the hands raised in defence and delivering cruel and brutal injuries. Rotating upwards, the sharpened edge caught and split open the lower part of the man's jaw, and with blood pouring across his chest Marke fell forward, his useless hands instinctively going to his wounded face, while he collapsed to his knees at the feet of the attacker. The downed man then turned his head upwards, and Tragen stood over him as he brought the blade back to his waist. Looking into the stricken man's eyes before stepping his right foot back to give more impetus, he pivoted around and, with such assault, delivered the long blade across in one easy motion, completely slicing through the neck of the man whose body crumbled and collapsed blood-soaked to the ground. Stooping to pick up the head and feeling no pity in his actions, he roughly grasped the thickened hair, and turning towards where the men stood transfixed on the walkway, he marched forward before tossing it down across the bridge where it rolled uncontrollably along the cobbles before coming to a stop.

In the immediate instant of seeing his brother's severed head, Rogan had reacted and screaming toward the warrior, his blade held firmly at the ready, he tore towards Tragen across the blood-streaked cobbles.

Their blades had instantly met, Tragen holding his blood-stained sword out and across his body to throw off the advancing stroke of Rogan's frenzied attack as the two came together. The steel of their weapons clashed time and time again, and as they fought, their short knives were also brought into play, and each stabbed forward, jabbing and lunging as they circled around. Finally, Tragen thrust at the rider as he moved aside, glancing a blow across Rogan's body in passing before turning and plunging the knife through the clothing and deep between the muscular shoulder blades. The man was instantly pushed forward while the warrior delivered another slicing blow across the back of his thighs, and the rider fell crippled to the floor, his sinews cut through as the blood poured down through the slashed, gaping trousers. Lying face down, his blade useless beneath his body, the man was now at the mercy of Tragen as he stood over him.

"You will pay in blood for the lives of my people!" he raged, and lifting his blade high, he brought the point down.

This final blow came without warning, the long sword piercing the back of the man's neck as it severed his spine and his closing minutes came to a sudden end as his shortening breaths finally ceased.

While Rogan had sought to avenge his brother and had lost his life in the doing, Roth and Statte had turned back toward where their once-known leader stood outlined in the shifting mist on the north side of the bridge. Seeing Gallius alone and aware of his injuries, they were quick to move forward and make good their assault. But as they approached, lifting their blades to hasten the attack, Brann appeared out of the haze to stand on his right while Darric, his white hair shining silver in the mist, moved across from the left, and the two stood in support. Both held their swords in readiness, their short knives handy at their belts, as the two men on the bridge came to a stop.

"I'll take the scrawny one," Statte had said, lowering his blade towards where the slim, lean figure of Darric stood. "He'll be easy enough meat for me," he continued, his surly voice matching the look which crossed his face, and gesturing with his blade, he called the young man forward in challenge as he moved across to his right. Beginning with a direct approach, Statte rushed towards the man, raising his blade as he came onward, and Darric was immediate in his response. As they both met, their weapons joining with an almighty crash as they crossed swords, the power behind the younger man's style and expertise of fighting came as a complete surprise to the unsuspecting solidly built rider as he was propelled backwards by the sheer violence of the initial sword blow. And soon, he was realising his error in judgement of the skinny man. The full force of Tragen's training and his unseen gifts given while in the Light of *Ra* were then brought into play and soon being delivered down upon the astonished rider, and while they fought, Darric forced Statte back further onto the bridge and beyond where Gallius and Brann were coming together in facing Roth.

Here Brann had initially taken the lead, swinging his sword forward to meet his opposition's challenge, but Roth was quick to show his strength driving the tracker backwards, and as they disappeared out of the clearing and into the mist on the northern side, both men fought hard, and the clash of blades rang out, echoing in unison with those of Darric and Statte, over the bridge of the Great Waters.

The fighting was quickly over in both contests, Statte being surprisingly overpowered as Darric had twisted around, and reaching forward, the knife had been delivered deep into the neck of his enemy. The rider was then swiftly despatched by a cruel cut across the throat, his body falling to join the two brothers amongst the mist-covered cobbles of the bridge. And while Roth had rained down his blows upon Brann, Gallius had strode up out of the murk, and coming from behind, he took the rider by surprise, grabbing him brutally around the neck with his good arm and struggling with his right, he had brought his knife round to sharply graze the skin of the exposed neck, the blade threatening to bite deeper.

"Drop it," Gallius snarled, and Roth had immediately raised his hands in submission, his blade falling from his fingers as Brann swiftly delivered a vicious punch first to his stomach and then his face before roughly patting him down and disarming the breathless, bloodied man of his weapons.

"Kill me, and you'll never know my purpose," Roth gasped as the blood foamed at his mouth, and as his head was pulled backwards it revealed the bearded throat with its ring of sweat and grime which remained around the man's neck, "you'll never be the wiser, Gallius!" he finished.

"On your knees," Gallius whispered into the ear of the man he had once known as brother, and forcing him down, he let Brann bring the man's arms around, and the traitor's hands were tied tightly in his back before he was dragged across the clearing, his body receiving many harsh kicks from both men as they bound him up against an unforgiving tree which bordered the wood.

After the fighting, the riders were now all dead, apart from Roth, and the threat of danger was past. Tragen and Darric had been quick in collecting the horses from the south side, where the nervous group had moved back into the grasslands as the men fought. They had stayed together and were found only a short distance in, their heads down as they pulled at the tufts of grass. Leading them across the bridge and alongside the bodies which lay there, Darric was keen to see them unpacked and settled, but they were immediately met by Malian. Seeing the animals appearing out of the mist, he had rushed across from the other side, where Gallius and Brann were dealing with Roth and where the others had gathered.

"Where is *Amaunet?*" he breathlessly demanded, coming forward in great haste as the horses were led towards him. "I must assure myself that she is safe." Coming alongside the horses, he plunged his hands deep into each of the packages which hung off the straps. Eventually, his search found nothing, apart from cold, dirty clothing and meagre rations, and his distress was beyond belief.

"Where is she?" he cried out, looking at Tragen and Darric as they stood holding the mounts still and steady in the mist while they were searched. "She must be here!" his anxious voice rose in its distress. "One of these men must have her," he then reasoned, and rushing backwards and forwards across the bridge, he stopped at each stricken body that lay upon the cobbles.

Each time he emerged empty-handed before leaving the overspan of the Great Waters and racing towards

338

Gallius, and there, passing through the assembled group, he stopped in front of the beaten figure of Roth and raised his finger in accusation.

"He must have her!" he shouted on seeing where the remaining rider had been dragged and tied. "Search him!" he demanded.

Roth was immediately untied, and searching through his outer clothing revealed the light pack worn secret and unseen under his jacket and which contained only one small item. There within the depths of the pack, the Icon of *Amaunet* had been wrapped around with a neck scarf before being stuffed inside a thick woollen sock and hidden away. Malian gently and reverentially took the figure out and placing it on the ground beside him, he carefully unwrapped the snake-headed bundle with shaking hands. Casting aside the offending wrappings, he exposed the statue, which in her loss, had been the cause of so much death, anguish and distress.

The goddess lay before him, her red eyes looking directly into his and as he picked her up in his bitterly cold fingers, he felt a sudden warmth flood his body, for she too recognised the sure and certain hands which closed about her and in the knowing released her powers. Holding her up for the gathered group to see, he presented her to those standing in the clearing, and for them, the moment had many different meanings. However, for Malian, it was one of overwhelming gratitude and a sheer joyful happiness at her finding.

"She is safe now," he cried with great thankfulness as he held the cherished Icon aloft, "and she will be returned to our people, and they will once again live in her warmth and prosperity." The ruby eyes of the tiny statue flashed as he spoke, and the hard gold of her body glowed within the altar tender's hands as he brought the figure around, the encircling cold of the invading chilly mist appearing to diminish and fade back northwards before the warmth of her image.

But after declaring her safely found, Malian was then just as quick in once more wrapping her away and protecting her, this time in his own scarf, and the cold which had been briefly subdued suddenly returned. The group instantly sought to shelter under the very edge of the trees and make their fire in the clearing while around the evening darkened, for the night was swiftly coming upon them.

Gallius, however, had other plans for the night, for having searched Roth and been witness to the finding of *Amaunet*, he had again also seen the talisman, which still hung around the man's neck, and he had suddenly been transported back into the tunnels of the Sleeping Caverns. Now seated in the cold dark of the growing night in front of the rider he had once thought of as brother, he wondered if there was more to come.

"Where did you come by this?" he questioned as he took time to speak with the subdued man, and pulling off the token, he examined its intricacy as it lay in his hand. The lightness felt was no surprise for such a small ring of metal, but the intricate markings carried around and across its front and back gave it more of a complexity as the woven letters intertwined, and Gallius twisted it this way and that to make some sense of it.

"Where did you get it?" he now demanded, still getting no reply but remembering at last where he had seen it before. "I've seen one of these the very same around the throat of Dedrick, and the two must surely have some connection."

Roth had again been bound and tied up tight against the tree, and as he sat unfeeling of the chill upon the stone-cold ground, his blank gaze looked out across to where the fire was blazing, and as Gallius sat before him, he made out to be slow and reluctant in his misleading reply.

"Connection, yes, I would think you right to say that," he began sneeringly, picking up on the one given word, "for it is given with that in mind and also in form of union. But above that, I'll say no more." The token which had been roughly torn from his neck, the chain biting deeply as it was removed, hung from Gallius' right hand while his other grabbed hard about Roth's throat, the tight grip forcing the man's head back against the rough hardness of the trunk of the tree.

"Connection and union," Gallius repeated, looking again at the flat cold metal as he slowly tightened his grasp, "perhaps…but now what of your purpose? You are alive because you spoke of that, so be clear. What was your purpose?" he snarled, "Tell me!"

But even in his pain and discomfort, Roth continued to remain dishonest as he responded, "I was commanded to take the Icon from you by whatever means necessary and to journey northwards with it," he whispered, his voice constrained by the fierce grip which choked his breathing and he began to cough. "To go north, and I would be contacted on the way."

"Who told you this?" Gallius asked, "Was it, Dedrick?" His face was only inches away from Roth's, and the stench of the traitor's breath caught deep in his throat as he reasoned, "But why would he do that? There would be no need of him to ask this of you when I was taking the Icon north to him anyway?" Gallius' hand closed further as his confusion grew, and the face before him began to contort under his force.

"I don't know who it was," Roth lied, his voice becoming almost inaudible as his breathing became shallow and the coughing continued, "the command was given, and I had little choice." He passed out, and Gallius had to be content for the moment, but he was sure that the man knew more, and he would have need to question him further. Removing his grip, he allowed the head of the unconscious man to fall sideways.

While Gallius sat in front of the bound man and asked his questions, both Tragen and Brann had dealt with the men taken down upon the Median Bridge. And the dead bodies had been stripped of arms before being roughly carried back to the southern grasslands and thrown down. Here they had been left upon the green turf for any passing animals who wished to scavenge their remains. That job done, the two then returned to the northern clearing where the horses had been tied in the shelter of the trees and where the fire was flaming, and they had all gathered in its warmth.

Seated around, the group still remained in some separation, for Gallius and Brann had positioned themselves together, their backs towards the horses and where Roth remained tied. While the women had moved in closer to the fire near to where Malian, Mentu and Theroc had already come to rest. Tragen and Darric sat opposite, and here they had gathered the assorted weaponry from the three dead men and had taken it upon themselves to sort through and add to their own hardware.

The darkness closed fast, and the mist, which had never fully lifted, began to slowly drift downward again as the cold air descended, and soon the clearing was deep in its own whiteness, the fire lighting up the surroundings with its flickering flame. Eventually, Gallius stood up, leaving behind Brann to watch over Roth, and walking the short distance, he joined Malian and the rest of the group where they sat.

"Gallius, you have our eternal thanks," Malian said as he saw the tall man approaching, "for you have helped us in regaining our Icon." Reaching up, he clasped the cold hands of the man who had sat down alongside. "And now we will keep our pledge made to both you and to Tragen." He looked across to where the huge warrior sat, surrounded by his increasing armoury, before continuing, "So tomorrow we shall be going into the northern lands, which are known to you, and there you will guide us back to your city. We must now look to getting back the Icon of *Naunet*, and we must also save your daughter."

"Yes, and we must move on swiftly," Gallius replied, aware that he was taking this group into uncertain territory. But at least he could be thankful that they now had horses to ride before his thoughts turned to those of his daughter. "We should be in the city in three to four days if our travel is quick and we have no delays." His fingers nervously worked themselves across the interlacing characters of the talisman, and the light of the fire glinted off its mirrored surface. Eventually, after many moments of unsure thought, he turned to Malian and offered over the metal ring.

"What do you make of this?" he asked, placing the cold token into the altar tender's warm hand and hoping for some enlightenment.

Malian had some wisdom in script and its writing, but the scribe who sat next to him was more proficient in this area, and after quickly glancing over the disc, Malian promptly offered it up to his right.

"This is more in your line, Mentu," he asked, presenting it over, "is it something that you recognise?"

"It's very elaborate," the scribe said after some moments in which he had turned it over time and time again, "but no, it's nothing that I am familiar with, except to say that the metal is old silver and the markings are of ancient script." He handed the token carefully back to Gallius before quietly asking, "How did you come by it?"

"From around his neck," he said angrily, gesturing towards where Roth remained unconscious, the cold mist creeping out from beyond the trees to collect around the stooped shoulders. "And I'm sure I've seen one before around the neck of King Dedrick. I feel it must have some import, but my mind still fails in its thinking."

"Well, let it rest, for the moment," Malian advised. "First, we must talk of what now becomes of *Amaunet*. She has been returned and is secure in our care, but we now need to ensure her safety." Looking sideways to where the scribe sat to his right, he then addressed his friend.

"Mentu," he said, his voice grave and serious as those around the fire sat and looked on, "I am here entrusting you to carry our Icon back into the sanctuary of the south, and there you must await my return at the Sleeping Caverns. But I would not have you return alone." He nodded towards where the Black Swan sat in the firelight next to her daughter. "Olor Ebon has consented to guide you across the grasslands and back into the safety of the caverns, and Theroc will also be joining you." He grasped the warm trembling hands of the elderly scribe as he continued, "But if I should not return before the next full moon, then it will be up to you to restore *Amaunet* to her rightful place in the valley and restore harmony back to our people!" He looked down to where the wrapped figure remained cradled in his lap before turning and looking deep into the man's eyes and finishing with, "I know that I can trust you beyond any other."

"You can trust me, Malian," Mentu said as he looked back, tears brimming his eyes. And with his voice full of kindness and satisfaction in the honour placed upon him, he said, "I will ensure *Amaunet* is surely returned to her rightful home."

The small statue was then replaced inside the pack that

had been carried by Roth, and Malian reluctantly gave up the valued Icon which he had been entrusted by the gods to reclaim. Knowing that the valley and its people would soon again feel her warmth and generosity, he handed over the responsibility to Mentu and whispered a small prayer.

"And now I think we should all rest," he slowly said. "Tomorrow, our groups will be parting, and our headings will take us both north and south, and we may all be riding into troubled times."

The group made ready to sleep, but Gallius remained wary, and after patrolling the clearing, he still felt they had need to keep guard. Mentu promptly volunteered to take first watch, for given that he would be travelling south and away from any danger, he said he could afford a sleepless night and would rest along the journey's course.

***

Away to the north, in the City of the High Places, King Dedrick sat upon the seat of power, the huge granite statues of his forefathers and past kings staring down over his shoulder while before him his returning men, their tiredness hanging off their bones, had assembled and offered up their hard-won prize.

The Icon of *Amun* lay in his lap, the dirty wrapping of grey cloth concealing its features and giving little shape to the figure, and as the king paid off the men, he finished by quickly dismissing all those gathered around with a wave of his hand. Now alone, apart from his trusted friend Serdos, he carefully opened the cloth to reveal the seventh Icon which had come into his possession. Knowing now that he was only one step away from the eight, he smiled, and the surrounding statues took in his unbounded delight at the coming destruction. Holding the figure up, he looked into the ruby eyes, which stared back out of the frog's head and handing it to his high priest, he ordered him to oversee its custody and safety.

CHAPTER NINETEEN

"Is your shoulder still troubling you?" Shuma whispered through the mists as she saw Gallius irritably trying to make himself comfortable on the hard ground under the trees. "Would you like me to take another look?" Wrapping her cover around her, she left behind her companions and the warmth of the fire and walked slowly towards where the two riders had made their beds. Brann was already asleep beneath his thick cloak, the heavy snoring giving evidence of his slumber. Gallius, however, remained wide awake, his injury and many unresolved thoughts adding to his restlessness. Uncovering his shoulder, the jagged stab wound, although still deep, appeared clean after Shuma's treatment of the previous night, and in making her assessment, she again tidied the edges before covering back over with the shirt collar.

"It needs little tending," she said abruptly, standing behind the rider, "just keeping clean. Time and rest should see it mended."

"Time I may have," Gallius replied, pulling his cloak around to keep off the night's chill, "but rest will not be easy to come by for any of us." He straightened his right arm and flexing his fingers, felt the slow return of his strength.

"That I know," the wise woman acknowledged, moving forward and seating herself between the bodies of the two men, "the time now is not to rest. Tomorrow there will be a separation of our ways, and while we shall be quickly heading north, Mentu, Olor and Theroc will be heading south. Malian is putting his entire trust in the scribe to ensure the safety of *Amaunet*, while we will be putting ours in your leadership and your guidance." She glanced sideways towards Brann as the man turned over in his sleep, and then their talk turned to the coming days.

As they talked, the tall shadow of the scribe keeping his watch passed by many times before he eventually appeared out of the fog. Wandering past the fire, he approached the two where they sat near the sleeping figure of Brann. Sitting down before them, he rubbed his cold hands together as he peered towards the rider.

"Would you mind if I have another look at that token, Gallius?" he asked, with a puzzled expression crossing his face. "For the more I think, the more it seems familiar, though my thinking is unsure of its significance. Do you mind if I take a closer look?"

Gallius removed the token and its chain from his pocket, and handing it with little fear or concern to Mentu, the scribe swiftly took it across to the blazing fire where the others still sat awake. Looking intently at the ring of metal as it shone in the firelight, the intricate letters intertwining in and around the circle, he studied it again with an even more bewildered look on his face. Eventually, he stood, and with Gallius and Shuma watching his movements, he slowly walked to where Roth remained bound. Stooping over the traitor, he pressed his question.

"What is this token?" he quietly asked, pushing the dangling relic towards the face of the seated man. "Can you tell me who you got it from?" Receiving no reply to his simple questioning, he then leant forward and, with his clenched hand, brought the token closer before the man's eyes. "Tell me," he softly threatened, his voice changing to take on a more sinister tone, "or I will not be held responsible for Tragen's actions against you. You know the man is filled with rage and revenge, and he will see great satisfaction in your torture and suffering before he sees to your death."

Roth looked across to where the vastness of the warrior sat, his large body stooped forward, and the blade of a small knife glinted as it was sharpened before the fire. And in his remembering, he saw again the severed head of Marke with its grimace of surprise as it rolled across the span of the Median Bridge, and quickly he gave his reply.

"The king in the north gave me the token." And with that, he looked directly up towards the scribe, his face emotionless and empty of any feeling.

"You are a liar," Mentu answered calmly and slowly, "tell me where you got it."

"From Dedrick, the king," Roth repeated, his voice flat and impassive.

"You're a liar, tell me the truth," Mentu's harsh voice made its demand but turned to a whisper as the scribe sunk to his knees, his left hand creeping up unseen towards his chest.

Seated before Roth, his back to the rest of the group, he then slowly parted his outer clothing and undershirt, revealing an almost identical silver token that he wore close to his heart. Hidden away around his neck, it had lain for countless years, concealed from any prying eyes and unknown to even his closest of friends. Roth looked in surprise at each of the discs in turn, recognising immediately that in having a thicker outer ring, the one worn by the scribe was of higher status than his own. His gaze was then drawn away and back to the eyes of the man who sat ahead of him. The fire at his back was casting the tall shadow forward to loom over him as he sat bound in his confusion, but then Mentu had promptly straightened his clothing and, staring across, had made his final appeal.

"I will ask you one more time," he again whispered, his voice now shaking. "Who did you get it from?"

349

"From the high priest," Roth quickly whispered back, his voice low and barely audible, "from Serdos, in the cause of the Snake."

"Good," Mentu whispered back, his face close to the ear of the rider. "That is as I expected." And with a smile creeping across his face, he slowly asked, "If I release you, will you take it upon yourself to guide me safely back to the city?" His voice dropped as he demanded, "Do you, as a sworn Brother of *Apep*, give me your oath?"

"Yes, I do," Roth quickly agreed, his prospect of escape allowing for some hope that he had not expected to find before this meeting. "I offer you my oath, and I also give my loyalty."

"Good. Then stay alert," Mentu came back. Turning his head both left and right to check the whereabouts of the group, he quickly stood, rising tall above the restrained man and straightening his clothes around him, whispered, "I'll return later and we'll see to making our escape."

The two men, in their exchange of words, had now acknowledged the Ancient Brotherhood to which they both belonged, and its guarantee had been given by the ownership and sighting of the talisman. Trust and conviction in each other was therefore, instantly held beyond any doubt. But on rising, Mentu knew he would have to resume his humble role for just a little longer, and slowly drawing his wrap around him, he headed back towards Gallius and Shuma, where he once more became mild and uncertain in his manner, and Mentu, the scribe again approached the seated figures.

"Did you find out anything?" Gallius asked as he watched the scribe make his slow way back.

"I found out nothing further in the firelight," he replied, swiftly handing the token over, "and he talked only of the king." He nodded his head to where Roth sat. "But I have said that Tragen may loosen his tongue tomorrow, and that should give him something to think on!"

With that, he left the two seated together and resumed his watch, keeping to the misty edges of the clearing as he circled the camp. But his hands would not rest and kept forever reaching towards his chest, and he had to force them down and hold both tightly behind his back to control his emotions as he patrolled.

Pacing around the clearing, he could hardly believe his good fortune, and a smile briefly crossed his lips. For earlier, Malian had simply handed over the Icon of *Amaunet* to him, and the altar tender had entrusted him with its return to its rightful place. And this he had vowed he would do in the keeping of the spoken word. Now again, accidental chance, or something of that kind, had given him one of their own to guide him directly to the city and back into the heart of the brotherhood.

***

The Brotherhood of *Apep* was an ancient society, for the forces of disruption and chaos had always existed since time began and had been worshipped by man since he first stood tall upon the earth. And in the beginning of the world, they had once held sway over the land before the gods put in place their command, and order overcame chaos. The god *Apep*, his representation being that of a coiled snake, had been there at the beginning, for he was said to have been born alongside the sun god *Ra*. Where there is light, there is always dark, and where there is order, there is also disorder.

And the gods, on seeing the daily fight between the two, had sought to bring about an end to their bitter discord and the golden statue which embodied *Apep* was cast down, cut up and melted, and the golden liquid of his manifestation had run hot. The gods had then created and fashioned out of the molten gold the Eight Icons, *Amun, Heh, Kek* and *Nun* the four frog-headed gods and their counterparts *Amaunet, Hauhet, Kauket* and *Naunet* the four snake-headed goddesses, all with eyes adorned with gemstones. Bestowing upon the couples the four individual forces of water, invisibility, infinity and darkness, they distributed them wide and far apart, seeking to separate the Eight and, in so doing, break and banish disharmony and bring unity to mankind.

But man was short in his memory and admiration, and the Eight Icons, which in their giving did initially bring about an overall unity were soon seen to transport the cities of the north and south into dispute, and over the countless centuries, all had eventually retreated behind their barricades and their strengths had diminished. This left only the barren wastelands beyond the city walls where the raiders roamed, and the occasional travellers risked their lives in keeping contact between the people.

The Brotherhood of *Apep*, however, had remained and, having lain low over time, had once again raised their head, as over the recent decades, the cause had taken advantage of the differences between man. Slowly the whereabouts of the Eight had been rediscovered, and the men of the High Places had swiftly been sent out. For only in the unity of the Eight can the forces of chaos be once again reborn, and the high priest could once more resurrect *Apep*.

***

Mentu softly repeated the high priest's name as he walked, as it had been years since he had last heard it spoken, for little contact had been received from the city since he left and began his lifetime studies at the Great House of Ran Agua in the Valley of the Vallenti. He had been so much younger then, but he could still remember the name and vaguely recalled the man, for they had schooled together in the big citadel where the cold winds of the north blew. The City of the High Places, however, he remembered only vaguely, for he had been sent away by his father before this king's father was in place, and the high priest at that time was Serdos' grandfather, for the brotherhood, like the kingship was handed down father to son.

He recalled, as he briefly touched the talisman which hung about his neck, the day that he knew his father was dead. For the parchments the scribes had risked in sending out in their yearly package from the north had contained a small parcel in his name, and on opening, the token had fallen out at his feet. That had been over thirty years ago, and since that time, the packages from the north and from any of the other cities had dwindled and eventually stopped arriving in the valley, and the scribe had been left to study the brotherhood in the darkness of the libraries and at his own leisure.

Around the clearing, the cloaked figure of Mentu could be seen at times as he patrolled the tree-lined edge, but much later, as the dawn approached, when he judged all to be asleep, the scribe had disappeared into the thickened undergrowth which tumbled through the tightly packed trees. Moments later, he had suddenly come up behind the bound man, and quickly untying the knots, he released Roth from his restraints. The two then edged further under the cold darkness of the undergrowth and into the mists of the wood before slowly turning back northwards and passing by where Brann slept, and Gallius lay in his unrest. The horses that Mentu had readied earlier had been slowly and quietly moved away from the others as he had completed his circuits through the night and now stood in wait on the very edge of the tree line above the clearing.

Around the fire, the remainder of the group had settled and also slept, their cloaks pulled high and around each recumbent figure as the fire dwindled down to a steady glow and the wisps of smoke floated steadily skyward. But suddenly, Shuma awoke into a darkened silence, and straining her ears, she heard the faintest of noises that she could not place. Sitting up, she saw that the mist had begun to clear, and a half-moon shone down through the trees casting blacker shadows into the greyness of the early morning. Picking up her bow, she slowly moved over towards the riders. There nudging Gallius awake with a sharp push to his left shoulder, she whispered, "I hear movement." And pointing the tip of the bow towards the north, she slowly crossed to the left-hand trees edge, and Gallius, quick to arm himself, followed quietly in her steps.

Staying alert, the two moved soundlessly through the wood until, seeing the darkened shapes of the horses appear out of the shadows, Gallius had paused before quickly rushing forward to where the two robed figures were mounting in readiness to flee. Roth was closest to him and, pulling the man down from the horse, he had thrown him upon the ground and, kneeling over the struggling figure, had, with one sharp blow, delivered his knife deep into his chest.

The other figure had quickly taken off, and Shuma, instantly positioning an arrow, let it fly with the black shaft cutting through the swirling night air. Quickly finding its target in the receding back of the rider, the cloaked shape had fallen heavy to the ground, and the horse which it rode had disappeared off into the dark. On release of the bow, Shuma had freed her knife and straightaway followed the flight of the dart. Chasing up, she arrived at where the body lay face down, the black feathers protruding out from the left shoulder, while the long arms were thrown upwards and out along the hard ground.

"Oh my god, it's Mentu!" she exclaimed, as on turning over the body of the man, the hooded cloak had gaped open to reveal the face of the scribe. "It's Mentu!" she repeated, hardly able to believe what she saw and what she had done. Her arrow had hit the back of the man's chest, directly tearing through the muscle and piercing the heart as it plunged through, and death had come instantly as the body hit the black dirt of the northern track. Putting away her knife and dropping to her knees, she held the warm hand of the scribe as the realisation that their accepted closeness was now in some dispute and a sudden shock and sickness gripped her as she looked down. The open eyes stared back at her, and slowly she lowered the lids to avert the gaze.

The whole of the camp was now awakened by the noise and disruption, Brann and Darric being armed and ready to fight in a matter of seconds, while Tragen and Theroc were only moments behind. Seeing the kneeling shadow of Shuma further out from the clearing, the four had immediately raced to her aid, but on hearing their approach, she had called back.

"Gallius needs help!" she shouted, pointing into the trees where the voices of the two men could be heard. "Help him!"

Brann, Darric and Tragen instantly changed direction, heading off to the left and into the dark denseness of the trees while Theroc continued towards Shuma, reaching her as she dropped the limp hand of the scribe. Looking up at the elder, she said softly in disbelief, "I've killed

Mentu. He's dead!" Rising, she sharply turned away from the scene and walked back towards the fire.

Further into the wood, in the darkness under the tall trees, Gallius was continuing in his struggle with the injured Roth. And both men were locked in fight, their bodies tumbling along the ground and through the thickness of the darkened undergrowth, the leader continuing to slash at Roth as they fought. But as the three men rushed through the forest edge and moved out from the clearing, the moon stabbed down through the trees, and the encounter was swiftly brought to a close as Tragen launched himself forwards.

Throwing the man off Gallius, he had thrust his knife deep into the already wounded fighter, pushing the blade into the softness of the belly and tearing quickly upwards in one stroke as the man lay face up on the covering of pine needles and his roar of instant agony echoed through the woods.

The fight was then soon over, with the bodies of the two men being either dragged or carried and returned to the clearing which they had so hurriedly wanted to leave. The dead body of the scribe had been carried unceremoniously between Theroc and Darric, and space was made by the fire which Olor Ebon and Anitta had resurrected from the dying embers. There he was placed while the rest of the group began to regather in their shocked silence.

Roth had also been delivered back to the camp, Tragen and Brann dragging the still conscious, badly wounded man through the harsh brushwood, and on checking his deep and bloodied injuries, Shuma had quickly shaken her head at Gallius. His knife had plunged deep between the ribs, slicing downwards into the lungs and releasing blood into the chest, and it would only be a short time before the man would labour to breathe, and he would drown in his own fluid. The stomach wound gaped open between his torn shirt, the blood trickling out across his hips and between his legs, but this was secondary to the first wound, for his breathing would stop long before this would give him any problem, and all the other wounds he had received were superficial. The chest wound now began to ooze with frothy pink blood, and his upper clothing quickly became soaked to match his lower as Roth struggled to drag in the air, and the breathing became more erratic and shallow. Gallius had seated himself down next to his once friend and second-in-command, and even in his own upset and fury, he knew he needed to push his questions in the hope of gaining some answers and making their journey into the north easier.

"Tell me what you know, Roth!" he demanded, looking at the man as he fought to breathe, and feeling the pull and irritation of his own injury, he supported his right arm across his chest in some hope of lessening the pain. "Tell me, Roth. For once, we were brothers, and that still could hold some measure to me if you are true to your word," he lied, and pleading in hope of gaining information, he moved closer to the dying man and took hold of his hand.

While Gallius sat and received no replies, Malian could be seen to be beyond himself in anger and anguish as he looked upon the body of Mentu. He had called the man friend and soon realised the implications of putting his entire trust in the scribe, for his judgement he felt now had been shown to be lacking. Quickly he set about searching the body of the dead man, his shaking hands delving under the clothing in his haste to find the Icon. The pack containing *Amaunet* had eventually been found around his side and instantly removed, and on checking, the wrapped figure still lay within its depths. But as he searched the clothing, the altar tender also come upon the talisman, which sat hidden against the scribe's chest as his skin began to cool.

"Look, Gallius," he quickly declared to the rider and in his dismay and disturbed surprise, he quickly removed the silvered disc, saying, "look what I've found. Here is another token." Handing the intricately decorated metal ring swiftly across to Gallius, the rider retrieved Roth's counterpart from his breast pocket. Holding each in his bloodied hands, he matched the two together, noting the slight difference in the design of the scribes with its extra inner ring and the thicker outer ring adding weight to the one which lay heavier in his left hand.

"Tell me about these, Roth," he had then eagerly pressed, bringing the two tokens forward, for he knew now they had some important meaning behind them, "what do they intend or stand for?" He pushed his hands closer in his growing anger. "Tell me, Roth, for you know you have little time left."

The dying rider had then smiled cruelly up into the recognised face of Gallius, and with a trickle of blood coursing down his bearded chin, he raised his hands to the two tokens and, touching them, advised in a slow whisper, "The…high…priest ordered me…to take the Icon to him…to him only…and not to the king!" And with that said, his last breath was taken, his hands quickly dropping empty to his sides, and the rider went quietly and with little regret into his solitary darkness, the blood seeping from the open mouth as his head rolled away from the light.

Gallius then looked away both in displeasure and annoyance from the dead man before repeating softly, "the high priest." For in its saying, he was still uncertain as to whether this had been given as guidance or in warning, and the malicious smile which had crossed

Roth's face had left a bitterness in his throat, which he spat to the ground in his temper.

Sitting back from the dead man, he tried to remember the shadowy figure who lurked behind the king's seat, but his recollection of Serdos was vague. He recalled that he had been high priest long in his remembering, and before that, his father, Setrii, had briefly occupied the position but had not lasted long nor lived up to his name. For the son had appeared overly eager to take the position, and rumour was rife that he had hastened his promotion, quickly stepping up and grasping the opportunity.

"The high priest, Brann. Do you remember him?" Quickly turning, he stood and asked the man who was returning across the clearing, his arms full of damp wood collected from around the camp.

"Serdos, yes, I recall him," came the reply as he dropped the bundle near the fire, "he's been high priest since I can remember." Throwing a thick branch into the blaze, which sizzled and smoked in the intense heat, the older rider then asked, "Does he have something to do with this?" He looked to where the two dead bodies lay, and unlike those who sat around, he felt neither fear nor sadness at either passing.

"I'm not sure," Gallius said slowly, his mind trying to look at all the possibilities, "but…" He stopped and, looking around at where the others sat in their discomfort, finished with, "come, let's get these bodies out of the way and try and get some rest."

Mentu and Roth were then removed from the hearth, their bodies being lain to one side under the trees. And the rest of the group could now feel better able to gather closer together in the warmth of the fire without their eyes falling on their bloodstained remains. But their confusion persisted as they sat, and the silence which collected was unnerving. On settling earlier that night, they had assumed some safety in where they lay, but the last hour had brought a dismay that had descended amongst them, and they were shaken to the core by its intimacy, and sleep would not again be found that night.

***

While the hush of confused silence reigned around the camp above the Median Bridge, Serdos, the High Priest of the Brotherhood of *Apep*, stood in front of the alabaster altar where the exquisitely carved representation of the snake god coiled its serpentine form high above. Rising up, its polished chiselled scales glinted in the flickering pale light of the many blood-red candles. Placing the figure of *Amun* at its base, he stood back and looked along either side to where the six other Icons had already been grouped, before his sinister gaze was drawn upwards to the sleek head of the serpent, its long, sharp ivory teeth protruding downwards as its hollowed eyes stared out overhead into the dark.

The wait would soon be over, he thought, for there was now only one more Icon to secure, and he knew that as he stood there in the shadow of the great god, that by now, it should be on its way north. A charge of utter excitement coursed through his body, and his hot hands trembled as he touched the token around his neck. The solid silver talisman now felt heavier as the day dawned and in its hopeful meaning, meant the return of more brothers to the cause, and his mind had immediately and with great hope gone to Roth. For the brother had been given a privileged task and, as second-in-command to Gallius, had been best placed to ensure the return of *Amaunet* to the Eight.

Along the wide, ivory coloured ledge, the golden figures had been placed into their couples; the Deities of

Darkness, *Kek* and *Kauket*, stood together just to the right, with *Heh* and *Hauhet*, with their Power of Infinity standing beyond, and on the left the Spirits of Water, *Nun* and *Naunet* had been placed in wait of the last two Icons. Each, with their eyes of precious stone, looked out into the vast darkness of the subterranean underworld where the brotherhood met and had been sent out on their search, for untold years.

The Brotherhood of *Apep* had come together since the City in The Mountains had been born and had always been governed by its religious order, for even kings had to bow to the high priest and the sacred rituals he was empowered to perform. But as Century passed into countless Century, his main objective and purpose in life had become to locate and assemble the Deities, and down the ages, father had instilled in son the desire and lust to see the resurgence once more of the Great Serpent of Chaos. Serdos could never have believed that this would happen in his time, but increasingly it looked like it could be, as the Icons were found and brought before the altar. For the finding and acquiring of each individual statue had happened only recently, and the ensuing disorder brought about throughout mankind had escalated the chance of finding the others.

The Eight Icons, when assembled, made up The Ogdoad, the Deities of the Primordial Chaos who, in their parting and scattering throughout the land by the collective gods at the beginning of time, had banished Chaos and Disorder off the land. But with their assembly and bringing together, they would be melted down, and the Great Golden Serpent could once again be cast and would manifest himself, and the oncoming duel between Lightness and Dark would again be fought.

Serdos, having placed *Amun* on the altar, stepped back and bowing to the floor before the watchful god, he turned and walked slowly back through the dark and past the seats where the brothers would sit, before coming to a halt and removing his snake-edged crown and golden robe. Wrapping himself in a simple cloak he pushed open the secret door, and stepping out into the palace and into the daybreak of the morning he greeted the new day.

***

Many miles away, the dawn of the day was also being witnessed by those who sat beside the fire, for no one had found sleep after the turmoil of the last few hours and a silence had gathered close around. The coldness drifting around their backs as the last wisps of clinging mist had lifted slowly revealed the grey of the northern sky.

The bodies of both Mentu and Roth, having been moved from the fireside and been placed out beneath the trees, had already cooled, and a stiffness had carved their features into waxen images, the closed eyelids retracting to slightly reveal the fixed stare of their unseeing eyes. And here they would be left for either bird or beast to savour, for neither Gallius nor Malian would allow one moment of time spent on seeing them buried. The group, in the cold light of the morning, then made ready to part in swiftness, for there was an eagerness to be on their way, away from this place.

Malian had now been left with only one option in returning *Amaunet* back to the valley but appeared slow in approaching the remaining elder who sat alongside the Black Swan, the fire warming their cold hands as in their tiredness, they thawed off the night's chill. He felt his recent decision-making had been awry of late, and the fear of any further failure weighed heavy on his shoulders.

"Theroc," he slowly began as he sat down, bringing

his cloak tightly about him, "you know I have no other to ask or place this duty on," he stopped as he put his cold fingers across the man's warming hand, "but if you feel it is too much or beyond you then now is the time to say." He looked to the last of the elders who had travelled with them, and in his heart, he hoped that the challenge would be taken up.

Theroc, however, remained quietly by his side, aware of what the duty meant, and the time slowly passed as they each sat in thought.

"Perhaps if the duty was shared?" Olor Ebon eventually queried, her voice becoming quiet as the camp was being taken apart and the horses made ready. And Theroc had nodded his head in agreement to divide the entrustment of *Amaunet*, and Malian, at last, felt some ease in this decision.

"Agreed!" Theroc had said, the reply being echoed by the Black Swan, and the three had joined hands in an understanding of the pledge given.

The two group's now made ready to part, and goodbyes were said on both sides as Olor Ebon and Theroc, the statue of the Icon hidden away once again in its pack, each mounted their horses and slowly rode back towards the Median Bridge.

The rest of the group came to see them off, with Malian saying his prayers and wishes for safe travel being given by the others with a hope of meeting again in the future. Shuma had already said her farewells to her mother, and on seeing the departing back of the tall woman as she sat her horse, she waved her hand and watched until the figures disappeared from the bridge.

The group which had set off many weeks ago had now parted with the hope that *Amaunet* was returning into safety. Now there were other promises to keep, and as Malian stowed his bag on the back of his mount, he hoped he would not be lacking in courage to face the future on his journey north and that the gods would once more guide his step.

***

Moving off the bridge and through the trees which surrounded the southern end of the bridge, Olor and Theroc returned into the south, their journey taking them back towards the Sleeping Caverns. Passing the already half-eaten, mauled bodies of Marke, Rogan and Statte as they lay scattered upon the turf, the two passed into the light of the grasslands and *Amaunet*, the Eighth Deity, began her passage home.

About The Author

Glennis Goodwin was born in Staffordshire and from an early age was often told she had a wanderlust about her – her nose was always in one book or another, whisking her away to some far-off land! Anything to do with the people or wildlife of Africa always held an attraction and in the early 1980s, she was fortunate to find herself living and working in Zambia, which lasted for five years before she returned to the UK.

In her working life, she has gone from Nursing to Retail and from Academic Publishing to PA, but she never lost the feeling Africa gave her, and in those years, she had several holidays in Egypt and Kenya. Egypt was fascinating with all its Ancient history, and walking around the Temples of Luxor and Karnak, she imagined herself back in those days!

In 2004, after a change in personal circumstance, she aimed to return to her Nursing career and, combining that with her love of travel, went to New Zealand on a refresher course. Settling into life over there, she continued to further her career, met her new husband and made her life there.

Sadly, a brain haemorrhage and slight stroke ended her study, but after her recovery, she found herself wanting to write, something she had longed to do but never seemed to have the time for. Returning to the UK in 2017, she settled down at her computer, revisiting an idea put aside years previously, and over the following months, the tales of The Eight Deities of the Ancient Egyptians came to life in the story of Malian, the altar tender!

Currently, she is working on her second book, *Brotherhood of Apep*, which continues Malian's tale.

www.blossomspringpublishing.com

Printed in Great Britain
by Amazon

37427323R00209